D0846716

Other Books by Ann & Jeff VanderMeer

Best American Fantasy 1
(with Matthew Cheney)

Best American Fantasy 2
(with Matthew Cheney)

The New Weird

Steampunk

Fast Ships, Black Sails

Last Drink Bird Head:
Flash Fiction for Literacy

The Kosher Guide to Imaginary Animals

Steampunk Reloaded

The Weird

Books by Jeff VanderMeer

FICTION

Dradin, in Love

The Book of Lost Places

Veniss Underground

City of Saints & Madmen

Secret Life

Shriek: An Afterword

The Situation

Secret Lives

Predator: South China Sea

Finch

The Third Bear

The Three Quests of the
Wizard Sarnod

NONFICTION AND
ANTHOLOGIES

Leviathan 1 (with Luke O'Grady)

Leviathan 2 (with Rose Secrest)

Leviathan 3 (with Forrest Aguirre)

Album Zutique

The Thackery T. Lambshead Pocket Guide
to Eccentric & Discredited Diseases
(with Mark Roberts)

Why Should I Cut Your Throat?

Booklife: Strategies & Survival Tips
for the 21st Century Writer

Monstrous Creatures: Explorations
of Fantasy

The Steampunk Bible
(with S. J. Chambers)

THE
Thackery T. Lambshead
CABINET of
CURIOSITIES

Exhibits, Oddities, Images, and Stories

from Top Authors and Artists

THE

Thackery T. Lambshead
CABINET of
CURIOSITIES

Edited by

Ann & Jeff VanderMeer

HARPER Voyager
An Imprint of HarperCollins *Publishers*

Page 317 serves as a continuation of the copyright page.

This book is a work of fiction. The characters, incidents, and dialogue are drawn from the author's imagination and are not to be construed as real. Any resemblance to actual events or persons, living or dead, is entirely coincidental.

THE THACKERY T. LAMBSHEAD CABINET OF CURIOSITIES. Collection copyright © 2011 by Ann and Jeff VanderMeer. All rights reserved. Printed in the United States of America. No part of this book may be used or reproduced in any manner whatsoever without written permission except in the case of brief quotations embodied in critical articles and reviews. For information address HarperCollins Publishers, 10 East 53rd Street, New York, NY 10022.

HarperCollins books may be purchased for educational, business, or sales promotional use. For information please write: Special Markets Department, HarperCollins Publishers, 10 East 53rd Street, New York, NY 10022.

A hardcover edition of this book was published in 2011 by Harper Voyager, an imprint of HarperCollins Publishers.

FIRST HARPER VOYAGER PAPERBACK EDITION PUBLISHED 2012.

Book designed by Paula Russell Szafranski

Library of Congress Cataloging-in-Publication Data has been applied for.

ISBN 978-0-06-211683-3

12 13 14 15 16   OV/RRD   10 9 8 7 6 5 4 3 2 1

Dedicated to the memory of Kage Baker,

a wonderful writer and a good friend of Dr. Lambshead.

You are not forgotten.

Contents

Microbial Alchemy and Demented Machinery: The Mignola Exhibits

The Miéville Anomalies

Further Oddities

Visits and Departures

A Brief Catalog of Other Items 293

THE
Thackery T. Lambshead
CABINET of
CURIOSITIES

Exhibits, Oddities, Images, and Stories
from Top Authors and Artists

A photograph of just one shelf in Lambshead's study displaying the "overflow" from his underground collection (1992). Some items were marked "return to sender" on the doctor's master list.

The Contradictions of a Collection: Dr. Lambshead's Cabinet

By the Editors

To his dying day, Dr. Thackery T. Lambshead (1900–2003) insisted to friends that he "wasn't much of a collector." "Things tend to manifest around me," he told BBC Radio once, "but it's not by choice. I spend a large part of my life *getting rid of things*."

Indeed, one of Lambshead's biggest tasks after the holiday season each year was, as he put it, "repatriating well-intentioned gifts" with those "who might more appropriately deserve them." Often, this meant reuniting "exotic" items with their countrymen and -women, using his wide network of colleagues, friends, and acquaintances hailing from around the world. A controversial reliquary box from a grateful survivor of ballistic organ syndrome? Off to a "friend in the Slovak Republic who knows a Russian who knows a nun." A centuries-old "assassin's twist" kris (see the Catalog entries) absentmindedly sent by a lord in Parliament? Off to Dr. Mawar Haqq at the National Museum in Kuala Lumpur, Malaysia. And so on and so forth.

He kept very little of this kind of material, not out of some loyalty to the Things of Britain, but more out of a sense that "the West still has a lot to answer for," as he wrote in his journals. Perhaps this is why Lambshead spent so much time in the East. Indeed, the east wing of his ever-more-extensive home in Whimpering-on-the-Brink was his favorite place to escape the press during the more public moments of his long career.

Regardless, over time, his cabinet of curiosities grew to the point that his semipermanent loans to various universities and museums became not so much philanthropic in nature as "acts of self-defense" (*LIFE* Magazine, "Hoarders: Curiosity or a New Disease?," May 19, 1975). One of the most frenzied of these "acts" occurred in "divesting myself of the most asinine acquisition I ever made, the so-called Clockroach"—documented in this very volume—"which had this ridiculous habit of starting all on its own and making a massacre of my garden and sometimes a stone fence or two. Drove my housekeeper and the groundskeeper mad."

Breaking Ground

This question of the cabinet's growth coincides with questions about its location. As early as the 1950s, there are rather unsubtle hints in Dr. Lambshead's journal of "creating hidden reservoirs for this river of junk" and "darkness and subterranean calm may be best for the bulk of it," especially since the collection "threatens to outgrow the house."

In the spring of 1962, as is well-documented, builders converged on Lambshead's abode and for several months were observed to leave through the back entrance carrying all manner of supplies while removing a large quantity of earth, wood, and roots.

Speculation began to develop as to Lambshead's intentions. "If even Dr. Lambshead despairs of compromise, what should the rest of us, who do not have

Floor plan found in Lambshead's private files, detailing, according to a scrawled note, "the full extent of a museum-quality cabinet of curiosities that will serve as a cathedral to the world, and be worthy of her."

the same privilege, do?" asked the editor of the *Socialist Union Guild Newsletter* that year, assuming that Lambshead, at the time a member, was building a "personalized bomb shelter with access to amenities many of us could not dream to afford in our everyday lives, nor wish to own for fear of capitalist corruption." In the absence of a statement from Lambshead, the Fleet Street press even started rumors that he had discovered gold beneath his property, or ancient Celtic artifacts of incredible value. Whatever Lambshead's motivations, he must have paid the builders handsomely, since the only recorded comment from the foreman is: "Something's wrong with the pipes. Full stop." (*Guardian*, "Avowed Socialist Builds 'Anti-Democracy' Bunker Basement," April 28, 1962)

Throughout the year, Lambshead ignored the questions, catcalls, and bullhorn-issued directives from the press besieging his gates. He continued to entertain guests at his by-now palatial home—including such luminaries as Maurice Richardson, Francis Bacon, Molly Parkin, Jerry Cornelius, George Melly, Quentin Crisp, Nancy Cunard, Angus Wilson, Philippe Jullian, and Violet Trefusis—and, in general, acted as if nothing out of the ordinary was occurring, even as the workmen labored until long after midnight and more than one guest reported "strange metallic smells and infernal yelping burps coming up from beneath the floorboards." Meanwhile, Lambshead's seemingly preternatural physical fitness fueled rumors involving "life-enhancing chambers" and "ancient rites." Despite being in his sixties, he looked not a day over forty, no doubt due to his early and groundbreaking experiments with human growth hormone.

Why the secrecy? Why the need to ignore the press? Nothing in Lambshead's journals can explain it. Indeed, given the damage eventually suffered by this subterranean space, there's not even enough left to map the full extent of the original excavation. We are left with two floor plans from Lambshead's private filing cabinet, one of which shows his estate house in relation to the basement area—and thus two contradictory possibilities. One of them, oddly enough, corresponds in shape to a three-dimensional model of an experimental flying craft. This coincidence has led to one of the stranger accusations ever leveled against Lambshead (not including those attributed to contamination scholar Reza Negarestani and obliteration expert Michael Cisco). Art critic Amal El-Mohtar, who for a time attempted to research part of Lambshead's cabinet, claimed that "It became obvious from Thackery's notes that he was creating a kind of specialized Ark to survive the extermination of humankind, each item chosen to tell a specific story, and his particular genius was to have all of these objects—this detritus of eccentric quality—housed within a container that would eventually double as a

3

Floor plan of what Amal El-Mohtar called "a nascent spaceshop nee Ark," with a front view of Lambshead's house beneath it.

spaceship." However, it must be noted that this theory, leaked to various tabloids, came to El-Mohtar during a period of recovery in Cornwall from her encounter with the infamous singing fish from Lambshead's collection. Not only had her writings become erratic, but she was, for a period of time, fond of talking to wild-flowers.

The most popular of other apocryphal theories originated with the performance artist Sam Van Olffen, who, since 1989, has seemed fixated on Lambshead and staged several related productions. The most grandiose, the musical *The Mad Cabinet of Curiosities of the Mad Dr. Lambshead*, debuted in 2008 in Paris and London, well after Lambshead's death. Perhaps the most controversial of Van Olffen's speculations is that Lambshead's excavations in 1962 were meant not to create a space for a cabinet of curiosities but to remodel an existing underground space that had previously served as a secret laboratory in which he was conducting illegal medical tests. A refrain of "Doctor doctor doctor doctor! / Whatcher got in there there? A lamb's head?" is particularly grating.

Certainly, nothing about the flashback scenes to the 1930s, or the hints of Lambshead's affiliation with underground fascist parties, did anything to endear Van Olffen's productions to fans of the doctor, or the popular press. *The Mad Cabinet of Curiosities* closed on both Les Boulevards and the West End after less than a month. The combined effect of media attention for this "sustained attack on the truth," as Lambshead's heirs put it in a deposition for an unsuccessful lawsuit in 2009, has been to distort the true nature of the doctor's work and career.

A Deep Emotional Attachment?

Despite irregularities and bizarre claims, one fact seems clear: Lambshead, especially in his later years, formed a deep emotional attachment to many of the objects in his collection, whether repatriated, loaned out, or retained in his house or underground cabinet.

A close friend of Lambshead, post–World War II literary icon Michael Moorcock, who first met the doctor in the mid-1950s at a party thrown by Mervyn Peake's family, remembered several such attachments to objects. "It became especially acute in the 1960s," Moorcock recalled in an interview, "when we spent a decent amount of time together because of affairs related to *New Worlds*," the seminal science fiction magazine Moorcock edited at the time. "For a man of science, who resolutely believed in fact, he could be very sentimental. I remember how distraught he became during an early visit when he couldn't find an American Night Quilt he had promised to show both me and [J. G.] Ballard. He became so ridiculously agitated that I had to say, 'Pard, you might want to sit down

One of Sam Van Olffen's stage sets for the supposed laboratory of Dr. Lambshead, taken from the Parisian production of the musical *The Mad Cabinet of Curiosities of the Mad Dr. Lambshead* and supposedly inspired by Van Olffen's own encounter with the cabinet several years before. (*Le Monde*, March 2, 2008)

The "secret medical laboratory" stage set for *The Mad Cabinet of Curiosities of the Mad Dr. Lambshead*. A much less grandiose version of the musical was eventually turned into a SyFy channel film titled *Mansquito 5: Revenge of Dr. Lambshead*, but never aired. (*Le Monde*, March 2, 2008)

One of Lambshead's few attempts at art, admittedly created "under the influence of several psychotropic drugs I was testing at the time." Lambshead claims he was "just trying to reproduce the visions in my head." S. B. Potter (see: "1972" in Visits and Departures) claimed the painting provided "early evidence of brain colonization."

awhile.' Then he felt compelled to tell me that he and his first—his only—wife, Helen, who had passed on two or three years before, had watched the stars from the roof one night early in their relationship, and had snuggled under that quilt. One of his fondest memories of her." (*Independent*, "An Unlikely Friendship?: The Disease Doc and the Literary Lion," September 12, 1995)

A fair number of the artifacts in the cabinet dating from before 1961 would have reminded Lambshead of Helen Aquilus, a brilliant neurosurgeon whom he appears to have first met in 1939, courted until 1945, and finally married in 1950 (despite rumors of a chance encounter in 1919). She had accompanied him on several expeditions and emergency trips, as a colleague and fellow scientist. She had been present when Lambshead acquired many of his most famous artifacts, such as "The Thing in the Jar," a puzzler that haunted Lambshead until his death (see: Further Oddities). She also helped him acquire a number of books, including a rare printing of Gascoyne's *Man's Life Is This Meat*. Some have, in fact, suggested that Lambshead turned toward the preservation of his collection and building of a space for it as a distraction from his grief following Helen's death in an auto accident on a lonely country road in 1960.

Other items had significance to Lambshead because he had had a hand in their discovery, like St. Brendan's Shank, or in their creation, like the mask for Sir Ranulph Wykeham-Rackham, a.k.a. Roboticus. Perhaps most famous among these is the original of his psychedelic painting *The Family* from 1965, which for a time hung in the Tate Modern's exhibit "Doctors as Painters, Blood in Paint." In the painting, Death stares off into the distance while, behind it, a man who looks like Lambshead in his twenties stands next to a phantasmagorical rendering of Helen and her cousins.

In many cases, too, these objects, as he said, "remind me of lost friends"—for example, St. Brendan's Shank, which he came to possess during World War II, and which, as he wrote in his journal, "I spent many delightful days researching along with my comrades-in-arms, most of them, unfortunately, now lost to us from war, time, disease, accident, and heartbreak."

One of the few museum exhibit loans ever to have been photographed (Zurich, 1970s)—presented as evidence to support Caitlin R. Kiernan's accusations of Lambshead using artifacts to convey secret messages. She claims that Russian artist Vladimir Gvozdev, the creator of the mecha-rhino above, does not exist, and is a front for the "Sino-Siberian cells of a secret society."

Dr. Lambshead's Personal Life

In searching for a theme or approach to the cabinet, it may be relevant to return to the subject of Lambshead's wife. Throughout his life, and even after her death, Lambshead kept his attachment to Helen almost as secret as his cabinet, and *The Thackery T. Lambshead Pocket Guide to Eccentric & Discredited Diseases* never mentioned her, or referenced the marriage. Aquilus, a Cypriote Greek, came from a long line of dissenters and activists, and had originally left Athens to go to school at Oxford. She was and, at first, often seen as a beard for the doctor, since he was known to be bisexual and somewhat hedonistic in his appetites.

Aquilus, though, was a force and a character in her own right: a groundbreaking neuroscientist and surgeon in an era when females in those fields were unheard of; a researcher who worked for the British government during World War II to perfect triage for traumatic head wounds on the battlefield; and a champion at dressage who combined such a knack for negotiation with forcefulness of will that for a time she entered the political sphere as a spokesperson for the Socialist Party. Possessed of prodigious strength, she could also "shoot like a sniper" and "pilot or commandeer any damn boat, frigate, sampan, freighter, destroyer, or aircraft carrier you care to name," Lambshead wrote admiringly in a late 1950s letter to Moorcock.

All that ended in the one-car accident that left Lambshead in shock and Aquilus dead, her remains cremated and buried in a small, private ceremony almost immediately thereafter. Lambshead would never remarry, and often spoke of Helen as if she were still alive, a tendency that friends at first found understandable, then obsessional, and, finally, just "a quirk of Thackery's syntax," as Moorcock put it.

From 1963 on, however, despite his journals containing any number of elaborate descriptions of medical exploration and of artifacts acquired or sent off, there is only one mention of Helen. "Helen chose a different life," he writes in 1965, on the anniversary of her accident. The words are crossed out, then reinstated and emphasized overtop of the cross-out, with a violence that has torn the page, and several pages after, so that many entries thereafter are marked by and linked to that one sentence.

What to make of the statement "Helen has chosen another life"? Since 2005, when the journals first became available to the public through the British Library, many a researcher has attempted to make their reputation on an interpretation—everything from psychological profiling to outright conspiracy theories. Riffing off of the ideas, if not the political inclination, of the second endnote in Reza

Negarestani's "The Gallows-horse" (see: The Miéville Anomalies), unexplained-phenomena enthusiast and self-described "heretic Lambsheadean" Caitlín R. Kiernan has speculated that "Helen Aquilus did not die in a car crash in 1960. She staged her own death to join a secret society devoted to radical progressive change in the world, and spent the next half-century of her life in that struggle until a car bomb in Athens took her life in 2005, the body unclaimed for forty-eight hours and then mysteriously disappearing."

Evidence for this claim is flimsy at best, although Kiernan cites the speedy cremation of the body, the lack of any follow-up report, "due to the actions of a sleeper cell" within the police department, and "a damning history of collusion between the timing of Lambshead's museum loans/artifact purchases and the movements of known spies and double agents in the area. It must be assumed that encoded into such transactions were secret messages, some of them from Helen and some of them from Lambshead to Helen." Kiernan also notes the rapid reversal of some museum loans; in one case, involving "The Armor of Saint Locust," Lambshead rescinded his approval for the loan five days after the exhibit had opened to the public. She also references "the timing of Lambshead's visits to the Pulvadmonitor" (see: "Pulvadmonitor: The Dust's Warning," The Mignola Exhibits).

Kiernan saves her most pointed commentary for specific evidence: the rolled-up piece of parchment found inside a mechanical rhino in Zurich in 1976. "The text and image on this paper is ostensibly a *maskh* spell for constructing a pod for a journey toward the afterlife of the Elysian Fields. The spell is comprised of four main elements: a body wrapped in a shroud, one square and one rectangular chart, and lastly a scorpion, which in Middle Eastern folklore and talismans plays the role of a delivery system or a catalyst (here the scorpion is the engine for the pod to the afterlife). The dimensions of the pod (the shrouded body) have been given in the spell. The word 'scorpion' in Farsi has been hidden in this spell in the form of a cipher that looks like an abstract scorpion (the mark just above the word 'Elysian' at the bottom of the drawing). But what's also been hidden here, encrypted, is a series of messages from a husband to his wife that, if ever properly deciphered, would no doubt prove to be a hybrid of a love letter and a complex series of orders or *recognition of receipt of commands* that might have agency over several years, if not decades. *That* is the true scorpion in this image."

All of this "information" has been gleaned from what Kiernan calls "further encrypted evidence in Lambshead's journals from 1965 on—the year he learned that Helen wasn't dead—and supported by such circumstantial evidence as their heated public argument in 1959," also documented in the journals, in which

11

Spell or secret communication? The page found inside of the mecha-rhino, as photographed by Zurich investigator Kristen Alvanson.

Lambshead confesses, with no small amount of anguish, that "Helen is much more radical than I could ever be. How am I supposed to follow her in that?" Kiernan points to Lambshead's writings on "the second life of artifacts" in his "The Violent Philosophy of the Archive," which she claims "isn't about the objects at all, but about their repurposing by him."

Kiernan further claims that Helen attended Lambshead's funeral, "the mysterious woman in white standing at the back, next to Keith Richards and Deepak Chopra." However, photographs from the funeral clearly show many older women "standing at the back," several of them mysterious in the sense that they cannot be identified and are not on the guest list.

A theory put forward by Alan Moore, who knew Lambshead late in life better than anyone, is more reasonable and doesn't presume conspiracy and collusion. Moore suggests merely that the hectic pace Lambshead set from 1963 until his death in 2003 came from a sudden resolve: "It was merely one of the oldest stories, you see. A man attempting to outrun the knowledge of the continuing absence of the love of his life." (In the subtext of his pornographic masterpiece *The Lost Girls,* Moore would reference both Lambshead and Helen, through the device of a mirror separating them forever.)

Loans with Strings Attached: The Museum Exhibits

Of all of Kiernan's "evidence," the most fact-based concerned Lambshead's eccentric attitude toward the visual documentation of the contents of his cabinet, whether parts of it were at home or roaming abroad. Although it's hardly evidence of secret messages being included with his loans, Lambshead usually forbid even the usual photographs a museum will commission for catalogs or postcards. His sole recorded explanation? "It creates greater anticipation if the public has no preconceived idea of what they may be about to encounter. A photograph is a sad and lonely idea of an echo of something real." (*Guardian,* "Sir Ranulph Wykeham-Rackham. a.k.a. Robotikus, Still on Loan to Imperial War Museum, But Nowhere to Be Seen," June 4, 1998)

However, as even the barely suppressed emotion evidenced by the quote may suggest, it seems more likely that Lambshead's intense personal commitment to the core collection made the loaning of items, while necessary and part of what the doctor considered his "civic duty," also painful, and that forbidding photographs gave him a measure of control, a way he could allow the public to experience his cabinet and yet keep it from the Public Eye. As might be expected, the compilation of a book chronicling highlights from Lambshead's cabinet has been made much more difficult due to this eccentricity.

The Doctor Versus the Collector

For the majority of his career, due to his insistence on remaining true to his main passions, Lambshead existed on the fringes of medical science. He was well-respected by some of the world's best doctors, but it was only by becoming a kind of cult figure in the 1960s and 1970s, when he forged friendships with many of pop culture's elite, along with "sheer bloody persistence and endurance," that his medical exploits began to receive the media attention he believed they deserved. Later on, there would even be factions of Lambsheadologists who clashed in their interpretations of the doctor's theories, with Lambshead rarely if ever willing to put an end to such conflict with a definitive conclusion. "Definitive conclusions are for politicians, proctologists, and those who wear mascot costumes," he liked to say.

Despite the time spent on his cabinet, Lambshead's interests always manifested most concretely in *The Thackery T. Lambshead Pocket Guide to Eccentric & Discredited Diseases.* First published in 1921, the *Guide* gave agency and credence to real but obscure and often only anecdotally documented instances of diseases, parasites, and tumors. Not only did many young doctors from all over the world, who would later publish influential findings, receive a sympathetic welcome from the doctor, but marginalized peoples often found the *Guide* took up their cause, sometimes creating publicity for situations that local governments and foreign-relief agencies wished would just go away.

Published almost continuously until the doctor's death, the *Guide* received a controversial send-off with Bantam Books' commemorative eighty-third edition in 2003. That reviewers and readers were often confused as to whether the

Legendary Czech artist and animator Jan Svankmajer's tongue-in-cheek tribute to Dr. Lambshead's so-called "Skull Cucumber" hoax, perpetrated on London's Museum of Natural History in 1992, during as Lambshead put it, "a period of extreme boredom."

book constituted fact or fiction was the result of a colossal blunder by Bantam's marketing and PR departments, which were, as would be well documented later, largely dominated by pot-smokers. However, the doctor's legacy was vindicated by the fact that a large number of medical libraries now carry that edition in their medical-guides section.

However, as should be clear, the doctor's career was only half the story. Just as his exploration of eccentric diseases forms a secret history of the twentieth century, so, too, his cabinet of curiosities, in all of its contradictions, provides an eclectic record of a century—through folly and triumph, organized, if you will, by the imaginations of the eccentric and the visionary.

Resurrecting the Cabinet

Not until well after Lambshead's death of banal pulmonary failure did anyone except for his housekeeper seem to have had even an inkling of the full extent of the underground collection. This situation had been exacerbated by the old man's knowledge of his impending extinction. He had, for three years, been issuing a "recall" of sorts on many of his permanent loans. (This fact did not go unnoticed by Kiernan, who claimed these particular exhibits "had expired in their usefulness for communication with Helen.")

A long process of discovery awaited those assigned by the estate to take care of the house, which still begs the question: Why did it take so long to unearth the collection? Estate representatives have been vague on this point, perhaps hinting at some private foreknowledge and personal plundering prior to the British government, in 2008, declaring the property a national treasure—nothing was to be touched, except with extreme care, and certainly nothing removed.

But it is also true that Lambshead had left enough aboveground to keep archaeologists and appraisers busy for several lifetimes. In later years, Lambshead's housekeeper had gotten lackadaisical, and Lambshead made eccentric purchases of furniture—which, the week before his death, he'd hired movers to stack against the front door, as if to barricade the house against what he must have known by then was coming.

An invention commissioned from Jake von Slatt demonstrating the doctor's commitment to the future as well as the past. Some have speculated this device supports Amal El-Mohtar's "space Ark" theory. As described by Annalee Newitz, this image "illustrates an ideal system, where the knobs on the lower right demodulate cultural transmissions, and the amplifier beneath the bell transmits a psionic signal that can reach any analog neurological entity within 7,000 kilometers." (See Newitz's extended description in the Catalog section.)

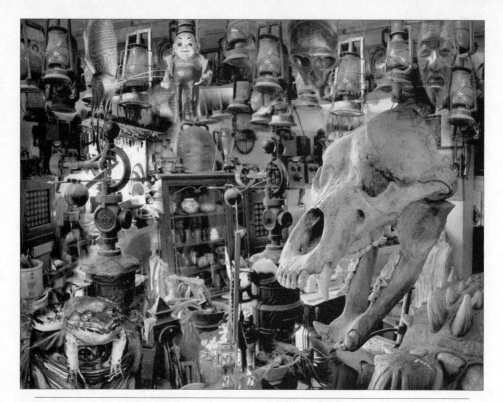

More evidence of the disarray of the cabinet space, in a photograph taken during a 2009 appraisal. (Found in the display case at the back, a half-finished letter penned by Lambshead: "As Lichtenberg said of angels, so I say of dust. If they, or it, ever could speak to us, why in God's name should we understand? And even if so, how then should we reply?")

Therefore, the man's house was in a catastrophic state of disarray, with letters from heads of state mixed in with grocery lists, major medical awards propping up tables or sticking enigmatically out of the many cat litter boxes, and several hundred volumes of his personal journals shoved into random spaces in a library as shambolic as it was complete. The only clean, uncluttered space was Helen's study, which remained as it had been upon her death.

No doubt because of this disarray, and the introduction of an administrative red herring—Moorcock has suggested that Lambshead left instructions for someone to "plant the herring, no matter how badly it might begin to smell"—indicating that the collection had long ago been sent into storage in Berlin, it took caretakers until last year to unearth perhaps "the most stirring find," as *Le Monde* put it. In the basement space, lost under a collapsed floor, were found the remains of a "remarkable and extensive cabinet of curiosities" that "appeared to have been damaged by a fire that occurred sometime during the past decade."

(*Le Monde,* "Une merveille médicale: Le curieux cabinet d'un médecin renommé enflamme l'imagination," April 14, 2010) Strangely, there is no report of *any* fire from the many years Lambshead owned the house, and we have only a brief anecdotal (and probably false) statement from the doctor's estranged housekeeper to guide us to any sort of conclusion.

The cabinet of curiosities took more than eighteen months to unearth, reconstruct, document, and catalog. Many of the pieces related to anecdotes and stories in the doctor's personal diaries. Others, when shown to his friends, elicited further stories. In many cases, we had only descriptions of the items. Still, we were determined to build a book that would honor at least the spirit and lingering ghost of Lambshead's collection. Thus, in keeping with the bold spirit exemplified by Lambshead and his accomplishments, we are now proud to present highlights from the doctor's cabinet. These have been reconstructed not just through visual representations but also through text associated with their history and (sometimes) their acquisition by Lambshead. (As with any cabinet, real or housed within pages, it is, as Oscar Wilde once said about an exhaustive collection of poetry, a "browsing experience, to dip into and to savor, rather than take a wild carriage ride through.")

We also have Lambshead's own wistful words from his diary, written on a long-ago day in 1964: "It is never possible to completely reconstruct a person's life from what they leave behind—the absurdity of it all, the pain, the triumphs. What's lost is lost forever, and the silences are telling. But why mourn what we'll lose anyway? Laughter truly is the best medicine, and I find whisky tends to numb and burn what's left behind."

OLY DEVICES
and Infernal Duds

The Broadmore
Exhibits

The Broadmore Exhibits

Greg Broadmore came by his interest in Lambshead's cabinet of curiosities honestly: through a familial connection. "Lambshead's family and mine were connected by an uncle, so even after my grandparents moved to New Zealand, they kept in touch."

On a trip to England at the age of twelve, Broadmore and his parents visited Lambshead. The artist remembers "a man in his eighties who looked more like fifty, but was as big a curmudgeon as you could possibly imagine. But he seemed to have a soft spot for me. At the very point where I was getting bored listening to them talk in the study, Lambshead suggested he step out to take me to the kitchen for some dessert . . . and instead he brought me down some steep steps into an underground space filled with wonders. The place was hewn out of solid stone and had that nice damp cool mossy smell you find in caves sometimes."

Broadmore remembers Lambshead giving him a wink and saying, "Don't break anything," and leaving him there with a glass of milk and some banana bread. "For me, it was like being given a free pass to an amazing fairyland—the outward expression of all of the visions in my head of anything miraculous. It had a deep and lasting effect on my art." For two hours, Broadmore roamed through Lambshead's collection, finding "countless old toys and ridiculously complex machines and scandalous artwork and comics and . . . well, I began to wonder what *wasn't* to be found there."

Broadmore never visited the cabinet again, and since then has, of course, gone on to forge a near-legendary career as an artist and creator aligned with Weta Workshop. "I was particularly saddened to hear of Lambshead's death a few years ago," Broadmore remembers. "It brought back all of those memories of those perfect hours in his cabinet of curiosities."

For this reason, among others, Broadmore kindly agreed to provide illustrative reconstructions for four of Lambshead's museum loans, which have never been photographed, even after his death, pursuant to instructions in his will.

The Electrical Neurheographiton

Documented by Minister Y. Faust, D.Phil

Constructed: March 14, 1914 (patent still pending)

Invented by: Nikola Tesla (Serbian subject of the Austrian Empire, later an American citizen, born July 10, 1856; "died" January 7, 1943)

History: Stolen from the "robotorium" (barn) of farmer-tinkerer Rhett Greene in St. John's, Dominion of Newfoundland, 1947, by Yugoslavian agents. Held in the Sub-Basement 6 of the Marshal Josip Broz Tito Museum of Yugoslavian Civilisation, until sold to Thackery T. Lambshead in 1997 and subsequently lent by his estate to the Slovenian National Museum of Electrical Engineering; L2010.01

Biographical Sketch

Few intellects in the history of Man achieved such Daedalian heights as those conquered by Serbian inventor, mechanical engineer, psychemetrician, and electrodynamist Nikola Tesla. Men as grand of conjecture and achievement as Tesla attract, along with their many accolades, such a volume of obloquy as to produce an aneurysm among all but the most robustly confident of souls. And while Mr. Tesla was confident indeed, even "galactically arrogant," as one detractor called him, he was also terrified of the charge that many of his foes in the scientific and journalistic establishments had hurled at him, *viz.*, that he was insane.

Indeed, as the twentieth century of our Lord unfolded, Tesla served for many cinematistes as the very archetype of the deranged natural physicist or "mad scientist." So it was that, in 1913, Tesla returned from his adopted America to the land of his birth to devote himself to constructing a mechanism that would ensure he never be chained in Bedlam's urine-spattered halls: the electrical neurheographiton (nyu-REY-o-GRAPH-i-ton, *lit.*, brain-wave writer).

Function of the Electrical Neurheographiton

Mr. Tesla's electrical neurheographiton (1914) was the forerunner of the electro-encephalogram and the electro-convulsive malady-eraser, and the estranged nephew of the intravenous mercury phrenological brain engine (known popularly as the "liquid silver guillotine").

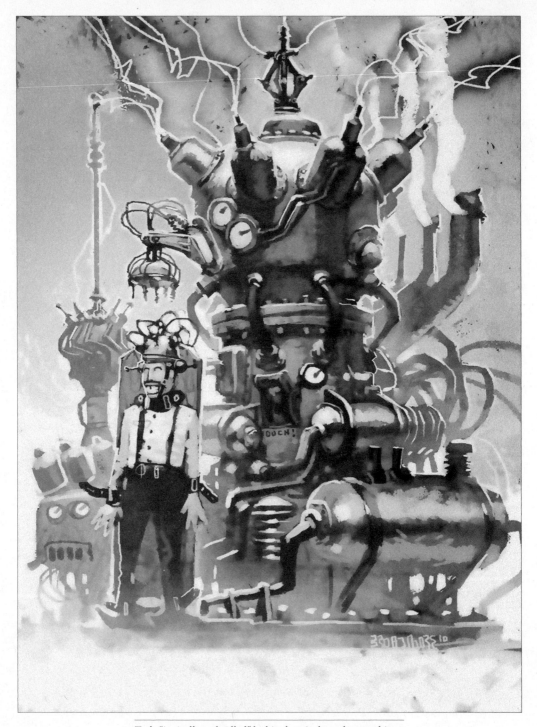

Tesla "ionically enthralled" by his electrical neurheographiton.

A massive mechanical device consisting of a generator and the most sophisticated magnetic-electrical scanner in the world at that time, the neurheographiton beamed electrical energy into a patient's cranium via a "healing helmet." The "electrical balm" demonstrably and immediately undercut the mania, enthusiasm, apostasy, anarchism, and other emotional morbidities of Tesla's numerous test subjects, apparently via relieving them of the burden of painful and traumatic memories (such as the recollection of childhood, adolescence, adulthood, and dotage), priming the patient's brain for emotional "rewriting" with whatever "biographical" data the therapist deemed appropriate. Following a single usage on himself, Tesla declared to his assistant, Mr. Igor Hynchbeck, that, "I'm cured, cured, cured, cured, cured, cured, cured, cured, cured, cured of all my obsessive impulsions! Absolutely, ab-solutely free of all of them!"

Electrophantasmic Discharges

A type of energetic pollution arising from the neurheographiton's manifold and highly charged internal mechanisms were what Mr. Tesla described in his *Apologia Electronika* as "electrophantasmic discharges"—plasmic fields that "disgorged horizontal ejaculations of lightning of a most disturbing and slaughterous composition." These discharges also warped light into phantasms that mimicked recognisable objects and people with resolute credibility. Such apparitions chiefly consisted of:

a. A Bosnian Coarse-Haired Hound eating a clown composed entirely of human kidneys.

b. A massive bust of influential English occultist Aleister Crowley that transmogrified into "a field of bunnies dancing with all the glee of becandied children."

c. A politely dressed Central European man offering a 1907–24 issue Hotchkiss No. 4 Paper Fastener (i.e., a stapler) to an unseen coworker.

Controversy and a Continent Torn Asunder

That final apparition proved most unfortunate for Gavrilo Princip, a nineteen-year-old Bosnian Serb and subject of the Austro-Hungarian Empire. On June

14, 1914, a hungry fifty-eight-year-old Tesla, desperate for a wealthy sponsor after so many investors had deserted him in favour of archrival American electro-tycoon Thomas Edison, sought to attract the royal patronage of Austrian archduke Franz Ferdinand.

Nikola Tesla ca. 1890, well before the majority of this troubles.

An overly enthusiastic Mr. Tesla bade his assistants wheel his neurheographiton into the streets of Sarajevo near Tesla's laboratory in search of the archduke's motorcade. Mr. Tesla planned to project its "plasmic balm" directly through the air and into the crania of the manifold madmen and wild women who prowled the city at all hours of the day and night, so as to prove his device's capacity to unleash a torrent of industrialism among the newly sane, for the betterment of the Austro-Hungarian Empire.

Tesla, a fine statistician in his own right, predicted the likelihood of the neurheographiton unleashing an electrophantasmic discharge as less than 1 per cent. Alas for Tesla, and even more for the archduke and the archduchess, that 1 per cent manifested as a crackle of electrons that bored directly through their bodies like any American accent through any English gathering. And, unfortunately for Gavrilo Princip, the electrophantasm happened to resemble him down to the last detail, with the apparitional stapler appearing to be, to all mortified onlookers, a Browning FN model 1910 pistol.

Princip's absolute innocence—Princip's whereabouts were verified by more than a dozen eyewitnesses at a local Bohemian "cheese shop" (opium den)—was of no defense, largely because, since age eleven, he'd told any Sarajevan who would listen to him that he longed for nothing more than the chance to execute "any Austrian royalist bastard I can get my grimies on." Indeed, Princip had only a fortnight previously completed a tattoo across his back (employing, ironically, another of Mr. Tesla's inventions, the electrographic somatic autodecorator), depicting himself decapitating Austrian emperor Franz Josef I with a cricket bat.

A Second Try in America

Fearing that it was only a matter of time before the authorities connected the archduke's accidental death (and the subsequent Great War that engulfed all of Europe) to the neurheographiton and to him (or assumed that Princip had been

Tesla's human weapon aimed at the archduke), Mr. Tesla returned to the United States to resume developing his mentation engine.

But Tesla quickly found that his funding troubles were as dire as ever. While his protracted conflict with Edison yielded him nothing but grief, his failed lawsuit against Guglielmo Marconi over the patent for radio left him even further in debt.

The following decades were unkind to Mr. Tesla, consisting of quixotic struggles that included a rapid opposition to the League of Nations and increasingly violent claims that "secretive operatives ensconced inside black submarinal vessels patrolled the very oceans, seas, lakes, and rivers in order to spy upon us all with their telescoping looking-glasses!" Tesla developed impulsions, including the unquenchable urge to orbit buildings three times before he entered them,

Aleister Crowley, in mushroom cap, during the majority of his troubles.

to have a stack of three folded napkins at every meal, and to produce neither less nor more than three bowel emissions at every 3 A.M. and 3 P.M. precisely. Finally, on March 3, 1933, Mr. Tesla's maddened certainty that he would win himself a sponsor granted him dividends. Word of his achievements and theories won him patronage of a Mr. Allen Dulles and a Mr. J. E. Hoover. For them, he constructed the Electrical Neurheographiton, Mark 2, which Tesla promised could not only rewrite mental histories but read them, making his device a deception-detector and espionage-recognition motor.

But, alas, patronage for Tesla was not to be. Mr. Tesla, in a bid to impress his sponsors that his device was no mere quackery or hocus-pocusion, arranged a private demonstration for Mr. Dulles and Mr. Hoover. While posterity does not record the contents of what Tesla revealed, Mr. Dulles was said to have quipped to a young Senator John Kennedy that Mr. Hoover found enormous distaste for Tesla's "sartorial speculations" about Mr. Hoover's leisure hours.

Triumph and Death of Tesla, and the
Disappearance of the Neurheographiton

Effectively indexed by the elites who could fund his research, Mr. Tesla embarked on a new odyssey: touring the United States with the smaller, more portable Electrical Neurheographiton, Mark 3, as part of "Genius Nikola Tesla's Electric Circus," announcing "electrical exorcism of various mental afflictions and neurological maladies." Mr. Tesla eventually made enough money (and trade in chickens and illicit spirits) from his circus to fund his various researches for the remainder of his life, including into "electro-transdimensional portals."

Finally tendering "exclusive" sales of the technical specifications of the Mark 4 to Warner Bros. Studios, Metro-Goldwyn-Mayer, and United Artists in 1939, Tesla departed from public life, offering occasional anti-Relativity screeds while devoting most of his time to developing a "teleforce projector," or death ray.

On January 12, 1943, Mr. Tesla was claimed to have died, although reports were conflicting. Many in Hollywood conjectured immediately that assassins in the pay of Big Cinema had done in the Serbian genius for selling them "exclusive" rights to a device whose blueprints contained, in tiny print, the phrase "I have omitted an explanation only for the motive unit which makes the entire machine work, in fear that the alchemists of celluloid might enthrall their nation and the world with ludicrous tales of vacuous lives." Others believed that Mr. Tesla's madness finally claimed him, inflicting him with a Jovian "brain burst" that produced not Minerva but rather a puddle of bloodied grey matter upon Tesla's hotel room floor. Among the modern-day Fraternal Society of Teslic Scientific Investigators, there remains the belief that Tesla's "corpse" was an electrophantasmic discharge that had merged with organic materials in the hotel room to produce a permanent simulacrum of Tesla, while the "real" man departed from this world to explore the Universe, unhindered by the constraints of mortals.

Documentation released following the dissolution of Yugoslavia at least identifies the path that Mr. Tesla's inventions took following their master's putative death. Farmer and amateur inventor Mr. Rhett Greene tracked down every working or dysfunctional electrical neurheographiton and, by means of wagon train, transported their many parts back to his "robotorium" (barn) in the then Dominion of Newfoundland, where he, without success, laboured for several years to make them work. Then, on Christmas Day 1947, Yugoslavian agents forcibly entered Mr. Greene's barn under cover of darkness and extracted all of Mr. Tesla's creations they found there.

The Lambshead Imperative

Dr. Thackery T. Lambshead, who had long enjoyed Mr. Tesla's invectives against Dr. Einstein's theories of special and general relativity, in 1997 tracked the remains of Tesla's most bizarre device (that had actually worked) to the Sub-Basement 6 of the Marshal Josip Broz Tito Museum of Yugoslavian Civilisation.

Apparently long-forgotten, the neurheographiton had been used to produce an indiscernible, global, mental domination, *viz.*, to effect the export and sale of the Yugo. Because the Bosnian-Herzegovinian state held no interest in the ravings of a Serbian "madman," Lambshead was able to acquire the entirety of the Tesla collection for the sum of 100 marka (about US $66). By the conditions of Dr. Lambshead's will, Lambshead's estate lent Tesla's materials to the Slovenian National Museum of Electrical Engineering (L2010.01), where they were nearly destroyed in a terrorist attack by members of the Church of Electrology.

St. Brendan's Shank

Documented by Kelly Barnhill

Museum: The Museum of Medical Anomalies, Royal College of Surgeons, London

Exhibit: St. Brendan's Shank

Medium: Copper, silver

Date: 1270s (?) (disputed)

Origin: The monks of the Isle of St. Brendan, also known as the Isle of the Blessed (disputed); the Faroe Islands (undisputed point of collection)

St. Brendan's Shank is a small device—eight inches long from tip to tip—made from thirty-seven interlocking copper globes, circular hinges, a narrow headpiece (with burrowing snout), and a winding key connected to a clockwork interior (silver alloy and iron). The device itself has an uncannily efficient winding system—a single turn of the pin sets its lifelike wriggle in motion for days, even months, at a time. More than one biologist has noted the device's astonishing mimicry of the movements, behaviors, and habits of a tiny subspecies of the Turrilepad, or armored worm, called the Turrilepus Gigantis, found in the North Sea and other cold-water locations. Like its prehistoric cousins, the segmented body of the Turrilepus Gigantis was covered in a tough, calcitic armor, had a sharp, burrowing snout, and exhibited a distinct lack of fastidiousness when it came to its diet.

The name of the Shank originates with the brethren of the Order of Brendan, although not from the saint himself. St. Brendan (called the Navigator, the Voyager, and the Bold) was no inventor, being far more interested in the navigational utility of the heavenly stars, the strange insistence of the sea, and, in one famously preserved quotation, the curious hum of his small boat's leather hull against the foamy breasts of the ocean's waves: "So like the suckling child, I return, openmouthed, to the rocking bosom of the endless sea." He was not a man of science, nor of medicine, nor of healing. He was known for his ability to inspire blind devotion and ardent love in his followers, who willingly went to the farthest edges of the known world to found fortresses of prayer, only to have their beloved abbott leave them behind.

One such monastery existed for many centuries on the cliffs of the Isle of

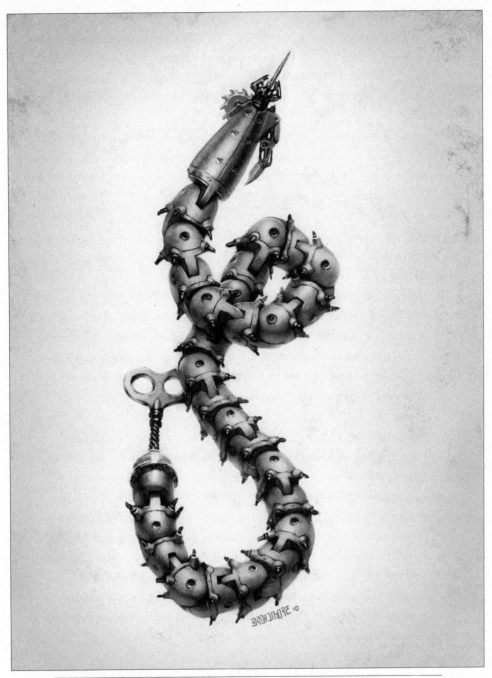

St. Brendan's Shank, made of interlocking copper pieces, with over thirty springs to keep the pieces in tension with one another.

St. Brendan—also known as the Isle of the Blessed—a lush, verdant island once inhabited by a strange pre-Coptic civilization that had since vanished, leaving only a series of man-made saltwater lakes that appeared to have some religious significance. The monks soon added to the many strange tales surrounding the place, for it was said that the monks themselves would never die unless they left the island.

It was here that the idea for the Shank appears to have originated, although the sophistication of the device has led to theories of outside collusion. Some, for example, believe that the device shows evidence of workmanship common to the Early Middle Period of Muslim scientific flowering in the 1200s, specifically the influence of the (nonmonastic) brothers known as Banu Musa, and their *Book of Ingenius Devices*. Given the amount of traveling the monks did over the centuries, it is not impossible that they came into contact with either the Banu Musa or equivalent.

Whether or not this legend is true, it seems incontestable that the development of the Shank followed eventually from an event in 1078, when the lonely order on the island found itself an unwilling host to the unstable and murderous son of Viking despot Olaf the Bloodless, King of Jutland. The arrival of the young Viking on the isle was recorded in the sagas of a bard known only as Sigi, who was present with the Viking entourage accompanying the prince.

> "The son of Olaf, upon hearing tell of an Isle populated by the Monks-Who-Cheated-Death, became inflamed by desire to find the place and conquer its secrets. The Isle, like a coward, made itself difficult to find, but the Prince did give chase through storm, through mist, and through ice until at last, the Isle was in our sights. We arrived with swords in hand, slicing open the first two monks who greeted us, as a demonstration of force and might. It was in this way that we learned that the Monks-Who-Cheated-Death had only cheated the death of cowards and slaves—a death in a bed, a death of age, a death of sickness. The death of Men cannot be cheated, nor can their Magics wish it away. And nothing, not even their craven God, is mightier than a Jutland sword. The monks knelt and trembled and wailed before us."

This account is contradicted in part by the journal of Brother Eidan, abbott of the order since the departure of their founder-saint: "The children of the children of the men who once laid waste to our homeland arrived upon our shores unexpectedly. They were tired and hungry and sick at heart. Our souls were moved to pity and we welcomed them with open arms. Their demands seemed beyond our abilities or strength to fulfill, but we had no choice but to try, as otherwise they would have put us all to the sword."

The prince suffered from a wasting disease that Sigi and other chroniclers had either covered up or had judiciously neglected to mention—this was the real reason the prince had come to the monks' island. What followed appeared to consist of a series of ablutions in the icy waters of the island's western bay. The monks told the prince they staved off death by stripping naked, bearing their skin to the morning light, and plunging into the water. Of course, if their other accounts are to be believed, any longevity, possible or impossible, came simply from prayer and from other essential properties of the island.

Nevertheless, after the young man stripped, winced, and shivered, submerging his body every morning for a full week, a miracle occurred. The son of King Olaf emerged from the water a new man, naked and shining, blessed with strength and health. "My disease is devoured and vanquished," he cried, and the Viking horde gave a halfhearted cheer. They left the island in a relatively unpillaged condition. No account tells of exactly *how* the prince was cured, however, despite the first reference in the literature to a "creature of healing." Nor is there any explanation for the prince's eventual death two years later, except for an obscure fragment from Sigi referring to "bleeding." Perhaps coincidentally or perhaps not, Brother Eidan died prior to the prince's recovery, and his successor, Brother Jonathan, notes only that "he made his sacrifice for our sake, and would that such a sacrifice not need be made again."[1]

A medieval representation of St. Brendan and his followers worshipping atop a floating sea monster.

The subsequent bleeding caught no one's attention, but news of the incredible healing spread slowly throughout Europe, with the result that many an expedition put forth into the northern seas. However, the island proved ridiculously difficult to find again. Many tried and failed, some sailing to their deaths. From these attempts grew the legend that the isle moved across the seas, from charted waters to the uncharted danger of "Here be dragons." Over the centuries, it would reportedly be sighted in view of the Canaries, in the midst of the Hebrides, off the coast of Newfoundland, and once apparently passed so close to Iceland that the bards sang of "waving at the holy men," interpreted by some scholars as a reference to extreme drunkenness instead.

If the monks' own records can be believed—and these accounts are vague on many points—by the late 1200s, the monks had succeeded, perhaps in partnership with Arab scientists traveling to Africa, in fashioning a mechanical equivalent to what presumably must have been a kind of symbiotic relationship with a form of Turrilepus Gigantis.

Over time—due in part to the creation of copies and the reduction in the number of monks from fatalities from drowning, slipping on wet stone floors, and the like—each monk came to be in possession of a replica of his own, although from the few descriptions, most of these may have been crude, nonfunctional copies.

The Shank—*our Shank*, the monks said fondly—soon became sanctified as a holy object. It became friend, confidant, and spiritual guide to every monk on the island, from the lowliest of the novitiate to the interim abbott. The monks carried the replicas around in their pockets, held them delicately (desperately) to their mouths, whispering secrets in the dark. Given the extraordinarily long lives of the monks, they had more secrets than most to confess to their small, metal friends.

After the silence of the Dark Ages, the Shank came once again to the notice of the burgeoning medical community in the West in the form of a smattering of accounts that hailed it as a kind of miraculous relic, but noting that even though healed, the recipients of the Shank suffered from a strange melancholy bordering on mania, following their treatment. Such patients drew pictures of the Shank—both the clockwork Turrilepad and the Turrilepad in the flesh. They painted portraits and composed sonnets and sang odes. They whispered the name of the lost saint in their dreams, and, as though suddenly losing sight of their senses, they would call out to him during the day, responding to the ensuing silence with fits of weeping. They left their families, left their businesses and affairs, and took to the sea, their eyes scanning the horizon for . . . well, they would not say. It was generally believed that they *could* not say.

Indeed, by the year 1522, Pope Adrian VI—having had enough of talk of floating islands, healing that resulted in death by melancholia, bleeding, or worse, and other rumors that, in his opinion, were, at best, due to the infernal influence of the followers of that fallen priest, Martin Luther, or, at worst (and Heaven forbid!), an insidious Ottoman plot—banned the use of the Shank, banned mention of the

Shank, and excommunicated the entire Order of St. Brendan. "Since the presence or absence of suffering is due wholly to the whims of God, it is a blasphemy and an insult to thwart the divine Plan," he wrote in October of that year, though, in his writings, he demonstrates an acute ignorance of *how* the Shank worked. He died a year later. It is doubtful that the monks on the wandering isle ever knew of their excommunication, or, indeed, that they would have cared.

Throughout the historical record, then, the actual *function* of the Shank had gone assiduously *unmentioned* in its brief appearances. The witnesses to the Shank merely attested that it *worked*, remaining curiously mum on other important matters for quite some time.

Perhaps because of this very mystery, Dr. Lambshead became keenly interested in locating one. Through his deep and multilayered explorations of the history of the medical arts, Lambshead had encountered several modern references to the Shank—particularly in his extensive rereading of *The Trimble-Manard Omnibus of Insidious Arctic Maladies*, edited by John Trimble and Rebecca Manard, long after his bitter and public feud with both Trimble and Manard—a kind of attempt through scholarship to reconcile. Still, he did not lay eyes on the object until many years later.

According to Dr. Lambshead's journals, volume 27, book 4, he finally encountered the Shank during World War II, while performing his duty as a surgeon on the Island of Mykines, the Faroe Islands still under the British flag. (He would soon return to his wartime efforts at London's Combustipol General Hospital.)

On October 5, 1941, the doctor wrote: "Patient arrived: an elderly gentleman, rapid heartbeat, high fever, terrible bleeding from the mouth and anus. Private Lansing informed me that the ancient man was found clinging to a leather-hulled skiff that had wedged between two large rocks at the lee of the island. The man was dressed in the manner of those bent toward monasticism—rough cloth, broken sandals, a rope binding the waist—and was impossibly old. His face had the look of leaves gone to mulch. His body was as light as paper and twice as fragile; his limbs fluttered and flapped as the breeze blew in cold gusts over the North Atlantic."

Lambshead further notes, and the duty log from the day confirms, that "He claimed to be an abbot in the Order of St. Brendan, and asked for forgiveness several times, but for what we had no clue, except for frequent references to his 'weakness.' Where he had come from, we had no idea—due to the currents in that place and a partial blockade by the Germans, it was all but impossible that he had sailed his boat from another part of the island—he had to have come from the sea." However, as Dr. Lambshead noted, there wasn't another island within one hundred miles, and the monk's boat could at best be classified "as a pathetic cockleshell."

The man carried with him "an intricate mechanical device that he clutched tightly in his hands." Although the artifact intrigued Lambshead, he had no time to examine it closely. The man was in need of immediate medical assistance. The bleeding was so profuse that it seemed to the doctor to have been caused by shrapnel, though that was "terribly unlikely." There had been no attacks in the last week against any of the islands—just a long, tense stalemate—and the wound "was fresh, and flowing."

The old monk explained that he had come from a place called Brendan's Isle after his craft became tempest-tossed in a sudden gale, and the island disappeared, and the monk was left alone on the undulating waves. Somehow, the doctor did not quite believe this explanation, although "to this day I couldn't say why I should doubt a dying monk."[2]

"Come back," the monk moaned, his eyes sliding past the rim of his sockets. "Oh, please come back with me."

"Does it hurt here?" the doctor asked, ignoring the monk as he palpated the belly.

"Was this the fate of our beloved Brendan?" the old man wheezed. "To realize too late that he was wrong to leave, that he wanted to come home." Tears leaked from the old man's rheumy eyes. "Always we wander, and it is so lonely. No matter where our island travels."

The doctor, assuming the man was raving, called the nurse to bring in the ether.

"Don't operate," the old monk raved, clutching his belly. "Oh, dear God, don't take it away."

"Don't take what away?" Lambshead said reasonably. "Your odd artifact is safe with us. You can have it back once we've operated." He wondered with growing irritation what on earth could be taking that nurse so long.

The monk's thin arm shot from the gurney, grabbed the doctor's crisp, white coat. "We were so alone," the monk whispered. "The Isle of the Blessed is a cold and lonely and desperate place without our beloved saint. And I am alone, and not alone. My brother! My brother! Don't take him!"

Lambshead reports that the monk shuddered so violently as the nurse came in, donning her surgical smock and mask, that he thought the monk might die right then, right there.

Five drops of ether, the doctor remembers thinking calmly. "Or, perhaps seven. Indeed, make it an even ten."

Soon, Lambshead opened up the anesthetized man's belly, and deep in the old monk's gut he found a very large tumor—nearly the size of a rugby ball, though three times as heavy—and inside the tumor, happily burrowing and eating away, "was a specimen of some form of Turrilepus Gigantis! The mirror image of the complex clockwork artifact we had found in the monk's pocket!"

After convincing the nurse to neither pass out nor leave the room, the doctor realized at once that the tumor, not the Turrilepus Gigantis—whether symbiotic or parasitic or belonging to some third classification—required immediate attention: "It was malignant and fast-growing, apparently too fast-growing to be mastered by the monk's little brother."

However, even Lambshead's best efforts were not enough.

"Exhausted and saddened by the outcome," Lambshead writes, "I nonetheless, in the interests of science, immediately performed an autopsy and attempted to preserve the Turrilepus Gigantis in an empty marmalade jar." What he found startled him: "This very old, tired man had had the organs and circulatory system of a twenty-five-year-old. If not for the aggressive growth of the tumor, a million-to-one anomaly that his symbiotic brother could not devour quickly enough, the monk might've lived another sixty or seventy years at least."

He also found that the mindless movements of the pre-wound replica had an oddly "hypnotic and vaguely dulling effect on me, its copper snout curling and uncurling rhythmically.

"What happened on the Isle of St. Brendan, I have no idea," Lambshead would write after the war, in a letter to the then-curator of the Museum of Medical Anomalies as part of the grant that included turning over the mechanical Shank and a half-dissolved, sad-looking Turrilepus Gigantis, "but I remain convinced that the last surviving member of Order of St. Brendan died on my operating table on 3 November 1941, and that this order had hitherto survived for centuries in part because of a symbiotic relationship with a creature that provided a high level of preventative medicine and thus conferred on these monks extremely long life. That extremely long life in such isolation may, in fact, be its own kind of illness I cannot speculate upon."

A month after the death and burial of the castaway monk, one Private Lansing wrote this in his journal: "Doctor Lambshead, always an odd duck, becomes odder by the day, afflicted as he is by a strange, growing sadness. He stands at all hours at the edge of the sea, his hand cupped over his eyes, scanning the horizon. He mutters to himself, and raves. And what's worse, he's given himself over to a bizarre religious fanaticism, calling out the name of a saint, waking, dreaming, again and again and again."

Whether this temporary melancholy was caused by the events of the war or by possession of the Shank is unknown, but in later years, Lambshead was known to remark, "I must say I was very happy to give the thing away."

Due to issues of medical ethics, the Shank displayed in this exhibit has yet to be tested on human patients. Nor have other specimens of this particular type of Turrilepus Gigantis ever been found.

ENDNOTES

1. There is unsubstantiated conjecture by Menard and Trimble that somehow the abbott conveyed his own seeming good health upon the Viking, as a way of saving the island, and that the monks then sought some way to avoid a similar catastrophe in future by creating an artifact that could, without a similar later sacrifice, perform the same function.

2. Later investigation would uncover nine reports from fishermen claiming to have found a castaway floating in the remains of a broken boat. Each report described a man dressed in the habit of a monk and impossibly old—a face like leaves gone to mulch, a body light as paper. Each man raved and raved about the Shank and a saint lost forever. In each instance, they died before reaching land, and their bodies were given over to the sea. If any of these men hid anything among their possessions, no record of it exists. What catastrophe they might have been fleeing is unknown, although German U-boat records do contain references to the sinking of at least two "ships" that do not correspond to any losses in the records of the Allies.

The Auble Gun

Documented by Will Hindmarch

Drs. Franz S. Auble and Lauritz E. Auble, Inventor/Designer

Auble Gun, 1884–1922

Purchased by Dr. Lambshead, January 1922

1922.11.1a&b

My goal is to create a new battlefield milieu in which a select few do battle for the sake of their ideals and their nations with science and engineering on their backs; a new generation of gallant combatants and miniaturized engines of war—knights not with horses and lances but with boilers and bullets.

—Dr. Franz Auble

The Development and Reputation of a Singular Weapon

According to Aidan Birch's book, *Cranks and Steam: The Story of the Auble Gun* (1921), Franz Auble came to America from Prague in 1855, at the age of eleven, with his mother. Though the Aubles were wealthy enough to buy Franz out of military service, due to a near-tragic misunderstanding he fought in the American Civil War as part of a Northern artillery battery and went deaf in his right ear as a result. Young Franz Auble's time among the deafening muskets and cannons may have inspired his idea for a shoulder-mounted weapon. "Franz Auble must very much enjoy being deaf," wrote Martin Speagel in the *St. Louis Gazette*, "for it means he hears only half of his bad ideas."

Although not widely known by the public, the Auble gun ranks among firearms and artillery enthusiasts as one of history's great curios. Not quite a personal firearm and not quite miniaturized artillery, the Auble is a man-portable, multibarreled *mitrailleuse* designed to be carried and fired on an operator's shoulder for "ease and haste of transport and displacement in tenuous battlefield circumstances," according to a lecture given by Franz Auble in 1882.

American humorist and essayist Edgar Douglas, while on a monologue tour in 1891, famously deemed it "the Awful gun." American shootists, in periodicals of the era, joked that it was the "Unstauble gun or Wobble gun."

The weapon's infamous instability was a result of the Aubles' innovative "human bipod" design. Franz Auble's vision cast able-bodied soldiers in the role of "specially trained mobile gunnery platforms," which would operate in three-man fire teams, triangulating on enemy positions. "Ideally," Franz Auble wrote, "the gun's very presence is enough to stymie or deter enemy soldiers, ending battles through superior military posture and displays of ingenious invention rather than outright bloodshed."

Word of Franz Auble's interest in "military posturing" over battlefield effectiveness led to his being labeled "a showman, not a shootist" by *Gentleman Rifleman* editor Errol MacCaskill in the periodical's winter 1882 issue. The Auble gun was still only in active development at the time. Billed as "a more personal approach to gentlemanly annihilation," perhaps tongue-in-cheek, an early hand-cranked prototype of the Auble gun debuted in 1883, just a year before the first demonstration of a proper machine gun: the Maxim gun, invented by Sir Hiram Maxim. Whereas the Maxim gun's reloading mechanism was powered by the weapon's own recoil action, the first Auble gun prototype was still powered by a hand crank. It looked somewhat like an oversized, shoulder-mounted film camera—and, indeed, some early design prototypes might have allowed shooters to shoot what they were shooting, so to speak.

When the Maxim gun first gained real attention, in the mid-1880s, Auble went back to the drawing board and the firing range. The era of the machine gun was coming, and in his journals, Franz would later bemoan his "fatally late understanding that the revolution would be in the field of ever-swifter reloading mechanisms, not the perfection of techniques to balance machinery on the human shoulder! Who knew?"

In the middle of 1884, however, Franz Auble was diagnosed with Brandywine syndrome, a rare and misunderstood disease in that day and age. Knowing he had limited time left to continue his work, he retreated to a cottage outside Boston, intent on designing a mechanism that would put the Auble gun into serious competition with the Maxim.

Journal entries from the time are chaotic—Franz combined his engineering notes with a dream journal analyzing months of fevered and torrid dreams of war and his dead wife—but on November 12, 1884, Franz wrote, "If I cannot escape my dreams, I must learn from them. I see smokestacks and gun barrels. I hear gurgling boilers and empty shells raining on cobblestones. It seems clear what the gun is asking me for!"

What he had arrived at was bold and, some said, insane: the creation of a steam engine to load rounds into the weapon automatically at the same time

The Auble Gun, probably being modeled by Dr. Lauritz E. Auble
(from a badly damaged photograph, ca. 1912).

that it discarded spent cartridges. He produced detailed drawings. He had patent
forms drawn up. He ordered smiths to forge new boilers and frames. He gave his
famous interview to *Cranks and Steam* author Aidan Birch. Then he died.

A Son Continues His Father's Uncertain Legacy

It was edging toward the spring of 1885. Snow was melting into the mud on the
day of Dr. Franz Auble's funeral in Massachusetts, and it seemed at first that his
work might never be completed. Lauritz was a dutiful son and devoted business
partner, but as he would later tell Aidan Birch, "I lacked my father's creative impulse. What came easily to him came to me with great difficulty. I did not have

his head for numbers or his vision." Birch is reputed to have replied that this might be more boon than curse, and when Lauritz asked him to elaborate, said that "vision is not the same as sight." Thus bolstered, Lauritz set out to forge a future for the Auble gun.

Lauritz's first goal was to improve the weapon's stability, especially after early tests with the portable boiler revealed the weapon to be dangerously inaccurate. Between the bubbling boiler and the rattling barrels, the gun proved good at providing a harrowing base of fire . . . but little else. The boiler chugged. The gun trembled. The shooter shook. In one well-photographed demonstration in 1885, the gun walked itself upward in such a flash that it hurled the test-shooter onto his back, cracking the boiler and belching steam onto the shooter and his handlers.

In response to the accident, Lauritz Auble experimented with orangutan shooters with Auble guns upon their backs, but no orangutan would come near the steaming device. "Only humans," Lauritz wrote in his journal, "are bold enough to master the Auble gun and its formidable report."

Abandoning his flirtation with trained animals, Lauritz devised new "human quadrapod" braces for would-be shooters. Each brace was bound to the shooter's shoulder and upper arm, affixed to a long, crutch-like leg extending down to a rubber foot. This gave the shooter two additional points of contact with the ground—one spar from each elbow—thereby stabilizing the shooter and the gun. This refined design is what Lauritz Auble took to the U.S. Army and Navy for demonstrations in the winter of 1885.

It did not fare well.

According to one military observer, the demonstration shooter "moved about like a newborn calf with a Gatling gun on its back; unsteady and uncertain. . . ." The Navy passed on the gun altogether. The Army ordered one revised Auble gun, but canceled their order within the week. Demonstrations for the British Army, the Canadian Army, and a small band of fanatical freemasons fared no better.

Seemingly, Lauritz was out of options. The unwanted gun had become a mechanical albatross, one that could counterintuitively kill with the slightest mis-shrug, yet could scarcely hit a target.

"My father wouldn't quit if he were here," Lauritz wrote in his diary. "In all the hours I spent watching him in his workshops, no lessons were more clear than these: That my father loved me and that he would not abandon his work for anything short of death.

"Neither shall I."

The Repurposing of the Gun for Entertainment

However, unnoticed by Lauritz, something positive was happening at his demonstrations—something that caught the attention of entrepreneur Luther Fafnerd: crowds of civilians were coming out to see the Auble gun in action.

By 1885, Luther Fafnerd was known for two things: his famed, contest-winning mustache, and the traveling circus shows he produced with his cousin, Thaddeus. Luther Fafnerd visited Lauritz Auble in January of 1886 at the Auble townhouse in Boston, and, over brandy and cigars, devised a new function for the Auble gun (and for Lauritz Auble).

As reported by the local paper, Fafnerd famously said after the meeting, "I know spectacle, and what Lauritz Auble has there is spectacular. Bring your eyeballs, ladies and gentlemen, and your earplugs—we have a new attraction!"

Lauritz tapped into his experiences pitching the Auble gun to military men to transform himself from businessman to showman. He traveled Europe and America with the next-generation Auble gun on his shoulder, demonstrating the weapon's incredible power and phenomenal noise for audiences from San Francisco to Prague. He wore a top hat and tuxedo and touted the Auble as a gentleman's engine of war.

Lauritz eroded dummy armies with a withering barrage of lead. Children marveled. Lauritz blasted plaster bunkers to bits. Crowds applauded.

While visitors were cheering, Lauritz was going deaf, like his father. So he incorporated that into the act. Cries of "Wot wot wot Lauritz?!" greeted him every time he ascended the stage.

Encouraged beyond his wildest dreams, and desperate to keep his audience—which he saw as "vindication of my father's work"—Lauritz devised increasingly theatrical shows, casting himself as a dramatic star and his Auble gun as a variety of famous weapons. He drew the gun from a papier-mâché stone and became King Arthur. Then he shot the stone to pieces and slew a dozen mannequin Mordreds. He strode across a rocky field, perched atop an elephant with an Auble on his shoulder, and became Hannibal blasting cardboard centurions apart with a steam hiss and a rattling thrum.

"People demand not just a performance," Luther Fafnerd once said, "but *heroics*!" Lauritz imagined that he was delivering just that.

His plans grew out of control. He devised a fifty-man stunt show called *The Battle of the Nile* that would pit Auble-armed stuntmen in boats maneuvering and firing blanks at each other off the Chicago lakeshore, but the Fafnerds refused to pay for it. They had something else in mind.

American "automotive inventor" James Tasker had come to the Fafnerds with a new contraption—the Tasker Battle Carriage—and a simple sketch for a show: pit the rumbling Battle Carriage against lifelike animals preserved with rudimentary taxidermy.

Best of all, for outlandish sums, private citizens brought in by one of the Fafnerds' circus trains could ride the Battle Carriage and hunt animals loosed from pens into Tasker's private ranch for the occasion. Tasker had effectively found a way to monetize the testing process for his new weapon-wagon. As Tasker wrote the Fafnerds in 1908: "Auble provides a weapon you want to see—I provide a weapon that spectators actually wish they could fire first-hand. For a few, we make that wish come true!"

Thaddeus Fafnerd signed the deal with Tasker in the summer of 1908 without telling Lauritz. Soon after, Lauritz was out of a job.

The Auble gun had failed as a weapon of war and had gone out in a hail of glory as a novelty. What could the future possibly hold? "Perhaps a joke, perhaps a curious footnote," Lauritz is said to have muttered on more than one occasion.

The Aftermath and Dying Fall of the Auble Gun

In the years that followed, Lauritz gradually faded from the spotlight, even for weapons enthusiasts. Young weapons designers tended to associate the Auble gun with sideshows, and thus any of his attempts to serve as a consultant failed.

Immediately following his circus departure, Lauritz started to woo Daisy Fafnerd, the forty-year-old widowed daughter of Thaddeus the ringmaster. Thaddeus, an ordained minister and never one to let business come before love, married them the same summer that the Auble shows were finally canceled: 1908. The new couple traveled with the Fafnerd Cousins Circus for years afterward, managing performances and arranging venues.

Just shy of fifty specimens of the Auble gun, in various makes and models, were put into storage in a Fafnerd Cousins warehouse in Nebraska—only to be destroyed in a tornado in 1912. One local headline read, "Circus Warehouse Destroyed, Nothing Valuable Lost, Show Must Go On." The field around the warehouse was littered with top hats, clown shoes, and bent Auble barrels. Clown makeup smeared the grass for years. Only one working Auble gun, a model used during the early circus days and kept in Lauritz Auble's Boston townhouse, now remained intact.

As the Fafnerd cousins grew older, they sold off their circus piece by piece and retired. Lauritz and Daisy lived for a few years off their savings, but the Auble

The Tasker Battle Carriage in action, re-created by Sam Van Olffen from period newspaper descriptions for use in one of his interminable performance art productions.

family fortune was gone—spent on Auble guns—and their circus money was rapidly dwindling. They sold the Boston townhouse and moved into an apartment, with, according to Birch, "a third of the space given over to half-finished inventions."

After the Great War exploded in Europe, Lauritz donated his time to the stateside war effort, assembling and testing weapons for the U.S. Army until peace came in 1918. That same year, Laurtiz was diagnosed with Brandywine syndrome, inherited from his father. Daisy passed away from a bout of pneumonia the following year.

In 1921, *Cranks and Steam* was published to widespread acclaim, much to Lauritz's dismay. Inside, the Auble was touted as a turn-of-the-century marvel of steam engineering and a bizarre breakthrough in firearms design. Yet the work was not quite a celebration of Auble ingenuity. The Auble gun was the steam, but the Auble men were the cranks. And there, on page 201, was an interview with James Tasker about his "profound vision" for the next-generation Battle Carriage, along with a smug quote about the Auble gun.

Humiliated by the book, Lauritz withdrew from society.

It was in the earliest weeks of 1922, when Lauritz Auble was dwelling alone in his tiny flat, quietly withering away, that a young Thackery T. Lambshead came calling. He wanted to buy the last remaining Auble gun—the gun he had marveled at so many years before from the stands of the Fafnerd Cousins Circus—and install it in his burgeoning collection of antiquities and curios. Lambshead was offering the Aubles some measure of recognition for the marvelous thing they'd created, ridiculous and grand.

"It's a grand and curious thing, that gun," Lambshead supposedly told Lauritz. "It's the gun that war didn't want." Lambshead reportedly spent the day with Lauritz, hearing tales of Franz Auble and Daisy and of Lauritz's time with the circus. They drank port and smoked cigars. "Your gun might not have shot anyone, but its report echoed in imaginations from the California coast to the uttermost edge of Europe," Lambshead recalls telling Lauritz. "That's quite a difficult shot to make."

Of Lauritz's reply, there is no record.

Dacey's Patent Automatic Nanny

Documented by Ted Chiang

From the catalog accompanying the exhibition "Little Defective Adults—Attitudes Toward Children from 1700 to 1950", National Museum of Psychology, Akron, Ohio

The Automatic Nanny was the creation of Reginald Dacey, a mathematician born in London in 1861. Dacey's original interest was in building a teaching engine; inspired by the recent advances in gramophone technology, he sought to convert the arithmetic mill of Charles Babbage's proposed Analytical Engine into a machine capable of teaching grammar and arithmetic by rote. Dacey envisioned it not as a replacement for human instruction, but as a labor-saving device to be used by schoolteachers and governesses.

For years, Dacey worked diligently on his teaching engine, and even the death of his wife, Emily, in childbirth in 1894 did little to slow his efforts.

What changed the direction of his research was his discovery, several years later, of how his son, Lionel, was being treated by the nanny, a woman known as Nanny Gibson. Dacey himself had been raised by an affectionate nanny, and for years assumed that the woman he'd hired was treating his son in the same way, occasionally reminding her not to be too lenient. He was shocked to learn that Nanny Gibson routinely beat the boy and administered Gregory's Powder (a potent and vile-tasting laxative) as punishment. Realizing that his son actually lived in terror of the woman, Dacey immediately fired her. He carefully interviewed several prospective nannies afterwards, and was surprised to learn of the vast range in their approaches to child-rearing. Some nannies showered their charges with affection, while others applied disciplinary measures worse than Nanny Gibson's.

Dacey eventually hired a replacement nanny, but regularly had her bring Lionel to his workshop so he could keep her under close supervision. This must have seemed like paradise to the child, who demonstrated nothing but obedience in Dacey's presence; the discrepancy between Nanny Gibson's accounts of his son's behavior and his own observations prompted Dacey to begin an investigation into optimal child-rearing practices. Given his mathematical inclination, he

Dacey's Patent Automatic Nanny in stand-by mode. In active mode, the arms meet so that the Automatic Nanny can rock the baby to sleep without the need for a cradle or even a blanket.

viewed a child's emotional state as an example of a system in unstable equilibrium. His notebooks from the period include the following: "Indulgence leads to misbehavior, which angers the nanny and prompts her to deliver punishment more severe than is warranted. The nanny then feels regret, and subsequently overcompensates with further indulgence. It is an inverted pendulum, prone to oscillations of ever-increasing magnitude. If we can only keep the pendulum vertical, there is no need for subsequent correction."

Dacey tried imparting his philosophy of child-rearing to a series of nannies for Lionel, only to have each report that the child was not obeying her. It appears not to have occurred to him that Lionel might behave differently with the nannies than with Dacey himself; instead, he concluded that the nannies were too temperamental to follow his guidelines. In one respect, he concurred with the conventional wisdom of the time, which held that women's emotional nature made them unsuitable parents; where he differed was in thinking that too much punishment could be just as detrimental as too much affection. Eventually, he decided that the only nanny that could adhere to the procedures he outlined would be one he built himself.

In letters to colleagues, Dacey offered multiple reasons for turning his attention to a mechanical nursemaid. First, such a machine would be radically easier to construct than a teaching engine, and selling them offered a way to raise the funds needed to perfect the latter. Second, he saw it as an opportunity for early intervention: by putting children in the care of machines while they were still infants, he could ensure they didn't acquire bad habits that would have to be broken later. "Children are not born sinful, but become so because of the influence of those whose care we have placed them in," he wrote. "Rational child-rearing will lead to rational children."

It is indicative of the Victorian attitude toward children that at no point does Dacey suggest that children should be raised by their parents. Of his own participation in Lionel's upbringing, he wrote, "I realize that my presence entails risk of the very dangers I wish to avoid, for while I am more rational than any woman, I am not immune to the boy's expressions of delight or dejection. But progress can only occur one step at a time, and even if it is too late for Lionel to fully reap the benefits of my work, he understands its importance. Perfecting this machine means other parents will be able to raise their children in a more rational environment than I was able to provide for my own."

For the manufacture of the Automatic Nanny, Dacey contracted with Thomas Bradford & Co., maker of sewing and laundry machines. The majority of the Nanny's torso was occupied by a spring-driven clockwork mechanism that controlled the feeding and rocking schedule. Most of the time, the arms formed a cradle for rocking the baby. At specified intervals, the machine would raise the baby into feeding position and expose an India-rubber nipple connected to a reservoir of infant formula. In addition to the crank handle for winding the mainspring, the Nanny had a smaller crank for powering the gramophone player used to play lullabies; the gramophone had to be unusually small to fit within the Nanny's head, and only custom-stamped discs could be played on it. There was also a foot pedal near the Nanny's base used for pressurizing the waste pump, which provided suction for the pair of hoses leading from the baby's rubber diaper to a chamber pot.

The Automatic Nanny went on sale in March 1901, with an advertisement appearing in the *Illustrated London News* (shown on the next page).

It is worth noting that, rather than promoting the raising of rational children, the advertising preys on parents' fears of untrustworthy nursemaids. This may have just been shrewd marketing on the part of Dacey's partners at Thomas Bradford & Co., but some historians think it reveals Dacey's actual motives for developing the Automatic Nanny. While Dacey always described his proposed teaching engine as an assistive tool for governesses, he positioned the Automatic Nanny as a complete replacement for a human nanny. Given that nannies came from the working class, while governesses typically came from the upper class, this suggests an unconscious class prejudice on Dacey's part.

Whatever the reasons for its appeal, the Automatic Nanny enjoyed a brief period of popularity, with over 150 being sold within six months. Dacey maintained that the families that used the Automatic Nanny were entirely satisfied with the quality of care provided by the machine, although there is no way to verify this; the testimonials used in the advertisements were likely invented, as was customary at the time.

What is known for certain is that in September 1901, an infant named Nigel Hawthorne was fatally thrown from an Automatic Nanny when its mainspring snapped. Word of the child's death spread quickly, and Dacey was faced with a deluge of families returning their Automatic Nannies. He examined the Hawthornes' Nanny, and discovered that the mechanism had been tampered with in an attempt to enable the machine to operate longer before needing to be rewound. He published a full-page ad, in which—while trying not to blame the Hawthorne parents—he insisted that the Automatic Nanny was entirely safe if operated properly, but his efforts were in vain. No one would entrust their child to the care of Dacey's machine.

Do not leave your child in the care of a woman whose character you know nothing about. Embrace the modern practice of scientific child-rearing by purchasing

DACEY'S PATENT AUTOMATIC NANNY

The ADVANTAGES of this UNIQUE SUBSTITUTE for a nanny are:

• IT TEACHES YOUR BABY TO ADHERE TO A PRECISE SCHEDULE OF FEEDING AND SLEEPING.

• IT SOOTHES YOUR BABY WITHOUT ADMINISTERING STUPEFYING NARCOTICS.

• IT WORKS NIGHT AND DAY, REQUIRES NO SEPARATE QUARTERS, AND CANNOT STEAL.

• IT WILL NOT EXPOSE YOUR CHILD TO DISREPUTABLE INFLUENCES.

CONSIDER THESE TESTIMONIALS FROM CUSTOMERS:

"Our child is now perfectly behaved and a delight to be near."
—Mrs. Menhenick, Colwyn Bay.
"An immeasurable improvement over the Irish girl we previously employed. It is a blessing for our household."
—Mrs. Hastings, Eastbourne.
"I wish I had been raised by one myself." —Mrs. Godwin, Andoversford.

THOMAS BRADFORD & CO.
68, FLEET STREET, LONDON; and MANCHESTER

To demonstrate that the Automatic Nanny was safe, Dacey boldly announced that he would entrust his next child to the machine's care. If he had successfully followed through with this, he might have restored public confidence in the machine, but Dacey never got the chance, because of his habit of telling prospective wives of his plans for their offspring. The inventor framed his proposal as an invitation to partake in a grand scientific undertaking, and was baffled that none of the women he courted found this an appealing prospect.

After several years of rejection, Dacey gave up on trying to sell the Automatic Nanny to a hostile public. Concluding that society was not sufficiently enlightened to appreciate the benefits of machine-based child care, he likewise abandoned his plans to build a teaching engine, and resumed his work on pure mathematics. He published papers on number theory and lectured at Cambridge until his death in 1918, during the global influenza pandemic.

The Automatic Nanny might have been completely forgotten were it not for the publication of an article in the *London Times* in 1925, titled "Mishaps of Science." It described in derisive terms a number of failed inventions and experiments, including the Automatic Nanny, which it labeled "a monstrous contraption whose inventor surely despised children." Reginald's son, Lionel Dacey, who by then had become a mathematician himself and was continuing his father's work in number theory, was outraged. He wrote a strongly worded letter to the newspaper, demanding a retraction, and when they refused, he filed a libel suit against the publisher, which he eventually lost. Undeterred, Lionel Dacey began a campaign to prove that the Automatic Nanny was based on sound and humane child-rearing principles, self-publishing a book about his father's theories on raising rational children.

Lionel Dacey refurbished the Automatic Nannies that had been in storage on the family estate, and in 1927 offered them for commercial sale again, but was unable to find a single buyer. He blamed this on the British upper class's obsession with status; because household appliances were now being marketed to the middle class as "electric servants," he claimed upper-class families insisted on hiring human nannies for appearance's sake, whether they provided better care or not. Those who worked with Lionel Dacey blamed it on his refusal to update the Automatic Nanny in any way; he ignored one business advisor's recommendation to replace the machine's spring-driven mechanism with an electric motor, and fired another who suggested marketing it without the Dacey name.

Like his father, Lionel Dacey eventually decided to raise his own child with the Automatic Nanny, but rather than look for a willing bride, he announced in 1932 that he would adopt an infant. He did not offer any updates in the following years, prompting a gossip columnist to suggest that the child had died at the machine's hands, but by then there was so little interest in the Automatic Nanny that no one ever bothered to investigate.

The truth regarding the infant would never have come to light if not for the work of Dr. Thackery Lambshead. In 1938, Dr. Lambshead was consulting at the Brighton Institute of Mental Subnormality (now known as Bayliss House) when he encountered a child named Edmund Dacey. According to admission records, Edmund had been successfully raised using an Automatic Nanny until the child was two years old, the age at which Lionel Dacey felt it appropriate to switch him to human care. He found that Edmund was unresponsive to his commands, and shortly afterwards, a physician diagnosed the child as "feebleminded." Judging such a child an unsuitable subject for demonstration of the Nanny's efficacy, Lionel Dacey committed Edmund to the Brighton Institute.

What prompted the institute's staff to seek Dr. Lambshead's opinion was Edmund's diminutive stature: although he was five, his height and weight were that of the average three-year-old. The children at the Brighton Institute were generally taller and healthier than those at similar asylums, a reflection of the fact that the institute's staff did not follow the still-common practice of minimal interaction with the children. In providing affection and physical contact to their charges, the nurses were preventing the condition now known as psychosocial dwarfism, where emotional stress reduces a child's levels of growth hormones, and which was prevalent in orphanages at the time.

The nurses quite reasonably assumed that Edmund Dacey's delayed growth was the result of substituting the Automatic Nanny's mechanical custody for actual human touch, and expected him to gain weight under their care. But after two years as a resident at the institute, during which the nurses had showered attention on him, Edmund had scarcely grown at all, prompting the staff to look for an underlying physiological cause.

Dr. Lambshead hypothesized that the child was indeed suffering from psychosocial dwarfism, but of a uniquely inverted variety: what Edmund needed was not more contact with a person but more contact with a machine. His small size was not the result of the years he spent under the care of the Automatic Nanny; it was the result of being deprived of the Automatic Nanny after his father felt he was ready for human care. If this theory were correct, restoring the machine would cause the boy to resume normal growth.

Dr. Lambshead sought out Lionel Dacey to acquire an Automatic Nanny. He gave an account of the visit in a monograph written many years later:

> [Lionel Dacey] spoke of his plans to repeat the experiment with another child as soon as he could ensure that the child's mother was of suitable stock. His feel-

ing was that the experiment with Edmund had failed only because of the boy's "native imbecility," which he blamed on the child's mother. I asked him what he knew of the child's parents, and he answered, rather too forcefully, that he knew nothing. Later on, I visited the orphanage from which Lionel Dacey had adopted Edmund, and learned from their records that the child's mother was a woman named Eleanor Hardy, who previously worked as a maid for Lionel Dacey. It was obvious to me that Edmund is, in fact, Lionel Dacey's own illegitimate son.

Lionel Dacey was unwilling to donate an Automatic Nanny to what he considered a failed experiment, but he agreed to sell one to Dr. Lambshead, who then arranged to have it installed in Edmund's room at the Brighton Institute. The child embraced the machine as soon as he saw it, and in the days that followed he would play happily with toys as long as the Nanny was nearby. Over the next few months, the nurses recorded a steady increase in his height and weight, confirming Dr. Lambshead's diagnosis.

The staff assumed that Edmund's cognitive delays were congenital in nature, and were content as long as he was thriving physically and emotionally. Dr. Lambshead, however, wondered if the consequences of the child's bond with a machine might be more far-ranging than anyone suspected. He speculated that Edmund had been misdiagnosed as feebleminded simply because he paid no attention to human instructors, and that he might respond better to a mechanical instructor. Unfortunately, he had no way to test this hypothesis; even if Reginald Dacey had successfully completed his teaching engine, it would not have provided the type of instruction that Edmund required.

It was not until 1946 that technology advanced to the necessary level. As a result of his lectures on radiation sickness, Dr. Lambshead had a good relationship with scientists working at Chicago's Argonne National Laboratory, and was present at a demonstration of the first remote manipulators, mechanical arms designed for the handling of radioactive materials. He immediately recognized their potential for Edmund's education, and was able to acquire a pair for the Brighton Institute.

Edmund was thirteen years old at this point. He had always been indifferent to attempts by the staff to teach him, but the mechanical arms immediately captured his attention. Using an intercom system that emulated the low-fidelity audio of the original Automatic Nanny's gramophone, nurses were able to get Edmund to respond to their voices in a way they hadn't when speaking to him directly. Within a few weeks, it was apparent that Edmund was not cognitively delayed in the manner previously believed; the staff had merely lacked the appropriate means of communicating with him.

With news of this development, Dr. Lambshead was able to persuade Lionel Dacey to visit the institute. Seeing Edmund demonstrate a lively curiosity and inquisitive nature, Lionel Dacey realized how he had stunted the boy's intellectual growth. From Dr. Lambshead's account:

> He struggled visibly to contain his emotion at seeing what he had wrought in pursuit of his father's vision: a child so wedded to machines that he could not acknowledge another human being. I heard him whisper, "I'm sorry, Father."
>
> "I'm sure your father would understand that your intentions were good," I said.
>
> "You misunderstand me, Dr. Lambshead. Were I any other scientist, my efforts to confirm his thesis would have been a testament to his influence, no matter what my results. But because I am Reginald Dacey's son, I have disproved his thesis twice over, because my entire life has been a demonstration of the impact a father's attention can have on his son."

Immediately after this visit, Lionel Dacey had remote manipulators and an intercom installed in his house and brought Edmund home. He devoted himself to machine-mediated interaction with his son until Edmund succumbed to pneumonia in 1966. Lionel Dacey passed away the following year.

The Automatic Nanny seen here is the one purchased by Dr. Lambshead to improve Edmund's care at the Brighton Institute. All the Nannies in Lionel Dacey's possession were destroyed upon his son's death. The National Museum of Psychology thanks Dr. Lambshead for his donation of this unique artifact.

HONORING LAMBSHEAD:

STORIES Inspired by the Cabinet

Stories Inspired by
the Cabinet

In early 2002, Ray Russell of prestigious specialty press Tartarus approached Lambshead about publishing a charity chapbook. It would celebrate Lambshead's life from an unusual angle: by focusing on the objects in the doctor's cabinet. Russell and Lambshead shared a fascination with supernatural literature that included a love for Arthur Machen, Elizabeth Jane Howard, and Thomas Ligotti. Several years earlier, Russell had even visited the cabinet for the express purpose of viewing some letters from Machen to Lambshead.

After some deliberation, Lambshead gave his blessing—"as long as all proceeds benefit the Museum of Intangible Arts and Objects and the Institute for Further Study," both of which he thought were underfunded and "staffed by wraiths in ragged clothes; it might be good for morale if they could afford sandwiches at least." Russell agreed and immediately embarked on the project, hoping to ride the coattails of the forthcoming Bantam/Pan Macmillan editions of *The Thackery T. Lambshead Pocket Guide to Eccentric & Discredited Diseases.*

Choosing from a list of items drawn up by Russell, several writers contributed, including the then-unknown Naomi Novik (who at the time wrote period ghost stories under the name N. N. Vasek). By January 2003, the chapbook was ready to be sent to the printer. It also included a somewhat overenthusiastic introduction titled "Virile Lambshead: Catch the Disease!," written by an editor at the medical journal the *Lancet.*

The inspiration for the stories varies greatly. For example, the actual foot that sparked Jeffrey Ford's "Relic" probably dates to the Crimean War's legendary Charge of the Light Brigade. As Lambshead put it, "unless the family mythology is wrong, this foot of my saintly grandfather was mummified due to the chance confluence of devastating military technologies and a freak dismount caused by a faulty stirrup." Similarly, Holly Black's story is mostly conjured up from the imagination, the item in question being "an odd Paddington knockoff that I felt sorry for."

However, Novik's teapot did, according to a Sotheby's auction catalog, belong to Edward John Moreton Drax Plunkett, a.k.a. Lord Dunsany. "Threads" by Carrie Vaughn gently mocks Lambshead's all-too-real predilection for scheduling interviews and then either not showing up or "observing my interview from afar." As for other allusions in the stories, Lambshead's involvement with various British secret service organizations is still murky, and the Meistergarten was probably never used by Lambshead to curb the rambunctious children of visiting relatives.

Unfortunately for readers, Lambshead died before publication, and the chapbook became a casualty of the free-for-all of lawsuits surrounding his estate. This decision was made easier for the estate because of an unfinished letter from Lambshead that began: "Dear Ray: Cease, desist, herewith take it upon yourself to remove me from . . ." (Russell claims the letter would have continued along the lines of either "from your overblown introduction" or "your annoying mailing list.")

Here, then, for the first time, in defiance of potential lawsuits, we are honored to publish those stories, along with all of the original art, sans Robert Mapplethorpe's piece for Novik's story. These tales do indeed form a bizarre tribute to Dr. Lambshead's cabinet, if not the man himself.

Threads

By Carrie Vaughn

Unicorn

For the twentieth time, Jerome reviewed the invitation that had brought him, more than prompt, to the parlor in the doctor's obscure manor house. *Mr. Kennelworth, Brief interview granted, ten minutes only, be prompt. Signed, Lambshead.* It appeared to be his actual signature, and not a note by some assistant.

The stooped housekeeper, who no doubt had been with Lambshead for decades, had guided him here to sit on a velvet-covered wingback chair and wait. The loudly ticking clock sitting at the center of the marble mantelpiece over the fireplace now showed that Lambshead was three minutes late. Would his ten-minute interview be reduced to seven minutes?

Not that sitting in the parlor wouldn't have been fascinating in itself, if he weren't so anxious. He'd arrived at the village the day before, to prevent any mishaps with the train, and spent the night in one of those little country inns with a decrepit public house in front and sparse rooms to let upstairs. The included breakfast had been greasy and now sat in his belly like lead. The village had exactly one taxi, whose driver was also the proprietor at the inn. Jerome had had to practically bribe him to drive him out here. He needed that interview, if for no other reason than to make sure the newspaper reimbursed him for his expenses.

But all he could do was wait. Breakfast gurgled at him. Perhaps he ought to review the questions he hoped to ask the doctor. *Doctor Lambshead, what of your sudden interest in occult experimentation? Is it true the Royal Academy has censured you over the debate about the veracity of certain claims made regarding your recent expedition to Ecuador?*

He ought to be making notes, so that his readers would understand what he was seeing. The parlor was filled with curios of the doctor's travels, glass-fronted cabinets displayed a bewildering variety of artifacts: elongated clay vases as thin as a goose's neck; squat, mud-colored jars, stopped with wax, containing who knew what horrors, wide baskets woven with grass in a pattern so complicated his eyes blurred. Weapons hung on the walls: spears, pikes, three-bladed daggers, swords as long as a man. Taxidermied creatures of the unlikeliest forms: a beaver that seemed to have merged with a lizard, a turkey colored scarlet.

The tapestry of a unicorn hanging in the center of one wall amid a swarm of serious-visaged portraits seemed almost ordinary—every country manor had at least one wall containing a mass of darkened pictures and a faded, moth-bitten Flemish unicorn tapestry. The beast in this one seemed a bit thin and constipated, gazing over a pasture of frayed flowers.

Jerome was sure that if he got up to pace, the eyes in the portraits would follow him, back and forth.

When he heard footsteps outside the parlor, he stood eagerly to greet the approaching doctor, and frowned when the doors opened and a young woman appeared from the vestibule. She stopped and stared at him, her eyes narrowed and predatory.

"Who are you?" they both said.

She wore smart shoes, a purplish skirt and suit jacket, and a short fur stole—fake, no doubt. A pillbox hat sat on dark hair that curled fashionably above her shoulders. She had a string of pearls, brown gloves, and carried a little leather-bound notebook and a pencil. He pegged her—a lady reporter. A rival.

In the same moment, she seemed to make the same judgment about him. Her jaw set, and her mouth pressed in a thin line.

"All right. Who are you with?" she said. Her accent was brash, American. An *American* lady reporter—even worse.

"Who are you with?" Jerome answered.

"I asked you first."

"It doesn't matter, I got here first, and I have an exclusive interview with the doctor."

"*I* have the exclusive interview. *You've* made a mistake."

He blinked, taken aback, then held out the note, which he'd crushed in his hands. Chagrined, he tried to smooth it out, but she took it from him before he could succeed. Her brow creased as she read it, then she shoved it back to him and reached into her handbag for a very similar slip of paper, and Jerome's heart sank. She offered it to him, and he read: brief interview granted, ten minutes only, for the exact same time. The exact same signature decorated the bottom of the page.

His spectacular opportunity was seeming less so by the moment.

"So the professor made a mistake and booked us both for exclusive interviews at the same time," she said.

"Evidently."

James A. Owen's depiction of the medieval tapestry from Lambshead's collection, the original so badly burned in the cabinet fire that only the fringe remains (now on display in the International Fabric Museum, Helsinki, Finland).

"Figures," she said. She crossed her arms, scanned the room, then nodded as if she had made a decision. Her curls bobbed. "Right, here's what we'll do. You get five minutes, I get five minutes. We coordinate our questions so we don't ask the same thing. Then we share notes. All right?"

"Hold on a minute—"

"It's the only fair way."

"I didn't agree to a press conference—"

"Two of us are hardly a press conference."

"But—"

"And don't try to blame me, it's the doctor who double-booked us."

I wasn't going to, Jerome thought, aggrieved. The afternoon was crumbling, and Jerome felt the portraits staring at him, a burning on the back of his neck. "I think that since I was here first it's only fair that I should have the interview. Perhaps you could reschedule—"

"Now how is that fair? I came all the way from New York to get this interview! You're from where, Oxford? You can show up on his doorstep anytime!"

He blinked again, put off-balance by her identifying his accent so precisely. He was the son of a professor there, and had scandalized the family by not going into academics himself. Roving reporting had seemed so much more productive. Romantic, even. So much for that. "I can see we've gotten off to a bad start—"

"Whose fault is that? I've been nothing but polite."

"On the contrary—"

Just then the double doors to the library opened once more, freezing Jerome and the woman reporter in place, her with one hand on her hip, waving her notebook; him pointing as if scolding a small child. The housekeeper, a hunched, wizened woman in a pressed brown cotton dress, scowled at them. Jerome tucked his hands behind his back.

"The doctor is very sorry, but he'll have to reschedule with both of you. He'll send letters to confirm a time." She stood next to the open door, clearly indicating that they should depart.

The woman reporter said, "Did he say why? What's he doing that he can't take ten minutes off to talk?"

"The doctor is very sorry," the housekeeper said again, her scowl growing deeper. She reminded Jerome of a headmistress at a particularly dank primary school. He knew a solid wall when he saw one.

Jerome gestured forward, letting the lady reporter exit first. She puckered her lips as if about to argue, before stalking out of the room. Jerome followed.

63

Once they were standing on the front steps of the manor, the housekeeper shut the door behind them with a slam of finality.

"Well. So much for that," he said. "I don't suppose you'd like to share a cab back to the village?"

"I'd rather walk," she said, and did just that, following the lane away from the building.

He watched her, astonished at the many unkind adjectives his mind was conjuring to describe her.

His cab arrived, and gratefully he rode it away, ignoring the hassled mutterings of the driver. They passed the woman reporter on the road, still marching, still with that look of witchy fury on her face, which was flushed now and streaked with sweat. A better man might have stopped and offered a ride yet again.

Further on the road, they passed an impressive black Bentley, filled with children. They seemed to be playing some game resembling badminton, in the backseat. And what were they doing, going to the doctor's manor? Lambshead didn't have children, did he? Grandchildren? Nieces and nephews? Jerome hadn't thought so, and he'd certainly never find out now.

He left it all—the doctor, the manor, the housekeeper, the car full of children, and the harridan of a reporter—behind, determined not to think on the day anymore. The pub and a pint awaited.

Mille-fleur

Their screaming certainly did carry in the close confines of the automobile.

The chauffeur scowled at Sylvia in the rearview mirror, and she turned away, her headache doubling.

"Children, please sit. All of you, sit now. Sit *down*." She had been instructed by Lady Smythe-Helsing not to raise her voice at the children, as that would damage their fragile psyches. She had also been instructed not to ever lay a hand on any of them in an effort to control them—such efforts led to violence, which could not be tolerated. If she ever did any such thing out of Lady Smythe-Helsing's view, the children would report it. Never mind them, the chauffeur would report it. And he had the gall to glare at her for their misbehavior.

So here they were, the four little darlings scrambling all over the seats and each other, throwing their dolls and stuffed bears and India-rubber balls, kicking at the windows and ceilings, punching and screaming. Alice, Andrew, Anna, Arthur.

"That famous doctor is opening his house for tours, just for the afternoon, take the children to visit, it will be so educational," Lady Smythe-Helsing had announced this morning. Commanded. "Simpson will drive you. Hurry along, won't you?" The children had been lined up, tallest to shortest, oldest to youngest, ages ten to five, looking smart and crisp, the boys in their pressed suit jackets and ties—real, not clip-on—the girls in their pleated skirts and snow-white blouses with lace-trimmed Peter Pan collars. So lovely, weren't they? Their mother had kissed their rosy cheeks as they beamed up at her. Then Lady Smythe-Helsing had left Sylvia alone with them while she went to lead the latest meeting of the Oakwaddling Village Improvement Society.

The children had looked at Sylvia with such a piercing sense of anticipation.

Now that they had turned the interior of the car into a rugby pitch, the chauffeur looked at Sylvia, clearly thinking, *How could you let them carry on so?* He'd report to the mistress how the incompetent governess couldn't control a few innocent children.

"Miss Sylvia, are we there yet?" said the youngest boy, Arthur.

"Not yet, dear."

"I want to be there *now!*"

"Unless you've found a way to alter space and time, you'll have to wait."

He bit his lip and furrowed his brow, as if considering. If anyone could find a way to disrupt the workings of the universe, it would be one of the Smythe-Helsing children.

Meanwhile, Sylvia stared out the window, wishing *she* could speed up time. They had reached the drive leading to Dr. Lambshead's manor when they passed a woman in a dress suit walking away. She seemed angry. They'd also passed a car earlier—so the doctor's tours of his manor were popular. That many more people to notice the unruly children and tsk-tsk the poor governess who couldn't control them. Sylvia sighed.

Finally, the car stopped before the manor's carved front doors. Sylvia struggled to pop the door open, succeeded, and the children exploded out of the car. They ran laps around it, pulled each other's hair and sleeves and skirts and ties. Sylvia couldn't tell if they were screaming or laughing. Well, if they ran it out now, maybe they'd actually sleep tonight.

She glanced at the chauffeur, intending to discuss procedures for getting them all home. "I'll wait," he said, glaring.

Sighing again—she probably sighed more than she spoke—Sylvia moved to the bumper to head off the latest lap around the car. Andrew pulled up short in front of her, and the others crashed into him. Sylvia pointed to the house. "That way."

Screaming, they rocketed toward the ancient-looking and no-doubt fragile front doors, which obediently opened inward. The housekeeper, a stern-looking woman who seemed even more ancient and weathered than the doors, stood by them. Even the children fell silent at her appearance.

The old woman glared at Sylvia and said, "Here for a tour, miss?"

Sylvia swallowed and nodded. "Yes, if you please. The children really aren't so bad—"

"This way." The housekeeper disappeared into a darkened vestibule.

Alice, the oldest, glanced at Sylvia, sizing her up.

"Go on," Sylvia said, but the children had already raced inside. Sylvia hurried to follow them.

Housekeeper and children waited by another set of doors at the end of the entryway.

"If you would kindly keep the children in the parlor." The housekeeper glared with her beady, crab-like eyes, and opened the door. Sylvia and the children inched inside.

When Sylvia saw the parlor, she nearly cried. So many *things*, all of them smashable. Pottery, glassware, trinkets with gears and levers, arcane instruments made of spindly wire, fabric to be soiled, paper to be torn, entire cabinets to be toppled, and a wall full of art to be destroyed. Almost lost among portraits whose gazes followed her hung a floral tapestry in faded colors, which looked like it would disintegrate if one merely breathed on it. It was an odd, blurred thing that almost seemed to change shape if she turned her head just so.

The children trembled—vibrating, anticipating, potential energy waiting to burst forth—hoping for the chance to get their dirty little claws on everything. The housekeeper closed the double doors, her gaze still boring into Sylvia, as if expecting the worst and knowing it would be the governess's fault if even the smallest sliver broke free from the leg of a chair. The children would destroy it all, and the doctor would report the horror to Lady Smythe-Helsing, and Sylvia would be fired.

And would that really be such a bad thing? Perhaps she could leave right now, climb out a window and run . . .

She put a hand against her forehead, trying to stave off the headache building behind her eyes. "Children, do *behave*," she said, by rote, out of habit, tired and unconvincing, even though the children hadn't moved since the closing of the door. It was only a matter of time before the human whirlwind.

Still, the children didn't move. Sylvia allowed herself to exhale. She attempted an actual instruction.

"Why don't you sit here on the sofa while we wait?" she said. Quietly, the children obeyed. They lined up on the sofa and sat, one after the other, no one pinching anyone.

Extraordinary. Truly extraordinary. Something was terribly, terribly wrong here.

Sylvia sat in a wingback chair across from them, watching. They sat, hands folded in laps, and waited, not making a sound, not even flinching. Somewhere, a clock ticked, and it sounded like the tolling of a funeral bell. Sylvia's heart was racing for no reason at all.

When the double doors opened again, she nearly shrieked, hand to her breast to still her heart. The children merely looked.

The housekeeper stood there, like a monk, in her brown dress. She frowned. "There's been a change of plans. I'm afraid the doctor has been unexpectedly detained. You'll have to come another time."

That was that. The whole afternoon for nothing, and now Sylvia was going to have to herd the children back outside, and back to the car for the ride home.

But they left the parlor quietly, single-file by height and age. Outside, on the front steps, they halted in a row, like little soldiers, while the car pulled around. They got in, sat quietly, and stayed that way until the car left the grounds of Lambshead's manor. Then, they burst into screams, the boys hit the girls, the girls pinched the boys, and everybody bounced against the ceiling. She could only watch. They were spring toys that had been let loose.

Terrifying.

The Girl at the Fountain

A week later, Jerome returned to the manor in a hopeful mood, eager, prepared. His newspaper had agreed that a second trip to Lambshead's manor was worth it, for the chance to recoup some of the expenses with an actual story. This attempt couldn't possibly go any worse than the last. He knocked on the door, which the scowling housekeeper opened, showing him into the foyer and pointing him to the library.

The lady reporter was in the library, standing before the tapestry of a girl at a fountain, nestled amid the staring portraits.

"Not you again!" he blurted, and she turned on him, gaze fierce. She had the most extraordinary green eyes, he noticed.

"Oh, give me a break!" she said.

"What are you doing here?"

"I'm here for my interview—what are you doing here?"

"*Your* interview, this is supposed to be *my* interview. How did you manage this?"

67

"Don't lay this on me, this isn't my fault!" She stepped toward him, pointing, and he took a step forward to keep her from getting the upper hand.

"You're trying to tell me that you aren't following me?" he said. "That you didn't arrange to be here simply to aggravate me?"

"Wait a minute—I was here first this time! Are *you* following *me*?"

"What? No!"

She was only slightly shorter than he was, but the heels of her shoes may have made her appear taller, just as they accentuated the curve of her calves and the slope of her hips inside their clinging skirt. Today, she wore navy blue, a well-tailored and flattering suit, a cream-colored blouse contrasting with the flush of the skin at her throat.

"I don't care who screwed up and who double-booked us," she said. "I'm getting my interview and you can't stop me." Her lips were parted, her eyes shining, and her hair seemed soft as velvet.

"I don't want to stop you," he said, and realized that he really didn't.

"Then you'll turn around and walk out of here right now?"

"I don't know that I'm ready to do that."

She tilted her head, her fury giving way to confusion, which softened her mouth and forehead and made her eyes wide and sweet. "But you won't stand in my way?"

"Well, I might stand in your way."

In fact, they had moved close enough together that they were only inches apart, gazing into each other's eyes, feeling the heat of each other's bodies.

"And why would you do that?" she said, her voice low.

"I think—to get a better look at you."

"Really?"

"Yeah." He couldn't see the rest of the room anymore.

"I have to admit, you're an interesting man— I . . . I don't even know your name."

"Jerome. Yours?"

"Elaine."

They kissed.

The shock that passed from his lips through his nerves to the tips of his toes came not only from the pressure of her mouth, the weight and warmth of her body pressed against him, her hands wrapped around the hem of his jacket to pull him closer—but also from the fact that he was kissing her at all. It should never have happened. It was meant to be.

The kiss lasted for what seemed a very long time, lips working between gasps for breath, hands on each other's arms. This, he thought, this was what he had come for.

Finally, they broke apart and stared at each other in wonder.

"What was that?" she—Elaine—said. Her cheeks were pink, and her breathing came quickly.

"It was perfect," he breathed.

"God, it was, wasn't it?" she whispered.

"Oh yes." He leaned forward for another kiss, but she interrupted the gesture.

"Let's go. The two of us, together, let's leave, go somewhere and never look back."

"What about your interview?" he said.

"What interview? Who?"

He could hardly remember himself. They were in this archaic parlor filled with artifacts, books, carved fireplace, stern portraits, and that faded tapestry, which hardly seemed a setting for passion—his heart was suddenly filled with fragrant gardens and winding paths where he could hold her hand and walk with her for hours.

He took both her hands and pulled her toward the door. "You're right, let's go."

A wide, glorious smile broke on her face, a flower unfolding, opening to him, filling him with joy, unbridled and bursting. Hand in hand, they left the parlor, breezed past the scowling housekeeper, and burst through the front doors to the outside, where the sun was shining gloriously and the shrubs seemed filled with singing larks. Jerome had an urge to sing along with them. Elaine was grinning just as wide as he was, and he'd never felt so much . . . *rightness* in being with someone.

They had to step aside for a passing car filled with countless children, whose screams were audible through the glass.

"Can I ask you a question?" Elaine asked.

"Of course." He would do anything for her.

"Do you want children?"

He thought a moment; he'd never really considered, and found he didn't much need to now. "No, not really."

"Good. Excellent." She smiled at him, and his heart nearly burst.

At the end of the drive, the boundary to the property, Elaine stopped. Her tug on his hand made Jerome stop as well. He blinked at her; her frown gave him the sense of a balloon deflating, of a recording of birdsong winding down to the speed of a dirge.

They dropped each other's hands. He was rather startled that he'd been holding it at all.

"What are we doing?" she asked. "We can't just run off like a couple of teenagers. This isn't like me *at all*."

"Nor me," Jerome said. "But . . . perhaps if you think that I simply couldn't help myself." That was true enough—whatever had happened, it was a surge of passion that seemed to have vanished, much to his regret. He wanted it back.

He tried on an awkward smile for her, and if she didn't return it, she at least didn't scowl.

"There's something really weird about that house," she said, looking back to the manor.

"Agreed," he said. "I find I don't want the interview so much after all."

"Yeah. You said it."

"Elaine, would you like to have dinner with me?" he asked impulsively, sure she would rail at him for it and not caring.

She studied him a moment, then said, "You know? I think I would."

The Hunt

The doctor's manor was an edifice of terror. The foundation stones exuded a fog of trepidation. Knowing that the children would be horrible would be easier than not knowing at all what they would do this time.

For yes, Doctor Lambshead had sent a note to Lady Smythe-Helsing, apologizing profusely for cutting short their previous tour and offering a second opportunity, which the lady accepted. Once again, Sylvia rode in the Bentley with the angry chauffeur and four screaming children. The housekeeper was waiting for them at the front doors. Once again, she directed them to the parlor. The children lined up next to her, and the doors closed.

Sylvia closed her eyes, held her breath. Waited for screams or sighs or giggles. Or quiet, obedient breathing. As it happened, she didn't hear anything. So she opened her eyes.

The children were gone.

She had no idea where to look for them, and studied the walls as if the children had melted into the wallpaper, as if she might see their faces staring out of the portraits or stitched into the threads of the tapestry, among the hunters and their spears surrounding the poor unicorn at bay.

A snap of a breeze touched her, and she flinched as something tugged at her hair. Reaching up, she picked at the curl tucked behind her ear and felt some foreign object. She untangled it and looked—a toothpick, perhaps. Or a tiny dart.

She looked to where it had come from and saw Andrew, the older boy, with none other than a blowgun in his hands. And the empty spot on the wall where he'd taken it from. Dear God, the heathen had fired at her.

He ducked behind the sofa and ran.

That was it. She'd had enough. She went after him, with every intention of laying a hand on him—only for as long as it took to throw him out of the house. All of them. Let Lady Smythe-Helsing fire her. Let the doctor report what an awful governess she was.

As she chased Andrew through the doorway from the parlor to the library, she tripped. Looking back, she saw why—Alice and Arthur, crouched on either side of the doorway, had pulled a length of rope across the passage, just as she stepped into it. Good heavens, what had gotten into them? They'd always been holy terrors but never truly malicious. The injuries they inflicted were usually accidental.

The two of them scrambled to their feet and ran back toward the parlor.

Rubbing a bruised elbow, she went to follow them. Four against one was terrible odds. Especially those four. How had she gotten into this? Oh yes, she needed a job. She had too much education for scut work but not enough for anything professional. Be a governess, that was the solution. Some of the very wealthy families still had them. What an opportunity. Better than regular teaching, and maybe she'd catch the eye of some wealthy gentleman who would take her away from all this.

Bollocks. All of it. This wasn't a job, it was a war.

She entered the parlor and paused—they'd hidden, and were being very quiet for once.

Several more weapons seemed to have vanished from their places on the wall, and she had a sinking feeling. She had already started backing away, step by step, when Arthur came at her with a spear that was larger than he was. Alice had a bow and quiver of arrows.

Sylvia turned and ran. Out of the parlor, through the kitchen, where she nearly collided with Andrew, who was now wielding an axe as well as the blowgun. Changing direction mid-stride, she made her way through a pantry to a scullery and then to a workroom, and from there to the foyer again, and to a second library, where she slammed shut the door and bolted it.

There, next to the wall, stood Anne. She'd been hiding behind the door, and Sylvia hadn't looked. Anne stared at her. In her hands, clutched to her chest, she held a cage the size of a shoebox, made of sticks tied together with twine. In the cage was a mouse, the small, brown kind that invaded pantries and scurried across kitchen floors. The creature huddled in the corner, sitting on its haunches, its front paws pressed to its chest, trembling. Its large and liquid eyes seemed to be pleading. Sylvia understood how it felt.

On the other hand, the girl's gaze was challenging. She looked up at Sylvia, who somehow felt shorter. Her breath caught, and when she tried to draw another, she choked. The corner of the girl's lips turned up.

Meanwhile, little hands had begun pounding on the door.

"All right," Sylvia said. "That's how it is, is it?" She unbolted the doors and flung them open. The other three children—spears, blowguns, axes, arrows, daggers, and scalpels in hand—were waiting for her. Little Anne stood behind her, wearing an expression of utter malice, like she was thinking of how to build a larger cage. "You lot will have to catch me, first," Sylvia said.

She shoved past them with enough force to startle them into stillness, just for a moment. Then, they pelted after her. This time, Sylvia made for the front door, breezing past the startled housekeeper. She wrestled opened the heavy front doors, didn't say a word to the chauffeur who was leaning on the hood of the Bentley and smoking a pipe. He stared after her wonderingly, but she didn't have time to explain, because the four little Smythe-Helsings were charging after her, silent and determined, weapons held to the ready. As she'd hoped they would.

The end of the drive was perhaps a hundred yards away. Sylvia wasn't an athlete, by any means, but she was no slouch, either, and herding these children for the last year had certainly kept her fit. All she had to do was reach the end of the property and not look back. But she could hear their footsteps kicking up gravel, gaining on her.

Then she was across the line marked by the brick columns at the end of the drive. If this didn't work, she was lost. She stopped and turned to see the four children running after her, murder hollowing their expressions. First Alice, then Andrew, then Anne, then little Arthur crossed the invisible line, and they all stopped and stared, bewildered, at the weapons in their hands.

Arthur dropped the spear and started crying.

"Oh, Arthur, hush now, it's all over now, it's all right." Sylvia knelt beside him and gathered him in her arms, holding him while he sobbed against her shoulder. Then all the children were crying, clinging to her, and she spread her arms to encompass them.

She made them wait by one of the brick columns while she went to fetch the car. They stayed right where she told them to, hand in hand, watching her with swollen red eyes her entire way back to the manor, where she told the chauffeur that they'd like to go home now, and didn't answer any of his brusque questions. The housekeeper watched her from the front steps, a glare in her eye and a sneer on her lips. Sylvia paid her no mind.

BACK AT THE Smythe-Helsing estate, the children were exhausted, and Sylvia gave them each a glass of water and a biscuit and put them to bed. She then went to see Lady Smythe-Helsing, who had returned from her watercolor class and was sitting in her parlor taking tea.

Sylvia approached. "Lady Smythe-Helsing, ma'am?"

"Yes, what is it?" She set aside her cup and scowled at the interruption.

Taking a deep breath, Sylvia said, "I quit."

The woman blinked, transforming her native-born elegance into a fish-like gawping. It made Sylvia stand a little taller. Without her furs and title, the lady was no better than her governess.

"What?" she finally said.

"I quit. I'm leaving. I've had enough. I quit." She felt like a general who'd won a battle.

"This is outrageous."

"This is not the Middle Ages," she said, imagining tearing that medieval tapestry to bits. "I can leave when I like."

"But what will you do? I certainly won't be writing you a referral after this."

"Anything I want," she shot back without thinking, then tilted her head, considering. "Maybe I'll go to America. Hollywood. I'll be a movie star."

"You're delusional."

"Perhaps. Perhaps not."

"You'll fail. And you'll never find another position as a governess."

"Thank God," Sylvia said, and went to fetch her things.

SYLVIA REACHED THE stairs that led down from the children's wing to the back door when a figure stopped her. Little Anne in her nightgown, hugging her flaxen-haired doll.

"Anne. Hello."

"Hello."

"And then good-bye, rather. I'm leaving."

"I know," the girl said. "I'll miss you."

"Pardon? Really?"

"You're the best governess we've ever had. You listen."

"Oh, Anne. But you understand that I have to leave."

"Oh yes. It's the only sane choice."

Sylvia smiled. "There's a good girl, Anne."

Anne smiled, too, and wandered back to bed.

73

Suitcase in hand, Sylvia left through the back door and walked away from the Smythe-Hesling manor with a spring in her step.

Storage

The housekeeper watched the Smythe-Helsing children and their governess depart, then went to the parlor, to the tapestry hanging in the center of a group of portraits. Odd, faded, ambiguous, it seemed to change shape based on how one tilted one's head when looking at it. A fascinating piece. The housekeeper took it down off its nail, rolled it up, and carried it to a downstairs room, to put with other ambiguous experiments. On the way, Lambshead removed the wig and false nose, and dispensed with the stooped posture that had transformed him.

There was nothing, he considered, like a little firsthand observation in one's own home.

Ambrose and the Ancient Spirits of East and West

By Garth Nix

Ambrose Farnington was not particularly well-equipped to live an ordinary life. An adventurer in the Near East before the Great War, the war itself had seen him variously engaged in clandestine and very cold operations in the mountains between Turkey and Russia; commanding an infantry battalion in France and Belgium; and then, after almost a day buried in his headquarters dugout in the company of several dead and dismembered companions, as a very fragile convalescent in a nursing home called Grandway House, in Lancashire.

Most recently, a year of fishing and walking near Fort William had assisted the recovery begun under the care of the neurasthenic specialists at Grandway, and by the early months of 1920, the former temporary Lieutenant Colonel Farnington felt that he was almost ready to reemerge into the world. The only question was in what capacity. The year in the Scottish bothy with only his fishing gear, guns, and a borrowed dog for company had also largely exhausted his ready funds, which had been stricken by his remaining parent's ill-timed death, his father putting the capstone on a lifetime of setting a very bad example by leaving a great deal of debt fraudulently incurred in his only child's name.

Ambrose considered the question of his finances and employment as he sorted through the very thin pile of correspondence on the end of the kitchen table he was using as a writing desk. The bothy had been lent to him with the dog, and though both belonged to Robert Cameron, a very close friend from his days at Peterhouse College in Cambridge, his continued presence there prevented the employment of bothy and dog by a gamekeeper who would usually patrol the western borders of Robert's estate. Besides, Ambrose did not wish to remain a burden on one of the few of his friends who was still alive.

It was time to move on, but the question was: on to what and where?

"I should make an appreciation of my situation and set out my qualities and achievements, Nellie," said Ambrose to the dog, who was lying down with her shaggy head on his left foot. Nellie raised one ear, but made no other movement, as Ambrose unscrewed his pen and set out to write on the back of a bill for a bamboo fishing rod supplied by T. H. Sowerbutt's of London.

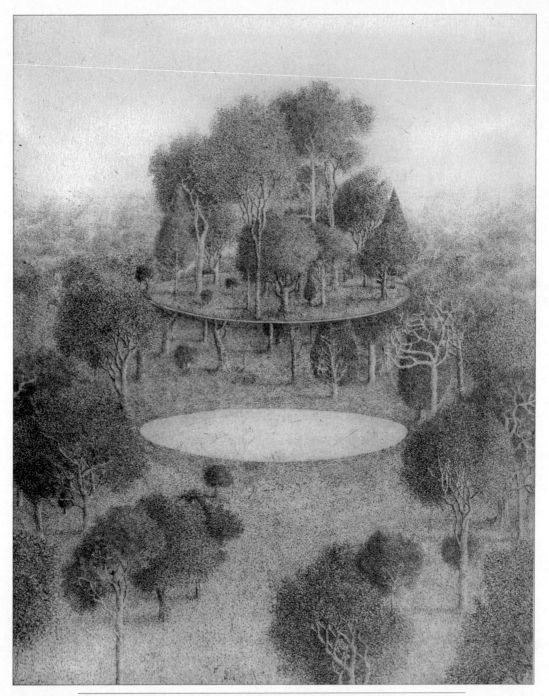

Jonathan Nix's etching "Tree Spirits Rising," honoring Dr. Lambshead's period of interest in "bushes, bramble, herbs, and eccentric ground cover."

"Item one," said Ambrose aloud. "At twenty-nine, not excessively aged, at least by time. Item two, in possession of rude physical health and . . . let us say . . . in a stable mental condition, provided no underground exercise is contemplated. Item three, a double-starred first in Latin and Greek, fluent in Urdu, classical Persian, Arabic, Spanish, French, German; conversant with numerous other languages, etc. Item four, have travelled and lived extensively in the Near East, particularly Turkey and Persia. Item five, war service . . ."

Ambrose put down his pen and wondered what he should write. Even though he would burn his initial draft on completion, he was still reluctant to mention his work for D-Arc. Even the bare facts were secret, and as for the details, very few people would believe them. Those people who would believe were the ones he was most worried about. If certain practitioners of some ancient and occult studies discovered that he was Agent çobanaldatan, the man who had so catastrophically halted that ceremony high on the slopes of Ziyaret Daği, then . . .

"I suppose if I am not too specific, it can't matter," Ambrose said to Nellie. He picked up the pen again, and continued to speak aloud as he wrote.

"Where was I . . . war service . . . 1914–1915. Engaged by a department of the War Office in reconnaissance operations in the region of . . . no, best make it 'the East.' Returned in 1916, posted to KRRC, rose to brevet lieutenant colonel by May 1918, commanded the Eighth Battalion, wounded 21 September 1918, convalescent leave through to 5 March 1919 . . . no, that looks bad, far too long, will just make it 'after convalescent leave' resigned temporary commission . . . how do I explain this last year? Writing a paper on the Greek inscriptions near Erzerum or something, I suppose, I do have one I started in '09 . . . let's move on . . ."

He paused as Nellie raised both ears and tilted her head towards the door. When she gave a soft whine and stood up, Ambrose pushed his chair back and went to the window. Gently easing the rather grimy curtain aside, he looked out, up towards the rough track that wound down from the main road high on the ridge above.

A car was gingerly making its way down towards the bothy, proceeding slowly and relatively quietly in low gear, though not quietly enough to fool Nellie. It was a maroon sedan of recent European make, and it was not a car that he knew. To get here, the driver had either picked or more likely cut off the bronze Bramah padlocks on both the upper gate to the road and the one in the wall of the middle field.

Quickly, but with measured actions, Ambrose went to the gun cabinet, unlocked it with one of the keys that hung on his heavy silver watch-chain, and took out his service revolver. He quickly loaded it and put the weapon and another five cartridges in the voluminous right pocket of his coat, his father's sole useful legacy, an ugly purple-and-green tweed shooting jacket that was slightly too large.

He hesitated in front of the cabinet, then, after a glance at Nellie and at a very old pierced bronze lantern that hung from a ceiling beam, he reached back into the cabinet for a shotgun. He chose the lightest of the four weapons there, a double-barrel four-ten. Unlike the other guns, and against all his usual principles, it was already loaded, with rather special shot. Ambrose broke it, whispered, *"melek kiliç şimdi bana yardum"* close to the breech, and snapped it closed.

The incantation would wake the spirits that animated the ammunition, but only for a short time. If whoever came in the maroon car was an ordinary visitor, the magic would be wasted, and he only had half a box of the shells left. But he did not think it was an ordinary visitor, though he was by no means sure it was an enemy.

Certainly, Nellie was growling, the hair up all along her back, and that indicated trouble. But the bronze lamp that Ambrose had found in the strange little booth in the narrowest alley of the Damascus bazaar, while it had lit of its own accord, was not burning with black fire. The flame that flickered inside was green. Ambrose did not yet know the full vocabulary of the oracular lantern, but he knew that green was an equivocal colour. It signified the advent of some occult power, but not necessarily an inimical force.

Readying the shotgun, Ambrose went to the door. Lifting the bar with his left hand, he nudged the door open with his foot, allowing himself a gap just wide enough to see and shoot through. The car was negotiating the last turn down from the middle field, splashing through the permanent mud puddle as it negotiated the open gate and the narrow way between the partly fallen stone walls that once upon a time had surrounded the bothy's kitchen garden.

Ambrose could only see a driver in the vehicle, but that didn't mean there wouldn't be others lying low. He raised the shotgun and thumbed back both hammers, suddenly aware of a pulsing in his eardrums that came from his own, racing heart. Nellie, next to his leg, snarled, but well trained as she was, did not bark or lunge forward.

The maroon sedan stopped a dozen yards away. Past the gate, and within the walls of the garden, which might or might not be significant. When he had first moved in, Ambrose had planted silver sixpences in every seventh stone, and buried three horseshoes in the gateway. That would deter most of the lesser powers, particularly those already distressed at being so far west of the old Giza meridian. Which meant that his visitor was either mundane or not one of the *lesser* powers that stalked the earth. . . .

The car door creaked open, backwards, and a tall man in a long, camel-coloured coat with the collar up and a dark trilby pulled down over his ears hunched himself out, his arms and legs moving very oddly—a telltale sign that told Ambrose all he needed to know. As the curious figure lurched forward, Ambrose fired the left barrel at the man's chest, and a split-second later, the right barrel at his knees.

Salt splattered across the target and burst into flame where it hit. Hat and coat fell to the ground, and two waist-high creatures of shifting darkness sprang forward, salt-fires burning on and in their mutable flesh.

Ambrose pulled the door shut with one swift motion and slammed down the bar. Retreating to the gun cabinet, he reloaded the shotgun, this time speaking the incantation in a loud and almost steady voice.

A hissing outside indicated that the demons had heard the incantation, and did not like it. For his part, Ambrose was deeply concerned that his first two shots had not disincorporated his foes; that they had freely crossed his boundary markers; and that they had got to his home without any sign of having aroused the ire of any of the local entities that would take exception to such an Eastern presence.

He looked around the single room of the bothy. The windows, though shut, were not shuttered, and there was probably not enough sunshine for the glass to act as mirrors and distract the demons. If they were strong enough to cross a silver and cold-iron border, they would be strong enough to enter the house uninvited, though not eager, which was probably the only reason they had not yet broken down the door or smashed in a window—

Nellie barked and pointed to the fireplace. Ambrose spun around and fired both barrels as the demons came roaring out of the chimney. But even riddled with ensorcelled salt, the demons came on, shadowy maws snapping and talons reaching. Ambrose threw the now-useless shotgun at them and dived to one side, towards the golf bag perched by his bed, as Nellie snarled and bit at the demons' heels.

Demon teeth closed on his calf as his hands closed on his weapon of last resort. Between the irons and the woods, Ambrose's fingers closed on the bone-inlaid hilt of the yataghan that bore the maker's mark of Osman Bey. Tumbling the golf bag over, he drew the sword, and with two swift strokes, neatly severed the faint red threads that stood in the place of backbones in the demons, the silvered blade cutting through the creatures' infernal salt-pocked flesh as if it were no more than smoke.

The demons popped out of existence, leaving only a pair of three-foot lengths of scarlet cord. Nellie sniffed at them cautiously, then went to nose at Ambrose's leg.

"Yes, it got me, damn it," cursed Ambrose. "My own fault, mind you. Should have had the sword to hand, never mind how ridiculous it might have looked."

Ambrose looked over at the oracular lantern, which had gone out.

"Possibly inimical, my sweet giddy aunt," he muttered as he pushed down the sock and rolled up the leg of his plus fours. The skin was not broken, but there was a crescent-shaped bruise on his calf. Next to the bruise, the closest half-inch of vein was turning dark and beginning to obtrude from the skin, and a shadow was branching out into the lesser blood vessels all around.

Ambrose cursed again, then levered himself upright and hobbled over to the large, leather-strapped portmanteau at the end of his bed. Flinging it open, he rummaged about inside, eventually bringing out a long strip of linen that was covered in tiny Egyptian hieroglyphics drawn in some dark red ink. Ambrose wrapped this around his calf, tapped it thrice, and spoke the revered name of Sekhmet, at which the hieroglyphics faded from the bandage and entered into his flesh, there to fight a holding battle against the demonic incursion, though it was unlikely that they would entirely vanquish the enemy without additional sorcerous assistance. Egyptian magic was older and thus more faded from the world, and though Ambrose had immersed the bandage on his last visit to the Nile, that had been many years before, so the hermetic connection was no longer strong.

Ambrose had nothing else that might work. Nor was there anyone he could easily turn to for assistance. In fact, he thought wretchedly, there were only two possible sources of the kind of help he needed within a thousand miles. One he had hoped to stay away from, and the other was very difficult to reach without extensive and unusual preparations that would simply take too long.

"First things first," muttered Ambrose. Using the yataghan as a crutch, but also to keep it close to hand, he limped to the table. Lighting a match against the back of his chair, he applied it to the bill for the fishing rod, and watched his recent appreciation crumble into ash, dousing the blaze with the last half-inch of cold tea from his mug when it threatened to spread to the other papers.

"Just like the war," he said wearily to Nelly. "Bloody thing was obsolete as soon as I wrote it. I suppose I shall have to—"

Nellie lifted her ears.

Ambrose whipped around to check the oracular lantern. The flame had relit and was even higher now, burning red and gold, signifying danger, but not immediate, and allies. Not friends, but allies.

"I'm not trusting you," Ambrose said to the lantern. Still leaning on the yataghan, he retrieved his shotgun and reloaded it, though this time he did not speak the words. Nellie stayed by his side, her ears up and intent, but she was not growling.

As the sound of a car being driven a shade too fast for the rough track grew louder, Ambrose cautiously opened the door and looked out.

He was not very much surprised to see that the second car was a green Crossley 20/25, the usual choice of the Secret Service Bureau and so also of its even lesser-known offshoot, D-Arc. He even recognized the two men in the front, and could guess at the other two in the backseat. Nevertheless, he kept the shotgun ready as the Crossley skidded to a halt behind the maroon sedan and the men got out. Three of them, two with revolvers by their sides and one with a curiously archaic, bell-mouthed musketoon, stayed close to the car, watching the bothy, the maroon car, and the hillside. The fourth, a man Ambrose knew as Major Kennett, though that was almost certainly not his real name, advanced towards the bothy's front door. The quartet were dressed for the city, not the country, and Ambrose suppressed a smile as Kennett lost a shoe in the mud and had to pause to fish around for it with a stockinged foot.

"I see we're a little late," said Kennett, as he pulled at the heel of his shoe. He was a handsome man, made far less so by the chill that always dwelt in his eyes. "Sorry about that."

"Late for what?" asked Ambrose.

"Your earlier guests," answered Kennett. He held out his hand. After a moment, Ambrose balanced the shotgun over the crook of his left arm and shook hands.

"You knew they were coming?" asked Ambrose.

Kennett shook his head. "We knew something was coming. Quite clever really. We've been keeping tabs on a private vessel for days, a very large motor yacht owned by our old friend the emir and captained by Vladimir Roop. It docked at Fort William, the car was lowered, and off it went. Nothing . . . unwelcome . . . touched the earth, you see, and it's a hardtop, windows shut, keeping out all that Scottish air and lovely mist and those who travel with it."

"Did you know I was here?"

"Oh yes," said Kennett. He looked past Ambrose, into the simple, single room of the bothy. "Rather basic, old boy. Takes you back, I suppose?"

"Yes it does," said Ambrose, without rancour. Kennett, like most D-Arc operatives, was from an old and very upper-class family. Ambrose was not. Everything he had achieved had come despite his more difficult start in life. He had taken a long series of steps that had begun with a scholarship to Bristol Grammar at the age of seven, the first part of a challenging journey that had taken him far, far away from the ever-changing temporary accommodations shared with his father, at least when that worthy was not in prison for his various "no-risk lottery" and "gifting circle" frauds.

"Each to his own," remarked Kennett. "I take it you've dealt with the visitors?"

"Yes."

"We'd best take you away then," said Kennett. "Lady S wants to have a word, and I expect you'll need that leg looked at. Demon bite is it?"

"Lady S can go—" Ambrose bit back his words with an effort.

"Quite likely," replied Kennett. "I wouldn't be at all surprised. But I don't see the relevance. Lady S wants to see you, therefore you will be seen by her. Unless, of course, you want to stay here and turn into something that will have every Gaelic-speaking entity of wood, air, and river rising up to assail?"

"No," replied Ambrose. He knew when it was pointless to rail against fate. "I don't want that. Do we have to go all the way to London? I don't think I can make—"

"No, not at all," said Kennett. "Lady S is on a progress through the far-flung parts of the D-Arc realm. She's in Edinburgh, taking stock of our new medical advisor."

"New medical advisor?" asked Ambrose. "What happened to Shivinder?"

Kennett turned his cold, cold eyes to meet Ambrose's gaze, and held it for a second, which was sufficient reply. Whatever had happened to Dr. Shivinder, Ambrose would likely never know, and if he did find out, by some accident of information, he would be best to keep it to himself.

"The new chap is quite the prodigy," said Kennett. "Oxford, of course, like all the best people."

Ambrose sighed and limped a step forward towards the car. There were tiny wisps of smoke issuing from under the hieroglyphic bandage, as the small angels of Sekhmet fought the demonic infestation. While it wouldn't actually catch alight, the pain was quite intense, which was another sign that the demons were winning.

"Spare me the jibes," he said. "Can we just go?"

"Yes, we should toodle along, I suppose," said Kennett. "Jones and Jones will stay to secure the place, and they can bring your gear along later and so forth. Do we need to shoot the dog?"

Ambrose bent down, gasping with the pain, and took Nellie by the collar.

Turning her head, he looked deeply into her trusting brown eyes, and then ran his hand over her back and legs, carefully checking for bites.

"No, she's clear," he said. "She can go back to the big house. Nellie! Big house!"

He pointed to the garden gate as he spoke. Nellie cocked her head at him, to make sure he was serious, yawned, to show her lolloping red tongue, and slowly began to pick her way through the mud.

She had only gone a few yards when Kennett shot her in the back of the head with his revolver. The heavy Webley .455 boomed twice. The dog was shoved into the puddle by the force of the impact, her legs continuing to twitch and jerk there, even though she must have been killed instantly. Blood slowly swirled into the muddy water, steam rising as it spread.

Ambrose fumbled with his shotgun, swinging it to cover Kennett. But it was broken open, and Kennett was watching him, the revolver still in his hand.

"There was demon-taint in her mouth," said Kennett, very matter-of-fact. "She wouldn't have lasted a day."

Ambrose shut his eyes for a moment. Then he nodded dully. Kennett stepped in and took the shotgun, but did not try to remove the yataghan that Ambrose used to lever himself upright.

"You're all right?" asked Kennett. "Operational? Capable?"

"I suppose so," said Ambrose, his voice almost as detached as Kennett's. He looked down at Nellie's body. Dead, just like so many of his friends, but life continued and he must make the best of it. That was the litany he had learned at Grandway House. He owed it to the dead, the dead that now included Nellie, to live on as best he could.

"Did you do that to test me? Did Lady S tell you to shoot my dog?"

"No," replied Kennett calmly. "I had no orders. But there was demon-taint."

Ambrose nodded again. Kennett could lie better than almost anyone he knew, so well that it was impossible to know whether he spoke the truth or not, unless there was some undeniable evidence to the contrary. And there could have been demon-taint. Of course, with the dog's head shattered by hexed silver fulminate exploding rounds, there was no possible way to check that now.

Leaning on his yataghan, Ambrose trudged to the standard-issue departmental car. He had hoped to avoid any further involvement with D-Arc, but he had always known that this was a vain hope. Even when he had left the section the first time in 1916, escaping to regular service on the Western Front, there had still been occasional reminders that D-Arc was watching him and might reel him in at any time. Like the odd staff officer with the mismatched eyes, one blue and one green, who never visited anyone else's battalion in the brigade but often dropped in on Ambrose. Always on one of the old, old festival days, sporting a fresh-cut willow crop, a spray of holly, or bearing some odd bottle of mead or elderberry wine. Ambrose's adjutant and the battalion's second-in-command called him "the botanist" and thought he was just another red-tabbed idiot wandering about. But Ambrose knew better.

Once in the car, Ambrose retreated almost immediately into a yogic trance state, to slow the effects of the demon bite. Possibly even more helpfully, it stopped him thinking about Nellie and the long roll-call of dead friends, and as it was not sleep, he did not dream. Instead, he experienced himself travelling without movement over an endless illusory landscape made up of Buddhist sutras.

Ambrose came out of this trance to find that the car had stopped. He looked out the window and saw that the sun was setting. The gas lamps had just been lit, but it was still quite bright enough for him to work out that they had reached Edinburgh, and after a moment, he recognized the street. They were in South Charlotte Square, outside what, at first glance, appeared to be a hotel, till he saw a small brass plate by the front door, which read ST. AGNES NURSING HOME.

"New Scottish office, more discreet," grunted Kennett, correctly interpreting Ambrose's expression. D-Arc's previous Scottish office had been co-located with the SSB, tucked away in a temporary building on the outer perimeter of Redford Barracks, a position that provided physical security but made more arcane measures difficult to employ.

Kennett led Ambrose quickly inside, through the oak-and-silver outer doors, past the mirrored inner doors, and across the tessellated, eye-catching tiled floor of the atrium, all useful architectural defences against malignant spirits. The demon had grown enough in Ambrose's leg for him to feel its attention drawn by the mirrors, and his leg twitched and twisted of its own accord as he crossed the patterned maze of the floor.

Kennett signed them into the book at the front desk, at which point Ambrose was relieved of his yataghan and revolver in return for a claim ticket, before being helped upstairs.

"Lady S will see you first," said Kennett. "Afterwards . . . I suppose the medico can sort out your leg."

Ambrose caught the implication of that phrasing very well. Any treatment would be dependent on Lady S and how Ambrose responded to whatever she wanted him to do: which was almost certainly about him returning to active duty with D-Arc again.

"In you go," said Kennett. He rapped on the double door, turned the knob to push it open a fraction, and released his supporting grip on Ambrose's elbow.

Ambrose limped in, wishing he was elsewhere. Kennett did not follow him, the door shutting hard on Ambrose's heels with a definitive click.

The room was dark, and smelled of orange zest and the sickly honey-scent of myrrh, which was normal for any chamber that had Lady S in it. Ambrose peered into the darkness, but did not move forward. It was better to stay near the exit, since he knew that only a small part of this room was actually connected to the building and to Edinburgh itself. The rest of the room was . . . somewhere else.

He heard a rustling in the dark, and swallowed nervously as the strange smell grew stronger. A candle flared, the light suddenly bright. Ambrose hooded his eyes and looked off to one side.

Lady S was there, some feet away from the candle, again as expected. He could see only her vague outline, swathed as she was in gauzy silks that moved about her in answer to some breeze that did reach the door.

"Dear Ambrose!" exclaimed the apparition, her voice that of some kindly but aged female relative welcoming a close but morally strayed junior connection. "How kind of you to call upon me in my hour of need."

"Yes," agreed Ambrose. "I could not, of course, resist."

Lady S laughed a hearty laugh that belonged to a far more full-fleshed person, someone who might have triple chins to wobble as they guffawed. The laugh did not match the narrow, dimly perceived silhouette in her fluttering shrouds.

"Oh you always could make me laugh," she said. "I don't laugh as much as I should, you know."

"Who does?" asked Ambrose, unable to keep the bitterness from his voice.

"Now, now, Ambrose," said Lady S. Something that might be a finger wagged in the air some distance in front of his face. "No petulance. I can't abide petulance. Tell me—your father, he of many names and aliases, may he rest in peace—his birth name was really Farnowitz and he *was* born in Germany?"

"You know he was," said Ambrose tightly. "It's in my file and always has been. My mother was English, I was born in Bristol, and what's more I have served my country more than—"

"Yes, yes dear," comforted Lady S. "We're not holding it against you. Quite the contrary. We need someone with a modicum of the art who also has German blood. Apart from the king, who naturally isn't available to us, the combination is rather scarce among our ranks."

"What do you need me to do, and what do I get out of it?"

"Oh, my dear young man, such impatience and, dare I say, rudeness will not serve you well. But perhaps it is the demon that is gnawing its way up your leg? I will make some allowance for that."

"I beg your pardon, Lady S," muttered Ambrose. Even at the best of times, it did not pay to offend Lady S, and this was far from the best of times.

"Oh, do call me Auntie Hester," cooed the apparition in the darkness. "You know I do like all my young men to call me Auntie Hester."

"Yes, Auntie Hester," said Ambrose reluctantly. He could not suppress a shiver, as he knew exactly what she was: a revenant who survived only thanks to powerful magic, numerous blood sacrifices, and a budget appropriation that was never examined in Parliament. Lady Hester Stanhope had been dead for eighty years, but that had not ended her career in one of the predecessor organizations of D-Arc. She had gone from strength to strength in both bureaucratic and sorcerous terms since then. Though she was severely limited in her physical interaction with the world, she had many other advantages. Not least were her unrivalled political connexions, which ran all the way back to the early nineteenth century, when she had managed the household of her uncle William Pitt the Younger, then prime minister of Britain.

"Very good. Now, it has come to our attention that someone exceedingly naughty in Solingen . . . the Rhineland, you know . . . is trying to raise a *Waldgeist*, and not just any sixpence-ha'penny forest spirit, but a great old one of the primeval wood. They've got hold of the ritual and three days from now they're going to summon up the old tree-beastie and set it on our occupying forces—and we can't allow that, can we? Therefore, Ambrose my darling, you will dash over to Solingen, call up this *Waldgeist* first, and bind it to our service, then have it destroy the second summoner. Are you with me so far?"

"I know very little Teutonic magic," said Ambrose. "Surely there must be someone else better—"

"You'll have a *grimoire*, dear," said Lady S. "You *can* read Old High German?"

"Yes, but—"

"That's settled then!" exclaimed Lady S. "Our new doctor will cut that demon out for you, he's a darling boy and such a fine hand with the blade. Major Kennett will accompany you to Solingen, by the way. In case you need . . . assistance."

"What about the attack on me today?" asked Ambrose quickly. The wind-swept figure was retreating further into the dark, and the candle was guttering. "They were Anatolian demons! Why would the emir be sending them against me now?"

"You will be protected," said Lady S. Her voice was distant now. "D-Arc takes care of its own."

"I know it does!" shouted Ambrose. "That's why I want to know who really sent those demons! Did you set this all in train—"

"*Au revoir*, my dear," said a very remote voice, no more than a whisper on the wind.

The door behind him snapped open, and an inexorable force propelled Ambrose back out through the doorway. Landing on his injured leg, he fell and sprawled lengthways across the carpeted hall. Kennett looked down at him for a moment, sniffed, and helped him up.

"Doctor Lambshead is all ready for you," he said. "Gunderbeg is standing by to eat the demon when it's cut out, and we have all the recuperative apparatus prepared. Best we get a move on, I think."

Ambrose looked down at his leg. The bandage of Sekhmet was now just a few strands of rag, and it was being chewed on by a mouth that had grown in his calf muscle, a black-lipped, razor-fanged mouth that was trying to turn itself upwards, towards his knee.

"Yes," said Ambrose faintly. "If you don't mind."

AT NOON THE next day, his leg salved, bandaged, and entirely demon-free, Ambrose was on the boat train to Dover and thence to Calais, with Kennett keeping company. An uneventful channel crossing was complete by midnight, and after only changing trains twice, they were in Solingen the following morning.

Ambrose spent a good part of their travelling time reading the *grimoire* that Kennett had handed to him in Edinburgh. The book had come wrapped in a piece of winding cloth cut from the burial shroud of the Scottish sorcerer Thomas Weir, a fabric made to stifle sorcery, indicating that the D-Arc librarian believed the *grimoire* had the potential to act of its own volition. Accordingly, Ambrose treated it with care, using reversed gloves to turn its pages and marking his place with a ribbon torn from a child's bonnet.

The *grimoire* was a typeset version of a much older text. It had been printed in the late sixteenth century, and a note with it attributed the book to the German sorcerer and botanomancer Bertin Zierer, though, as the flyleaf was missing and the original binding has been replaced several times, this was noted as being speculation rather than fact.

The section of the *grimoire* dealing with the *Waldgeist* of the Primeval Wood that had once stretched across much of modern Germany was, as per usual, couched in rather vague language, apart from the description of the actual ritual. It did not describe the form the *Waldgeist* usually took, or go into any details of its powers, beyond a warning that these would be employed against anyone who dared wake it who was "not of the blood of Wotan." The only clue to the nature of the *Waldgeist* came from an etching that showed a disc of ground covered in trees rising from a forest. Titled, in rough translation, "Tree Spirits Rising," it did not help Ambrose very much, though it did make him wonder if the *Waldgeist* manifested as some sort of gestalt entity composed of a whole section of modern forest.

Apart from the *grimoire*, the duty librarian had also included a large-scale map of the area around Solingen and some typed pages of research and observation. The map indicated that the locus of the *Waldgeist* was in the middle of a small but very old wood some twenty kilometers south of Solingen. The notes cross-referenced the ritual cited in the *grimoire* with other known practices of Teutonic magic, and affirmed that it looked to be complete and not designed to trap or harm the caster by some omission or intentional change.

Shortly before their arrival, both men assumed their appointed disguises, which had been placed by unseen hands in the next-door compartment. Ambrose became a full colonel from the staff sent to join the British forces of occupation on some mission that was not to be denied or enquired about by anyone. Kennett, on the other hand, simply put on a different and more conservative suit, topped with a grey homburg identical to that worn by the late King Edward, and thus assumed the appearance of a mysterious civilian from the upper echelons of Whitehall.

They were met at the Ohligs Wald station in Solingen by a young subaltern of the Black Watch, whose attempt at an introduction was immediately quashed by Kennett.

"You don't need to know our names and we don't want to know yours," he snapped. "Is the car waiting? And our escort?"

"Yes, sir," replied the young second lieutenant, a blush as red as the tabs on Ambrose's collar spreading across his cheeks. "As per the telegraph message."

"Lead on then," said Kennett. "The sooner we take care of this the better."

The car, commandeered from the divisional general, was accompanied by four motorcycle outriders and three Peerless trucks carrying the nameless subaltern's infantry platoon and a machine gun section.

"We hardly need all this carry-on," protested Ambrose as he settled into the grandly upholstered backseat of the general's car, and Kennett climbed in next to him. "Surely it would be better for me to get changed and just walk into the wood as a tourist or something?"

"I don't think so," replied Kennett. "The fellow who is hoping to . . . carry out his deed . . . is the leader of a gang of militants called Die Schwarze Fahne and they have quite a membership of former soldiers and the like. We'll have these lads establish a cordon around the wood, then you and I will go in."

"You're coming with me?" asked Ambrose. "The *grim—*"

He stopped himself, aware that the driver and the subaltern in the front seat were so obviously trying to not listen that they must be able to hear everything, even over the noise of the engines as the whole convoy got under way. "That is, the reference is specific about German heritage and the . . . subject's response if . . . ah . . . in contact with others."

"M' grandmother was Edith Adler, the opera singer," drawled Kennett out of the side of his mouth, so only Ambrose could hear. "So I have a drop or two of the blood. But I'll keep well back, just the same."

Ambrose nodded slightly and tried not to show how much he was discomfited by Kennett's disclosure. Even from such slight information, he would now be able to positively identify the man. Which meant that Kennett was either taking him into some inner echelon of trust, or he didn't think Ambrose would be around long enough for it to matter.

It only took forty minutes to reach the fringes of the wood. Ambrose sat in the car for a few minutes while everyone else got out, and read the relevant pages of the *grimoire* for perhaps the twentieth or thirtieth time. The ritual was not complex, but he had to memorise it. It would not be possible to refer to the book in the middle of the process.

He felt quite calm as he slipped the *grimoire* inside his tunic and did up the buttons. They looked like the usual brass, but were, in fact, silver-gilt, part of the sorcerous protection that Ambrose hoped would help him if things went only slightly awry. Of course, when dealing with an entity like a primeval tree spirit, it was far more likely that if something did go wrong, it would be on a scale so immense that no amount of sorcerous protection would make the slightest difference.

The lieutenant's platoon, under the direction more of a leather-lunged sergeant than the pink-faced officer, were forming up in three ranks on the verge. The trucks were parked across the road to block other vehicular traffic, and the Vickers machine gun was in the process of being emplaced on its tripod some way off, up a slight rise, to enfilade the road.

Ambrose got out and orientated the map to north by the sun, shifting it slightly to get the road in the right relationship, map to real topography. The map indicated the beginning of a footpath a dozen or so yards beyond the machine-gun position, and sure enough, there was a stone cairn there and a rotting wooden signpost that once upon a time had something written on it.

"We'll follow the footpath," said Ambrose, indicating the way. He folded the map and slipped it in with the *grimoire*. "It goes to the . . . the agreed rendezvous."

Kennett nodded and turned to the anxiously waiting lieutenant.

"Send one section to patrol the perimeter of the wood to the west and one section to the east. Keep one section here. Your men are not to enter the wood, no matter what you hear. Cries for help, orders that sound like they come from me or the colonel, all are to be ignored unless we are actually in front of you. If we do not come out within three hours—my watch says ten twenty-two, set yours now—return to Solingen, report to your CO, and tell him to immediately contact General Spencer Ewart at the War Office and relay the code phrase *'defectus omnes mortui.'*"

"But that's . . . uh . . . fail . . . failing . . . failure . . . all dead," said the lieutenant, busy trying to scribble the phrase in his notebook and set his watch, all at the same time.

"Did I ask you to translate?" snapped Kennett. "Do you have the code phrase?"

"Yes, sir!" replied the lieutenant. He closed his notebook and managed to successfully set his watch, his platoon sergeant surreptitiously leaning in to make sure he'd got it right.

"Finally, fire two warning shots over the heads of anyone approaching. If they continue, shoot to kill. It doesn't matter who they are. Civilians, women, children, whoever. Here is a written order to that effect."

"Yes, sir," said the lieutenant. There was considerable doubt in his voice and his hand shook a little as he unfolded the letter, his eyes flickering across the typewritten lines before widening enormously as they came to the short signature—just a first name and a capital letter—at the bottom of the page.

"Yes, sir!" he repeated, much more vigorously.

"Presuming we return, I'll want that back," said Kennett. "Carry on."

The lieutenant saluted and whirled about, speaking quickly to his sergeant, who a moment later began to bellow orders. Ambrose ignored the sudden bustle of military activity and began to walk towards the footpath. His eyes were on the fringes of the wood, looking for signs of arcane disturbance. But there were none visible. This part of the wood was composed of beech trees, their trunks green and mossy, their foliage a darker green. The light changed under the trees, gaining a soft, green tinge, but this was the natural magic of leaves and sun, not anything sorcerous.

It was also cooler under the canopy of the forest. Ambrose led the way with Kennett a dozen yards behind. They walked in silence, save for the occasional squelch of soft ground, or the snapping of a fallen twig where the footpath wound through higher, drier ground.

A half-mile or so in, the beeches began to give way to oaks. They were much older, and grew closer together, the footpath leading into relative darkness. As they left the beech forest behind, Ambrose noticed that it was quieter among the oaks as well. All the bird-sound had vanished, and all he could hear were his own and Kennett's footsteps. Then, not much farther on, Kennett's footsteps stopped.

Ambrose looked back. Kennett was leaning against the broad trunk of one of the ancient oaks. He nodded and waved Ambrose on. Clearly, this was as far as Kennett cared to go into the heart of the wood, and, as he was far more in practice and so currently more attuned to the occult than Ambrose, this probably meant he had sensed the locus of the *Waldgeist* somewhere close ahead.

Indeed, no more than fifty yards ahead, there was a forest glade where the oaks parted around a clear expanse of grass. In the middle of this small clearing was an incredibly ancient, stunted tree, a king-oak that could well be thousands of years old. Blown over by some long-forgotten storm, it still lived, its branches spreading horizontally, its trunk twisted and gnarled, its bark as hard as iron.

Ambrose could feel the *Waldgeist* now, the sense of the sleeping spirit that had been born of thirty million trees, and would not fade until the last of those trees was gone. Humans had decimated the primeval forest, but the spirit still remained. It only slept, and in Ambrose's opinion, it would be best left to do so. But he knew he had no real choice. If Lady S wanted the *Waldgeist* awoken, then it had to be awoken.

He knelt by the trunk of the king-oak, and paused, just for a moment, to gather his thoughts, mentally going through each step of the ritual. Satisifed that he had remembered it all, he laid out everything he needed on the forest floor.

First of all was the silver *athame*, his sacred knife, the one he had used in Turkey and thought lost when he was at the Front, only to find it had been stored away in the D-Arc armoury against his later use. They had always presumed he would come back.

Second was an acorn from this same wood, though from long ago. It was so old it was almost petrified, and though he had been assured its origin had been checked by thaumaturgic assay, as well as in the D-Arc records, it was the one element that he doubted. If it was from somewhere else, it might well help to raise the *Waldgeist*, but it would not be a friendly awakening.

The third thing was not in the ritual. Ambrose took his revolver from its holster and laid it down, to be ready at hand. If things went very badly wrong, he intended to shoot himself. It would be a far quicker and kinder way to die. Ancient spirits were not known for their sense of mercy.

That done, it was time to start. Ambrose began to recite the words of the waking ritual. His voice was steady, and he spoke carefully, as he sliced the end of his left thumb with the *athame* and let the bright blood drip onto the ancient acorn. As the blood dripped, the words became a chant, rhythmically repeated over and over again.

The acorn soaked up the blood like a sponge. When nine drops had fallen, Ambrose cut his right thumb and let another nine drops fall, without faltering in his chant. The guttural Old High German words sounded very loud in the stillness of the wood, but Ambrose knew it wasn't so much the words themselves that mattered. It was the thoughts behind them, the blood, and the aged seed.

He finished the chant at exactly the same time he pushed the acorn into the soil with both his bleeding thumbs, and sat back.

Nothing happened. Ambrose waited, sitting cross-legged next to the ancient oak, his hand on the butt of the revolver, ready to lift it up to his temple and fire.

A slight breeze swooped down and rustled the leaves on the low, spreading branches. It was cold, ice-laden, and out of time and place, in this splendid German summer.

"So it begins," whispered Ambrose. He could feel the *Waldgeist* stirring all around, the spirit waking in the wood. He looked up and saw the branches of the king-oak lifting, and then a moment later the trunk groaned and creaked, as it began to straighten up. It was becoming the great tree of old, when it had stood sixty feet high or more, tall and straight and strong.

If it was a typical manifestation of a tree spirit, the tree itself would respond to Ambrose's summoning, either to whisper with the soft sussuration of leaves, or to pin him down with a heavy branch and send a thousand green shoots to penetrate his body, slowly growing through skin and flesh until they did fatal damage to some vital organ. Or, even worse in some ways, the *Waldgeist* might force itself into Ambrose's mind, remove everything of his personality, and create for itself a human puppet. That was likely one of Kennett's main reasons for accompanying him, to guard against this eventuality with his revolver and its exploding silver bullets.

The wind blew stronger, and the tree grew taller. Ambrose made his fingers uncurl from the revolver, though he kept his hand close. It was important not to appear with weapons in hand, for that in itself might sway the *Waldgeist* to enmity.

Then the ground shivered and sank beneath Ambrose. It was an unwelcome sensation, delivering sudden uncertainty, and even worse, the sharp memory of being buried alive. Wildly, he looked around, and saw that just as in the etching in the *grimoire*, the king-oak and all the trees around the glade had risen from the surrounding forest, as if a disc had been cored out and lifted straight up.

Ambrose looked down, and saw the earth crumbling beneath him. His fingers closed on the revolver and he managed to get it halfway to his head before he was suddenly pulled down, taken into the earth as a shark drags down a swimmer, without mercy or any possibility of resistance.

The ground closed over Ambrose's head, the revolver landing with a thud to mark the spot. Grass grew in an instant through the bare soil, eager tendrils of green wrapping around the blued metal of the gun, until in a moment it was covered in green and lost to sight.

Deep underground, Ambrose screamed and screamed and screamed, all inside his head, for his mouth was shut with soil. He relived the sudden concussion of the German shell, the blankness in his ears, the earth silently cascading into the dugout, the last glimpse of Peter's terrified face, the lantern snuffed out in an instant . . . and then the darkness, the pressure of the earth, everywhere about him save for a tiny air pocket between two fallen beams, where he had pressed his face.

Then there had been the terrible, never-ending time of being trapped, not knowing whether he would ever see daylight again, or breathe the clean air, untainted by earth and fumes and the slowly building stench of the corpses of his friends as they began to rot around him. Alone in the earth, held in an implacable grasp and wreathed in silence. Slowly dying, but not quickly enough for it to be an escape.

Now it was all happening again.

But it was not the same, some fragment of Ambrose's still-screaming mind observed. He was completely buried in the earth, this time, and so should already be well on the way to asphyxiation. But he felt no need to breathe.

Also, he could hear. He could hear his own heartbeat, beating a sharp tattoo of panic, but he could also hear the movement of the earth. But there was something else, as well, something that, as his panic lessened, he realised was a voice, the voice of the *Waldgeist*.

What he heard was not words, at least not in any human language. It was the sound of the forest, of the wind, and the trees, and the birds and the insects, somehow ordered and structured to become something that he could understand.

The *Waldgeist* of the primeval forest was whispering to him, as it took him into its embrace. Its true heart was down in the tangled roots where he lay, not in the tree above. He could feel those roots now, twining around him, gripping him lightly, but ready to rend him apart should the spirit's feelings change.

It wanted to know why he had awoken it, and for what purpose.

Ambrose told it, not bothering to open his mouth. It took his explanation and went into his mind for more, its presence like a sudden shadow on a summer's day, cool and crisp as it slowly spread through his memories and mind. Ambrose's panic shrank before this shadowy touch, and he grew quiet, almost asleep himself, the *Waldgeist* growing more awake.

As the tree spirit wandered in his thoughts, Ambrose relived them, too, slowly and sleepily. All the wonders and horrors of his life, from his earliest recollections to the events of the last few days. All were examined by the tree spirit, and as they progressed, in no particular order, Ambrose felt that each memory, and everything he had done or not done, was being weighed up and catalogued, added to the *Waldgeist's* careful inventory of all the other living things in its forest domain.

Eventually, it finished looking. Ambrose was very tired by then, so tired that he could barely formulate the question that constituted his mission, visualising each word in his mind as if he were writing it down on an order pad, the question carefully contained within the rectangular grid.

So	you	will	not	answer	this	other sum-moner
in	the	days	to	come?	and you	will
be	content	to	rest	until I	call	you
from	your	sleep	again?			

No answer came. Ambrose tried to ask the question again, but he was too tired. Fear and panic had exhausted him, but now he felt a different weariness. He was warm, and comfortable, and the tree roots that cradled him felt as familiar as the ancient armchair by the fire in the bothy, the one with the sheepskins laid over its creased and faded leather upholstery.

Ambrose slept, and did not dream.

When he awoke, it was with a start. There was bright sunshine on his face, making him blink, and the blue sky above was bordered with green. He sat up and saw that he was at the foot of the king-oak, which was once again bent and bowed by the passage of time. There was no sign of his revolver or *athame*, but when he stood up, and checked himself over, everything else seemed to be unchanged. The *grimoire* was still in his tunic, as was the map. There was some earth caught under his Sam Browne belt, and his uniform was somewhat mussed, but that was all.

Everything else looked normal. There was no risen disc of trees, and though he could feel the *Waldgeist*, it was very faint. It slept again, and was sleeping very deep. Whether he had convinced it or not to remain quiescent, it would take far more than the blood of two thumbs and the ritual he had used to wake it now.

Ambrose frowned, but it was a merry frown. He didn't really understand what had happened, but he knew his object had been achieved. He also felt surprisingly good, almost as happy in himself as he had been in the far-off, golden days before the War.

He clapped his hand against the king-oak in friendly farewell, and set off along the path. Several paces along, he was surprised to find himself whistling. He frowned again, and stopped, standing still on the path. He couldn't remember when he had last felt like whistling.

There was a rustle up ahead. Ambrose's attention immediately returned to the present. He snuck off the path and crouched down behind a lesser but still substantial oak, regretting the loss of his revolver. Someone was coming very cautiously up the path, and it could be a German anarchist as easily as Kennett, and even if it was Kennett, Ambrose couldn't be sure of his intentions, and he was no longer so ready to just let Kennett kill him. There would be time enough to join his friends.

"Ambrose?"

It was Kennett. Ambrose peered around the trunk. Kennett was coming along the path, and he wasn't brandishing a weapon. But very strangely, he was no longer wearing the same suit with the grey homburg. He was in tweeds, with a deerstalker cap, and there was something about his face . . . a partially healed scar under his eye that hadn't been there . . .

"Ah," said Ambrose. He stepped out from behind the tree and raised his hand. "Hello, Kennett. How long have I been away?"

Kennett smiled, a smile that, as always, contained no warmth whatsoever, and was more an indication of sardonic superiority than any sense of humour.

"A year and a day," he said. "Just as the *grimoire* said."

"Not the copy you gave me," said Ambrose.

"Naturally," replied Kennett. "You might have refused to go. But from the whistling, the general spring of the step, and so forth, I presume the cure has been efficacious?"

"I do feel . . . whole," admitted Ambrose. He paused for a moment, eyes downcast, thinking of his own reactions. "And I believe . . . I am no longer afraid to be underground."

"That's good," said Kennett. "Because we have a job to do, and I'm afraid a great deal of it is deep under the earth. High, but deep. I'm not fond of the Himalayas myself, but what can you do?"

"Was there actually a German adept who wanted to raise the spirit?" asked Ambrose, as they began to walk together back along the path.

"Oh yes," said Kennett. "It's doubtful if he would have succeeded, and the timing was not quite what we said, but Lady S thought we might as well try to get two birds with one stone. The new doctor brought it to her attention that this old spirit had a twofold nature, that as well as trampling the undeserving and so on, it also traditionally sometimes healed the sick and those of 'broken mind.'"

"Broken mind," repeated Ambrose. "Yes. I suppose that I wasn't really getting any better where I was. But those demons—"

"They *were* the emir's," interrupted Kennett. "Forced our hand. Couldn't be helped."

"I see," said Ambrose, with a swift sideways glance at Kennett's face. He still couldn't tell if the man was lying.

They walked the rest of the way out of the wood in silence. At the road, there was a green Crossley 20/25 waiting, with Jones and Jones leaning on opposite sides of the bonnet, each carefully watching the surrounding countryside. They nodded to Ambrose as he walked up, and he thought that Jones the Larger might even have given him the merest shadow of a wink.

Ambrose's yataghan was on the floor behind the front seat, and there was a large cardboard box tied with a red ribbon sitting in the middle of the backseat. Kennett indicated the box with an inclination of his head.

"For you," he said. "Present from Lady S."

Ambrose undid the ribbon and opened the box. There was a velvet medal case inside, which he did not open; a silver hip flask engraved with his name beneath a testimonial of thanks from an obscure manufacturer of scientific instruments in Nottingham; and a card with a picture of a mountaineer waving the Union Jack atop a snow-covered mountain.

Ambrose flipped open the card.

"Welcome back," he read aloud. "With love from Auntie Hester."

Ivica Stevanovic's "Relic with Fish," part of his series "The Silence of Many Pattering Feet: Saints and the Bits They Leave Behind."

Relic

By Jeffrey Ford

Out at the end of the world, on a long spit of land like a finger poking into oblivion, nestled in a valley among the dunes, sat the Church of Saint Ifritia, constructed from twisted driftwood and the battered hulls of ships. There was one tall, arched window composed of the round bottoms of blue bottles. The sun shone through it, submerging altar and pews. There was room for twenty inside, but the most ever gathered for a sermon was eleven. Atop its crooked steeple jutted a spiraled tusk some creature had abandoned on the beach.

The church's walls had a thousand holes, and so every morning Father Walter said his prayers while shoveling sand from the sanctuary. He referred to himself as "father" but he wasn't a priest. He used the title because it was what he remembered the holy men were called in the town he came from. Wanderers to the end of the world sometimes inquired of him as to the church's denomination. He was confused by these questions. "A basic church, you know," he'd say. "I talk God and salvation with anyone interested." Usually the pilgrims would turn away, but occasionally one stayed on and listened.

Being that the Church of Saint Ifritia could have as few as three visitors a month, Father Walter didn't feel inclined to give a sermon once a week. "My flock would be only the sand fleas," he said to Sister North. "Then preach to the fleas," she replied. "Four sermons a year is plenty," he said. "One for each season. Nobody should need more than four sermons a year." They were a labor for him to write, and he considered the task as a kind of penance. Why he gave sermons, he wasn't sure. Their purpose was elusive, and yet he knew it was something the holy men did. His earliest ones were about the waves, the dunes, the sky, the wind, and when he ran out of natural phenomena to serve as topics, he moved inward and began mining memory for something to write.

Father Walter lived behind the whalebone altar in a small room with a bed, a chair, a desk, and a stove. Sister North, who attended a summer sermon one year, the subject of which was The Wind, and stayed on to serve Saint Ifritia, lived in her own small shack behind the church. She kept it tidy, decorated with shells and strung with tattered fishing nets, a space no bigger than Father Walter's quarters. In the warm months, she kept a garden in the sand, dedicated to her saint. Although he never remembered having invited her to stay on, Father Walter proclaimed her flowers and tomatoes miracles, a cornucopia from dry sand and salt air, and recorded them in the official church record.

Sister North was a short, brown woman with long, dark hair streaked with grey, and an expression of determination. Her irises were almost yellow, cat-like, in her wide face. On her first night amid the dunes, she shared Father Walter's bed. He came to realize that she would share it again as long as there was no mention of it during the light of day. Once a season, she'd travel ten miles inland by foot to the towns and give word that a sermon was planned for the following Monday. The towns she visited scared her, and only occasionally would she meet a pilgrim who'd take note of her message.

In addition to the church and Sister North's shack, there were two other structures in the sand-dune valley. One was an outhouse built of red ship's wood with a tarpaulin flap for a door and a toilet seat made of abalone. The other was a shrine that housed the holy relic of Saint Ifritia. The latter building was woven from reeds by Sister North and her sisters. She'd sent a letter and they'd come, three of them. They were all short and brown, with long, dark hair streaked with grey. None had yellow eyes, though. They harvested reeds from the sunken meadow, an overgrown square mile set below sea level among the dunes two miles east of the church. They sang while they wove the strands into walls and window holes and a roof. Father Walter watched the whole thing from a distance. He felt he should have some opinion about it, but couldn't muster one. When the shrine began to take form, he knew it was a good thing.

Before Sister North's sisters left to return to their lives, Father Walter planned a dedication for the relic's new home. He brought the holy item to the service wrapped in a dirty old towel, the way he'd kept it for the past thirty years. Its unveiling brought sighs from the sisters, although at first they were unsure what they were looking at. A dark lumpen object, its skin like that of an overripe banana. There were toes and even orange, shattered toenails. It was assumed a blade had severed it just above the ankle, and the wound had, by miracle or fire, been cauterized. "Time's leather" was the phrase Father Walter bestowed upon the state of its preservation. It smelled of wild violets.

There was no golden reliquary to house it; he simply placed it in the bare niche built into the altar, toes jutting slightly beyond the edge of their new den. He turned and explained to the assembled, "You must not touch it with your hands, but fold them in front of you, lean forward, and kiss the toes. In this manner, the power of the saint will be yours for a short time and you'll be protected and made lucky."

Each of them present, the father, Sister North and her sisters, and a young man and woman on their honeymoon, who wandered into the churchyard just before the ceremony got under way, stepped up with folded hands and kissed the foot. Then they sat, and Father Walter paced back and forth, whispering to himself, as was his ritual prior to delivering a sermon. He'd written a new one for the event, a fifth sermon for the year. Sister North was pleased with his industry and had visited his bed the night he'd completed it. He stopped pacing eventually and pointed at the ancient foot. The wind moaned outside. Sand sifted through the reeds.

Father Walter's Sermon

When I was a young man, I was made a soldier. It wasn't my choosing, I don't know. They put a gun to my head. We marched through the mud into a rainy country. I was young and I saw people die all around me. Some were only wounded but drowned in the muddy puddles. It rained past forty days and forty nights and the earth had had its fill. Rivers flooded their banks and the water spilled in torrents from the bleak mountains. I killed a few close-up with a bayonet and I felt their life rush out. Some I shot at a distance and watched them suddenly drop like children at a game. In two months time I was savage.

We had a commanding officer who'd become fond of killing. He could easily have stayed behind the lines and directed the attack, but, with saber drawn, he'd lead every charge and shoot and hack to pieces more of the enemy than the next five men. Once I fought near him in a hand-to-hand melee against a band of enemy scouts. The noises he made while doing his work were ungodly. Strange animal cries. He scared me. And I was not alone. This Colonel Hempfil took no prisoners and would dispatch civilians as well as members of his own squad on the merest whim. I swear I thought I'd somehow gone to hell. The sun never shone.

And then one night we sat in ambush in the trees on either side of a dirt road. The rain, of course, was coming down hard and it was cold, moving into autumn. The night was an eternity I think. I nodded off and then there came some action. The colonel kicked me where I sat and pointed at the road. I looked and could barely make out a hay cart creaking slowly by. The colonel kicked me again and indicated with hand signals that I was to go and check out the wagon.

My heart dropped. I started instantly crying, but as not to let the colonel see me sobbing, I ran to it. There could easily have been enemy soldiers beneath the hay, with guns at the ready. I ran onto the road in front of the wagon and raised my weapon. "Halt," I said. The tall man holding the reins pulled up and brought the horses to a stop. I told him to get down from his seat. As he climbed onto the road, I asked him, "What are you carrying?" "Hay," he replied, and then the colonel and the rest of our men stormed the wagon. Hempfil gave orders to clear the hay. Beneath it was discovered the driver's wife and two daughters. Orders were given to line them all up. As the driver was being escorted away by two soldiers, he turned to me and said, "I have something to trade for our freedom. Something valuable."

The colonel was organizing a firing squad, when I went up to him and told him what the driver had said to me. He thanked me for the information, and then ordered that the tall man be brought to him. I stood close to hear what he could possibly have to offer for the lives of his family. The man leaned over Hempfil and whispered something I could not make out. The colonel then ordered him, "Go get it."

The driver brought back something wrapped in a dirty towel. He unwrapped the bundle and, whisking away the cloth, held a form the size of a small rabbit up to the colonel. "Bring a light," cried Hempfil. "I can't see a damn thing." A soldier lit a lantern and brought it. I leaned in close to see what was revealed. It was an old foot, wrinkled like a purse and dark with age. The sight of the toenails gave me a shiver.

"This is what you will trade for your life and the lives of your family? This ancient bowel movement of a foot? Shall I give you change?" said the colonel and that's when I knew all of them would die. The driver spoke quickly. "It is the foot of a saint," he said. "It has power. Miracles."

"What saint?" asked the colonel.

"Saint Ifritia."

"That's a new one," said Hempfil and laughed. "Bring me the chaplain," he called over his shoulder.

The chaplain stepped up. "Have you ever heard of Saint Ifritia?" asked the colonel.

"She's not a real saint," said the priest. "She is only referred to as a saint in parts of the Holy Writing that have been forbidden."

Hempfil turned and gave orders for the driver's wife and daughters to be shot. When the volley sounded, the driver dropped to his knees and hugged the desiccated foot to him as if for comfort. I saw the woman and girls, in their pale dresses, fall at the side of the road. The colonel turned to me and told me to give him my rifle. I did. He took his pistol from its holster at his side and handed it to me. "Take the prisoner off into the woods where it's darker, give him a ten-yard head start, and then kill him. If he can elude you for fifteen minutes, let him go with his life."

"Yes, sir," I said, but I had no desire to kill the driver. I led him at gunpoint up the small embankment and into the woods. We walked slowly forward into darkness. He whispered to me so rapidly, "Soldier, I still hold the sacred foot of Ifritia. Let me trade you it for my life. Miracles." As he continued to pester me with his promises of blessings and wonders, the thought of killing him began to appeal to me. I don't know what it was that came over me. It came from deep within, but in an instant his death had become for me a foregone conclusion. After walking for ten minutes, I told him to stop. He did. I said nothing for a while, and the silence prompted him to say, "I get ten yards, do I not?"

"Yes," I said.

With his first step, I lifted the pistol and shot him in the back of the head. He was dead before he hit the ground, although his body shook twice as I reached down to turn him over. His face was blown out the front, a dark, smoking hole above a toothful grimace. I took the foot, felt its slick hide in my grasp, and wrapped it in the dirty towel. Shoving it into my jacket, I buttoned up against the rain and set off deeper into the woods. I fled like a frightened deer through the night, and all around me was the aroma of wild violets.

It's a long story, but I escaped the war, the foot of Saint Ifritia producing subtle miracles at every turn, and once it made me invisible as I passed through an occupied town. I left the country of rain, pursued by the ghost of the wagon driver. Every other minute, behind my eyes, the driver's wife and daughters fell in their pale dresses by the side of the road in the rain, and nearly every night he would appear from my meager campfire, rise up in smoke, and take form. "Why?" he always asked. "Why?"

I found that laughter dispersed him more quickly. One night I told the spirit I had plans the next day to travel west. But in the morning, I packed my things up quickly and headed due south toward the end of the world. I tricked him. Eventually, the ghost found me here, and I see him every great while, pacing along the tops of the dunes that surround the valley. He can't descend to haunt me, for the church I built protects me and the power of Saint Ifritia keeps him at bay. Every time I see him his image is dimmer, and before long he will become salt in the wind.

The impromptu congregation was speechless. Father Walter slowly became aware of it as he stood, swaying slightly to and fro. "The Lord works in mysterious ways," he said, a phrase he'd actually heard from Colonel Hempfil. There was a pause after his delivery of it, during which he waved his hands back and forth in the air like a magician distracting an audience. Eventually, two of the sisters nodded and the honeymoon couple shrugged and applauded the sermon.

Father Walter took this as a cue to move on, and he left the altar of the shrine and ran back to the church to fetch a case of whiskey that the Lord had recently delivered onto the beach after a terrific thunderstorm. The young couple produced a hash pipe and a tarry ball of the drug, which bore a striking resemblance to the last knuckle of the middle toe of Saint Ifritia's foot.

Late that night, high as the tern flies, the young man and woman left and headed out toward the end of the world, and Sister North's sisters loaded into their wagon and left for their respective homes. Father Walter sat on the sand near the bell in the churchyard, a bottle to his lips, staring up at the stars. Sister North stood over him, the hem of her habit, as she called the simple grey shift she wore every day, flapping in the wind.

"None would stay the night after your story of murder," she said to him. "They drank your whiskey, but they wouldn't close their eyes and sleep here with you drunk."

"Foolishness," he said. "There's plenty still left for all. Loaves and fishes of whiskey. And what do you mean by murder?"

"The driver in your sermon. You could have let him live."

He laughed. "I did. In real life, I let him go. A sermon is something different, though."

"You mean you lied?"

"If I shot him, I thought it would make a better story."

"But where's the Lord's place in a story of cold-blooded murder?"

"That's for Him to decide."

Sister North took to her shack for a week, and he rarely saw her. Only in the morning and late in the afternoon would he catch sight of her entering and leaving the shrine. She mumbled madly as she walked, eyes down. She moved her hands as if explaining to someone. Father Walter feared the ghost of the driver had somehow slipped into the churchyard and she was conversing with it. "Because I lied?" he wondered.

During the time of Sister North's retreat to her shack, a visitor came one afternoon. Out of a fierce sandstorm, materializing in the churchyard like a ghost herself, stepped a young woman wearing a hat with flowers and carrying a travel bag. Father Walter caught sight of her through blue glass. He went to the church's high doors, opened one slightly to keep the sand out, and called to her to enter. She came to him, holding the hat down with one hand and lugging the heavy bag with the other. "Smartly dressed" was the term the father vaguely remembered from his life inland. She wore a white shirt buttoned at the collar, with a dark string tie. Her black skirt and jacket matched, and she somehow made her way through the sand without much trouble in a pair of high heels.

Father Walter slammed shut the church door once she was inside. For a moment, he and his guest stood still and listened to the wind, beneath it the distant rhythm of the surf. The church was damp and cold. He told the young lady to accompany him to his room where he could make a fire in the stove. She followed him behind the altar, and as he broke sticks of driftwood, she removed her hat and took a seat at his desk.

"My name is Mina GilCragson," she said.

"Father Walter," he replied over his shoulder.

"I've come from the Theological University to see your church. I'm a student. I'm writing a thesis on Saint Ifritia."

"Who told you about us?" he asked, lighting the kindling.

"A colleague who'd been to the end of the world and back. He told me last month, 'You know, there's a church down south that bears your saint's name.' And so I was resolved to see it."

Father Walter turned to face her. "Can you tell me what you know of the saint? I am the father here, but I know so little, though the holy Ifritia saved my life."

The young woman asked for something to drink. Since the rainwater barrel had been tainted by the blowing sand that day, he poured her a glass of whiskey and one for himself. After serving his guest, he sat on the floor, his legs crossed. She dashed her drink off quickly, as he remembered was the fashion in the big cities. Wiping her lips with the back of her hand, she said, "What do you know of her so far?"

"Little," he said and listened, pleased to be, for once, on the other end of a sermon.

Mina GilCragson's Sermon

She was born in a village in the rainy country eighty-some odd years ago. Her father was a powerful man, and he oversaw the collective commerce of their village, Dubron, which devoted itself to raising plum fish for the tables of the wealthy. The village was surrounded by fifty ponds, each stocked with a slightly different variety of the beautiful, fantailed species. It's a violet fish. Tender and sweet when broiled.

105

Ifritia, called "If" by her family, wanted for nothing. She was the plum of her father's eye, her wishes taking precedence over those of her mother and siblings. He even placed her desires above the good of the village. When she was sixteen, she asked that she be given her own pond and be allowed to raise one single fish in it that would be her pet. No matter the cost of clearing the pond, one of the larger ones, she was granted her wish. To be sure, there was much grumbling among the other villagers and even among If's siblings and mother, but none was voiced in the presence of her father. He was a proud and vindictive man, and it didn't pay to cross him.

She was given a hatchling from the strongest stock to raise. From early on, she fed the fish by hand. When she approached the pond, the creature would surface and swim to where she leaned above the water. Fish, to the people of Dubron, were no more than swimming money, so that when Ifritia bequeathed a name on her sole charge, it was a scandal. Unheard of. Beyond the limit. A name denotes individuality, personality, something dangerously more than swimming money. A brave few balked in public, but If's father made their lives unhappy and they fell back to silence.

Lord Jon, the plum fish, with enough room to spread out in his own pond and fed nothing but table scraps, potatoes, and red meat, grew to inordinate dimensions. As the creature swelled in size, its sidereal fish face fleshed out, pressing the eyes forward, redefining the snout as a nose, and puffing the cheeks. It was said Jon's face was the portrait of a wealthy landowner, and that his smile, now wide where it once was pinched, showed rows of sharp, white teeth. A fish with a human face was believed by all but the girl and her father to be a sign of evil. But she never stopped feeding it and it never stopped growing until it became the size of a bull hog. Ifritia would talk to the creature, tell it her deepest secrets. If she told something good, it would break out into its huge, biting smile; something sad, and it would shut its mouth and tears would fill its saucer-wide eyes.

And then, out of the blue, for no known reason, the fish became angry with her. When she came to the edge of the pond, after it took the food from her hand, it splashed her and made horrid, grunting noises. The fish doctor was called for and his diagnosis was quickly rendered. The plum fish was not supposed to grow to Lord Jon's outsized dimensions, the excess of flesh and the effects of the red meat had made the creature insane. "My dear," said the doctor in his kindest voice, "you've squandered your time creating a large purple madness and that is the long and short of it." The girl's father was about to take exception with the doctor and box his ears, but in that instant she saw the selfish error of her ways.

After convincing her father of the immorality of what they'd done, she walked the village and apologized to each person privately, from the old matrons to the smallest babies. Then she took a rifle from the wall of her father's hunting room and went to the pond. A crowd gathered behind her as she made her way to the water's edge. Her change was as out of the blue as that of Lord Jon's, and they were curious about her and happy that she was on the way to becoming a good person. She took up a position at the edge of the water, and whistled to the giant plum fish to come for a feeding. The crowd hung back, fearful of the thing's human countenance. All watched its fin, like a purple fan, disappear beneath the water.

Ifritia pushed the bolt of the rifle forward and then sighted the weapon upon a spot where Jon usually surfaced. Everyone waited. The fish didn't come up. A flock of geese flew overhead, and it started to rain. Attention wandered, and just when the crowd began murmuring, the water beneath where Ifritia leaned over the pond exploded and the fish came up a blur of violet, launching itself the height of the girl. Using its tail, it slapped her mightily across the face. Ifritia went over backwards and her feet flew out from under her. In his descent, Jon turned in midair, opened his wide mouth, and bit through her leg. The bone shattered, the flesh tore, blood burst forth, and he was gone, out of sight, to the bottom of the big pond, with her foot.

She survived the grim amputation. While she lay in the hospital, her father had the pond drained. Eventually, the enormous fish was stranded in only inches of water. Ifritia's father descended a long ladder to the pond bed and sloshed halfway across it to reach Lord Jon. The creature flapped and wheezed. Her father took out a pistol and shot the fat, odious face between the eyes. He reported to others later that the fish began to cry when it saw the gun.

The immense plum fish was gutted and Ifritia's foot was found in its third stomach. Her father forbade anyone to tell her that her foot had been rescued from the fish. She never knew that it stood in a glass case in the cedar attic atop her family home. As the days wore on and her affliction made her more holy every minute, the foot simmered in Time, turning dark and dry. She learned to walk with a crutch, and became pious to a degree that put off the village. They whispered that she was a spy for God. Dressing in pure white, she appeared around every corner with strict moral advice. They believed her to be insane and knew her to be death to any good time.

Mina held her glass out to Father Walter. He slowly rose, grabbed the bottle, and filled it. He poured himself another and sat again.

"Did she make a miracle at all?" he asked.

"A few," said Mina and dashed off her drink.

"Can you tell me one?"

"At a big wedding feast, she turned everybody's wine to water. She flew once, and she set fire to a tree with her thoughts."

"Amazing," said Father Walter. He stood and put his drink on the desk. "Come with me," he said. "There's something I think you'll want to see." She rose and followed him out the back door of the church. The sand was blowing hard, and he had to raise his arm in front of his eyes as he leaned into the wind. He looked back and Mina GilCragson was right behind him, holding her hat on with one hand. He led her to the shrine.

Inside, he moved toward the altar, pointing. "There it is. Saint Ifritia's foot," he said.

"What are you talking about?" said Mina, stepping up beside him.

"Right there," he said and pointed again.

She looked, and an instant later went weak. Father Walter caught her by the arm. She shook her head and took a deep breath. "I can't believe it," she said.

"I know," he said. "But there it is. You mustn't touch it with your hands. You must only kiss the toes. I'll stand outside. You can have a few minutes alone with it."

"Thank you so much," she said, tears in her eyes.

He went outside. Leaning against the buffeting wind, he pushed aside the bamboo curtain that protected the shrine's one window. Through the sliver of space, he watched Mina approach the altar. Her hands were folded piously in front of her, as he'd instructed. He realized that if she'd not worn the heels, she'd never have been able to reach the foot with her lips. As it was, she had to go up on her toes. Her head bobbed forward to the relic, but it wasn't a quick kiss she gave. Her head moved slightly forward and back, and Father Walter pictured her tongue passionately laving the rotten toes. It both gave him a thrill and made him queasy. He had a premonition that he'd be drinking hard into the night.

After the longest time, Mina suddenly turned away from the foot. Father Walter let the bamboo curtain slide back into place and waited to greet her. She exited the shrine, and he said, "How was that? Did you feel the spirit?" but she never slowed to answer. Walking right past him, she headed toward the outhouse. The sand blew fiercely, but she didn't bother to hold her hat and it flew from her head. Mina walked as if in a trance. Father Walter was surprised when she didn't go to the outhouse, but passed it and headed up out of the valley in the dunes. On the beach, the wind would have been ten times worse. As she ascended, he called to her to come back.

She passed over the rim, out of sight, and he was reluctant to follow her, knowing the ghost of the driver might be lurking in the blinding sandstorm. He turned back toward the church, his mind a knot of thoughts. Was she having a holy experience? Had he offended her? Was she poisoned by the old foot? He stopped to fetch her hat, which had blown up against the side of the outhouse.

That night, his premonition came true, and the whiskey flowed. He opened Mina GilCragson's travel bag and went through her things. By candlelight, whiskey in one hand, he inspected each of her articles of clothing. When holding them up, he recognized the faint scent of wild violets. He wondered if she was a saint. While he was searching for evidence in the aroma of a pair of her underpants, Sister North appeared out of the shadows.

"What are you up to?" she asked.

"Sniffing out a holy bouquet. I believe our visitor today may have been a saint."

"She was nothing of the sort," said Sister North, who stepped forward and backhanded Father Walter hard across the face. His whiskey glass flew from his grasp and he dropped the underpants. Consciousness blinked off momentarily and then back on. He stared at her angry, yellow eyes as she reached out, grabbed his shirt, and pulled him to his feet. "Come with me," she said.

Outside, the sandstorm had abated and the night was clear and cool and still. Not letting go, she pulled Father Walter toward the shrine. He stumbled once and almost fell, and for his trouble, she kicked him in the rear end. Candlelight shone out from the shrine's one window, its bamboo curtain now rolled up. Sister North marched the father up to the altar and said to him, "Look at that."

"Look at what?" he said, stunned by drink and surprise.

"What else?" she asked.

And, upon noticing, he became instantly sober, for the big toe of the holy foot was missing. "My God," he said, moving closer to it. Where the toe had been was a knuckle-stump of sheered gristle. "I thought she was sucking on it, but in fact she was chewing off the toe," he said, turning to face Sister North.

"You thought she was sucking on it . . ." she said. "Since when is sucking the holy toes allowed?"

"She was a scholar of Saint Ifritia. I never suspected she was a thief."

Sister North took a seat and gave herself up to tears. He sat down beside her and put his arm around her shoulders. They stayed in the shrine until the candles melted down and the dawn brought bird calls. Then they went to his bed. Before she fell asleep, the sister said to him, "It happened because you lied."

He thought about it. "Nahh," he said. "It was bound to happen someday." He slept and dreamt of the driver's wife and daughters. When he woke, Sister North was gone.

Sister North's Sermon

Father—By the time you find this, I'll already be four miles inland, heading for the city. I mean to bring back the stolen toe and make amends to Saint Ifritia. She's angry that we let this happen. You, of course, bear most of the responsibility, but I, too, own a piece of the guilt. It may take me a time to hunt down Mina GilCragson. I'll try the university first, but if she's not a scholar, I fear she might be a trader on the black market, trafficking in religious relics. If that's the case, the toe could at this moment be packed on the back of a mule, climbing the northern road into the mountains and on through the clouds to the very beginning of the world. If so, I will follow it. If I fail, I won't be back. One thing I've seen in my sleep is that at the exact halfway point of my journey, a man will visit the church and bring you news of me. If he tells you I am dead, then burn my shack and all my things and scatter the ashes over the sea, but if the last he's seen of me I'm alive, then that means I will return. That, I'm sure of. Wake up and guard the foot with your very life. If I return after years with a toe and there is no foot, I'll strangle you in your sleep. Think of me in bed, and in the morning, when you shovel sand, pray for me. There are four bottles of whiskey under the mattress in my shack. You can have three of them. I spent a week of solitude contemplating your sermon and realized that you didn't lie. That you actually killed the driver of the hay wagon. Which is worse? May the sweet saint have mercy on you.

—*Sister*

TWO DAYS LATER, Father Walter realized he'd taken Sister North for granted, and she was right, he had killed the driver just as he'd described in his sermon. Without her there, in her shack, in the shrine, in his bed, the loneliness crept into the sand dune valley and he couldn't shake it. Time became a sermon, preaching itself. The sand and sun and sand and wind and sand and every now and then a visitor, whose presence seemed to last forever until vanishing into sand, a pilgrim with whom to fill the long hours, chatting.

Every one of the strangers, maybe four a year and one year only two, was asked if they brought word from Sister North. He served them whiskey and let them preach their sermons before blessing them on their journeys to the end of the world. Sometimes an old man, moving slowly, bent, mumbling, sometimes a young woman, once a child on the run. None of them had word from her. In between these occasional visits from strangers lay long stretches of days and seasons, full of silence and wind and shifting sand. To pass the long nights, he took to counting the stars.

One evening, he went to her shack to fetch the second bottle of her whiskey and fell asleep on her bed. In the morning, there was a visitor in the church when he went in to shovel. A young man sat in the first pew. He wore a bow tie and white shirt, and even though it was in the heart of the summer season, a jacket as well. His hair was perfectly combed. Father Walter showed him behind the altar and they sat sipping whiskey well into the afternoon as the young man spoke his sermon. The father had heard it all before, but one thing caught his interest. In the midst of a tale of sorrows, the boy spoke about a place he'd visited in the north where one of the attractions was a fish with a human face.

Father Walter halted the sermon and asked, "Lord Jon?"

"The same," said the young man. "An enormous plum fish."

"I'd heard he'd been killed, shot by the father of the girl whose leg he'd severed."

"Nonsense. There are so many fanciful stories told of this remarkable fish. What is true, something I witnessed, the scientists are training Lord Jon to speak. I tipped my hat to him at the aquarium and he said, in a voice as clear as day, 'How do you do?'"

"You've never heard of a connection between Saint Ifritia and the fish?" asked Father Walter.

The young man took a sip, cocked his head, and thought. "Well, if I may speak frankly . . ."

"You must, we're in a church," said the Father.

"What I remember of Saint Ifritia from Monday Afternoon Club, is that she was a prostitute who was impregnated by the Lord. As her time came to give birth, her foot darkened and fell off just above the ankle and the child came out through her leg, the head appearing where the foot had been. The miracle was recorded by Charles the Bald. The boy grew up to be some war hero, a colonel in the war for the country of rain."

The young man left as the sun was going down and the sky was red. Father Walter had enjoyed talking to him, learning of the exploits of the real Lord Jon, but some hint of fear in the young man's expression said the poor fellow was headed all the way to the end, and then one more step into oblivion. That night, the father sat in the churchyard near the bell and didn't drink, but pictured Sister North, struggling upward through the clouds to the beginning of the world. He wished they were in his bed, listening to the wind and the cries of the beach owl. He'd tell her the young man's version of the life of Saint Ifritia. They'd talk about it till dawn.

For the longest time, Father Walter gave up writing sermons. With the way everything had transpired, the theft of the toe, the absence of Sister North, he felt it would be better for the world if he held his tongue and simply listened. Then, deep in one autumn season, when snow had already fallen, he decided to leave the sand dune valley and go to see the ocean. He feared the ghost of the driver every step beyond the rim but slowly continued forward. Eventually, he made his way over the dunes to the beach and sat at the water's edge. Watching the waves roll in, he gave himself up to his plans to finally set forth in search of Sister North. He thought for a long time until his attention was diverted by a fish brought before him in the surf. He looked up, startled by it. When he saw its violet color, he knew immediately what it was.

The fish opened its mouth and spoke. "A message from my liege, Lord Jon. He's told me to tell you he'd overheard a wonderful conversation with your Sister North at the Aquarium restaurant one evening a few years ago, and she wanted to relay the message to you that you should write a new sermon for her."

Father Walter was stunned at first by the talking fish, but after hearing what it had to say, he laughed. "Very well," he said and lifted the fish and helped it back into the waves. When he turned to head toward the church, the driver stood before him, a vague phantom, bowing slightly and proffering with both hands a ghostly foot. "Miracles . . ." said a voice in the wind. The father was determined to walk right through the spirit if need be. He set off at a quick pace toward the sand dune valley. Just as he thought he would collide with the ethereal driver, the fellow turned and walked, only a few feet ahead of him, just as they had walked through the dark forest in rain country. In the wind, the holy man heard the words, "I get ten yards, do I not?" repeated again and again, and he knew that if he had the pistol in his hand, he'd have fired it again and again.

With a sudden shiver, he finally passed through the halted ghost of the driver and descended the tall dune toward the church. The words in the wind grew fainter. By the time he reached the church door and looked back, the driver was nowhere to be seen along the rim of the valley. He went immediately to his room, took off his coat, poured a glass of whiskey, and sat at his desk. Lifting his pen, he scratched across the top of a sheet of paper the title: "Every Grain of Sand, a Minute."

When he finished writing the sermon, it was late in the night and, well into his cups, he decided on the spot to deliver it. Stumbling and mumbling, he went around the church and lit candles, fired up the pots of wisteria incense. As he moved through the shadows, the thought came to him that with the harsh cold of recent days, even the sand fleas, fast asleep in hibernation, would not be listening. He gathered up the pages of the sermon and went to the altar. He cleared his throat, adjusted the height of the pages to catch the candlelight, and began.

"Every grain of sand, a minute," he said in a weary voice. With that phrase out, there immediately came a rapping at the church door. He looked up and froze. His first thought was of the driver. The rapping came again and he yelled out, "Who's there?"

"A traveler with news from Sister North," called a male voice. Father Walter left the altar and ran down the aisle to the door. He pushed it open and said, "Come in, come in." A tall man stepped out of the darkness and into the church's glow. Seeing the stranger's height, he remembered the driver's, and took a sudden step backward. It wasn't the ghost, though, it was a real man with thick sideburns, a serious gaze, a top hat. He carried a small black bag. "Thank you," he said and removed his overcoat and gloves, handing them to Father Walter. "I was lost among the dunes and then I saw a faint light issuing up from what appeared in the dark to be a small crater. I thought a falling star had struck the earth."

"It's just the church of Saint Ifritia," said the father. "You have news of Sister North?"

"Yes, Father, I have a confession to make."

Father Walter led the pilgrim to the front pew and motioned for the gentleman to sit while he took a seat on the steps of the altar. "Okay," he said, "out with it."

"My name is Ironton," said the gentleman, removing his hat and setting it and his black bag on the seat next to him. "I'm a traveling businessman," he said. "My work takes me everywhere in the world."

"What is your business?" asked the father.

"Trade," said Ironton. "And that's what I was engaged in at Hotel Lacrimose, up in the north country. I was telling an associate at breakfast one morning that I had plans to travel next to the end of the world. The waitress, who'd just then brought our coffee, introduced herself and begged me, since I was travelling to the end of the world, to bring you a message."

"Sister North is a waitress?"

"She'd sadly run out of funds, but intended to continue on to the beginning of the world once she'd saved enough money. In any event, I was busy at the moment, having to run off to close a deal, and I couldn't hear her out. I could, though, sense her desperation, and so I suggested we meet that night for dinner at the Aquarium.

"We met in that fantastic dining hall, surrounded by hundred-foot-high glass tanks populated by fierce leviathans and brightly colored swarms of lesser fish. There was a waterfall at one end of the enormous room, and a man-made river that ran nearly its entire length with a small wooden bridge arching up over the flow in one spot to offer egress to either side of the dining area. We dined on *fez-menuth* flambé and consumed any number of bottles of sparkling Lilac water. She told me her tale, your tale, about the sacred foot in your possession.

"Allow me to correct for you your impressions of Saint Ifritia. This may be difficult, but being a rationalist, I'm afraid I can only offer you what I perceive to be the facts. This Saint Ifritia, whose foot you apparently have, was more a folk hero than a religious saint. To be frank, she went to the grave with both feet. She never lost a foot by any means. She was considered miraculous for no better reason than because she was known to frequently practice small acts of human kindness for friends and often strangers. Her life was quiet, small, but I suppose, no less heroic in a sense. Her neighbors missed her when she passed on and took to referring to her as Saint Ifritia. It caught on and legends attached themselves to her memory like bright streamers on a humble hay wagon."

"The foot is nothing?" asked Father Walter.

"It's an old rotten foot," said Ironton.

"What did Sister North say to your news?"

Ironton looked down and clasped his hands in his lap. "This is where I must offer my confession," he said.

"You didn't tell her, did you?"

"The story of her search for the missing toe was so pathetic I didn't have the heart to tell her the facts. And yet, still, I was going to. But just as I was about to speak, beside our table, from out of the man-made river, there surfaced an enormous purple fish with a human face. It bobbed on the surface, remaining stationary in the flow, and its large eyes filled with tears. Its gaze pierced my flesh and burrowed into my heart to turn off my ability to tell Sister North her arduous search had been pointless."

Father Walter shook his head in disgust. "What is it she wanted you to tell me?"

"She wants you to write a sermon for her," said Ironton.

"Yes," said the father, "the news preceded you. I finished it this evening just before your arrival."

"Well," said the businessman, "I do promise, should I see her on my return trip, I will tell her the truth, and give her train fare home."

For the remaining hours of the night, Father Walter and his visitor sat in the church and drank whiskey. In their far-flung conversation, Ironton admitted to being a great collector of curios and oddities. In the morning, when the visitor was taking his leave, the father wrapped up the foot of Saint Ifritia in its original soiled towel and bestowed it upon his guest. "For your collection," he said. "Miracles."

They laughed and Ironton received the gift warmly. Then, touching his index finger and thumb to the brim of his hat, he bowed slightly and disappeared up over the rim of the dune.

More time passed. Every grain of sand, a minute. Days, weeks, seasons. Eventually, one night, Father Walter woke from troubling dreams to find Sister North in bed beside him. At first, he thought he was still dreaming. She was smiling, though, and her cat eyes caught what little light pervaded his room and glowed softly. "Is it you?" he asked.

"Almost," she said, "but I've left parts of me between here and the beginning of the world."

"A toe?"

Sister North's Sermon

No, only pieces of my spirit, torn out by pity, shame, guilt, and fear. I tracked Mina GilCragson. She's no scholar, but an agent from a ring of female thieves who specialize in religious relics. The toe was sent along the secret Contraband Road, north, to the beginning of the world. I travelled that road, packing a pistol and cutlass. And I let the life out of certain men and women who thought they had some claim on me. I slept at the side of the road in the rain and snow. I climbed the rugged path into the cloud country.

In the thin atmosphere of the Haunted Mountains, I'd run out of food and was starving. Unfortunately for him, an old man, heading north, leading a donkey with a heavy load, was the first to pass my ambush. I told him I wanted something to eat, but he went for his throwing dagger, and I was forced to shoot him in the face. I freed the donkey of its burden and went through the old man's wares. I found food, some smoked meat, leg bones of cattle, and pickled plum fish. While

I ate, I inspected the rest of the goods, and among them I discovered a small silver box. I held it up, pressed a hidden latch on the bottom, and the top flipped back. A mechanical plinking music, the harmony of Duesgruel's *Last Movement*, played, and I beheld the severed toe.

I had it in my possession and I felt the spirit move through me. All I wanted was to get back to the church. Taking as much of the booty from the donkey's pack as I could carry, I travelled to the closest city. There I sold my twice-stolen treasures and was paid well for them. I bought new clothes and took a room in a fine place, the Hotel Lacrimose.

I spent a few days and nights at the amazing hotel, trying to relax before beginning the long journey home. One afternoon, while sitting on the main veranda, watching the clouds twirl, contemplating the glory of Saint Ifritia, I made the acquaintance of an interesting gentleman. Mr. Ironton was his name and he had an incredible memory for historical facts and unusual opinons on the news of the day. Having travelled for years among paupers and thieves, I was unused to speaking with someone so intelligent as Ironton. We had a delightful conversation. Somewhere in his talk, he mentioned that he was travelling to the end of the world. At our parting, he requested that I join him for dinner at the Aquarium that evening.

That night at dinner, I told Ironton our story. I showed him the toe in its small silver case. He lifted the thing to his nose and announced that he smelled wild violets. But then he put the toe on the table between us and said, "This Saint Ifritia, you speak of. It has recently been discovered by the Holy of the Holy See that she is in fact a demon, not a saint. She's a powerful demon. I propose you allow me to dispose of that toe for you. Every minute you have it with you you're in terrible danger." He nodded after speaking.

I told him, "No thank you. I'll take my chances with it."

"You're a brave woman, Ms. North," he said. "Now what was the message you had for your Father Walter?"

As I told him that I wanted you to know I was on my way, and to write a sermon for me, an enormous violet fish with a human face rose out of the water of the decorative river that ran through the restaurant next to our table. It startled me. Its face was repulsive. I recalled you telling me something about a giant plum fish, Lord Jon, and I spoke the name aloud. "At your service," the fish said and then dove into the flow. When I managed to overcome my shock at the fish's voice, I looked back to the table and discovered both Ironton and the toe had vanished.

I had it and I lost it. I felt the grace of Saint Ifritia for a brief few days at the Hotel Lacrimose and then it was stolen away. I've wondered all along my journey home if that's the best life offers.

SISTER NORTH YAWNED and turned on her side. "And what of the foot? Is it safe?" she asked.

He put his arm around her. "No," he said. "Some seasons back I was robbed at gunpoint. A whole troop of bandits on horses. They took everything. I begged them to leave the foot. I explained it was a holy relic, but they laughed and told me they would cook it and eat it on the beach that night. It's gone."

"I'm so tired," she said. "I could sleep forever."

Father Walter drew close to her, closed his eyes, and listened to the sand sifting in through the walls.

Lord Dunsany's Teapot

By Naomi Novik

The accidental harmony of the trenches during the war produced, sometimes, odd acquaintances. It was impossible not to feel a certain kinship with a man having lain huddled and nameless in the dirt beside him for hours, sharing the dubious comfort of a woolen scarf pressed over the mouth and nose while eyes streamed, stinging, and gunpowder bursts from time to time illuminated the crawling smoke in colors: did it have a greenish cast? And between the moments of fireworks, whispering to one another too low and too hoarsely to hear even unconsciously the accents of the barn or the gutter or the halls of the public school.

What became remarkable about Russell, in the trenches, was his smile: or rather that he smiled, with death walking overhead like the tread of heavy boots on a wooden floor above a cellar. Not a wild or wandering smile, reckless and ready to meet the end, or a trembling rictus; an ordinary smile to go with the whispered, "Another one coming, I think," as if speaking of a cricket ball instead of an incendiary; only friendly, with nothing to remark upon.

The trench had scarcely been dug. Dirt shook loose down upon them, until they might have been part of the earth, and when the all-clear sounded at last out of a long silence, they stood up still equals under a coat of mud, until Russell bent down and picked up the shovel, discarded, and they were again officer and man.

But this came too late: Edward trudged back with him, side by side, to the more populated regions of the labyrinth, still talking, and when they had reached Russell's bivouac, he looked at Edward and said, "Would you have a cup of tea?"

The taste of the smoke was still thick on Edward's tongue, in his throat, and the night had curled up like a tiger and gone to sleep around them. They sat on Russell's cot while the kettle boiled, and he poured the hot water into a fat old teapot made of iron, knobby, over the cheap and bitter tea leaves from the ration. Then he set it on the little camp stool and watched it steep, a thin thread of steam climbing out of the spout and dancing around itself in the cold air.

Yishan Li's depiction of Lord Dunsany's Teapot, from the forthcoming Novik-Li graphic novel "Ten Days to Glory: Demon Tea and Lord Dunsany."

The rest of his company were sleeping, but Edward noticed their cots were placed away, as much as they could be in such a confined space; Russell had a little room around his. He looked at Russell: under the smudges and dirt, weathering; not a young face. The nose was a little crooked and so was the mouth, and the hair brushed over the forehead was sandy brown and wispy in a vicarish way, with several years of thinning gone.

"A kindness to the old-timer, I suppose," Russell said. "Been here—five years now, or near enough. So they don't ask me to shift around."

"They haven't made you lance-jack," Edward said, the words coming out before he could consider all the reasons a man might not have received promotion, of which he would not care to speak.

"I couldn't," Russell said, apologetic. "Who am I, to be sending off other fellows, and treating them sharp if they don't?"

"Their corporal, or their sergeant," Edward said, a little impatient with the objection, "going in with them, not hanging back."

"O, well," Russell said, still looking at the teapot. "It's not the same for me to go."

He poured out the tea, and offered some shavings off a small, brown block of sugar. Edward drank: strong and bittersweet, somehow better than the usual. The teapot was homely and common. Russell laid a hand on its side as if it were precious, and said it had come to him from an old sailor, coming home at last to rest from traveling.

"Do you ever wonder, are there wars under the sea?" Russell said. His eyes had gone distant. "If all those serpents and the kraken down there, or some other things we haven't names for, go to battle over the ships that have sunk, and all their treasure?"

"And mermen dive down among them, to be counted brave," Edward said, softly, not to disturb the image that had built clear in his mind: the great writhing beasts, tangled masses striving against one another in the endless cold, dark depths, over broken ships and golden hoards, spilled upon the sand, trying to catch the faintest gleam of light. "To snatch some jewel to carry back, for a courting gift or an heirloom of their house."

Russell nodded, as if to a commonplace remark. "I suppose it's how they choose their lords," he said, "the ones that go down and come back; and their king came up from the dark once with a crown—beautiful thing, rubies and pearls like eggs, in gold."

The tea grew cold before they finished building the undersea court, turn and turn about, in low voices barely above the nasal breathing of the men around them.

IT SKIRTED THE lines of fraternization, certainly; but it could not have been called deliberate. There was always some duty or excuse which brought them into one another's company to begin with, and at no regular interval. Of course, even granting this, there was no denying it would have been more appropriate for Edward to refuse the invitation, or for Russell not to have made it in the first place. Yet, somehow, each time tea was offered, and accepted.

The hour was always late, and if Russell's fellows had doubts about his company, they never raised their heads from their cots to express it either by word or look. Russell made the tea, and began the storytelling, and Edward cobbled together castles with him, shaped of steam and fancy, drifting upwards and away from the trenches.

He would walk back to his own cot afterwards still warm through and lightened. He had come to do his duty, and he would do it, but there was something so much *vaster* and more dreadful than he had expected in the wanton waste upon the fields, in the smothered silence of the trenches: all of them already in the grave and merely awaiting a final confirmation. But Russell was still alive, so Edward might be as well. It was worth a little skirting of regulations.

HE ONLY HALF-HEARD Russell's battalion mentioned in the staff meeting, with one corner of his preoccupied mind; afterwards, he looked at the assignment: a push to try and open a new trench, advancing the line.

It was no more than might be and would be asked of any man, eventually; it was no excuse to go by the bivouac that night with a tin of his own tea, all the more precious because Beatrice somehow managed to arrange for it to win through to him, through some perhaps questionable back channel. Russell said nothing of the assignment, though Edward could read the knowledge of it around them: for once, not all the other men were sleeping, a few curled protectively around their scratching hands, writing letters in their cots.

"Well, that's a proper cup," Russell said softly, as the smell climbed out of the teapot, fragrant and fragile. The brew, when he poured it, was clear amber-gold, and made Edward think of peaches hanging in a garden of shining, fruit-heavy trees, a great, sighing breath of wind stirring all the branches to a shake.

For once, Russell did not speak as they drank the tea. One after another, the men around them put down their pens and went to sleep. The peaches swung from the branches, very clear and golden in Edward's mind. He kept his hands close around his cup.

"That's stirred him a bit, it has," Russell said, peering under the lid of the teapot; he poured in some more water. For a moment, Edward thought he saw mountains, too, beyond the orchard-garden: green-furred peaks with clouds clinging to their sides like loose eiderdown. A great wave of homesickness struck him very nearly like a blow, though he had never seen such mountains. He looked at Russell, wondering.

"It'll be all right, you know," Russell said.

"Of course," Edward said: the only thing that could be said, prosaic and untruthful; the words tasted sour in his mouth after the clean taste of the tea.

"No, what I mean is, it'll be all right," Russell said. He rubbed a hand over the teapot. "I don't like to say, because the fellows don't understand, but you see him, too; or at least as much of him as I do."

"Him," Edward repeated.

"I don't know his name," Russell said thoughtfully. "I've never managed to find out; I don't know that he hears us at all, or thinks of us. I suppose if he ever woke up, he might be right annoyed with us, sitting here drinking up his dreams. But he never has."

It was not their usual storytelling, but something with the uncomfortable savor of truth. Edward felt as though he had caught a glimpse from the corner of his eye of something too vast to be looked at directly or all at once: a tail shining silver-green sliding through the trees; a great green eye, like oceans, peering back with drowsy curiosity. "But he's not *in* there," he said involuntarily.

Russell shrugged expressively. He lifted off the lid and showed Edward: a lump fixed to the bottom of the pot, smooth, white, glimmering like a pearl, irregular yet beautiful, even with the swollen tea-leaves like kelp strewn over and around it.

He put the lid back on, and poured out the rest of the pot. "So it's all right," he said. "I'll be all right, while I have him. But you see why I couldn't send other fellows out. Not while I'm safe from all this, and they aren't."

An old and battered teapot made talisman of safety, inhabited by some mystical guardian: it ought to have provoked the same awkward sensation as speaking to an earnest spiritualist, or an excessively devoted missionary; it called for polite agreement and withdrawal. "Thank you," Edward said instead; he was comforted, and glad to be so.

Whatever virtue lived there in the pitted iron, it was no more difficult to believe in than the blighted landscape above their trenches, the coils of hungry, barbed, black wire snaking upon the ground, and the creeping poisonous smoke that covered the endless bodies of the dead. Something bright and shining ought not to be more impossible than that; and even if it was not strong enough to stand against all devastation, there was pleasure in thinking one life might be spared by its power.

THEY BROUGHT HIM the teapot three days later: Russell had no next of kin with a greater claim. Edward thanked them and left the teapot in a corner of his bag, and did not take it out again. Many men he knew had died, comrades in arms, friends; but Russell lying on the spiked and poisoned ground, breath seared and blood draining, hurt the worse for seeming wrong.

Edward dreamed of sitting with Russell: the dead man's skin clammy-grey, blood streaking the earthenware where his fingers cupped it, where his lips touched the rim, and floating over the surface of the tea. "Well, and I was safe, like I said," Russell said. Edward shuddered out of the dream, and washed his face in the cold water in his jug; there were flakes of ice on the surface.

He went forward himself, twice, and was not killed; he shot several men, and sent others to die. There was a commendation, at one point. He accepted it without any sense of pride. In the evenings, he played cards with a handful of other officers, where they talked desultorily of plans, and the weather, and a few of the more crude of conquests either real or hoped-for in the French villages behind the lines. His letters to Beatrice grew shorter. His supply of words seemed to have leached away into the dirt.

His own teapot was on his small burner to keep warm when the air raid sounded; an hour later, after the all-clear, it was a smoking cinder, the smell so very much like the acrid bite of gas that he flung it as far up over the edge of the trench as he could manage, to get it away, and took out the other teapot, to make a fresh cup and wash away the taste.

And it was only a teapot: squat and unlovely except for the smooth, pearlescent lump inside, some accident of its casting. He put in the leaves and poured the water from the kettle. He was no longer angry with himself for believing, only distantly amused, remembering; and sorry, with that same distance, for Russell, who had swallowed illusions for comfort.

He poured his cup and raised it and drank without stopping to inhale the scent or to think of home; and the pain startled him for being so vivid. He worked his mouth as though he had only burned his tongue and not some unprepared and numbed corner of his self. He found himself staring blindly at the small, friendly blue flame beneath the teapot. The color was the same as a flower that grew only on the slopes of a valley on the other side of the world, where no man had ever walked, which a bird with white feathers picked to line its nest so the young, when they were born, were soft grey and tinted blue, with pale yellow beaks held wide to call for food in voices that chimed like bells.

The ringing in his ears from the sirens went quiet. He understood Russell then finally; and wept a little, without putting down the cup. He held it between his hands while the heat but not the scent faded, and sipped peace as long as it lasted.

The teapot is unremarkable in itself: a roundbellied, squat thing of black, enameled iron, with the common nail-head pattern rubbed down low over the years and a spout perhaps a little short for its width; the handle has been broken and mended, and the lid has only a small, stubby knob. Dr. Lambshead is not known to have used the teapot, which wears a thin layer of grey dust, but a small attached label indicates it was acquired at an estate auction held in Ireland circa 1957.

Lot 558: *Shadow of My Nephew* by Wells, Charlotte

By Holly Black

As an auctioneer, I can tell you that there are only two things that make buyers bid on a piece. They want it for the money or they want it for the story.

And even when they want it for the money, it's the story that keeps them bidding as the numbers spiral higher and higher, past the reasonable limit they set, upward, to sweaty and exultant triumph. A young man looking to invest in an artist whose name he mispronounces—but knows is worth a lot—might actually be sold on his own story. Born in a grubby apartment to parents who never finished college, but look at him now—look at all that art on his walls—what a man of taste he must be! Or maybe he's sold on the story of the artist himself, who died young and in debt—a tragedy that our investor finds romantic from his penthouse apartment with park views. Or perhaps it is the story of the piece itself that evokes a single memory—the tilt of the neck on a beautiful girl our investor never got the courage to approach but still burns for in his fitful dreams.

Well, take a look at this next piece and see if its story appeals to you.

Take a good, long look.

It might appear to be a contemporary found-object sculpture, with its speaker-heart and diamond eyes. You might guess it came from a gallery in SoHo, but this piece actually dates from the turn of the century.

The artist, Charlotte Wells, was born in a logging camp in the northeastern part of Maine. Her father was a cook. He and his wife lived in a ramshackle cabin with their three children—John, Toby, and baby Charlotte.

In the winter, food was scarce, and that February had been worse than most. When a black bear was spotted, the loggers tracked it back to its lair and shot it for meat and the warmth of its pelt. As they made ready to drag the dead bear's body back to camp for butchering, they realized it wasn't alone in the cave. A bear cub cried weakly for its mother.

Not sure what to do with it, the men brought the cub back to camp and dumped it in the snow outside the cook's cabin. The bloody flesh of its mother

Eric Orchard's "Portrait of a Bear Unbound (with speaker)"

was brought inside, along with her pelt. Young Toby and John found it and begged their mother to let them keep the little bear.

"There's no food to spare," her husband warned.

"Nonetheless," said Mrs. Wells and nursed the bear cub along with Charlotte.

Mrs. Wells would rest each of them on opposite hips, as though they were twins. It got to be that the bear seemed like just another baby, even sleeping beside Charlotte in her crib, thick fur tickling her nose and teaching her his bestial scent.

They had to call him something, so Mrs. Wells named the bear Liam, after a cousin of whom she'd always been fond.

Liam followed Charlotte around, never wanting to be parted from her side. When she began to crawl, he tottered around on all fours. When she began to walk, he stood up, too, much to the consternation of Mr. and Mrs. Wells.

Charlotte's first word was "Mama."

Liam's first word was "Lottie."

Mr. and Mrs. Wells were surprised, but pleased. Liam turned out to be a quick learner. He had trouble holding an ink pen, and although his penmanship was to be despaired of, he was very good with sums.

And when Charlotte was given a bear-fur cape, made from the pelt of Liam's bear mother and lined in velvet as bright red as droplets of blood in snow, he did not mourn. He barely seemed to recall another life. And if sometimes he grew silent or withdrawn, Charlotte quickly jollied him out of his sulks with some new game.

If Liam and Charlotte were inseparable as children, they were even closer in adolescence, always climbing trees and playing games and pulling at one another's hair. But Liam never seemed to stop growing. Mrs. Wells had to use curtains and bedsheets sewn together for his shirts and trousers. Shoes were hopeless. And no matter how much food he ate, Liam's stomach was always growling for want of enough. He gulped down huge portions of soup, drank the whole kettle's worth of tea, ate an entire loaf of bread at a time, and, on at least one holiday, devoured an entire haunch of salt-cured venison.

By the time he was fifteen, he towered over Mr. Wells and could carry a felled tree on his back. His strength was so great he could no longer control it. One afternoon, while playing a game of tag, he reached for Charlotte, and instead of touching her shoulder lightly with the pad of his paw, he slashed her cheek with his nails.

She screamed, blood soaking her dress, and soon the whole camp was gathered around Liam, looking at him through narrowed eyes. A few had brought rifles.

"He didn't mean to," Charlotte shouted, burying her face against his fur.

The crowd dispersed slowly as she wept, but not before Liam saw in each of their faces that they were afraid, that they had been afraid for a long time. He would never be one of them. Mrs. Wells saw it, too.

"Liam," Mrs. Wells said, later that night. "You can't stay here anymore. It's not safe."

"But Mother," said the bear. "Where will I go?"

"Perhaps it is time for you to be among your own people," said Mrs. Wells.

He looked around the far-too-small kitchen, where even if he hunched over, the tips of his ears scraped the ceiling. He touched the stool that creaked underneath him and glanced across the table at the tiny, bird-boned woman with the silvering hair. "I do not know their ways," said Liam.

Mrs. Wells stroked his cheek like she had when he was small. "Then go to the big city down east. All manner of folk live there. All manner of different customs. Maybe there'll be a place for you, too."

Liam nodded, knowing that she was right. "I will leave in the morning," he said.

Mrs. Wells packed up cheese, bread, apples, preserves, and sausages for his journey. Mr. Wells gave Liam five shiny dollar coins to get him started. John gave him a fishing pole so he'd be able to catch some lunch any time he wanted. Toby gave him a Bible and a flask of the strong liquor they distilled from potato peels. It wasn't a small flask, but in Liam's paw, it might as well have been a thimble.

"Where's Charlotte?" Liam asked. "Won't she come and kiss me good-bye?"

"She's taking this very hard," Mr. Wells said. "Feels responsible."

"Is she very hurt?" asked Liam, thinking of the marks on her face. Wondering if they would scar. Wondering how it would be for her if they did, for she was thought of as a great beauty and much admired. Would that change?

"She'll get better," said John. "Lottie knows you didn't mean to hurt her."

"And we all know she's not vain," said Toby, which made Liam feel even worse. Toby's mouth lifted on one side. "I wager you'll always be her favorite."

"Tell her," Liam said in his deep, growling voice. "Tell her that I will write."

"Of course," said Mrs. Wells, neither of them mentioning that mail took ages to find its way up to their town.

He embraced them, one by one. He tried to be as gentle as he could, tried not to crush them against him, tried not to press his nose against their necks as he drew the scent of them into his lungs one final time.

Then, sack of food tied to the fishing pole, fishing pole slung over his shoulder, Liam started the long journey south.

He walked for half the day, stopping to eat everything Mrs. Wells had packed for him. His stomach hurt less, but self-pity still gnawed at his gut.

That night, he slept under the stars. A cool breeze tickled his fur, his ears twitched, and he could almost imagine that he had always lived this way. He was tempted to throw away his rod and flask, to strip off his clothes, and never to walk upright again.

It thrilled him and made him afraid, all at once.

For three days and three nights, he journeyed thus. He spoke no words on his journey—there was no one to speak to—and although sometimes the smells of humans and woodsmoke gusted toward him, they were being replaced with the vivid smells of crushed pine needles and the clotted sap of trees.

One morning, he stopped at a river to catch his breakfast. Slowly, he waded into the water on all fours, the bright, bubbling river shockingly, joyously cold. He felt every pebble against the pads of his paws. He reached out to sweep a silvery fish into the air, where he knew he would catch it between his teeth. Just then, the wind changed directions, blowing a familiar scent to his twitching nose.

He stood and lumbered into the woods.

Charlotte was running toward him, wrapped in the fur of his mother, the cloak's lining as bright as blood. A dirty and tear-stained bandage still covered her face.

Her eyes went wide.

For a moment, he imagined roaring up and striking her down. He imagined chewing her up, sinew and bones. He imagined being a bear and nothing more.

Then he remembered himself.

"Charlotte," he said, his voice cracking with disuse. Three long days in the forest had almost made him lose his human speech.

She was shivering with cold. She went to him and pressed herself against him, so that, with her cloak, he didn't know where he ended and she began.

"I'm sorry," he said gruffly, trying not to rest his claws against her, even gently. He was apologizing for what was beneath the bandages, but also for the terrible thoughts he tried to put out of his mind. "Very, truly sorry."

"What you are is wet," she said, with a laugh. "And your nose is cold."

With those words, he knew he was forgiven.

He gathered wood and Charlotte made a fire, talking the whole time. She told him about her plan to sneak out and come with him. She told him how cleverly she'd snuck out of the house with her little suitcase and waited for him by the ford in the road. But, as time passed, she realized he must have taken a different road entirely. She headed out after him, thinking she might yet catch him, but by nightfall, although she was sure she was following the right road, there was no sign of Liam.

"And such sounds the night makes!" she told him. "I was sure I was going to be eaten up by wolves. I barely slept a wink!"

Her relief was so great that she couldn't stop talking. His happiness was so great that he was content to listen.

"But why did you come?" he asked finally.

"I can't let you have all the adventures," she told him. "The world is bigger than one logging town, big enough for you. And since I am so small, I figure I might be able to fit in it, too."

He smiled big enough to show a row of white teeth.

And so, together, they journeyed south. Charlotte picked berries from bushes and Liam fished from streams and lakes without his rod, wading in and tossing gleaming trout onto the bank.

Sometimes Charlotte set traps and caught tiny birds that crunched between Liam's teeth.

At night, Charlotte and Liam covered themselves in a blanket of leaves and curled up together, telling stories until they fell asleep.

Finally, they saw the city in the hazy distance. It seemed to be sculpted from red brick and chimney smoke. As they drew closer, they passed more and bigger houses. Motorcars whizzed by, ladies turning their scarved heads to stare at the bear and his sister.

Liam stared back, full of awe.

"We will make our fortunes here," Charlotte said, dancing her way across the cobblestones, her scuffed boots as elegant on her as any slipper. "Here, everything is going to happen."

They were poor, but they managed to rent a little apartment, and when Liam's head brushed the lintel, it made them smile.

Liam got work loading boxes along the docks while Charlotte made a little money by sweeping up for a taxidermist whose office was a few streets over. He specialized in creating curiosities like fishes covered in fur, chimeras, tiny griffins, and fossilized fairies. Sometimes he let her stroke her finger carefully across a fox pelt before attaching chicken wings to the creature's back.

Sometimes, too, they would go to the cinema, where movie villains tied bow-lipped starlets to the tracks. Liam had to sit in the back, because he was so large, but Charlotte sat with him and they shared candy corn in little funnel cups.

Liam loved the city. He was strange, but in a place that delighted in strangeness. Everywhere that Liam turned, there were odd fashions, unfamiliar foods, and stores selling things of which he never could have dreamed. And he loved his job—unloading and loading exotic things heading from and to far-off places. Occasionally, one of the boxes didn't make it to its destination, and those nights Liam brought home a cloudy bottle of bourbon or a pound of coffee beans so strong that they woke the whole building when they were brewed. Just the scent of them was enough to make your heart race.

And, heart already racing, Liam met a girl. Her name was Rose, and the first time he saw her, she'd just broken the heel off of one dove-grey shoe. He carried her all the way to the boardinghouse where she lived. The other girls giggled when they spotted the bear lumbering up the steps, and the stern woman running the place even let him take a cup of tea in the kitchen, remarking that she'd never seen shoulders as broad or teeth as white on Rose's other suitors.

Turned out, Rose was a seamstress. When her long hours in the factory were over, she sewed herself smart dresses, each more beautiful than the last.

By the time he got back to their apartment, Charlotte could see that Liam was in love.

All he talked about was Rose. He told Charlotte about her soft hands, the way her bright blond hair fell around her face in soft curls, the way her clothes were always stiff with starch and freshly pressed, the no-nonsense way she told him about nearly getting arrested for smoking. She and her friends had to run away from a policeman, in their stiff corsets, ducking into a sweet shop and hiding in the bathroom. According to Rose, it had been a near thing.

Rose was always getting into scrapes. She had dozens of friends, most of them male. And she always had perfume to dot behind her ears and at the pulse points of her wrists.

Charlotte didn't like Rose, but she bit her tongue to keep from saying so. For so long it had just been Charlotte and Liam in the world, but though they had endured all other things together, love was something they must each endure alone.

"I want to marry her," Liam said.

Charlotte just nodded as she rolled out dough for pie. Cooked all together with gravy, the bits and pieces of the week's meals tasted just fine. She made two—a generous slice for her and the rest for Liam—then, as an afterthought, sliced a piece that he could take to Rose.

"She will be like a sister for you," Liam said.

Charlotte nodded again. The taste of copper pennies flooded her mouth, she was biting her tongue so hard.

Sometimes, when he was with Rose, Liam wished he could open up his fur like it was a cloak and wrap it around her.

But he did what he thought was expected of him. He looked for a better job and found one—as a stonemason, lifting slabs of marble and setting them with precision. He took Rose to his apartment, where Charlotte cooked them a whole ham. He bought her a pair of gloves sewn of lace so fine he was afraid his claws would pull it. When he asked Rose to marry him, he went to one knee, although he still towered over her chair, and shut his eyes. He could not bear to see her expression.

In lieu of a ring, he had scrimped and saved to buy her a pair of diamond earrings. They sparkled in their box like tiny stars. His palm quavered with nerves.

"I cannot marry you," Rose said, "for you are a bear and I am a woman."

And so he went away and wept. Charlotte made him a gooseberry pie, but he wouldn't eat it.

When he returned, he brought with him a long strand of pearls, each one fat and perfect as the moon.

Although Rose wrapped the strand around her neck three times, she replied again, "I cannot marry you. You are a bear and I am a woman."

Again he went away and wept. This time, Charlotte baked him scones. He picked at a few of the raisins.

"If she doesn't love you," said Charlotte, "she will only bring you sorrow."

"I love her enough for us both," said Liam and Charlotte could say no more.

The third time he went to Rose, he brought with him a golden ring as bright as the sun.

This time, greed and desire overtook her, and she said, "Even though you are a bear and I am a woman, I will marry you."

The bear's happiness was so vast and great that he wanted to roar. Instead, he took her little hands in his and promised her that he would put aside his bear nature and be like other men for as long as they were wed.

This time, Charlotte baked them a wedding cake, and Liam and Rose ate it together, slice by slice.

After Liam and Rose married, Charlotte moved out of the little apartment and took a room above the taxidermist's shop.

She had more time to help out, and so the taxidermist showed her how to cut wires and wrap them in perfumed cotton to give life to the skins. He showed her how to choose glass eyes that fit snugly in the sockets. He told her about Martha Maxwell, one of the founders of modern taxidermy, whose work he had once seen.

Time passed and Liam seemed happy as ever, doting on Rose. But Rose grew distant and vague. She stopped sewing and sat around the house in a dressing gown, plates piling up in the sink.

"What's wrong?" Charlotte asked, when she came over to bring them her very first attempt at taxidermy—a tiny bird with black eyes and feathers it had taken her a whole day to arrange. The taxidermist had told Charlotte that she had the touch, nodding approvingly as he walked around the piece.

Rose curled her lip at the sight of it. "Liam's not home."

"Can I leave it for him?" Charlotte asked.

Rose looked resigned, but allowed her into the house. As Rose turned, Charlotte saw the swell of her stomach.

She grinned and would have embraced Rose, would have babbled on with congratulations, would have offered to knit blankets and pick out ribbons, but Rose gave her such a look that Charlotte hesitated and only set the little bird down very carefully on the arm of Liam's chair.

Two nights later, Liam roused Charlotte from her bed in the middle of the night.

"There's something wrong with her," the bear said. "She's dying, Charlotte."

"What happened?" Charlotte said.

He shook his massive head. "She took something—I found the vial. To get rid of the baby. She said she could feel the little claws scratching at her insides. She said she dreamed of sharp teeth."

There was no doctor for many streets, so Charlotte woke the taxidermist from his bed, thinking he might know what to do. Rose had gone into labor by the time they got there.

All night long they laid cold compresses on her brow and grabbed her hands as she screamed through contractions. But the poison in the vial had stained her tongue black and robbed her of strength.

After hours of struggle, the child was born. A small bear child, already dead.

Rose died soon after.

Liam fell to all fours. "I tried to live as a man," he said, "but I am a bear in my blood."

"Liam!" Charlotte called, running to him and touching his back, sinking her fingers into his fur. "Bear or man, you are my brother."

133

But he turned away, lumbering down the stairs. He cast away his clothes and his boots as he came to the outskirts of the city. He entered the forest and would never walk upright or speak again.

Charlotte held the bear child to her, though it was cold as snow.

"I will call the necessary people," said the taxidermist. He looked uncomfortably at Rose's body, growing pale and strange. Death was something he was used to seeing at a remove. "You shouldn't have to see this—a young lady like you—"

But Charlotte ignored him. She recognized the scent of the child, the smell of Liam, as familiar as her own. "He's warming up," said Charlotte.

The taxidermist frowned. "The child is dead."

"Can't you hear him?" she asked. "He's crying for his father."

"Please, Charlotte, you must—" began the taxidermist, but then he paused. He could hear a low, thready sound, like weeping.

Closer and closer he came, until he was sure the sound came from the body in her hands.

"We will save him," Charlotte said.

They made this piece together, imbedding a speaker in the little bear's chest to amplify the sound and giving him Rose's diamond earrings in place of eyes. This, the first of many marvelous and wonderful creations by Charlotte Wells. Each one, it is said, came nearly alive under her touch. Nearly.

But does it still cry? I'm sure that's what you're wondering. Come closer, lean in. The little bear has something different to tell each one of you.

Lottery ticket numbers.

Messages from lost lovers.

Predictions for the future.

Oh, you want to know what *I* heard when I leaned near the speaker? Only this—that whomsoever is the next buyer will have luck and fortune for the rest of his days!

Think of the story.

I believe it's time for the bidding to begin.

A Short History of Dunkelblau's Meistergarten

By Tad Williams

One of the more unusual education devices ever designed was the Meistergarten of Ernst Dunkelblau, the "Pedagogue of Linz." When it was first presented to the public in 1905, it was called "The Eighth Wonder of the World" by some newspapers of the day, "The Devil's Carousel" by others. All agreed, however, that its like had never been seen before.

"It resembles a Lazy Susan," commented a reporter for America's *New York World,* "but instead of spinning to present dishes to be served, its revolutionary motion is meant to deliver children to Scholarship."

The Inventor: Ernst A. Dunkelblau

Little can be understood of either the Meistergarten or its products without first examining the life of its creator, Ernst Adelbert Dunkelblau.

Dunkelblau was born in a suburb of Linz, Austria, in 1859. His father was one of the engineers who designed and built the first iron bridge over the Danube, but his mother, Heilwig, had even bigger plans for her only child, and from a very early age little Ernst was given the benefit of her fascination with childhood learning. The acknowledged star of European education at the time was Friedrich Fröbel, famous for his ideas of the kindergarten—a place where children would learn through play. Frau Dunkelblau, however, was a stern woman who felt that the currently fashionable dogma was totally reversed—that children should learn by suffering, not play. She developed her own method, which she called *"Arbeit und Verletzung,"* or "Work and Injury," and employed it along with a very ambitious curriculum for her infant son, which she had determined would prepare him to enter a good Austrian university by the time he was twelve years old. In fact, Ernst Dunkelblau was accepted to the Karl-Franzens-Universität, better known today as the University of Graz, at the prodigious age of ten.

Young Dunkelblau never graduated from the university, however. Rumors of the day linked him to a scandal with a much older woman, the wife of a university custodian, who claimed that young Dunkelblau offered her a florin to "nap upon her bosom." Accounts subsequent to his death suggest that Dunkel-blau never entirely overcame this troubling propensity for offering money to women not of his own family; in later years the significance of this weakness became so divisive among European Freudians that there were violent differences of opinion about it—indeed, there are reports of a famous fight in a London café between Otto Rank and Melanie Klein, in which Klein was said to have slapped Rank so hard and so often that he was led away weeping and for weeks would only see patients with a scarf draped over his face.

Much of Ernst Dunkelblau's personal history between the years of 1871 and 1899 is hazy, little more than rumor and innuendo. It is known that he served briefly in the Austro-Hungarian army as a telegrapher, but was discharged because so many of his messages contained interpolated phrases such as "Ernst is scared," "sleepy dumplings," or simply the word *"Mutti"* ("Mommy") typed over and over, none of which bore any relationship to the military messages young Dunkelblau had been tasked with sending.

Apparently, he also found time during these years to finish his education, graduating from a small university in Triesen, Liechtenstein, called the Tod-krank-Igil Institute. Little more is known, because the university was subsequently burned to the ground by local villagers and its records lost.

Many of Dunkelblau's later experiments in pedagogy, including the famous Meistergarten, seem to have roots in his Liechtenstein student period, because his adult writings on the subject of educational psychology frequently contain phrases, such as "two-schilling Vaduz Mustache" and "bloody Triesen pitch-forks ouch ouch," which seem to trace to this time.

However, with 1899 and his return to Linz, we see the triumphant execution of designs and ideas that had obviously been building in Dunkelblau's mind for some time, culminating that year in the opening of the St. Agnes Blannbekin Private School for Boys and Girls, an institute under Dunkelblau's personal supervision. The doctor was described by one of the school's first students as "a great, smiling, bearded Father Christmas of a man" and "a performing bear, quick to growl, quick to eat off the plates of others, but also swift with a booming laugh or a sudden storm of tears caused by the frustrations of his work."

In 1905, after some period of experimentation with mechanical equipment and the selection of a first set of human test subjects, Dunkelblau unveiled his magnum opus to the Austrian and international press: the Meistergarten.

John Coulthart's painstaking reconstruction of the Meistergarten.

The Meistergarten

The machine itself was described in a subsequent legal deposition by a lawyer for the family of one of the children:

> It was the size of a very small fairground ride, and, in fact, bore much of the appearance of a children's carousel, being circular, a little less than three meters in diameter, and profusely decorated in the very ornamented style of the time with baroque leaves and vines. At the center, a bit larger than the human original it sought to emulate, was the bronze head that contained the speaking tube and the audio tubes and various other bits of the mechanism that would allow it to interact with the youthful subjects.

The machine itself (although most of the gears and tubes were hidden from view by the panels on the outside of the Meistergarten) was designed as both a teaching resource and a self-contained supply of everything by way of health and nurture that the child subjects would need. The bronze head that took pride of place at the center of the Meistergarten, perched much as a bride and groom might stand in the middle of a wedding cake, was created in the image of a classical sculpture of a goddess, but with a hinged jaw and small lightbulbs behind the isinglass of the eyes. It would turn on a swivel to listen or speak to the children in turn. A correct answer would solicit a mechanical smile (signaled by a grinding noise as the jaws rubbed together) and various invisible caresses on the student's unprotected skin within the body of the machine. A wrong answer would cause the automaton's eyes to flash red and its mouth to gape widely as it gave forth a loud klaxon that some observers called "horrifying," but Doktor Dunkelblau called "usefully arresting."

Other facilities for the better promotion of learning had been built into the Meistergarten but were not immediately revealed by the staff of the St. Agnes Blannbekin school.

The Subjects

"Die Berühmten Fünf," or "The Famous Five," as the first child subjects were known, had been handpicked by Dunkelblau himself because he felt they would be "uniquely susceptible" to this new kind of learning, which he sometimes referred to as his *"Automatische* Super-Mama," but more often as simply "The System."

The names of these first volunteers, or at least the names by which they were known in the literature surrounding the experiment, were:

Trudl K., 7 years old, from Linz

Wouter S., 9 years old, from Passau

Franz F., 8 years old, from Linz

Helga W., 8 years old, from Scherding

Lorenz D., 7 years old, from Radstadt

These students (or, rather, their parents) had agreed that they would spend at least the next three years as part of Dunkelblau's experiment—joined to the apparatus, with all their needs satisfied by the machine while they received the most complete and thorough education of any human child ever. Or so was Dunkelblau's assertion; the results of his groundbreaking experiment and the value of his data are still in dispute to this very day.

Some later researchers have claimed that Ernst Dunkelblau chose his subjects by nonstandard criteria that included "interesting distress noises," "shape of feet and nose," and, in one case, that of Helga W., because the young girl had "a tantalizingly brilliant future in Music or the Arts," epitomized by her singing voice and early grace at the Austrian *Boarischer*, the polka, and other folk dances.

The Experiment

The name of Dunkelblau's invention, Der Meistergarten, was a play on Fröber's famous "kindergarten"—a children's garden. Ernst Dunkelblau, though, did not plan simply to educate children, but to create "masters," students who would be superior to ordinary children in every way, as Dunkelblau had felt himself to be.

"I was a nightingale in a cage full of croaking ravens" is how he once described his time at the University of Graz. "My little, sweet, and sensible voice could not be heard above the cacophonous din of the other so-called scholars. . . ."

So it was that the Famous Five were "assigned to the System," in Dunkelblau's phrase, in September 1905 at his school in Linz. Completely immobilized by machinery from the neck down, the children were catheterized for waste disposal and fitted with feeding tubes that periodically pumped meals (a slurry of oats, root vegetables, and some meat products) directly into their stomachs. The inside of the Meistergarten device also contained a number of specialty appendages, which were not displayed to the children, capable of administering to their hidden bodies comforting pats and caresses as well as pinches and slaps.

The Meistergarten was then closed and the neck-rings sealed, so that all that could be seen of the subjects were their heads, all facing in toward the center of the circular Meistergarten, which was set in an otherwise empty, mirrored hall specially prepared by Dunkelblau at the St. Agnes Blannbekin school. Observers watched the experiment from behind the one-way mirrors lining the large room. From that moment on, the subjects had no other direct human contact. The machinery of the Meistergarten itself was serviced during the subjects' sleeping period by silent custodial workers and mechanics dressed in black robes and hoods. If the children seemed restless on service nights, a mixture of nitrous oxide and chloroform was pumped into the System Hall so that they would not be unduly bothered by the presence of the dark figures.

From the moment of their introduction into the Meistergarten until their release, the subjects interacted only with the bronze head at the center of the machine, nicknamed Minerva. In an effort not to confuse the subjects with old associations, Dunkelblau decided against an overly sympathetic "female presence" for his invention: at the last moment, he cancelled a contract with well-known stage actress Lottelore Eisenbaum, who would have contributed Minerva's voice, and took on the role himself, speaking to the students in a strained, falsetto, "female" voice with as little emotional inflection as possible, attempting to create what he called "a true Machine Mother Sound." One of his research assistants said that twenty years later she still "woke up wailing and weeping" after dreaming of the Minerva voice.

The children were roused from sleep each morning by the sound of Minerva's wake-up call, a loud, ratcheting shriek based on Dunkelblau's idea that, of all noises, the most perfect focus of attention could be created by the sound of an industrial accident coupled with an expression of human terror. After the previous night's meal had been pumped out of their system and a new meal pumped in, the students began a long and rigorous day of history, mathematics, natural sciences, Greek and Latin, and some unusual coursework of Dunkelblau's own devising, including Lesion Studies, Practical Engorgement, and Social Attack Theory. They were taught by the rote method, instructed by "Minerva" (in reality, Dunkelblau, of course, watching from the far side of a one-way mirror and speaking into a tube) and immediately corrected for each error on a rising scale of reprisal that began at "Lightly Bruising Pinch with Flashing Eyes" and peaked at "Flare, Shriek, and Scourge" (at which point, the subject usually had to be sedated for at least twenty-four hours to allow recovery and what Dunkelblau termed "deeper learning").

Correct answers received praise from "Minerva" and sometimes also the singing of a verse of *"Hejo, Spann den Wagen an,"* one of Dunkelblau's favorite songs from his childhood:

Hey ho! Hitch up the cart,
For the wind brings rain over the land.
Fetch the golden sheaves,
Fetch the golden sheaves . . .

The student who answered Minerva correctly was also rewarded by the activation of certain bladders within the machinery that, when inflated, gave a pleasurable sensation.

Problems

The first real controversy about Dunkelblau's experiment came in December 1905, when the parents of Trudl K. asked that their daughter be released from the System for the Christmas holidays and were refused. They were denied a similar request at Easter as well. In her unhappy missive to the doctor, Frau K. wrote, "Our daughter's letters appear to be written by someone other than our daughter. The last three have all said exactly the same thing, 'Do not come visit—it will interrupt the important work we are doing here, work that will forever confound the servile devotees of that ape Fröbel and his "Child-Garden"!' We find it hard to believe," Mrs. K continued, "that our daughter cares greatly about Friedrich Fröbel, who died almost a half century before she was born, and we have also heard disquieting rumors from neighbors of the St. Agnes school that children can be heard throughout the day and night, moaning, weeping, and even barking like distressed dogs. . . ."

A year later her parents were given permission by the Bildungsministerium, the Austrian educational authority, to remove their daughter from Dunkelblau's machine. Perhaps piqued by their withdrawal from the experiment, Herr Doktor Dunkelblau ordered that Trudl be delivered to her parents' house at night in a device he called an "Egress Chrysalis," which the K. family claimed was little more than a conventional straitjacket augmented with a canvas sack over the patient's head.

Schooling continued for the other four subjects despite some odd malfunctions from the Meistergarten, in which Minerva continued to speak as though the missing child was still part of the experiment and would even dole out stinging electrical shocks to the remaining subjects for "teasing poor little Trudl."

The End of the Experiment

The remaining four children all stayed in the Meistergarten for the duration of the planned three-year period, without parental interference. In fact, by the time the Meistergarten was opened and the students removed, the parents of Franz F. and Lorenz D. could not be easily located. The family of Franz F. proved to have moved to Swabia in Germany and at first maintained that they had no child. The D. family, still in Linz, did not deny young Lorenz was theirs, but argued that they had "sold" him to Dunkelblau and that, by giving him back, Dunkelblau was reneging on their agreement.

The scandal over Trudl K. had died down at last, but when little Franz F., now almost eleven years old and newly returned home, attacked and bit a postman so badly that the man nearly bled to death, the newspapers again picked up the story, many of them painting Dunkelblau as "irresponsible" and "unscientific." Dunkelblau responded in a famous letter to the editor of the *Linzer Volksblatt*, stating "the hounds of Conventionality can sniff my arse to their hearts' content—all they will discover is the scent of Genius leaving them far behind!"

The Aftermath

Ernst A. Dunkelblau never published his results of his experiment, claiming that "the general population is not capable of understanding the sublime heights of Truth we have scaled here." In later years, the St. Agnes Blannbekin school was closed by the Linz authorities. A special squadron of Bundesheer troops took away the Meistergarten itself, which had fallen into disrepair—the head of Minerva was currently being used by the school as a gramophone horn for folk-dancing practice—but the final disposition of the rest of the famous device is unknown. The Minerva head was reportedly displayed in a 1938 British auction house catalog, listed as "macabre pseudo-classical ash tray," but its current whereabouts are also a mystery.

Dunkelblau himself died in Linz in 1932, in the Altstadt apartment of a "working woman," murdered by parties unknown. At the time of his death by strangulation, the doctor was dressed in the costume of a nineteenth-century schoolboy, complete with rucksack (which, for some reason, was stuffed full of boiled eggplant) and a false mustache. The false mustache was a particularly odd detail, because it was smaller than the doctor's own mustache, over which it had been affixed.

The Lives of the "Famous Five"

TRUDL K.: After she was removed from the Meistergarten and the school, little is known about this subject. In the 1920s, when Dunkelblau was much in the news, various stories appeared in the newspapers to suggest she had become a (not very successful) music-hall performer or acrobat in Vienna. None of this was ever proved, although to this day, in Austria, a street mime is still called a "Shrieking Trudl." When she died in 1948 in a Graz hospital, her obituary noted only that she had "been part of a famous educational experiment, and later married a Polish animal trainer."

FRANZ F.: Although best known for his attack on a postman in 1908, Franz F. had perhaps the most unusual history of any of the Meistergarten subjects. When the Great War began, he enlisted under an assumed name in the Austro-Hungarian army and rose through the ranks by dint of almost heedless courage under fire. He was nicknamed *Der Werwolf* by his comrades and reputedly crossed no-man's-land every night to bedevil the enemy, dressed only in a kilt made from the scalps of his victims. In fact, a vast collection of body parts in glass jars, known as "Franz's Toys," is reportedly still hidden in a back room of the Museum of Military History in Vienna. After the war, Franz F. disappeared from public view, although a few historians insist he was eventually hunted down and killed in the Bohemian Forest by a specially trained team of Austrian police led by an American Cherokee Indian tracker, William First Bear.

LORENZ D., described by Dunkelblau as "a quiet, unassuming child," never spoke a distinguishable word after being part of the Meistergarten system, although he sang wordlessly and laughed and even screamed without visible cause for the rest of his life. He was institutionalized in 1916 and began to paint, primarily "huge, barren landscapes peopled by burning mice and human-headed octopuses," as a nurse described them. He also climbed walls with great skill, and was often to be found by his caretakers curled up in the institution's overhead light fixtures, asleep. Lorenz D.'s family never questioned their own judgement in letting him be part of Dunkelblau's experiment, and described those who criticized their choice as "pitiful" and "jealous," despite their own lack of interest in visiting Lorenz after he was institutionalized.

HELGA W., whose "brilliant future" in the arts never materialized, nevertheless did become a performer of sorts. Witnesses in the 1930s identified her as the "Hard-Boiled Egg Woman" in Berlin's infamous Der Eigenartige Wandschrank club, who was said to be able to fling an egg fifteen meters with her reproductive parts while leading the crowd in singing *"Wir Wollen Alle Kinder Sein!"*

WOUTER K., the most materially successful of the doctor's subjects, founded a number of private hospitals for the care of "difficult children" (which, some alleged, were merely "holding cells" for the unwanted offspring of the wealthy) and then funneled the profits into the manufacture of chemical agents such as mustard gas, which was banned after the Great War by all sides but still bought and stockpiled by many nations for years after, so that Wouter K. became known in international military circles as "Meister Senf," or "Mister Mustard." Soon his factories were making many other kinds of poisons as well, and his scientists are linked to the discovery of the infamous G-series poison gases, including sarin, tabun, and cyclosarin. Wouter K. made millions but used the money primarily to shield himself from the public eye, and was not heard from again until he issued the following "proclamation" to the world's leading newspapers in early 1939:

The work of Doktor Adelbert Dunkelblau has been much maligned in the international press, especially by those whose minds are too small to understand his vision. What his work proved was not that the Meistergarten was unworkable, or a "crackpot" scheme, as some have termed it, but simply that the experimental sample was too small. I was one of five subjects, and I have become one of the world's most successful and richest men. Surely a success rate of twenty percent is not to be mocked, especially with a discovery that will *literally change the world.* A generation of supermen is a goal that no one can fault, and I will provide the first seeds for that wondrous human accomplishment. Twenty percent. It is something to think about—something to thrill the human soul!

I have purchased a quantity of land—no one will know where!—and on that site I shall build Dunkelblau's Meistergarten anew. But instead of five, I shall commit five hundred or even five thousand subjects to the test (there are orphanages the world over that will happily contribute their superfluity), and from these humble materials will our first generation of *"Meistermenschen"* be born. But unlike the clownish National Socialists of the current German government, our gifted ones will not reveal themselves, let alone brag of their superiority, but instead they will turn around and create newer, larger generations of others like them, until one day we shall emerge from the wild places where we have hidden ourselves and take our true place as leaders of a fallen, but not entirely hopeless, world. Be warned! On that day, *everything* will change.

It was rumored in some circles that throughout the 1920s and 1930s "Wouter K." secretly bought extensive tracts of land in the largely unexplored Chaco Boreal region on the border between Paraguay and Bolivia. Others claim his major holdings were uninhabited volcanic islands in the South Atlantic and Southern Ocean. In either case, to this day, nothing definitive has ever been heard of the last Dunkelblau test subject, and although a few businesses with the name "Meistergarten" have shown up in international registries from places as distantly separated as Franz Joseph Land in the Arctic and Dar Es Salaam, Tanzania, no sign of the promised "first generation of *Meistermenschen*" has yet been seen. However, it is clear that even at this late date, the book on Dunkelblau's experiment cannot quite be closed for good.

MICROBIAL ALCHEMY and Demented Machinery

The Mignola Exhibits

The Mignola Exhibits

The artifacts researched as part of the Mignola Exhibits tend to reflect *Hellboy* creator Mike Mignola's own fascination with Lambshead's cabinet. Mignola says he first remembers reading about Lambshead "in a comic when I was nine—it was one of those two-page spreads they used to fill space, with a title like 'Strange but True.' It might've been a *Tales from the Crypt*."

The images of such iconic Lambshead pieces as the Clockroach were originally intended for an abandoned Mignola project titled *Subsequently Lost at Sea*, which would have been a detailed illustrated chronicle of, as Mignola puts it, "important stuff that got lost at sea." The book would have reached back as far as the Romans with their "often unreliable galleys." Mignola feels the results "would've been as important to the study of all kinds of crap lost at sea as Alasdair Gray's *Book of Prefaces* is to the study of the English language."

The pieces documented herein were initially lost at sea in the spring of 2003, following an urgent directive from Lambshead that rescinded the museum loans on the Clockroach, Roboticus mask, Shamalung, and Pulvadmonitor.

Lambshead's directive sent the exhibits to the Museum of Further Study in Jakarta, Indonesia, all by circuitous routes. Roboticus and Shamalung left via the HMS *Dorsal Fin of God*, which disappeared seventy miles west of the Canary Islands. The USS *Jeraboam II*, carrying the Clockroach, was captured by pirates off the coast of Somalia, led by, as the BBC put it, "What looked like someone's Greek great-grandmother with a knife in her teeth," who managed to elude U.S. and British naval units during a heavy storm. *The Baalbek*, flying the Libyan flag and carrying a twice-hermetically sealed Pulvadmonitor, vanished off the Horn of Africa. (Some—specifically, Caitlín R. Kiernan—have suggested that the route of the freighters and the points at which they disappeared form a complex message from Lambshead "to parties unknown," if we could only interpret it.)

By then, the good doctor's heart had finally given out and his heirs countermanded his orders, an act that seemed to have no agency. However, astoundingly enough, Roboticus, Shamalung, and the Pulvadmonitor (babbling incoherently) turned up at Lord Balfoy's Antiques on London's Portobello Road two years later, selling for fifty pounds apiece. The artifacts were turned over to the Museum of Intangible Arts and Objects in Saragossa, Spain, where experts eventually confirmed that all three pieces now met "all of our requirements regarding Immateriality, Intangibility, Elusiveness, and the Ephemeral." When the objects were returned to their respective museums, the attendants therein seemed united behind Billy Quirt—thirty-year velvet-rope veteran of Imperial War exhibits—in believing that the artifacts are "a bloody lot more and a bloody lot less than they were before they went traveling."

The predicament does underscore one reason Mignola abandoned the book: "Too much stuff eventually washes up. Sometimes just when you'd like it to stay lost. I'd rather just draw stuff that's always there, like monsters."

Addison Howell and the Clockroach

Documented by Cherie Priest

Museum Name and Location: The Stackpole Museum of Prototypical Industry; Port Angeles, Washington

Name of Exhibit: Pioneer Myths and Lore in Peninsular Victoriana

Category information

    Creator: Addison Sobiesky Howell (alleged); American, born 1828 in Chicago, Illnois. Died 1899 in Humptulips, Washington

    Title: "Clockroach," built 1878(?)

    Medium: Mixed, primarily steel, cast iron, rubber tubing, and glass

    Source: Donated in 1953 by the Museum of History and Industry in Seattle, Washington, at cost of transportation—and a gentleman's agreement with regards to subsequent restoration and display

Accession number: 1953.99

Exhibit Introduction Panel: Pioneer Myths and Lore in Peninsular Victoriana

The Olympic Peninsula has long been home to a number of Native American tribes, including the Hoh, Makah, and the Quileute; but it was not until the second half of the nineteenth century that it became settled by white homesteaders. Primarily, these homesteaders were farmers and loggers, lured by the Homestead Act of 1862 and the promise of a temperate climate.

Though much can be said about the Native traditions and myths, this exhibit focuses on the rural homesteaders and their inevitable bedtime or campfire stories—some of which were regarded with a seriousness that borders on the charmingly naïve or dangerously optimistic, as evidenced by the items on display.

Highlights of the collection include:

(1908.32, items a-g) Filbert Seyfarth's assortment of "vampire-killing" poisons. These anti-undead concoctions were understandably unpopular—considering that, given a vampire's traditional diet, the poisons must first be consumed by a potential victim (presumably, of the suicidally game-for-anything variety).

(1912.11) Earl Lenning's Skoocooms Mesmerizing Ray (patent no. D224,997), a trigger-operated light-projecting contraption intended to befuddle a creature now better known as "Sasquatch." The existence of this device leads some researchers to suspect that a Native American practical joker enjoyed a hearty laugh at Mr. Lenning's expense.

(1953.99) Addison Howell's "Clockroach," a one-man, quasi-lobster-shaped vehicle allegedly designed and driven by an aloof, peculiar craftsman who was rumored to be the devil himself.

We at the Stackpole Museum of Prototypical Industry would like to welcome you to this exhibit and invite you to ask questions. However, we ask that you not touch the Clockroach—nor allow children to climb upon it and make the *choo-choo* noise, as this is both contextually inappropriate and bound to result in tetanus shots for all concerned.

Clockroach: The Legend

(Oral tradition transcribed by UW graduate student Gregory Blum from an interview with Petra Oberg [1902–1996], daughter of Isac and Emma Johnson—two of Humptulips' original settlers.)

Addison Howell didn't so much arrive in Humptulips as appear there sometime around 1875. He had money, which set him apart from everybody else—because everybody else was working for the logging company, and mostly they didn't have a pot to piss in, as my daddy put it.[1]

Mr. Howell built himself a house, way outside of town, a big three-story place set back in the hills—and you couldn't see it until you were right on top of it, what with all the trees.

He had a wife with him at one point, but she died up there. Folks said he'd murdered her with an ax, but there was never any proof of that and we didn't have any law at the time nohow, not a sheriff or anything, much less a jail. We had a mayor, though—a fellow named Herp Jones—and I think if Herp could've rounded up enough warm bodies, he would've seen to a lynch mob.[2] But everyone he might've asked was either working or drinking, so I guess that didn't happen.

The town gave Mrs. Howell a Christian burial in a little plot back behind the only church we had, and her guilty-as-sin husband paid a pretty penny to have a crypt built up around her. It was a real big deal, because nobody else in town had ever gotten a crypt, and only about half the folks who ever died even got a tomb

Addison Howell on his Clockroach

stone.[3] Then Mr. Howell went back to his house in the trees, and, for the most part, nobody hardly ever saw him again.

A few years later, as I heard it, Addison Howell was out and about doing whatever it is a wicked man does on a Sunday, and he came across a homesteader's camp just off the old logging road. There was a wagon with a broken axle, and two dead men lying beside a campfire. It looked like they'd been tore up by wolves, or maybe mountain lions, or somesuch creature. But inside the wagon he heard a little girl crying. He looked inside and she screamed, and she bit him—because like attracts like, I suppose, and the girl had a bad streak in her, too. That's why he took her home with him.

She was maybe eight or nine when he brought her inside, and legend has it she was mute. Or maybe she didn't feel like talking, I couldn't say. . . . [4] . . . Anyway, he raised her as his own, and they lived together in the house in the hills, and nobody ever visited them because everybody knew they were doing evil things up there.[5]

But people started telling stories about hearing strange noises out there at night, like someone was whacking on metal with a hammer, or sawing through steel. Word got around that he was building a machine that looked like a big bug, or a lobster, or something. It had a big stack on top and it was steam-powered, or coal-powered, or anyway it was supposed to move around when he was sitting inside it.

I don't know who was fool-headed enough to get close enough to listen, but somebody did, and somebody talked.

And later on, the mayor and some friends of his, all of them with guns and itchy trigger fingers, went up to that house and demanded to know what was going on up there. For all they knew, he was summoning Satan,[6] or beating up that girl,[7] or raising whatever kind of hell I just don't know.

Addison Howell told them they were welcome to look around, so they did. They didn't find anything, and they were mad about it. They asked the girl what was going on, but she wouldn't say nothing and they thought maybe she was scared of Howell, and that's why she wasn't being helpful. But she was a teenager by then, or old enough that she could live there with a dirty old man if she felt like it, and people'd look askance, but no one would take her away.

Not long after that, Addison Howell went into town to do some business—he was over at the logging foreman's place, and nobody has any idea why, or what they were talking about. They got into some kind of fight—the foreman's wife overheard it and she came out and saw them struggling, so she took her husband's shotgun and she blew the back of Addison Howell's head clean off, and he died right then and there.

The foreman went and got Herp Jones, and between 'em, they figured it was good riddance. They decided they should just leave him in the crypt with his wife, since there was a slot for him and everything, and that's what they did. They wrapped up his body and carried it off.

When they got to the crypt, they found that one of the doors was hanging open—and that was odd, but they didn't make nothing of it. They thought maybe there'd been an earthquake, a little one that wasn't much noticed, and the place had gone a little crooked. It happens all the time. But inside the thing, they found the floor all tore up. There used to be marble tiles down there, and now they were gone. Nothing but dirt was left.

I expect they wondered if someone hadn't gotten inside and stolen them. Marble might've been worth something.

They didn't worry about it much, though. They just dumped old Addison Howell into his slot, scooted the lid over him, and shut the place up behind them. Then they remembered the girl who lived at Howell's place—nobody knew her name, on account of she'd never said it—and they headed up there to let her know what had happened.

I think privately they thought maybe now she'd come into town and pick a husband, somebody normal and good for her. There weren't enough women to go around as it was, and she was pretty enough to get a lot of interest.

When they told her the news she started screaming. They dragged her into town to try and calm her down, but she wasn't having any of it. Around that time there was a doctor passing through, or maybe Humptulips had gotten one of its own. Regardless, this doctor gave her something to make her sleep, trying to settle her. They left her in the back room of the general store, passed out on a cot.

And that night, the town woke up to a terrible commotion coming from the cemetery behind Saint Hubert's. Everybody jumped out of bed, and people grabbed their guns and their logging axes, and they went running down to the church to see what was happening—and the whole place was just in ruins. The church was on fire, and the cemetery looked like someone had set off a bunch of dynamite all over it. The Howell crypt was just a bunch of rubble, and there was a big old crater where it used to be.

And by the light of the burning church, the mayor and the logging foreman and about a dozen other people all swear by the saints and Jesus, too . . . they saw a big

machine with a tall black stack crawling away—and sitting inside it was the demon

Addison Howell, driving the thing straight back to hell. Some said he was laughing, some said he was crying. Most everyone said they were glad he was gone.

ENDNOTES

1. Colloquialism for severe poverty. I offered to amend the "i" in "piss" to an asterisk for the sake of decency, but head of antiquities Dr. Meagher said to leave it alone, surprising no one even a little bit.

2. Census records for this region are all but nonexistent until well into the twentieth century, so little is officially known about the town's population; but anecdotal evidence and extensive, thankless, unpaid legwork by a graduate student (who is poor enough to warrant an analogy in need of an asterisk) suggests that fewer than three hundred people were in residence at the time.

3. Records kept at Saint Hubert's Church imply an average of half a dozen deaths per year—startling only if one fails to consider that Humptulips was a logging town. As a side note, it turns out that St. Hubert is the patron saint of woodsmen.

4. Mrs. Oberg took this opportunity to speculate with regards to what wild animals might have eaten the girl's family, and then suggested that maybe she was too traumatized to speak thereafter. She also brought up the possibility that Mr. Howell was a pedophile, though that isn't the term she used. As Mrs. Oberg went on at great length upon the subject, her digression has been edited out. After all, an endnote is in better taste, unless Dr. Meagher wants a protracted diatribe about body parts and their respective fluids described with a good number of Anglo-Saxon, consonant-heavy words engraved on a plaque right there on the exhibit, surely prompting a number of embarrassed parents[4a] to answer many awkward questions on the way back to the car.

4a. Do they still let children scale the Clockroach and pretend it's a train? That was always my favorite part of school field trips to the SMPI, until one day I fell off and impaled my foot on a rusty spring. They made me get a tetanus shot.

5. When asked precisely how everybody knew this if no one ever visited them, Mrs. Oberg's iron-clad logic went as follows: "If they weren't up to any mischief, they would've just moved to town like civilized people."

6. This seems rather unlikely.

7. The interviewer considered the wisdom of interrupting to ask if the girl was made of metal, given Mrs. Oberg's previous statement, but resolved instead to save his breath. After all, he wasn't getting paid by the word. Or at all.

Clockroach: The Facts

(Fact-checking provided courtesy of Julia Frimpendump, professor emeritus of regional history, University of Washington. Sponsored in part by the West Coast Pioneer Bibliography Project, but not sponsored so extensively that the graduate student who was stuck typing out Dr. Frimpendump's notes was compensated one red cent for his efforts.)

Though Saint Hubert's church was, in fact, subjected to a fire in 1889, it did not burn in its entirety, and most of its records were preserved. There is a record of burial for a woman named "Rose M. Howell" on October 2, 1878, lending credence that the story of Addison Howell may hold a grain of truth; but there is no record for Mr. Howell's death, nor any subsequent burial.

After consulting with an archeo-industrialist in Cincinnati, I have concluded that the peculiar device known locally as "the clockroach" is very likely intended for use in the logging industry. Its forward claws suggest a machine capable of carrying tremendous weight, and the multiple legs imply that it could have traversed difficult terrain while successfully bearing a load.

Based on this information, one could speculate a kinder story for the tragic Addison Howell. It's reasonable to guess that he might have been a lonely man who adopted an orphaned girl, and in his spare time he devoted himself to tinkering . . . eventually coming up with this peculiar engine that might have revolutionized the industry, had it been adopted and mass-produced. His conversation-turned-argument with the logging foreman may have been some patent dispute, or an altercation over the invention's worth—there's no way to know.

The casual record-keeping and insular nature of a tiny homesteader's town has left us little with which to speculate.

However, the remains of a marble crypt can be found in Saint Hubert's churchyard. The church's present minister, Father Frowd, says that it collapsed during an earthquake well before his time—and to the best of his knowledge, it was salvaged for materials.

As for the wagon with the murdered occupants and the sole surviving child, evidence suggests that a family by the name of Sanders left Olympia, Washington, intending to homestead near Humptulips in 1881. This family consisted of a widower Jacob and his brother Daniel, and his brother's daughter Emily. The small family never reached Humptulips, and no record of their demise or reappearance has ever been found.

In one tantalizing clue located (once again) via Saint Hubert's, a spinster named "Emily Howell" reportedly passed away in 1931, at the estimated age of sixty. Her age was merely estimated because she never gave it, and she passed away without family members or identification. She was found dead alone in the large home she kept outside the city limits—her cause of death unknown.

But she is buried behind the church, and her tombstone reads simply, EMILY HOWELL, D. 1931. SHE NEVER FORGOT HIM, AND NEVER FORGAVE US.

Sir Ranulph Wykeham-Rackham, GBE, a.k.a. Roboticus the All-Knowing

Documented by Lev Grossman

Museum: Imperial War Museum, London

Exhibit: Military Miracles! Medical Innovation and the Great Wars

Category: Full-body prosthetic

Creator: Diverse hands, including Marcel Duchamp, Pablo Picasso, Thackery T. Lambshead, Adolf Hitler, and Andy Warhol

Medium: Stainless steel, rubber, enameled copper, textile

Sir Ranulph Wykeham-Rackham was born in 1877. As heir to the legendary Wykeham-Rackham wainscoting fortune, he was assured a life of leisure and privilege, if not any particular utility. But no one suspected that his life would still be going on 130 years later, after a fashion.

A brilliant student, he went up to Oxford at the age of sixteen and was sent down again almost immediately for drunkenness, card-playing, and lewdness. Given the popularity of these pastimes among the undergraduate body, one can only imagine the energy and initiative with which young Ranulph pursued them.

Although he had no artistic talent himself, Wykeham-Rackham preferred the company of artists, who appreciated his caustic wit, his exquisite wardrobe, and his significant annual allowance. He moved to London and rapidly descended into dissipation in the company of the members of the Aesthetes, chief among them Oscar Wilde. Wykeham-Rackham was a regular presence in the gallery during Wilde's trial for gross indecency, and after Wilde's release from prison, it is strongly suspected that wainscoting money bankrolled the elaborate ruse surrounding Wilde's supposed death, and his actual relocation to a comfortable island in the remote West Indies where such advanced Victorian ideas as "gross indecency" did not exist.

The real Wilde died in 1914, leaving Wykeham-Rackham alone and feeling, at thirty-seven, that his era was already passing away. Pater and Swinburne and Burne-Jones and the other aesthetes were long gone. The outbreak of World War

I further deepened his pessimism about the future of modern civilization. Rich, bored, and extravagantly melancholy, he enlisted in the Twenty-eighth Battalion of the London Regiment, popularly known as the "Artists Rifles," because, as he said, he "liked the uniform, and hated life." One can only imagine his surprise when the Artists Rifles were retained as an active fighting force and sent on a tour of the war's most viciously contested battlefields, including Ypres, the Somme, and Passchendaele. All told, the Artists Rifles would sustain more personnel killed in World War I than any other British battalion.

But Wykeham-Rackham survived, and not only survived but flourished. He discovered within himself either an inner wellspring of bravery or a stylish indifference to his own fate—the line between them is a fine one—and, over the course of three years of trench combat, he was awarded a raft of medals, including the Military Cross for gallantry in the face of the enemy at Bapaume.

His luck ran out in 1918, during the infamous hundred-days assault on Germany's Hindenburg line. Wykeham-Rackham was attempting to negotiate a barbed-wire barrier when a sharpshooter's bullet clipped a white phosphorus grenade that he carried on his belt. White phosphorus, then the cutting edge of anti-personnel weaponry, offered one of the grimmest deaths available to a soldier in the Great War. In short order, the chemical had burned away much of Wykeham-Rackham's lower body, from the hips down. As he writhed in agony, the German sharpshooter, evidently not satisfied with his work, fired twice more, removing the bridge of Wykeham-Rackham's nose, his left cheekbone, and half his lower jaw.

But not, strangely, ending his life. The former dandy's soul clung tenaciously to his ruined body, even as it was trundled from aid station to field hospital to Paris and then across the channel to London. There he became the focus of one of the strangest collaborations to which the twentieth century would bear witness.

At that time, the allied fields of prosthetics and cosmesis were being marched rapidly out of their infancy and into a painful adolescence in order to cope with the shocking wounds being inflicted on the human body by the new mechanized weaponry of World War I. Soldiers were returning from the battlefield with disfigurements of a severity undreamt of by earlier generations. When word of Wykeham-Rackham's grievous injury reached his family, from whom he had long been estranged, rather than attend his bedside personally, they opted to send a great deal of money. It was just as well.

In short order, Wykeham-Rackham's feet, legs, and hips had been rebuilt, in skeletal form, out of a new martensitic alloy known as stainless steel, which had just been invented in nearby Sheffield. They were provided with rudimentary muscular power by a hydraulic network fashioned out of gutta-percha tubing. The whole contraption was then fused to the base of Wykeham-Rackham's spine.

It was a groundbreaking achievement, of course, but not without precedent. The field of robotics did not yet exist—the word "robot" would not be coined till 1920—but the history of prosthetic automata went back at least as far as the sixteenth century and the legendary German mercenary Götz von Berlichingen, who lost his right arm in a freak accident when a stray cannonball caused it to be cut off with his own sword. The spring-loaded mechanical iron arm he caused to be built as a replacement could grip a lance and write with a quill. (Wykeham-Rackham was fond of quoting from Goethe's *Goetz von Berlichingen,* based on von Berlichingen's life, in which the playwright coined a useful phrase: *"Leck mich am Arsch,"* or, loosely, "Kiss my ass.")

To replace Wykeham-Rackham's shattered face, a wholly different approach was required. When he was sufficiently recovered from his first operation, Wykeham-Rackham was removed to Sidcup, a suburb of London, home to a special hospital dedicated to the care of those with grotesque facial injuries. It was an eerie place. Mirrors were forbidden. Throughout the town were placed special benches, painted blue, where it was understood that the townspeople should expect that anyone sitting there would present a gravely disturbing appearance.

Wykeham-Rackham's old artist friends, those who were left, rallied around him. Facial reconstruction at that time was accomplished by means of masks. A plaster cast was made of the wounded man's face, a process that brought the patient to within seconds of suffocation. The cast was then used to make a mask of paper-thin galvanized copper. Prominent painters competed with one another to produce the most lifelike reproduction of Wykeham-Rackham's vanished features, which were then reproduced in enamel that was bonded to the copper.

In all, twelve such masks were produced, suitable for various occasions and displaying a range of facial expressions. On seeing them for the first time, Wykeham-Rackham held one up, like Hamlet holding up Yorick's skull, and quoted from his old friend Wilde: "Man is least himself when he talks in his own person. Give him a *mask,* and he will tell you the *truth.*"

Following the end of the war, Wykeham-Rackham enjoyed a second heyday. His fantastical appearance made him the toast of the European avant-garde. A pioneer of kinetic sculpture, Marcel Duchamp was enraptured by Wykeham-Rackham, who agreed to be exhibited alongside Duchamp's other "ready-mades"; he even allowed Duchamp to sign his steel calf with his distinctive "R. Mutt."

Man Ray photographed him. Cocteau filmed him. Stravinsky wrote a ballet based on his life, choreographed by Nijinsky.

Picasso created a special mask for him, a Cubist nightmare that he never wore. (Wykeham-Rackham remarked that Picasso seemed to have missed the point, as the mask was more grotesque than what lay beneath it, not less.) Prosthetics became increasingly fashionable, and not a few deaths and grievous injuries among the fashionable set were explained as attempts to reproduce Wykeham-Rackham's distinctive "look."

Meanwhile, he was continuously undergoing mechanical upgrades and improvements as the available technology progressed. He regularly entertained whole salons of inventors and engineers who vied to try out their innovations on him. Nikola Tesla submitted an elaborate, wildly visionary set of schematics for powering his movements electrically. They were, characteristically for Tesla, the subject of a defamation campaign by Edison, then a blizzard of lawsuits by others who claimed credit for them, and then, finally and decisively, lost in a fire.

But as time wore on, Wykeham-Rackham became increasingly aware that while his metal parts were largely unscathed by the passage of time, his human parts were not. At a scandalous fiftieth birthday party thrown for him by the infamous Bright Young Things of London, Evelyn Waugh among them, Wykeham-Rackham was heard to remark that he was both picture and Dorian Gray in one man.

It was not long afterwards, in 1932, that Wykeham-Rackham opted to have the remainder of his face removed. He was tired, he said, of having his mask touched up to look older, to match his surviving features. Why not become all-mask, and look however he wished? It is not known with any certainty who performed this "voluntary disfigurement" operation, but it is strongly suspected that Lambshead's steady if not overly fastidious hand held the scalpel, judging by the fact that Wykeham-Rackham took a sub-rosa trip to Madagascar at around this time.

Meanwhile, storm clouds of international tension were once again massing. For a brief period, Wykeham-Rackham's lower limbs were declared a state secret, and he was required to wear specially designed pantaloons to conceal them. There were numerous attempts by Soviet emissaries to lure Wykeham-Rackham to Moscow—Stalin was said to have been obsessed with the idea of acquiring a literal "man of steel" to lead the glorious proletariat revolution.

No one was wholly surprised when Wykeham-Rackham reenlisted following Germany's invasion of Poland in 1939. He had grown increasingly disenchanted with twentieth-century urban life, with its buzzing electric lights, blaring radios, and roaring automobiles, even though he himself existed as its living, walking avatar. (He had reluctantly submitted to the electrification of his nether regions in the mid-1920s, after a series of messy, embarrassing hydraulic failures at public functions.) He mourned the elegance of his vanished late-Victorian world.

He was also lonely. His romantic life had stalled, in part because he lacked anything in the way of genitals. (It is rumored, although not confirmed, that attempts to add sexual functionality to Wykeham-Rackham's steel groin had to be abandoned after a catastrophic injury to a test partner.) At one time, he had hoped that the same procedure that made him what he was would be performed on others, who would share his strange predicament. But all attempts to repeat the experiment failed. It has been argued, most notably in Dominic Fibrous's definitive *Wykeham-Rackham: Awesome or Hokum?*, that this is because Wykeham-Rackham's condition was "medically impossible" and "made utterly no sense at all."

His one, platonic, romance seems to have been with a young mathematician and computer scientist named Alan Turing. Their dalliance led to the latter's formulation of his famous Wykeham-Rackham Test, which raised the question of whether it would be possible to devise a robot so lifelike that it would be impossible to tell it apart from a human being while making love to it.

Now in his sixties, Wykeham-Rackham was far too old for active service, but the physical stamina resulting from his unusual physical make-up, and his value to the troops as a source of morale, made him indispensable. For public-relations purposes, he joined the invasion of Normandy on D-Day, and the famous photograph of him striding from the surf onto Omaha Beach, his steel pelvis dripping sea foam, a bullet pinging off his enamel face, remains one of the iconic images of World War II. The American GIs cheered him on and called him "Tin Man."

But Wykeham-Rackham's excessive bravery was again his downfall. Emboldened by this taste of his former glory, he refused the offer of transport back to England and stayed with the Allied forces pressing forward through the Norman hedgerows. A close-range encounter with the infamous German *Flammenwerfer* seared his arms and torso almost to the bone. Once again, he made the perilous journey back across the Channel to the hospitals of London. This time, it was necessary to replace almost his entire upper body, leaving only his head and major organs in place.

Astoundingly, he lived on.

Indeed, some began to speculate that out of the crucible of the world wars, humanity's first immortal being had emerged. Wykeham-Rackham showed no obvious signs of aging, apart from his mane of white hair, which he took to dyeing to match its original lustrous black.

But inside, his soul was wasting away. A dark time began for Wykeham-Rackham. Owing to the precipitous decline in sales of wainscoting and wainscoting accessories since the Victorian period, his family fortune had dwindled almost to nothing. He was able to survive only on his military pension, and whatever he received making promotional appearances for the British Armed Forces. Twice he was caught stealing lubricants for his joints and convicted of petty larceny. He became silent and morose. He sold off eleven of his masks, and the Picasso, leaving only the one titled "Melancholia." It was, he said, the only one he needed.

Wykeham-Rackham's last moment in the spotlight came in the 1960s, when he became one of the oddities and grotesques taken up by Andy Warhol and the Factory scene in New York. He appeared in several of Warhol's movies, to the lasting detriment of his dignity, and was, of course, the subject of Warhol's seminal silkscreen *Wykeham-Rackham Triptych*. It was at Warhol's suggestion that Wykeham-Rackham commissioned the final surgery that turned him into an entirely synthetic being: the replacement of his skull with a steel casing, and his brain with a large lightbulb.

Conventional wisdom would argue that this was the end of Wykeham-Rackham's existence as a sentient being, but in truth, it was difficult to tell. As the 1960s wound down, he had spoken and moved less and less. One Warhol hanger-on remarked, in a display of sub-Wildean wit, that after the operation his conversation was "more brilliant than ever."

But Warhol cast Wykeham-Rackham off as lightly as he took him up, and the old soldier passed the 1970s and 1980s in obscurity. It's difficult to track his movements during this lost period, but curatorial notes found in Lambshead's basement suggest that some of Warhol's junkie friends eventually sold him to a traveling carnival, where he was put to use as a fortune-telling machine.

Even there, he was exiled to a gloomy corner of the midway. The proprietors despaired of ever making money off him, because, they said, no matter how they fiddled with his settings, he only ever predicted the imminent and painful demise of whoever consulted him.

His glorious past had been entirely forgotten but for a single trace. On the sign above his booth was painted, in swirly circus calligraphy, a quotation from Oscar Wilde:

"A mask tells us more than a face."

Sir Ranulph Wykeham-Rackham in his full sartorial (and metallic) splendor

Shamalung
(The Diminutions)

Documented by Michael Moorcock

SIR JOHN SOANE'S MUSEUM

13 Lincoln's Inn Fields, London, England

St. Odhran's coll

Reverend Orlando Bannister 1800–1900

Miniaturisation experiment? (c. 1899)

Organic material (wood, etc.) plus metals (various)

Loaned by the Barbican Begg Bequest at the City Museum (note, proprietorship

challenged by Battersea Municipal Museum, by the Lambshead Trust, and by

Greyfriars School, Kent)

L1922.11. bmm/LT/GFS

(Private viewing and reading of associated notes by appointment only.)

Notes

Greyfriars School in Kent claims this odd piece on the grounds that (a) Reverend Bannister was an ex-pupil still funded by the school to perform certain scientific investigations and experiments, and (b) the piece is possibly the work of another of its alumni, the sculptor and scientist John Wolt. Wolt disappeared from his lodgings in 1899, leaving only a brief note suggesting that he intended to take his own life ("My final journey, undertaken voluntarily, should not prove a difficult one, and I could ultimately come face to face with my Creator. Even if a little discomfort is felt, it will be as nothing compared to the joy of bringing the word of Our Saviour to God's tiniest creatures. B. has convinced me of their intelligence and individuality, and therefore they must be possessed of souls, just as St. Francis, apparently, believed that animals, too, have souls. I am filled with humility and ecstasy when I consider that I was their first missionary. Though the transition be painful and not a little difficult, I am assured by B. that all will be well in the ultimate."). This note and others are attached. In Reverend Bannister's remaining journal fragments (the majority were eaten by rats while in storage), he writes for January 1, 1900: "W. proves to be an enthusiast, perfectly willing to aid me in my work. We both feel God has chosen us."

One of the early cases of Seaton Begg ("Sexton Blake," as he was known to readers of detective fiction) was reported as "The Fairy Murders" in the *Union Jack* magazine, a patriotic weekly, of February 16, 1901, featuring Griff the Man-Tracker, probably an invented creature.

This manuscript being by far the most complete, believed the work of Sir David Garnett Blake, great-great-grandson of Sir Sexton Blake of Erring Grange, Erring, Sussex.

The bare facts of the case were as bizarre as they were brief: The small daughter of a Bermondsey tailor claimed that her half-grown cat, Mimi, had eaten a fairy. Of course, no one would believe her, even though she insisted she had seen Mimi nosing around a tiny leg. Rebecca, of course, was rightly punished for telling stories. But a few days later, she came to her mother holding triumphantly a little human ear. The Rabinowitzes, her parents, were unusual in those days in that they were vegetarians. The only meat they bought was for their cat. It came from their local butcher, Jacob "Cocky" Cohen. They inspected the ear and decided it was not human. When they went to Cocky's next, they would complain that monkeys and possibly other animals had been used in the preparation of his cats' meat.

Then Rebecca found part of a miniature arm, dressed in what appeared to be a tiny silk blouse sleeve, and brought this to her horrified parents, who could no longer hide the truth from themselves. The following Tuesday, they confronted the butcher.

Suspecting them of an extortion plan, so before witnesses, including PC Michael McCormac, Cocky began to sort through his supply of cats' meat in order to prove the Rabinowitzes wrong.

To his shocked astonishment, he discovered several items of what could only be human remains, but of such tiny proportions, they were immediately called "Lilliputian," by one of his witnesses, a Dr. Jelinek, Bohemian music teacher, originally of Prague, who would later give his part of the story in German to his sister. Upon informing the police, the witnesses were sworn to secrecy and made to sign Her Majesty's Official Secrets Act, but this did not stop the disgusted Cocky Cohen from taking the case to a young consulting detective who had recently set up practise in Norfolk Street, London E.

Seaton Begg (not yet knighted) would become famous under another name when his adventures were sensationalised and written up for a popular weekly,

An unfortunate participant in an ill-fated conversion

but in those days, he was scarcely a household name. He worked at that time with a gigantic creature of no known breed, whom he had raised and trained and named "Griff," or sometimes "Man-Tracker." An invaluable asset. Begg eagerly undertook to investigate the case, and within hours, Griff had found the source of the butcher's meat. A Battersea slaughterhouse advertised as The Metropolitan Meat Supply Co., which supplied sausages, animal food, fertilizer, and pie-filling to the trade, the firm seemed conscientious as far as its sanitary arrangements were concerned, and had passed its recent inspection with colours flying. When he confronted them, Begg himself considered their professional ethics beyond reproach.

With the help of his strange, unhuman assistant, Griff, Begg next discovered that Metropolitan Meat was being used by a corrupt entrepreneur known as Moses Monk to get rid of unwanted flesh. Aided by an accomplice on the premises, he introduced the meat into MMP's supply. Monk made most of his money by working as a "waste-disposal merchant," employed by unscrupulous merchants to get rid of organic material local councils refused to handle. However, Monk had a rather grislier arrangement with the Brookgate undertakers Ecker and Ecker to dispose of what they termed their "overspill"—paupers who had died without relatives in surrounding London boroughs. The council paid the Eckers by the corpse, supposedly buried in consecrated ground in simple lead coffins. It was far more profitable to let Monk handle the business, no questions asked, and sell the spare plots to grieving relatives. Yet this still did not explain the tiny "fairy" body parts discovered in Bermondsey. Under threat from young Begg and his strange assistant, Griff, Monk eventually confessed.

Of course, it was completely against the law to mix human remains with meat sold for consumption by animals, so Begg was at least responsible for bringing that filthy practise to an end.

The central mystery remained. Who were the "Lilliputians" and why was the government covering up their existence? Once again, Begg decided to put Griff the Man-Tracker on the case. Here is a description of Griff from the original fictionalised report in *Union Jack* no. 356, quoted on the Blakiana Web site:

> Can it be a man—this strange, repulsive creature so stealthily stealing along? Surely no human being was ever so repulsively formed as this? Yet it is garbed as a man!
>
> A bowler hat, long, loosely fitting black overcoat, baggy trousers, tan-coloured spats, and great, ill-shaped boots. But the face! How can we possibly

describe it—or, rather, the little that can be seen of it? The bowler hat is full large for the head, and is drawn down over the forehead and skull, and rests upon large, outstanding, and hair-covered ears. Great blue spectacles, of double lens, cover the eyes and some portion of the visage. The nose is very flat, and of great width of nostrils. The unusual sight of a "respirator" can be seen well covering up the mouth. A great and light-coloured muffler also is so arranged that chin and jaws are both concealed; but what little of the face that can be detected is covered to the cheekbones with short and stiff-looking hair of a dull-brownish colour.

There is something strangely inhuman in the general expression, while the small, round eyes peer through the deep blue glasses like two brilliant sparks of fire.

Of wonderful breadth of shoulder, girth of chest, and length of arm, this is an individual who must be endowed with prodigious strength. A crooked back and bowed legs greatly add to the general grotesque hideousness of the figure as a whole.

This would be the first time that the government stepped in to dissuade Begg from unleashing his horrid assistant (ultimately, Griff would be housed at a facility—he died some time in 1918, where he had been employed in the bloody trench fighting which developed during the first world war), for, within an hour or two of putting Griff on the scene, Begg was summoned to the offices of the Home Secretary Lord Mauleverer, who told him that, since he could not put Begg (younger son of his good friend General Sir Henry Begg) *off* the scent, then he had better put him *on* it. There were two conditions: (1) Griff must be "retired" as soon as possible, and (2) Begg must sign the Official Secrets Act and consider himself to be working not for Cocky, the Bermondsey butcher, but for His Majesty the King. Begg agreed. Turning over all available evidence in the case, Mauleverer commissioned Begg, under oath to the monarch, to investigate the matter as discreetly as possible.

The fictional version is, of course, well known. Clue by clue, Begg tracked down the fairy murderer to a deserted mill in the heart of Kent, where, with a secret grant from "Blackmonk Academy" (easily identified as Greyfriars School), mad scientist "Professor Maxwell Moore" had found a way to grow plants so much like human beings they deceived everyone. His aim was to breed a race of "peace-loving plant people," who would eventually take over from the human race. Begg's first clue was in the cat's refusal to eat vegetable matter.

Typical story-paper rubbish, of course, which satisfied the rumour-mongers when inevitably the tale got out in a garbled form. The truth was far more startling.

At this stage, we must introduce one of the key players—if not *the* key player—in this melodrama:

Orlando Bannister, D.D., the so-called Barmy Vicar of Battersea, at that time enjoying the living of St. Odhrán's, a Methodist and a master of the Portable Harmonium, also amateur inventor, had successfully weighed the human soul but not the mind. As a missionary, he had served for some years in the jungles of Guatemala, where he had become known for his unorthodox views concerning the nature of both dumb animals and even dumber plants. His scientific investigations informed the nature of his theological views. His book *Our Lord in All Things*, in which he argued that every individual blade of grass, every leaf or flower, possessed a rudimentary soul, went into many editions and was in the library of every sentimental lady in the land. The Blavatskyians embraced him. Sales from his book funded his travels and his scientific investigations. A devout Methodist, he was of a missionary disposition and had travelled everywhere on what he amiably called "the Lord's work."

With a fellow evangelist Sir Ranald Frieze-Botham, D.D. founded missions not only in several leading zoological gardens but also a score or so of botanical gardens, most of them in New Zealand.

Having done all he could do for the creatures of the land, at least for the moment, Bannister turned his attention to the deep. He built his rather spectacular Underwater Tramway, or Submersible Juggernaut, in order to carry the story of Creation to the creatures of the sea. He had pretty much exhausted his attempts to bring the Gospel to the Goldfish (as the vulgar press had it) when he happened upon Pasteur's study of microbes and realized his work had hardly begun.

Bannister and Frieze-Botham spent long hours discussing what means they could employ to isolate and introduce the word of God to the world of microorganisms. They did, in fact, receive some funding from Bannister's old school after he had persuaded the board of governors that, if a will to do evil motivated those microbes, then the influence of the Christian religion was bound to have an influence for good. This meant, logically, that fewer boys would be in the infirmary and that, ultimately, shamed by the consequences of their actions, the germs causing, say, tuberculosis would cease to spread.

The crucial step, of course, was how to reduce a missionary, complete with all necessary paraphernalia, to a size tiny enough to contact individual—or, at any rate, small groups of—microbes.

As it happened, Frieze-Botham was in regular correspondence with the inventor Nikola Tesla, who at that point had lost his faith in his adopted homeland of the United States and planned to emigrate to England, where he felt his less conservative ideas would find more fruitful ground. Upon disembarking from the S.S. *Ruritania*, he was at once met by the two divines, who hurried him off to Bannister's vicarage in leafy Balham.

There, Tesla was allowed to set up his Atomic Diminution Engine in what had been the vaults of an old abbey created on the site by the so-called Doubting Friars, or Quasi-Carmelites, in the thirteenth century.

Tesla needed an assistant, so the obvious person was John Wolt, who had been at school with Bannister and Frieze-Botham and was a great admirer of Tesla. He had already read his hero's paper *On Preparing a True Atomic Diminution Engine*, printed privately in Chicago, and could think of no better way of serving both God and Science than helping carry the scriptures to the germs. "Better than trying to persuade the Germans," he quipped, referring to Tesla's humiliating experience in Berlin, which had rejected his electric recoilless gun, among other inventions.

Their work began apace.

Tesla, Wolt, and Frieze-Botham set to work unpacking and assembling the massive crates as they turned up from America. Soon an entire machine took shape in the church basement, and Tesla's mood became increasingly elevated as his dynamos set to mumbling and whistling, then yelped into sudden life, drowning all other sound before being brought under purring control by their master.

"Messieurs, we have our power," declared Tesla in his preferred language. His wife had always preferred it, too.

From what Begg pieced together and lodged under the "50 Years Act," we can see that only Tesla, and perhaps Bannister, survived their attempts to shrink through what Tesla named "metamultiversal plates" down through the alternative universes to near-infinity. Practicing first on dead animals, then on human corpses obtained from Monk (which was what was turning up as parts of "fairies" or "Lilliputians" in the "meat" Monk disposed of through his usual means), the inventor and his colleagues were soon prepared to experiment on living animals and eventually on human subjects—and then themselves. All human subjects were volunteers and paid well, but only advanced to the first and second levels. Four died, all at what was called "the first level of descent." Which was when Monk, who had supplied the corpses, now offered to take them off the vicar's hands. He was growing rich on what they paid him and rather neglecting his usual dumping business.

When Tesla was satisfied that no harm could possibly come to human organs subjected to his electrics, he announced that he was ready to send a living creature straight through into what he termed the Intra-Universe, or Second Aether, down to worlds subtly different but ranged according to scale and mass so that the smaller one became the denser one, and the larger the more amorphous. The process had to be endured by degrees, stepping down a level at a time. All the laboratory guinea pigs used returned safely and indicated what was likely to happen to a human subject. At the first level, one remained small but visible and yet one's normal weight. At the second level, one vanished from human sight, though one's weight could still be measured as identical and the subject could be observed through a microscope; and at the third level, far more powerful instruments were needed until the traveller vanished completely from the scale, and weight became meaningless in the context. Wolt would, at his own request, be the first to be sent "downscale."

Tesla was by no means oblivious of concern. He was nervous. He asked Wolt over and over if he felt ready. He received a steady affirmative. And so, the process began as Wolt stepped into the apparatus and the tall bell jar was lowered over him until it came to rest on the sturdy mahogany plinth. Lights and gauges let into the wood indicated the progress as Tesla's dials and graphs began precise measurement of the man's molecular structure before sending him on the first stage of his journey. Wolt carried with him portable versions of the crucial instruments, together with Dr. Bannister's patented Portable Harmonium and a case of Bibles. On his left were the controls he would use for his return through five groups of six levels. Before returning, however, he would establish a base camp, where, before he returned, he planned to leave the majority of items he took with him.

The others watched eagerly and with concern the first transition, which the guinea pigs were known to have survived. Before their eyes, within a glorious, pale green aura, Wolt grew smaller and smaller until, triumphantly brandishing his Bible, he disappeared from view—to reappear in the viewing screen of the electric microscope still waving, evidently in good health. Another stage, and Wolt could be observed staring in awe at the lush, almost infinite world of the Submicroscopic.

He could be seen to consult his Bible at this point, and begin to preach. He was still preaching when he vanished at last from human ken, beyond the range of all Tesla's detection devices.

Now the men waited impatiently. Would Wolt return safely?

Hours went by. Tesla, who always ate voraciously when nervous, sent out for sandwiches.

And then, as dawn began to touch the horizon with a delicate grey, Wolt's image popped onto the microscope lens, and soon he was looking up at them and showing them that apart from his crucifix, he was empty-handed.

Another ten minutes, and a breathless, grinning Wolt stepped from his plinth with stories of wonderful landscapes, new spectra, and sometimes dangerous types of flora and fauna—all, he felt sure, waiting to be instructed in the ways of the Bible. He was full of the emotions and feelings he had experienced in the other world. He had feared he might be descending into Hell, but instead he had been close to Heaven. "Ah, the ecstasy." He had felt at one with the raw stuff with which God made the world. Far from reporting failure, Wolt was almost raving about his success. There were intelligent creatures in our bloodstreams, discussing ideology that could destroy or save our world, and when their fight was decided, so our fate was decided. Not only could these creatures learn from the Bible; it was a matter of grave urgency that they be converted to the Christian faith as quickly as possible. "Whole armies of missionaries are needed down there!" Wolt insisted. He would help train them, perhaps draw maps from the sketches he had made.

Overjoyed, the three Methodists congratulated Tesla, who was anxious to remind them that the work was still at an early stage. Privately, he wondered if Wolt had experienced a series of delusions and was merely mad.

As Begg wrote in his report to the Home Office: "They did not know what the effects on a living human brain might be, let alone to what harm his body had been exposed. There could be terrible side-effects, which might materialise in days or even years, produced by the rapid change of size while retaining the same mass."

Wolt spoke of "making holes in the cosmos," and nobody was sure what that meant. Nonetheless, the experiment seemed to have proven everything they had considered in theory. Bannister, in particular, was anxious to make the next trip. Wolt drew him a map, showing where, protected from the strange elements of the submicroscopic world, he had left the Bibles, the Portable Harmonium, and all the other materials that had accompanied him. With more Bibles, perhaps some firearms for self-defence, and provided with food and a few other necessities, they could probably remain in the Second Aether for months. The four men celebrated, inflamed by the knowledge that they had found new worlds to conquer for their beloved Saviour.

Although Wolt was anxious to return, they decided to send another of their company and drew lots, Frieze-Botham winning the right to be the next to descend. He took another case of Bibles, more supplies of soap, tinned butter, bully beef and so forth, ammunition and firearms. His experience was pretty much identical to Wolt's. He reported a rather peaceful scene, with herds of oddly shaped herbivores moving placidly through dimensionless veldts and forests whose crowns were invisible. More like fresh coral than anything above the waves, said Frieze-Botham on his return. He said he felt like some heavy sea-beast brought by gravity to the only depths it could comfortably negotiate. And, at last, it was the eager cleric's turn to experience what he had, after all, first sought to explore. Equipping himself with more Bibles, bully beef, and bullets, he gave the signal to Tesla and ultimately was gone.

This time, however, the hours became slow days as the trio prayed that no accident had come to Bannister. Tesla cursed himself for not rigging up some kind of subatomic telephone. A week was to pass before the apparatus began to flicker and spark, and still the men did not dare to hope. When all was over, they stared into an empty stage. Only the controls and wires were to be seen, perfectly intact, as also were the levers and gauges.

Before the others could stop him, Wolt had vaulted the brass rail and given the signal to raise the bell. "It's up to me to find him. Don't try to stop me. I know those timeless, dimensionless spaces like the back of my hand." He then remembered to call for the last Portable Harmonium, the only instrument to send out sounds loud enough for the reverend to hear. His crucifix clutched to his chest, Wolt gave the signal to begin the descent across the planes of the multiverse into what were essentially alternate worlds. Tesla and Frieze-Botham remained to operate the equipment and rack their brains for further means of communicating with the micronauts.

This time, the apparatus was back in minutes, rocking crazily and empty of most supplies. A crazed and battered Wolt, his clothing in shreds, fell from the gigantic bell and reeled to the rail of the crypt, mouthing a single word: *"Sham-alung."* And that was all. Next, he seemed to remind himself of something and, reaching into the jar, clambered back aboard the machine. He pulled two levers, then waved from the apparatus as it disappeared on another journey down the dimensions. The two observers were at a loss to control what was happening.

But the next time it returned, it came bearing a different passenger successfully up through stage five and four, and made it shakily through three before jamming at two, showing a small Orlando Bannister, brass crucifix in one hand, a Bible lying on the surrounds of the ruined electrics next to some loose notes,[1] as if from a book,[2] and a small Portable Harmonium, which, on further inspection, proved to be a perfect working model. The figure of Bannister appeared to be made of a very heavy metal, so far unidentified, and was exquisitely carved, impossible to tell from its original.

Tesla and the others knew exactly what had happened, realising the effect of repeated atomic shifts on a living creature, especially a creature of Bannister's venerable years. His atoms had atrophied, as the few knowledgeable scientists of the day described the process. What was a lifelike statue to the world, was really the last remains of a brilliant scientific mind and a man of almost childlike faith in the workings of his Maker. The apparatus was eventually dismantled, after Tesla and Frieze-Botham had worked for almost a year attempting to reverse time and to rescue Wolt, but it was as if, said Frieze-Botham, growing increasingly spiritual, the Almighty had made it clear that these experiments, however innocent and moved by faith, were to cease.

To this day, people interested in such things continue to debate the meaning of the word "Shamalung," but, as yet, no credible interpretation has been offered. It could be from any one of millions of microbe languages.

ENDNOTES

1. Subsequently much enlarged, each a perfect page of writing, sadly not sequential, in OB's hand.
2. See above.

Pulvadmonitor:
The Dust's Warning

Researched and Documented by China Miéville

British Dental Association Museum
64 Wimpole Street, London

Xanthe Serkis (British, 1903–1953), Thomas Thomas (British, 1890–1964)
Pulvadmonitor; the Dust's Warning (c. 1937–1952, 1952–1986)
Glass, wood, brass, leather, wire, mechanisms, dentures, dust
Undocumented (twice)

To be discovered is the task and telos of an artefact. Its historic mission is to be born, midwifed into the light like any other whelp, pulled out of the earth or delivered from a long-forgotten cupboard womb. It dies when it is born, of course: and its post-birth duties in the museum where we trap it are an afterlife in a most literal sense, and as drab, doubtless, as quotidianly dull as the afterlives that await us. It is best to avoid consideration of what it is we commit when we investigate: curation is an unkindness we perpetrate against objects and we must hope their revenge is endlessly deferred. After all, we must do it. To be themselves, all artefact are born once.

—THACKERY T. LAMBSHEAD, "THE VIOLENT PHILOSOPHY OF THE ARCHIVE"

when because it comes and
what may we say among those things
shall not be if we have shame enough for truth
that we were not warned

—UNKNOWN, "ODE TO EVERYTHING"

1. The Second Birth

In 1986, under a brisk new administration, the British Dental Association Museum, until then an institution that had been allowed to tick over in a relatively sedate manner, somewhat insulated from the ravages of visitors, was subjected to a vigorous clearout and cleaning. What, in their later paper, the Trades Union Congress called "this notorious Cleansing Event" was conducted in an atmosphere of laissez-faire vim, blamed by some participants for several breakages and the disappearances of at least four artefacts. Considerably less discussed— meriting only an oblique and en passant mention in *Thatcher's Mops*, Cecily Fetchpaw's otherwise exhaustive book on the subject—is what was uncovered in the museum attic as it was emptied of cardboard boxes, spider corpses, and long-ossified cleaning products.

The agency staff, they later testified, hesitated as they ascended the stepladders at a sound they thought was a gas leak. When, gingerly, their team-leader raised her head through the hatch and scanned the area with her torch, she was shocked initially to realise how much further the unlit room extended. Immediately, she was shocked, and much more violently, again, when the light reached into a low triangular nook below a staircase at the windowless chamber's rear, onto the heads of a sarcophagus and an antique Anubis, various other items of Egyptiana, and a bell jar containing a head, on the floor, eyes at the level of her eyes. What caused her, it emerged, to stagger on her precarious perch, fall, and break her hip, was when the ash-coloured lips behind the glass moved.

Word spread, of course. A number of staff bypassed the inefficient, jury-rigged security and went to look. This was an age before camera phones, but someone procured the Polaroid used for artefact records, and there exist three bad pictures of inquisitive students of dental surgery and museum workers ranged around the bell jar in what looks like worship. Even such inadequate still images give a sense of the atmosphere at the scene. According to those present, the head, though it did not at any point open its eyes, moved its mouth and bit startlingly white teeth, hard enough that the chattering was audible through the bell-jar glass. Next to it, wired up to it, hissing faintly and clattering like a telegraph machine, was a battery or engine, with gently pulsing gauges.

"We didn't shine the lights on it too hard," according to one of the cleaners. "Not too often. It seemed like that might be a bit . . . much for its eyes." "It definitely wasn't alive," according to the Head of Dentures. "No way. Yes, I know it was moving. But it was grey, grey, grey. And dry. Mummified or saponified or something. No, I don't know how it was moving. Electricity or something. No, I don't know. I have nothing more to say."

Even by the indirect light, the extraordinary texture of the head was clear. It moved in small spasms, creasing its dun self in unnatural directions. "Not like a head," one witness said. Its teeth, gleaming from behind dirt-coloured lips,

Another unfortunate participant

ceramic-white and vivid, look in the photographs overlaid on the picture like a crude collage, part of a wholly different image with a quite different palate. At seconds when the dials on the little motor twitched, the face might slightly crease its eyes or wince as if in pain, in response or cause, it was impossible to say.

It was not long until a small team of uniformed men and women arrived and declared the attic out of bounds. They hauled equipment up the ladder and in, and the staff on duty on the floor below grew used to the scuffing sounds of whatever their investigations were. It was two days before anyone from the museum realised that what the visitors wore were not scene-of-crime police overalls, although similar. The women and men who had received the information about the find and were performing their forensics in the attic were not police. (It was, indeed, for exactly such exigencies as this accidental discovery, and not for the spurious reasons set out elsewhere in this volume, that Professor Lambshead kept his extensive network of sleeper agents on retainer at most museums worldwide.) Before any scandal could ensue, Lambshead himself had arrived from his Polish trip and arranged a private meeting with the head of the Dental Museum, in the aftermath of which the police were never called and the cut of the director's clothes improved.

> it is not through pages turning to elements
> nor through liminals nor tumbling streets
> and there is no etherized sky above us as we
> that we walk only rather by this cleanest
> steel yet this steel glass this tough clean material
> also sheds time's exhaust

—UNKNOWN, "ODE TO EVERYTHING"

1.2. The Damascene Moment

The famous Lambshead passage at the start of this entry, from the "Violent Philosophy . . . ," has been repeatedly parsed and interpreted, according to most hermeneutics going. What had, until the discovery in the Dental Museum attic, been less universally considered was the asterisk that beckoned at that paragraph's end, to whisper its content from page bottom: "*At least* once, we should say. And what of the artefact that is born twice? What of such ontological profligacy? Deep understanding seems to slide with appearance, reappearance; now inspiring, now gone."

The existence of the object in the museum attic was no secret from Lambsheadians from the time of its discovery, but it was not considered a major piece, and was not much studied (even allowing for difficulties of access), until events at the notorious 2005 Conference on Lambshead Studies drew researchers' attention to it. Auto-argumentative footnotes such as the one quoted here have always commanded the attention of a small subgroup of specialist Lambsheadologists; dissidents among dissidents, the Digressionists, who insisted that these were the keys, bloated with import, master codes, the texts to which they pretended to be adjuncts, messages to be unpicked. Condemned by more traditional textualists as tendentious, they insisted that this particular passage, for example, must refer to an artefact known not merely to have been found and lost again, but to have been discovered twice, unique and different each time.

Determined to humiliate them and destroy the credibility of these avant-garde heretics, the leading scholars of mainstream Lambsheadianism invited Simone Mukhopadhay, the most eloquent of the Digressionists, to a debate with Alan Demont, secretary of Lambshead Studies. As Demont started his careful demolition job, focusing on what he insisted was the lack of deep meaning in the "Twice-born Footnote" above, as it was called, from "The Violent Philosophy of the Archive," his eight-year-old daughter (who was present at the session, crèche facilities unavailable, and who was drawing a tiger on the back of, and a forest in the margins of a printout of his paper) interrupted him, in front of the audience, to point out that the first letters of the last, oddly syntaxed sentence of that footnote spelled out a message. (She had picked out the relevant letters with crayoned flowers.)

Lambshead, it transpired, was more than a curator of this piece; he was, indeed, unusually active in its creation. From that Rosetta-stone footnote moment, identifying as it did the object of its own attention, it was a relatively short time until, by dint of intense and sometimes destructive rummaging through the doctor's effects, papers, and above all his diaries, first the identity, then the story of the twice-found object and, to a limited extent, Lambshead's peripheral and unclear role in its creation, came out. So many mentions of so many objects litter those extraordinarily extensive records that it is often only with such external prods that the distinctions between items of importance, and pretty rocks or banged together bits of wood with which Lambshead was momentarily taken, can be ascertained. These passages had been read many times, but no one had put them together, until that acronym came to light, and the memory of the attic, and the specific anecdote became important.

Here the focus must be on the reconstructed story: the history, prehistory, and two births of the artefact itself, the Pulvadmonitor. Or, in the name given it by Lambshead's acronym, about the deep understanding that seems to slide with appearance, and so on: the Dust's Warning.

> *will you your will?*
> *will it to me.*
> *I will you mine.*

—Unknown, "Ode to Everything"

2. The First Birth

The professor, though a man of science, was a polymath. He enjoyed the company of, and endeavoured to participate in salons and discussion groups with, artists, writers, poets, and various other representatives of *La bohème.* One from such a milieu was the literary critic Thomas Thomas. It was to Lambshead that Thomas came in 1952, begging his help, bearing a large box and several books. Lambshead was surprised to see him, as their particular circle had mostly attenuated by the mid-1940s, and it was some years since he and Thomas had been in each other's company.

After abbreviated pleasantries, Thomas explained his message and presence. He had been put in an awkward position, he explained, by Xanthe Serkis, and seeking Lambshead's advice. Serkis was a critic, known to the professor, but only very slightly, a good decade previously. When he had met her, she had been working on a book about David Gascoyne and other British surrealists.

"That's correct," Thomas told him. "She still is. That's rather the point."

In a pre-echo of Thomas's approach to Lambshead, Serkis, who had absented herself from the poetic and critical scene for several months, had recently and aggressively contacted Thomas, demanding to see him. Some months earlier, Serkis had received, she told him, a copy of Gascoyne's *Man's Life Is This Meat,* preceding the 1936 Parton Press edition. She had shown it to him, and he described it to Lambshead: imperfectly printed, the publisher Down-Dandelion Press, its colophon showing a stylised upside-down flower, its roots above the earth, its bloom below. In content, it was largely the same as the later official editions, except for a few differences of punctuation, and, the one substantial difference, a whole extra poem inserted into the text. Its title was "Ode to Everything."

Serkis had received the book in the post. That she did not remember ordering it did not surprise her overmuch: as a critic of solid though unorthodox reputation, she received a good deal of material unsolicited, most of it from small presses anxious to gain her mention. There was, however, no return address, no covering note, no enclosure of any kind. She could find no details on Down-Dandelion Press from any of her usual sources, and later and exhaustive searches failed to turn up any more copies of the book. Gascoyne himself, whom she knew though not well, denied any knowledge of the copy or the poem, and seemed mildly amused but not very interested by them.

In truth, Serkis hadn't felt much different at first, thinking the book some illicit curio, a mischievous thing put together from a proof, leaked to her with, she vaguely assumed, the "Ode . . ." inserted to draw attention—camouflaged by Gascoyne's minor but real reputation—to another, shyer poet's work. "She told Thomas," Lambshead's journals read, "that she had included a one-line mention of the odd edition in her monograph. Then padded that one line with another. Returned again, to add some few words, on the subject of the ode itself, interpreting it, with a tendentious and provocative heuristic, as if it *were*, in fact, one of Gascoyne's, to see what it told us about the rest of his corpus."

The teleology is clear. Lambshead recounts Thomas's recollections. "What started as that mention became a paragraph, then a chapter—a chapter devoted to an interloping poem!—then a whole section. Abruptly, it was the subject of her book, still at first, in an increasingly absurd pretence, discussed as if Gascoyne had written it, until the title had been changed to *Anon's Ode*. But that was not the end of it, either. Her focus did not stop. Had continued down like the switching and switching of a microscope's field of focus, probing no longer the whole poem but one section, stanza, on down."

Thomas had brought a copy of the "Ode to Everything," the initial stanzas of which read to Lambshead, he tells us, like a rather too-unreconstructed riff on one thing or another, though here and there, a turn of phrase—"this minatory summer," he mentions; "your felt-silenced castanets"; "the slander that a lizard feels no love"—startled him. (The few snips and stanzas that he reproduces, in passing praise, reproduced again here, are all we have. The poem, indeed the book, the few details available, are untraceable. Nor does the Internet help us, whatever the search string.)

Months of research, she had told Thomas; hundreds of pages of notes; reams of started, interrupted, and restarted chapters—all of which she brought out in sheaves and bundles and laid across his desk to prove her point—and Serkis had been moved to write her monograph entirely on one line: "What does the dust wish to tell us?"

"That's the question," she told Thomas. "That's the only question."

Thomas, quailing, had gently prodded, offered to read her book, and she had looked at him with bewildered anger. She swept her papers off his table. Forget the book, she said. The book, she assured him, was no longer the focus of her work. Thomas had understood abruptly that what had been a project of interpretation had become one of lunatic detection. She was not, as he had thought at first, applying her considerable critical skills to the eight-word question: she was, rather, attempting to answer it. What does the dust wish to tell us?

She had opened her box. She had brought out for Thomas a glass dome, its base connected to that mockery of a battery. From the front of the dome jutted a flared tube, and rattling around within the glass, unsecured, were a pair of dentures. The two of them had regarded the collection of equipment for some time, in silence. "It took me three years of physics," Serkis said, "but I worked out how to build it."

"I need you to look after it," Serkis said. "I have a fear."

" 'By this time, old man, as you can imagine,' Thomas said to me, 'I had my doubts about poor old Xanthe's sanity,' " Lambshead wrote. " 'And where are you going?' I asked her. Answer, as she left, came there none." Thomas, aware in vague terms of his friend's interests and predilections, had immediately decided to bring it to Lambshead. As for Xanthe, neither Thomas, nor Lambshead saw her again.

What would have looked to the nonspecialist like a disconnected pile of rubbish was not something Lambshead, with his considerable experience, would ever dismiss out of hand, of course. For two weeks, he fiddled. He put his ear close to the speaking tube. He tinkered with the battery. When one combination of switches were switched, he records, he heard a tiny hiss: pushed another way, he heard nothing. What the dials measured remained opaque to him, but measure it they did, tweaking and jumping in response to he knew not what. He, attuned to the importance of time, left the bell jar alone for several days. He waited, one of his assistants reported, "with more than mere patience." On his return, all was as it had been.

"I gave it one last shake," he writes, "listened to the rattle of the teeth through that upturned speaking trumpet, and nothing else."

A year and three months after his visit from Thomas—during one of his periodic clear-outs of artefacts for which he no longer had space, or in which he no longer had interest, or which were "not working"—the professor is believed to have given what we later came to know as the Pulvadmonitor to the Dental Museum; on the grounds, presumably, that what it appeared to be designed to showcase, if for reasons beyond him, were the disaggregated dentures. In the museum itself, sterling detective work has uncovered an acquisition note for what is recorded simply as "Item," on which note is an irate scribbled exchange in two hands: "What the hell am I supposed to do with this?" "Bung it in the bloody attic."

Where, undisturbed, it did not so much languish as prepare itself for its second birth, for more than thirty years.

> beyond any fog
> in which copyright has been asserted
> is where the geese live

—UNKNOWN, "ODE TO EVERYTHING"

3. The Internatal Decades

Lambshead quickly ascertained, after the second birth of what was later named Pulvadmonitor, that it was too fragile to be moved. It remained, and remains, in the attic of the Dental Museum. It was simple, with the resources and unorthodox measuring equipment to which Lambshead had access, to ascertain that, contrary to the assumption made by all other observers in the team, no long-mummified head had been placed within the container to be minutely animated by current from the battery. There was no residue of any matter transference. The head was not a speaker of, or for, the dead.

The realisation came, at last, according to the simpler exigency of placing a hand over the mouth of the trumpet, and observing the start of a slow collapse and agitation in the face within, that rather than a speaking tube leading out, it was a funnel drawing in.

A little super-gentle unscrewing of the outer rim, and Lambshead uncovered a filter like a finely holed sieve, clogged by now with three decades of hairs and larger airborne particles. This he cleaned and replaced. There was another, finer-grained filter further down the tube. The inside of the bell jar was under constant negative pressure. Air emerged from the grille at its base, but it was sucked in fractionally quicker through the trumpet, and from it was removed in stages the larger scobs of airborne debris, so that what it deposited at last within the long-undisturbed glass was a constant, extraordinarily slow, stream of London dust.

And it was from thirty-plus years of that dust that the head within had slowly self-organised. Around the palate and fake gums and teeth from which it could make a mouth.

"She did it," Lambshead was to write. "My poor lost friend Serkis. She found a means to give the dust a voice."

neither lens nor cheque can clear for you
nor shall this cat and nor shall these beaked bones intervene

—UNKNOWN, "ODE TO EVERYTHING"

4. The Dust's Warning

With this realisation, it became doubly imperative that the object not be moved, the battery not turned off (not that any researcher knew what combination of dials and switches might perform that action, nor how it had been left in an "on" position initially). The tiny chatterings and whisperings of the head were already enough to strain the integrity of the desiccated coagulum, held together by air pressure and the willpower of dust clearly desperate to communicate a message.

If the mouth opens—for it opens still now—more than the tiniest crack, the lines of the face go deep, and a little avalanche of mouse-back-coloured substance spills away. Its shape is constantly replenished by the slow intake from the funnel, and so long as the losses occasioned by such linguistic exigencies are in balance with that new matter, the head can sustain itself. A sudden movement, a loss of power, and the face-slide would be catastrophic.

Anyone who wishes to study or learn from the Pulvadmonitor must scooch uncomfortably down on the attic floor, to its eye level, more or less, making their notes in the dim illumination of field lights (more permanent alterations to the room to accommodate a better display would cause vibrations that might destroy the emissary).

Almost all our questions remain unanswered. Why does the dust not open its eyes? What nature of eyes exist, indeed, if any, below those powder lids? Was it some sense of propriety that led the dust to construct the top of a collar, as if it was the bust only of a full person? As if, having decided to mimic our shape to make the transmission of information easier, in consideration for our psychology, there was no point in doing less than a thorough job. And, on the other side, what uncanny intuition for transubstantial courtesy was it that led Xanthe Serkis to place teeth ready for the soft-palateless dust, that it had grown around and constructed its dust-lips around, to ease its shaping of our words?

Of course, the main question has always been, what is the dust's warning?

no

no no no

o really?

yes no

—Unknown, "Ode to Everything"

5. The Tragedy of Design

There can be no doubting the urgency of whatever message it is the dust wishes to convey. Whenever footprints, be they ever so careful, cross the floor towards it, it appears to become aware that it has watchers. Its mouth moves as quickly as it dares, it speaks as eagerly as its substance allows, its teeth, those little ceramic flashes in otherwise quite matt, quite indistinguishable dun skin, chatter like a telegraph operator. It wants to tell us something.

The funnel is just in front of its lips, so tantalisingly like the speaking tube we know it is not. It might even operate like one, amplifying its breathless voice enough for us to hear, but that the soft current of air from *out to in* effaces whatever minutely whispered phrases the head might speak. Its voice is so faint that not even stethoscopes on the glass can help. It is simply inaudible. Only the click of those teeth can be heard, and if they tap in code, it is not one amenable to our codebreakers.

Of course, lip-readers of countless languages have been brought to watch the head, to decipher its words. What is most frustrating of all to dust-watchers is not that none of them can discern any meaning but rather that they often see a few phrases, always disputed, never quite clear.

Two English-speaking lip-readers have claimed the dust said *this dog will never be your friend* amid a stream of meaningless syllables. An Italianophone claimed that it told her three times to *cross the bridge. It is too late for the light* has been seen spoken in four languages. In 2002, a Hindi reader and a Finnish one both claimed to have read the lips *at the same moment,* the first seeing *stop up all these gaps before it comes,* the latter *consider where your own bones go.*

Opinion is divided as to how to proceed. Lambshead was a pessimist on this issue. "As Lichtenberg said of angels," he wrote in one of his last letters, "so I say of dust. If they, or it, ever could speak to us, why in God's name should we understand?"

Two things remain unclear, and intemperately debated. One is the origin of the quiet Egyptian heads that watch the Pulvadmonitor, the Dust's Warning, approvingly. They were not a gift from Lambshead. No one knows their provenance, and there is no record of their arrival.

185

The second concerns the "Violent Philosophy of the Archive." This essay, in which is the footnote where first is mentioned the Dust's Warning, and which hints at the importance of its (second) birth, was found in a sheaf of Lambshead's papers dating from the mid-1980s and published posthumously. What is controversial is precisely when it was written. Textual evidence suggests that while it might have been just after, it could very well have been just before, the nook in the museum attic was uncovered. The question is whether, in other words, Lambshead was musing on something recently discovered; or was waiting impatiently for something that he had prepared to be found again.

The dust doubtless knows the answer, and its agitated efforts notwithstanding, can tell us, and warn us of, nothing.

The Miéville Anomalies

The following art from China Miéville and accompanying descriptions by writer Helen Oyeyemi and "philosopher prince" Reza Negarestani first came to our attention by an exceedingly circuitous route that started with an anonymous e-mail that linked to a long article on Lambshead's "secret past" published by an Athens newspaper. A week later, a letter with a Malaysian postmark arrived from someone named only "Incognitum," who claimed to belong to a secret radical society devoted to change "through extreme re-contextualization and cross-pollination." The envelope contained a key to decode the article. Two weeks after that development, the editors of this volume had an unpleasant encounter with a masked stranger who shadowed the house for two weeks before leaving a rather less encrypted message on the garage door.

Decoding the article revealed the text for "The Very Shoe" and "The Gallows-horse." Photographs of the crudely related pictographs on the garage door with the initials "CM" scrawled beside them were sent to the agent of China Miéville, whose sole response was to provide the two images reproduced herein. Failed attempts were made to telephone both Helen Oyeyemi and the Philosopher Army or "Shield Wall" dedicated to preventing Reza Negarestani from being contaminated by the world.

Although these inquiries yielded no direct results, we subsequently received permissions to reprint from the same Malaysian address, which a Google Earth search revealed to be an empty lot in Kuala Lumpur. Thus, while we present this material as "in the spirit" of the cabinet, we cannot verify that Dr. Lambshead ever possessed such a shoe, or such a gallows-horse. As of this writing, there seem few options for obtaining further information. (It was a condition of Miéville's participation in this compilation "and any future project that you may wish to pursue with him until either his demise or your own," per telephone conversations with his designated "metamorphosis attaché," that we not question him further on the subject.)

The Very Shoe

As Told to and Compiled by Helen Oyeyemi

Created: circa 1940–1941

Creator: Radim Kasparek (1901–1971) of Bohumil, Moravia

Materials: Silk and canvas, with leather uppers, glass strip (3 cm), pinewood heel. Antenna: galvanized steel. Inner compartment (low-grade balsa wood, cotton lining) and accompanying window (low-grade balsa wood, 10 denier nylon) at the front of the outer sole added at a later date by person/s unknown

Property of: Petra Neumann née Tichy (1970–), legal owner of shoe as per inheritance. Lambshead's diary notes that "the most curious shoe" arrived in the first post on September 28, 1995, in a box postmarked Lausanne, accompanied by a note dated "October 1990": "I trust you, Lambshead—inasmuch as I can be bothered to trust anybody. We are forbidden to bring material possessions to the monastery, so I leave this in your hands. Its value is beyond measure to me. It is my great-aunt's shoe—the other one is lost, but the story in the family is that when Ludmila first saw the pair she was absolutely thrilled, clasped her hands together, and said in her best English: 'They're just too very very!' So I call it 'the Very Shoe.' This thing is a witness, my friend. It stands by and it does not change its story. Extend the antenna and listen. Then tell me: am I mad, or are there still miracles in the world?" It can be seen that the doctor underlined the words "the monastery" and surrounded them with red exclamation marks, and indeed, the location and affiliation of this "monastery" Neumann mentions is unknown; subsequently, so are Neumann's current whereabouts. The only other extant note from Neumann to Lambshead mentioning this institution is found among his papers—Neumann describes "the monastery" as "a place you go to learn conversation with stones, to find out what it is stones know."

Accession number: L1990.43

The story of this shoe is quite a plain one, I'm afraid—the shoe has no ethnographic significance, nor does it have anything as exciting as a curse or a long-standing feud associated with it. It was made by a man who was not exactly poor, but close enough. He was awkward-looking, and he stammered because he was shy, and he always said the wrong thing to women, so they didn't like him. He believed that he was born to loneliness. He ended up alone, so maybe he was. There was a William Blake poem that he muttered to himself as he worked, joining soles and heels:

> *Man was made for joy and woe;*
> *And when this we rightly know*
> *Through the world we safely go . . .*

(there's more but it is a long poem)

> *. . . Every night and every morn*
> *Some to misery are born.*
> *Every morn and every night*
> *Some are born to sweet delight.*
> *Some are born to sweet delight,*
> *Some are born to endless night.*

And yet, and yet, Radim got a wife. A woman of elegance, a dancer. Ludmila. She had dainty, beautiful feet, with the highest and most pliant arches Radim had ever seen. The glass panel on the side of the shoe is titillation, designed to show a mere hint of a beautiful curve. Ludmila was of the Romani. One day, some soldiers and some doctors came to Bohumil, and they separated the Romani men from the Romani women, and made inspections of their health. The soldiers and the doctors found Ludmila even though she lived in a house with Radim—vigilant neighbours informed them that some of the Romani lived in houses now, so they knocked on doors. Ludmila's health was excellent, and the following week she was sent a letter, ordering her to settle her affairs before a certain date, twenty-eight days away. Then, on the date given, she must go to a camp at Lety and serve as a labourer. Radim began to make plans for the two of them to run away together, but Ludmila would not run. Radim applied to go to the labour camp with her, but his application was refused. So he made her a pair of shoes, because he didn't know what else to do. Ludmila danced for him the night before she went to the camp, and he was afraid that he'd made the heel too high. The next afternoon, Radim's younger brother, Artur, went around to Radim's shop to see how he was holding up after Ludmila's departure. Radim told him about the dancing: "At one point she was simply spinning, round and round. And so fast, her face was a blur. It looked dangerous. And she said—*I can't stop! Catch me!* And I did. But what about when she's over there? What if—"

(What if she can't stop? It was silly to ask such a question. That would be the least of her worries; even a fool could see that.)

Years later, Radim and Artur Kasparek went to that camp at Lety, where many, many Czech Romani were sent—the brothers went down on their knees amongst others who were also on their knees, and they searched a great hill of shoes, listening to cries of grief and cries of dismay: "They all look the same. . . ."

When they found this shoe, the brothers knew that Ludmila had died at Lety. They would not have to go to Auschwitz, where some five hundred of the labourers had been sent, and search the shoes there. Radim and Artur puzzled over the addition of the window to the structure of the shoe; then, with a finger, Radim pierced the scraps of stocking that hung over the window and brushed gnawed bits of newspaper out of the compartment, newspaper and breadcrumbs and little bits of crumbled sugar. A mouse had been nesting in there. A pet—Ludmila had had a pet, at least. Radim looked for the second shoe. He looked and looked, but he couldn't find it. Night came, and he and Artur slept beside the pile, woke at dawn and kept searching, but by the end of the second day, they knew the other shoe was gone.

(For validation purposes, I should perhaps say something about who I am, and how I have come by this information. I am Antonin Neumann, Petra Neumann's husband. The first time I took her to dinner, she told me she could never love anyone who ate their soup the way I did. I didn't see anything wrong with the way I ate my soup, but I tried to change it. She laughed, and repeated herself. It demoralized me. I was reduced to asking for a very simple thing: her friendship, her respect. Then she made a U-turn and said she didn't care either way, but we could get married if I liked.

I am a jeweller by trade, and I can say, without overstating my situation in any respect, that I am a rich man. Still, I have not known happiness for many years. Petra went off on her wild-goose chase without doing me the courtesy of announcing her plans, and I haven't heard from her since. Talking to stones . . .

I suppose I could fall in love with someone else, or, at the very least, distract myself with some other love, but I don't want to. I've been tracing Petra's family tree instead. With money, you can buy whole lives; you have only to wait until they have been lived. I've been reading diaries, reading letters of the most trivial kind, travelling, looking into the faces of her forebears and finding her there. I don't think I'll show her anger when she returns: my time has not been wasted. Somehow we've grown closer, much closer than we could have grown if she had been sat by my side all these years, much closer than most lovers ever get. Needless to say, I'm grateful to have been asked to produce the notes on this item.)

I'll get on with it now.

Radim Kasparek's younger brother, Artur, is still living. The things I have written are things he dictated to me. He says that Radim first saw Ludmila at a bonfire—there was a fiddler there, and he saw her at the edge of the crowd, knee-deep in shadow, and she chose his shadow, Radim's shadow, and she danced with it, and she came near . . . and he thought—"Is it *me* she's coming to? Can she mean it? She cannot mean it." Radim wrote this down. His thoughts about Ludmila. She was like a reed—when she moved, you saw her and you saw what moved her. She opened her hand to him. Here is the wind. She came still nearer, and Radim offered her his cup, and she drank mead from it, and she greeted him in a language he didn't understand.

Artur says he didn't talk to Ludmila much. She was only interested in Radim, and dancing, and her people.

"Want to know what that brother of mine spent his life savings on?" Artur asked when I visited him. He still lives in Bohumil with his wife, two doors away from the shop and the flat above it, where Radim and Ludmila lived for two years. He showed me a blackened patch on the roof, where lightning had struck years ago; he showed me two blocks of space that were lighter than the tile that surrounded them. At first, I didn't really take in what he was telling me, because I was nervous that he should fall or injure himself in some other mysterious way that only those over eighty are capable of.

But the gist of the matter is this: Radim Kasparek bought two wide-ranging transmitters, hi-tech stuff back then, though it looks almost pre-mechanical now. He placed the transmitters on the roof, and he played music for Ludmila to dance to. Nothing especially tasteful, or sophisticated, nothing that outlasted the era—saccharine waltzes, mainly. And he recorded his voice, and he transmitted that, too. He'd only say a couple of things—he was none too imaginative, and he was unsure that the messages would really go from Bohumil to Lety, and he was wary, too, of saying too much, of his voice being heard by others tuned into that frequency. Still, it was a nice idea. When he returned from his trip to the camp of Lety, he stopped the transmissions, though he left the transmitters on the roof, left everything in place until the storm that finished it all off six or seven years later.

That's the story of the Very Shoe—but there's just one thing more. On the back of one of my Petra's letters to him, Lambshead scrawled some words I recognize.

Ludmila, jsem s tebou.

Miluju tě, Ludmila, víc než kdy jindy . . . víc než kdy jindy.

How do I recognize these words?

I have heard them.

Don't ask me how this works, reader, when the transmitters are gone, and the man and the woman involved are deep in the ground, miles and miles apart. And anyway, even if the transmitters were still there, they would be in Moravia, and this shoe is now in Wimpering-on-the-Brook! I don't know how this works, and it's a headache even trying to think my way around it, but—pick up this shoe, reader, this pretty, sturdy thing. You've picked up the Very Shoe? You're holding it? Good. Now—extend the antenna—slowly, carefully, so that it will continue to work for the next listener, and the next. First, you will only hear crackling; almost deafening white noise. Then you will hear some music . . . something silly and light, just barely melodic, in three-quarter time. Then you will hear a voice—deep and strong, speaking phrases broken with emotion. The man stammers. Allow me to translate for you:

> Ludmila, I am with you.
>
> I love you, Ludmila, more than ever . . . more than ever.

We cannot truly know what happened to Ludmila at Lety, how much she suffered, whether she danced there at all, whether she heard the music or the words. We don't know anything about Ludmila Kasparek, not even what her surname was before she married. We just have one of her shoes, one transmission—we don't even know the content of the other transmission. We only know that Ludmila Kasparek could dance, and that she inspired a devotion that lasted a long time. From then until now, and who knows how much longer . . .

Yes, that's all we know about her. But I think she would have liked that.

The Gallows-horse

Documented by Reza Negarestani

Museum: Museum of Intangible Arts and Objects, Saragossa, Spain

Exhibitions: The Secret History of Objects; The Center for Catoptrics and Optical Illusions; Hall of the Man-Object

Creators and Causes: Objects themselves; Deviant phenomenal models of reality; Neurolinguistic and cognitive distortions

Dates of manifestation: May 4, 1808–1820(?); July 1936–January 1961; January 2003

Title: The Gallows-horse

Objectal mediums: Gaspar Bermudez (Spanish, 1759–1820), Thackery T. Lambshead (British, 1900–2003)

Also known as the Edifice of the Weird, the gallows-horse is the highlight of the Museum of Intangible Arts and Objects. Simultaneously being displayed in three distinct and permanent exhibitions, the gallows-horse presents the four basic criteria of the museum—Immateriality, Intangibility, Elusiveness, and Ephemeral Manifestations. Gallows-horse was first brought to the attention of the museum's board of experts and trustees by an international collective of researchers consisting of art and science historians, linguists, and philosophers, who were commissioned by the Universities of Oxford and Exeter to index and organize the notes and memoirs of the late Dr. Thackery T. Lambshead, a prominent British medical scientist, explorer, and collector of esoteric arts and exotic objects. These notes, according to the research collective, include references to various objects and artworks collected by Dr. Lambshead during his lifetime. Whilst the majority of these references have been traced to tangible corporeal objects currently on display in various international museums, there were also scattered allusions to objects that did not have any record in museums or private collections. Either ravaged by a fire that broke out in Dr. Lambshead's private residential collection, or lost during his lifetime, nearly all of these objects—thanks to engineering and technological interventions—are now visually reconstructed through digital simulation.

In the late stages of documentation, however, the research collective came upon a concluding remark written by Dr. Lambshead regarding an alleged and final item added to the collection before his death. In a presumably closing remark marking the completion of the collection, Dr. Lambshead writes:

> January 28, 2003: It is not about the question of part-whole relationships, it is not even about the question of possible combinations of different objects, it is about the self-improvising reality of objects—unapproachable and incommensurable with our perception—that could give rise to gallows-horse just as it could rise to either horse or gallows, or something fundamentally different, or nothing at all. Even in its most kitsch material forms, the gallows-horse rises from the pandemonium of objects. A collection without such a thing is simply a tawdry carnival that spotlights human perception and displays our mental bravado instead of objects themselves. [. . .] Today I erected the gallows-horse as the final and crowning piece of the wonder-room.

"It is this emphatic reference to the *final* and *crowning* piece that made us reexamine [his] notes in search of the gallows-horse," says Professor Rachel Pollack, one of the researchers appointed to index and categorize the bulk of writings penned by Dr. Lambshead. The first reference to the gallows-horse dates back to January 10, 1936, when Dr. Thackery T. Lambshead writes in his journal: "The sky is clear and the gallows-horse reigns; canaries sing from crogdaene." For more than two decades, references to the gallows-horse persist always in the context of such enigmatic sentences that undulate between brief cryptic notes and self-invented semantic structures, and are always preceded by an exact date. For example, a note from July 15, 1953, reads, "The Salamian began to sink Ariabignes' boat. When a man runs out of the steam of history, it is in our best interest to restore the history to a previous state, when that man did not exist, or make that man mount the gallows-horse." Or "December 3, 1958: In the wake of recent incidents, my pain is rekindled every night either by the fear of death or even worse, by the fear of riding the gallows-horse at a gallop."

I. Gallows-horse at The Secret History of Objects (second floor, room 6)

The letter to the Museum of Intangible Arts and Objects states that none of the early references to the gallows-horse written between 1936 and 1959 described or even identified it as an object or a *thing*. During this period, the gallows-horse continually appeared in the form of a chameleonic crypt or a cipher that opportunistically mimicked the semantic context of the sentence or the phrase it inhabited. It has been unanimously confirmed by the members of the research collective that, in its larval stage of development between 1936 and 1959, before it began to fully appear as an object—at least as objects are commonly known— the gallows-horse has been a linguistic crypto-object with parasitic behaviors. "Like a menace that must be assimilated by its foes to defeat them from within," the research collective emphasizes, "the early form of the gallows-horse tends to adapt—in the most esoteric way—whatever meaning the sentence that hosts it conveys. This uncanny linguistic crypto-object dem- onstrates its independent reality by mould- ing the world of the conscious and thinking subject around itself, literally thinking the subject that thinks it."

During its incubation period, the gal- lows-horse was simply feeding off of con- texts and linguistic connections in Dr. Lambshead's notes and memories in or- der to build an empty cognitive carapace around itself. In this period, therefore, the gallows-horse cannot be understood in terms of an emerging thing, whether this new thing would be an idea, a thought, or a corporeal object. Adamantly refusing to be considered as something (let alone a uni- fied thing made of a gallows and a horse), the gallows-horse is *the very personifica- tion of the primordial death of all meaning par excellence* that oscillates be- tween sense and non-sense, depending on its mode of deployment against the parameters of human perception. In this early linguistic incubation period, the deeper you dig into the context where the gallows-horse is buried, the more pro- miscuous you find the gallows-horse is in relation to its semantic and semiotic neighbors. In digging for the true gallows-horse, you simply dig out nothing. In its basal form—that is, before it is born as a distinct idea and is manifestly imagined—the gallows-horse can be anything precisely because it is nothing.[1]

The Secret History of Objects is proud to present *Naught-horse-Naught- gallows,* an equivocally inexistent object that linguistically manifested as the gallows-horse from 1936 and 1959 throughout notes attributed to Thackery T. Lambshead—a meaning-feigning crypto-object that not only reveals a tenaciously alien yet meaningless expanse behind its ideated components, which are "horse" and "gallows," but also worms itself into the semantic foundation of its context, eroding it so thoroughly that only a depth devoid of meaning, significance, and ghosts remains.[2]

II. Gallows-horse at the Center for Catoptrics and Optical Illusions (second floor, room 9)

The second life of the gallows-horse as an intangible object began December 15, 1959, when for the first time Dr. Lambshead directly addressed the gallows-horse as an object by obliquely writing on the ambivalent aspects of the gallows-horse:

> I dreamed of myself dancing on the gallows-horse, hanging to its neck, swaying on its back, trotting with the rest of the herd. How can a horse take you to the gallows when the gallows is the horse? It is not a euphemism for death nor does it realize the literality of a horse carrying the convict to the gallows. As far as the nomenclature is concerned, it can be the horse-gallows as much as it can be the gallows-horse. There is no distance between the gallows and the horse to be either stretched or traversed. Yet despite the absence of such a distance, the gallows and the horse retain their distinct identities, the horse is still a horse and the gallows is still an inanimate edifice. But the curious aspect of this object is how can the horse and the gallows be united as one without one being the extension of the other or without a substantial change in their nature so as to make the intimacy and entanglement of the animate with the inanimate possible?

For less than two years, a scarce number of comments on the gallows-horse were made by Dr. Lambshead. These comments have frequently been presented in the form of bewildering riddles regarding the unified nature of the gallows-horse as one object in which both the gallows and the horse retain their distinct identities in one way or another without veering toward monstrous or marvelous categories. This "period of second advent" (as it is stated in the letter to the Museum of Intangible Arts and Objects) lead the research collective to believe that what Dr. Lambshead was calling the gallows-horse should be none other than the Equcrux, which is also known as the cross-horse or the Spanish sphinx.

During the Spanish War of Independence (1808–1814), two days after civilian residents of Madrid stood in rebellion against the occupation of the ruthless

French army and one day after the massacre of the same Spanish civilians by Bonaparte's army, on May 4, 1808, on a hilltop outside of Madrid, a small French task force handpicked by Marshal Joachim "Dandy King" Murat had prepared the gallows for hanging a Spanish traitor who was also a renowned and talented portraitist named Gaspar Bermudez. Being an artist friend of Francisco Goya, Bermudez certainly did not share Goya's more patriotic sentiments. He had been providing the French troops with vital military and inside-palace information since the beginning of war. But on the first of May, he had inadvertently given erroneous information to the French army stationed in Madrid, contributing to the rebellion of the second of May and the flowing of French blood in the streets of Madrid. Marshal Murat had ordered the execution of Bermudez immediately after repressing the uprising, but he later changed his mind and decided to subject the Spanish artist to a humiliating mock execution instead. This was mainly due to the popularity of Bermudez as a gifted portraitist among royal and wealthy French patrons, including Murat, who had Bermudez paint seven different portraits of himself.

Reportedly, minutes before sunrise, the French soldiers take Bermudez to the gallows riding on a horse; they perform their short everyday ritual by putting the noose around Bermudez's neck and charging the horse. The gallows having been manipulated by the French soldiers possessed two adjacent nooses, a fake and a real noose. Once the horse leaps forward, Bermudez finds himself—perhaps after a minute or two lost in terror—with a second noose around his neck, fallen on his chest on the ground. As he raises his head, he sees the sun dawning and an opaque light that permeates between the gallows, the neighing horse, and a patch of swampy ground in which the horse is rearing, transiently filling the gap between all three objects (that is, the waterlogged patch of earth, the horse, and the gallows). And Gaspar Bermudez beholds what he later calls the Equcrux, a spectral object consisting of three distinct identities (the soggy earth, the horse, and the gallows) seamlessly fixed upon each other in a fashion that the horse was beheaded by the gallows and the quaggy patch of earth was inseparable yet categorically distinct from the hooves. The Equcrux, according to the Spaniard himself, was an object that had been created outside of the infinite possibilities given to the worlds of the horse, the gallows, the waterlogged earth, and even the aurora as separate objects; it was a spectral gradient between the animate and the inanimate, a frozen instance of transgression from the realm of the individual objects toward a universe in which things were always anonymous until now.

The figure of the Equcrux enjoyed a brief popularity after the war, when Bermudez claimed himself as a war hero and mass-produced the spectral object as a kitsch symbol of the horrors of war branded as the Spanish sphinx, an object made of stuffed leather and wood in the form of a horse in rearing position, whose body was attached to a modeled gallows from the base of the neck so that it had as its head, literally, the gallows. However, due to production constraints and additional costs, it had been decided by Bermudez himself to abandon the third object, the quaggy patch of water, which in the first models was unsuccessfully made of straw mixed with resin. In the course of a few years, the Spanish sphinx lost its national popularity after Gaspar Bermudez was finally brought to the Spanish court as a traitor and a national shame. The last vestiges of the Spanish sphinx as a figure of terror were erased from memories and flea markets when Francisco Goya's *Disasters of War* was finally published in 1863.

As a part of the Center for Catoptrics and Optical Illusions, an inoperative replica of the Spanish sphinx has been installed with a patch of wet soil, a taxidermized horse, and a wooden gallows brought together in an illuminated cubicle, where these objects can no longer be conceived as the gallows-horse.

III. Gallows-horse in the Hall of the Man-Object (third floor)

In 1920, an unpublished essay by the Russian psychoanalyst Sabina Spielrein, titled "Gaspar Bermudez: A Case Study in the Spontaneous Shape of Trauma," recounts a different analysis of the Spaniard's spectral object. As Spielrein writes in the introduction to her essay, through a German collector she came across a surprisingly well-preserved copy of a personal diary attributed to a Spanish portraitist named Gaspar Bermudez and became increasingly interested in the life of this obscure artist and his vision of the cross-horse. The diary, as Spielrein remarks, opens a secret passageway into the life of this enigmatic Spanish artist. A major portion of the diary deals with Bermudez's intimate fascination with horses, which obsessively asserts itself as a form of identification of his self with a horse or a drove of horses. The diary reveals that in conjunction with his main profession as the portraitist of Spanish and French nobles, yet hidden from the eyes of the public, Bermudez had the habit of making self-portraits of himself as horses with different—subtly human— postures and facial expressions. This complete identification of his self and ego with a horse, Spielrein argues, eventually became a mental basis for the figure of the Equcrux, or the cross-horse. During the mock execution, the humiliating blow that was inflicted on Bermudez's outgrown and mutated ego forced the self—that is, the Spaniard's self—to shed part of itself in order to cope with the extreme and unbidden force of trauma that asserted itself not as a French executioner but as the gallows that firmly stood before his overthrown self and prostrate ego.

The act of shedding a part of the self in order to save the rest is, in fact, common among organisms (such as lizards shedding their tails or the so-called scratching tic) as a primitive yet powerful means of self-preservation. The curious and interesting aspect of Bermudez's traumatic experience is that while he was degraded at the foot of the gallows, it was not his human self that cut off a part of itself but his earlier identification of his *self* with a horse. Since Bermudez's ego had already fully identified with a horse, at the moment of the traumatizing blow, it was his equine self that cut parts of itself in order to save the integrity of the rest of the horse (or, more accurately, Bermudez's full mental identification with a horse). When Bermudez's ego dismembered itself to ensure the survival of the greater part, a void was left in his nervous system, a deep hole punctured in the horse that had already replaced the mental human image of the self. Knocked down at the foot of the gallows and his ego dismembered, Bermudez's equine self had no option to restore its "lost chunk" (Spielrein) other than by filling in the new cavity with the invasive force of trauma that could neither be expelled nor be allowed to shatter the entire nervous system. The cross-horse is precisely the mental object created by these traumatic tensions and breaches in Bermudez's psychic structure, the beheaded horse was permanently trephinated by the gallows, which was but the mental identification of the traumatic force. Spielrein writes that not only the damaged cervical vertebrae of the horse tightly locked into the wooden end of the gallows but also the intrusive traumatic force of the gallows impaled the horse from precisely where it had already torn off one of its parts. The upright pole of the gallows was re-erected as the restored cervical vertebrae of the horse, the triangle formed by the cross-beam its new cranium and the noose-hole the space between the mandible and the higher jaw.

An offspring of a traumatic invasion, a traumatic object with a spontaneous anatomical structure, the Equcrux intriguingly does not signify a receding tendency toward earlier states of the evolutionary chain. In other words, for Bermudez, the trauma of the mock execution did not—unlike other instances of trauma and toppling of the ego—cause the individual to relapse into an earlier state of evolution when the species was still crawling, due to the lack of spinal developments. On the contrary, the Equcrux melds the bestial locomotion or four-legged model of walking with the anatomy of a straightened spine, which characterizes the bipedal species. The quadrupedal horse gets a new spine that exhibits the traits of a straightened—perhaps even too straightened—spinal curvature that has been transplanted by the L-shaped and the obsessively perpendicular composition of the gallows. For this reason alone, the spinal anatomy of the Equcrux cannot be compared with the spinal formations in monstrous mental categories, such as that of a centaur, in which the curved spine of the horse shifts to the less curved spine of the human. In the Equcrux, the spinal curvature is not produced by extending a more curved spine to a less curved one; it is the creation of a mathematical marriage between a curve (the quadrupedal spine) and a straight line (the gallows).

Spielrein continues by stating that from the day of the great humiliation onward, the Equcrux became the sole mental and artistic image of the Spanish portraitist, for it was not really a passing traumatic object anymore but his very self and psychic structure that had turned into a full-fledged object. After a month-long pause, Bermudez recommenced writing his diaries, which were, this time, exclusively dominated by his ambitious rants about replicating the Equcrux by any means or method of fabrication, and his immutable and recurring dreams, wherein he was always a drove of gallows-horses rushing down in great numbers from a hilltop toward a city.

The Equcrux, or Gaspar Bermudez, as he was traumatically conceived in the form of the gallows-horse, is currently kept in the Hall of the Man-Object in an empty vitrine labeled *Gaspar Bermudez, the gallows-horse.* A motto runs under the label: *¡Suelta a los raros!*

ENDNOTES

1. "It has been suggested that mimicry such as that of a chameleon is an impulse for dissolving back to the environment from which the individual was once relatively segregated; it is a force that is temporarily lent to the individual entity by nature. In using mimicry, the individual unconsciously utilizes the impulse for dissolution (or death) in order to gain some kind of profit (surviving, preying, or living in harmony with something else). But in reality, in using mimicry, the individual exercises the indifference of its environment to meaningful change and intention, that nature does not have any interest or motive to create meaningful differences, and that even in its most cunning and meaningful acts, the individual affirms the dissolution whereby all differences (including its own) and meanings are eradicated. The semantic mimicry that the gallows-horse undertakes is, in the same vein, neither a tendency to return to a meaningful semantic environment nor a meaningful yet cryptic act in itself. Instead, it is an act that reveals the fragile construction of meaning as the aftereffect of a compulsion to return to a meaningless abyss that precedes all patterns, signs, and signifiers. The gallows-horse communicates a meaning by mimicking its sentential environment, and in doing so, it demonstrates how meaning is the result of mimicry, which is, in fact, a compulsion to flatten all semantic differences and return once again to the meaningless abyss that lingers behind the words *horse* and *gallows*, as well as any other word, sign, idea, or image." (Richard Graansvort, *From Cryptography to*

Neurolinguistic Mimicry in Thackery T. Lambshead's Memoirs, London: Samuel Buscard Institute, 2009)

2. Shortly after the death of Dr. Thackery T. Lambshead and the publication of a number of his memoirs, the pseudonymous Pravda Online columnist Novena Brines published an exposé on the life of the British scientist. According to Brines, Lambshead was an overseas coordinating officer of MI6, whose scientific journeys and seemingly scandalous Communist sympathies were only shields to protect his true identity. Among the documents and sources that Brines cites as evidences and clues, are Lambshead's memoirs. Brines particularly focuses on the name "gallows-horse." She considers gallows-horse as a codename or what she calls an operation-marker. Brines argues that in the majority of cases, the name "gallows-horse" marks an imminent launch of an operation. In her exposé, Brines cites as an example the note "January 10, 1936: The sky is clear and the gallows-horse reigns; canaries sing from crogdaene." She explains that the note is dated one day before the British MI6 officers departed from Croydon Airport toward the Canary Islands in order to move and protect General Francisco Franco for the nationalist military coup that began with the code "Over all of Spain, the sky is clear" and ignited the Spanish Civil War. Brines, however, fails to provide any more convincing examples or concrete documents and mostly resorts to rumors to the extent that, in a public apology, *Pravda*'s editor in chief called Brine's speculation "a wild conspiracy theory more fitting for an American gossip column than *Pravda*."

FURTHER ODDITIES

Further Oddities

Through the catalyst of a generous grant from the Institute for Further Study, additional research into Lambshead's cabinet was undertaken expressly for this volume. Each item selected has been the subject of intense debate by Lambsheadeans and Lambsheadologists for years, while Lambshead's own attachment to these items varied from indifference to obsession.

For example, although Lambshead took it upon himself to document (admittedly, in a sardonic mood) the provenance of the Sir Locust armor, it was found upon his death in his clothes closet—wearing lingerie and a sunflower hat, with an Oxford jacket draped over it. One armhole had been turned upward and blocked off with an ashtray that overflowed with Punch cigar stubs. *The Thing in the Jar*, on the other hand, as chronicled by Michael Cisco, seemed to inspire not just a flurry of speculation as to its origins, but also a pervasive emotion of profound regret, along with bald-faced fictions of a sort not displayed by Lambshead elsewhere in his long recorded history. Items like the two art pieces, *The Singing Fish* and *Taking the Rats to Riga,* Lambshead kept in a small locked room, along with a scandalous Chagall and a Picasso titled *Quarantine for the Infected.* The two times Lambshead possessed *The Book of Categories*, it also resided therein. The room could only be opened using the Castleblakeney key, which tended to discourage idle curiosity.

Some might question the editorial decision to include research from Amal El-Mohtar and Caitlín R. Kiernan, given their criticism of, and wild theories about, Lambshead. However, it should be noted that the doctor himself, in his will, cited both "as members of the loyal opposition" who should be given "as much equal opportunity to feast on my corpse as anyone else. They've earned it."

The Thing in the Jar

Researched and Documented by Michael Cisco

The Thing in the Jar was presented to Dr. Lambshead by an African anthropologist specializing in the study of Europeans, one Prof. Manjakanony Ramahefajonatana, of the University of Antananarivo, Antananarivo, Madagascar, in exchange for some assistance rendered in accumulating a representative collection of items of contemporary everyday English use. The object was discovered by Prof. Ramahefajonatana's principal research assistant, Vololoniaina Rasendranoro, who, owing to a condition of amnesia brought on by a clout she received on the head as she was escaping from a burning barn in Essex, was entirely unable ever to account for how she came across it. The only definitely known fact about the jar's past is that it was found in England, and does not appear to have originated elsewhere.

The object is a cylindrical glass jar, fifteen inches tall and six inches in diameter, weighing about twenty-five pounds, with a bronze base and lid. The bottom is wrapped in a fringed skirt of faded red velvet with gold tassels, and bears at its center an engraving of an owl in semi-profile and the legend "Griscyple Bros.—1737." The top is hermetically sealed with black wax.

The jar contains an anthropic creature.

This object is associated with a manuscript in Dr. Lambshead's own hand, consisting of a great many sheets of different hotel stationery, contained in a manila file folder. The folder's projecting tab is covered with a stack of adhesive labels, one laid atop another. The exposed, uppermost label had something written on it which was then aggressively scribbled over, and the rest of the folder is leopard-spotted with scribbled-out words or phrases. The only unmarred writing on the folder itself consists of three words inscribed in a column on the inner surface of the front, or untabbed, half of the folder. They are, from top to bottom: MUSHROOMS, BACON, OVALTINE.

Not unlike the folder, the manuscript is also heavily emended, with many strikethroughs and insertions. The battered, fraying pages show signs of having been much handled. Not only are all the pages from different hotels, but they are written and marked in a variety of media, including ink, pencil, lipstick, crayon, pastels, and, in one case, a dry and crusty reddish-brown fluid that has the characteristics of blood. The alterations are, more often than not, written in a medium different from that of the older text. The implements used also must have been highly varied, ranging from rare and expensive Sheaffer or Pelikan fountain pens to the quills of exotic birds to ordinary run-of-the-mill ballpoint pens and No. 2 pencils to sharpened fragments of bone or medical implements dipped in ink or stain. In one case, a correction is actually cut into the paper with a sharp instrument, perhaps a scalpel, and there are minute discolorations around the incisions suggesting the scalpel had been in surgical use quite recently when the correction was made, or, perhaps, that Dr. Lambshead had been struck by an idea in the very midst of performing an operation, and had paused to make the change in the text using literally what he had in his hand just at that moment.

In content, the manuscript consists of a list and seven fragmentary narratives or descriptions, all of which seem intended to account for the existence of the Thing in the Jar. All of them are, also, mutually exclusive, and it is impossible to ascertain which of them, if any, is the true explanation.

The list reads, in part, as follows:

imp / witch's brat

immature yeti

immature yama / yamantaka

buffalo spirit

buffalo minotaur

hoax by M.

motile fruiting body from enormous Kamchatkan mycelium

found in meteor / chrysolite

automaton replacement for lost child, abused, becomes monster

Japanese legend: pregnant mother murdered, stillborn child avenger

stillborn specimen, ankylopsoriasis

found blocking sewer drain under big city

infant gorilla raised by crocodiles

wandered into small German town in 1762 with note

discovered in exhumed coffin in place of body: cadaver changeling

conceit of insane taxidermist

small island North Atlantic where wrecked Vikings married wolves

mature specimen of gnome

"Thing in Jar" as first reproduced within Ramahefajonatana's dissertation, *Les Articles des Usages Quotidiens des Communautes Rurales et Semi-Rurales de l'Angleterre du milieu du Siècle Vingtième* (Paris: Plon, 1957)

According to the first narrative, the Thing is a fetish, created for some religious purpose. A sentence to the effect that it was made by the Akimel O'odham people of the American Southwest is struck out and somewhat ambiguously modified to mean something else that isn't exactly clear. The intention seems to be that this fetish was found among or traded from, or possibly to, the Akimel O'odham, and/or might be Aztec in origin. The text does clearly state that the fetish was placed in the jar by a white American individual who acquired it by theft. Many possible names for this recipient, or thief, are given, all of them crossed out: Buckwaldo Mudthumper, Eustace Bucke, Cornelius Abereustace, Haldernablou Yuchachev, Steven Williams, Shi Mu-ke, Beldu Terrance, Josephine Mouse, Melinda Post-office, Macfitzhugh O'Donaldin, Wigberto Fuentes, Mustafa Mukhtar al Kateb, Bradford Frederic. The story breaks off after mention of this person, with no indication of its intended ending.

The second manuscript bluntly identifies the Thing as an aborted minotaur. This is cancelled and replaced with the phrase "reverse minotaur," meaning not the offspring of a bull and a woman, as in the fable, but of a man and a cow. A partial list of the less well-known of the Greek islands is included; most likely, Dr. Lambshead intended to select one of these as the setting for his story, but abandoned it altogether before doing so.

The third and longest fragment is a rambling narrative, based on documented events, of an expedition to Saibai in the Torres Strait, and the Biak-Numfoor rain forests of the Schouten Islands. After many pages of laborious description mainly devoted to detailing their efforts to capture a living specimen of the Biak Naked-backed Fruit Bat (*Dobsonia emersaa*), Dr. Lambshead turns his attention to the island of Saibai and the Zaman Wislin cargo cult he and his companions discovered there. One practitioner in particular, a "pariah" who was compelled to live apart from the other inhabitants of the island, was rumored to have made strange use of an infant for magical purposes. Deleted segments of the story made this person a member of the cult in good standing at first, then "a demented European convert," but in the end Dr. Lambshead chose the native pariah variant. It was said that this man ["woman" was written first, then struck out] used to put a baby in a pot of boiling elixir ["water" had been written first, then struck out]. There is a careted phrase for insertion that indicates this was to be after incantations had been chanted over the baby for . . . and then this is followed by only a blank, presumably to be filled in later, but which remains empty.

When the enchanted baby would be placed in the pot, the boiling fluid would recoil away from the baby's body. Unharmed in any way, the baby would go to sleep in the warm pot, "in a kind of magnetic bubble" that prevented the fluid from injuring it. Meanwhile, "the crazed practitioner would solemnly open an elaborately carved box, and, with many gestures of sanctification and holiness, take out from the box a battered, ramshackle pair of aviator headphones. Handling them with exaggerated care, he would insert the plug at the end of the headphone cable into a crude, jury-rigged jack, basically just a hole cut into a large, hollow nut, affixed to the side of the pot by a stinking lump of coal tar. Then, placing the headphones on his own head, this man would pantomime efforts to 'tune' the pot by turning knobs he'd fashioned out of spools, and attached to a board. Through these headphones, the man claimed to be able to hear the voices of ancestral spirits, and of the gods themselves, talking to him. When asked what they sounded like, he raised his voice to a high falsetto and faintly repeated distinct phrases, much separated in time. While some were in Kalau Kauau Ya [the native language], most were American English. I plainly heard him say, 'I am the one who does not come when called.' What could be discerned of the remainder in English consisted of fragments: '. . . the water of skulls . . .' '. . . too much is happening when I try to sleep . . . sleep . . . sleep . . . in my sleep . . .' '. . . anyone dead must be treated or they may do more . . .' With this last, he began to shake violently, and threw a fit that seemed to me to have no obvious somatic cause."

The rest of the account slides back and forth; in some passages, it seems the doctor continues, as in the above quotation, to put himself on the scene observing the practitioner at work. In others, however, he comes to the island only after the death of the outcast, and receives the entire story secondhand. In both versions, however, the infant is initially normal, becoming less and less normal, more and more inhuman as the rituals are repeated, finally dying of an excess of mutation, at which point it is collected or traded for by Dr. Lambshead.

The fourth story is the outline of a work that, had it been written, would have run as long as a good-size novel. It was set on a farm in Indiana around the first few decades of the twentieth century, and was permeated with "a bittersweet air of nostalgia, the haunting poignancy of remembered youth, the amber radiance of sanctified recollection, the gentle grief of hindsight softened by the passing of time, the tender longing for bygone scenes, the pathos of enduring love devoted to people and things that have yielded themselves unto the Destroyer, the ghostly romance of innocent boyhood fantasy, the eerie melancholy of brooding and incommunicable childhood secrecy, and the wistfully spectral yearning for unseen and beautiful things that abide beyond the limits of life."

The main character, a boy of about nine, has an imaginary friend who "may be more than mere imagination," and which corresponds in description to the Thing in the Jar. Interspersed among typical domestic and rural scenes, "tinged ever with a foreboding of darker things," and described in lofty, high-minded prose poetry, are a series of lethal mishaps that would appear to be revenge for slights against the boy, although he is always obviously innocent of any connection to these suspiciously frequent and numerous accidents. Whatever his other reasons for not undertaking the composition of this novel, the notes show clearly Dr. Lambshead's indecision about the outcome of the story. The imaginary friend is now a disowned, disfigured twin brother—presumed dead, now a creation of the boy's own mind—a figure so intensely visualized and otherwise invested in by the boy as to take on physical, independent form, as a kind of projection of the boy's unconscious, yet now the imaginary friend is an alternate personality, and yet now it is a demon, now a ghost.

The fifth story is a terse, telegraphic account of an earthquake in Mexico, and is the only really complete piece in the folder. The setting is an ancient Olmec ritual center, only recently uncovered by archaeologists. Twenty minutes or so before the earthquake hits, the carvings ornamenting certain of the site's structures begin to come to life. They flee the site, crawling, flying, hopping, slithering, burrowing, throwing themselves into a swiftly flowing river nearby, flapping off among the clouds, or creeping hurriedly away toward the distant mountains. The carvings all escape except one, which is killed when a piece of debris dislodged from a hillside falls, striking it. This creature, collected by the archaeological team, is the Thing in the Jar.

The sixth item is lengthy and so extensively revised that it is very difficult to read. In it, Dr. Lambshead, or his source, lays out a theory of modified reincarnation redefining the idea of the *"bardo"* condition, originally found in the spiritual teachings of Tibetan Buddhism. By tradition, the *bardo* is a sort of pause between incarnations, where the souls of the dead linger for a time. The theory set down by Dr. Lambshead is that, under certain circumstances, some souls enter into a physical *bardo* condition involving the organic remains of their former bodies, although the process often introduces strange alterations in these bodies, coupled with some kind of machinery. Neither the provenance of the machinery nor the details or causes of the "process" alluded to can be made out in the garbled text of the description. The result is a hybrid being, part cadaver, part machine, which houses the soul during its *bardo* period. Dr. Lambshead calls these beings *"sarkoforms."* The only further information that can be extracted from this text is that the Thing is believed to be a bungled *sarkoform,* consisting of weirdly mutated and miniaturized remains drifting through time until they find their correlative machinery.

The seventh and final manuscript in the folder is included here in its entirety, as a sample of the general condition of the whole of the folder's contents.

The Seventh Manuscript

Once upon a time there was a man who loved volcanoes. ~~From birth or not~~. At first, his instincts were innocent. ~~His father his mother his uncle Brobisher~~ His father had told him once of a volcanic eruption ~~of Kraka of Herac Pomp~~ of Krakatoa, and he'd done a book report in school in grammar school that had been well received that had won him his first real praise in school. ~~He became a vulcanologist. Amateur~~. When he went to university he devoted himself to the study of vulcanology and in time became a professor of that subject, although his chief love was not in teaching about volcanoes in the classroom nor even of lecturing on volcanoes or conducting most forms of research into, for example, the history of volcanoes ~~of volcanic of vulcanic vuel~~ vulcanism and humans in human history. His great love was in visiting volcanoes and it was during one such visit that he realized his interest was sexual. When in the presence of erupting volcano he would experience all symptoms of intense arousal, including tumescence, tension in the groin, shortness of breath, an increase in temperature, a flush in the face, anxious nervous excite intension tension in the thorax. He often found that he'd be so lost in amorous contemplation of the gushing crater that he had made no observations of any scientific ~~use~~ utility. But only had penned such empty chestnuts as magnificent, breathtaking, beautiful, thrilling etc.

Finally taken aside by so-called "friend" and colleague.

"You had better be careful," his friend said. "Now, you wouldn't want to be catching 'volcano fever.'"

"Why is now a bad time to catch 'volcano fever'?"

"It happens to every vulcanologist, sooner or later," he ~~added~~ muttered a moment later ~~after a long pause~~ hastily. "The intellectual ~~intelligentsual~~ passion spontaneously develops a sensual dimension, the dense, shielding foam that protects the gem facet of eroticism lamentably dissolves to expose the bare and tinglingly sensitized surface to the ~~polyfluous exagamies of hermitanical and phantasmic erotimoids~~ . . ."

"I gather your meaning—[Here is interposed a long list of possible names for the interlocutor of the stricken vulcanologist. In the interests of economizing our use of space, only a few examples will be given: "Earthflounder . . . Soildozer . . .

Marldozer . . . Dozemarl . . . Claybeater . . . etc."]—Your prognosis is ~~a fetishistic transference~~ a common, everyday ~~fetishistic~~ transference."

"I'm glad we had this little talk, DAQUIRI." ["DAQUIRI" being the name attributed to the afflicted vulcanologist, in this line only. The paper shows signs of a name that was written, erased, and rewritten again and again, until the name DAQUIRI was allowed to remain on the smudged and badly roughened paper.]

Finally, on occasion of witnessing eruption and heavy flow at close hand, perfectly understandable given the circumstances loses all self control and experiences spontaneous orgasm ~~deliberately gets no accidentally~~—somehow ejaculates copiously into lava torrent before dragged away by hysterical, overreacting and narrow-minded assistant ~~who's too busy prying into other people's affairs to mind his own bloody business~~.

Few years later ~~stories~~ local legends begin to be told about a curious little man-like figure observed gamboling on slopes. Volcano's slopes. Thought to be a child in outfit. Costume. Very young. Too young for costumes really. At play unattended, dangerous locations. Virtually in the flames at times, untroubled. Found eventually curled in blazing hot alcove, in softened recess, sucking at unusually rounded ~~stalagmite tite mite TITE damn~~ stalagTITE. Netted. Snared. Resemblance. Faint. Distorted. Yet, somehow plain. Unmistakable. Creature radiates fantastic heat. Handler must wear aluminium suit.

Recognition mutual?

Escapes.

Winter. Volcano enters less active stage, coincidence.

Child found dead. Hypothermia.

Cools to room temperature.

Transferred to jar. Former contents, a salted lammergeier chick, sent to taxidermist [seven pounds ten shillings] for stuffing never retrieved. Jar sent to the farmhouse in Essex.

Grief of the father.

The Singing Fish

Researched and Documented by Amal El-Mohtar

This exciting find, titled *Der singende Fisch* ("The Singing Fish," pen and ink with watercolour, circa 1860), is a rare reproduction of the last known work of artist, artisan, and poet Edith Abendroth. She created *Der singende Fisch* during her incarceration in the Lunatic Asylum at Eberbach Abbey from 1861 until her death in 1869. Until now, only scattered descriptions of the piece were available, reproductions suppressed by the unusual events following Abendroth's death, which resulted in the superstition that surrounds *Der singende Fisch* to the present day.

The image contains the distorted proportions characteristic of all Ms. Abendroth's work, but there are more symbols at work here: consider that the critic is cock-eyed, seen in profile, which associates him with the noble figure of one-eyed Odin, the Norse God of the gallows, who sacrificed an eye in order to gain all the world's wisdom. Yet instead of Huginn and Muninn, Odin's twin ravens named Thought and Memory, two parrots perch on his shoulders, symbolic of meaningless chatter and thoughtless repetition. Still there are ravens in the image, after a fashion: two raven feathers (one from Thought, one from Memory?) peek out of the well of Imperial Ink at the critic's feet, suggesting that he has sacrificed Thought and Memory to produce the ink with which he will write his vicious tracts.

The fact that the critic leans against a stack of books could indicate any number of things: that he leans on the works of his betters without understanding them; that all his learning is useless to him as a means of understanding the singing fish; that all he can do is parrot the words of his educators without contributing thoughts of his own. Consider that he covers his mouth with his hand, and that he is dressed all in black—almost as if he had bathed himself in the death of Thought and Memory.

But where the critic's mouth is covered, the fish's mouth is wide-open; where the critic is silent, the fish sings.

What bait could hook such a throat?

Early Portrait of the Artist

Ms. Abendroth was born in Berlin in 1821 to Karl and Frieda Abendroth, who kept a prosperous print shop in the city, out of which they also taught drawing, painting, and etching. She showed a keen interest in these arts from an early age, and quickly grew quite skilled, in spite of—or perhaps partly due to—suffering from severe migraines. During such episodes she sometimes claimed to perceive things as larger or smaller than they truly were, and described the sensation in detail:

> It is as if the pain in my head comes from the swelling of the object in my sight—as if the table captured by my eye has grown too big for my head to contain without agony. Yet while these things grow, I think surely I must shrink, must be dwindling to a speck, and tremble to look at my hands for fear of seeing them become either a bird's or a giantess's. It hurts—and yet I think there must be something terribly splendid in being able to see the world as in a story book, that perhaps I am a heroine of some sort, yet to discover my purpose. It is all terribly interesting.[1]

The uniqueness of her perspective can be readily appreciated in her work, and is perhaps what suited it to the entertainment of children: giant frogs squat in well-upholstered seats, tiny horses pull carriages for damsel-fly nobility, and enormous mice-gentlemen dance with delicate ladies at a masque. She wrote

Edith Abendroth's "The Singing Fish"

charming books of fairy-tale verse in which such animals spoke and had adventures; these she illustrated herself, most often working in a combination of pen, ink, and watercolours, materials she had mastered by the time she composed *Der singende Fisch*. She sometimes turned toy-maker when a story became particularly popular: resin castings of Gren Ouille, hero of *Der stolze kleine Frosch* ("The Proud Little Frog"), and his good friend Hop, still command high prices at antique auctions. Happily, Dr. Lambshead's cabinet includes a model of her *Die Auferstehung des Frosches* ("Frog Resurrection"), which captures in surprising detail the most poignant moment of little Gren Ouille's struggle with pride, when he must humbly harness himself to a wagon in order to carry Hop's coffin into the revivifying light of Venus.

Ms. Abendroth's ability to mine her own work for inspiration was admirable, as was her skill at using it to generate multiple streams of revenue. She never married, but from her twenties on she was able to support herself comfortably without recourse to her parents' estate, though she continued to live with them until their death. She participated in Berlin's high society and was modestly admired and respected as a lady of good breeding; she enjoyed a passionate friendship with actress Gertrude Nadel, a woman renowned for her controversial portrayals of Dr. Faustus on stage. Ms. Nadel would later be instrumental in the preservation and presentation of Ms. Abendroth's oeuvre—however, it is ironically thanks to Ms. Nadel that Ms. Abendroth's renown in artistic and literary circles is less for her published material than for the rumour of a small satirical manuscript, *Leitfaden der Kritik* ("The Manual of Criticism"), of which *Der singende Fisch* would have been the final illustration.

The Regrettable Influence of Klaus Mehler

It was at one of Ms. Nadel's salons that Ms. Abendroth met Klaus Mehler, the man who would have an incalculable influence on her life and work. Nine years her junior, he was a former student of the Royal Prussian Academy of Arts turned critic, and was, according to Ms. Abendroth, very forceful in his interactions with her:

> I cannot say for certain how tall he is, and I think perhaps this infuriates him; sometimes he seems a comically little man, and I must squint to see him clearly in the shadow of a chair or soup tureen—yet at other times I feel like a beetle beneath the heel of his gaze. I do not like him—Gertrude does not like him, only she sighs and says his sister has influence at court and she simply *must* invite him

to her every gathering. He does not leave me alone, he does not even ask me to dance, but will insist instead upon debating my opinions on the merits of aquatint and Imperial Ink. I think I would be more interested in his conversation if he ever seemed to listen to what I had to say, but he does not—it is as if he listens with his eyes, watches my mouth to grasp my arguments, and so does not make any *sense* when he says I am wrong, wrong, wrong. I wonder if it is all women he dislikes, or all women artists, or me alone.[2]

It was not long after meeting Mehler that Ms. Abendroth ceased to write in her diary. Stephen Kurtz, who up until quite recently was the leading authority on Ms. Abendroth's career, suggests that her thoughts with regard to him were of so intense a nature that she recoiled even from articulating them to herself, preferring to retreat into increasingly escapist art. Helena Rothschild, however, disagrees, saying that the cessation of her diaries after keeping them meticulously for twenty years was a clear symptom of her growing terror of the man; Ursula Nussbaum suggests that Ms. Abendroth did keep writing, but later destroyed her journals to prevent them from falling into Mehler's hands while she was incarcerated.

The latter two conclusions are no doubt unnecessarily alarmist, but what little we do have of Ms. Abendroth's thoughts on Mehler indicates beyond any

Ron Pippin's model of Abendroth's *Die Auferstehung des Frosches* (Frog Resurrection)

doubt that she found him unsettling and relentless in his attention—behaviour that would only intensify when he began publicly criticising her work:

> Ms. Abendroth is certainly talented, and it is therefore all the more lamentable that she should turn her not inconsiderable skill to grotesque drolleries and fantastical nonsense. Her lines bespeak a steady hand, but her vision is wobbly; her choice of subjects speaks clearly of an immaturity of spirit, a child's mind in a woman's body. In this, it is true, she is not far different from most of her sex, but progress being what it is one has come to expect better of our city's women, and consequently one holds them to the highest possible standard.[3]

Taken alone, such comments might not, perhaps, have had quite the effect they did on Ms. Abendroth—but it was sadly at this time that her mother passed away, likely from some form of cancer, and was followed shortly thereafter by her father. Not very long afterwards, Ms. Abendroth moved into Ms. Nadel's home (as she, too, was unmarried), which should have been a comfort to the newly orphaned artist but made her rather an easier target for Mehler's savagery:

> One could perhaps surmise that Ms. Abendroth's art is the stunted result of a woman kept incomplete: were she to marry, to have a child of her own, it is possible that she would no longer present herself as one in her work. One suspects, however, that Ms. Abendroth thumbs her nose at such decency, preferring her twilight world of mannish actresses, spear-shaking frogs, and singing fish to the land of the living.[4]

It seems likely that Mehler was jealous of Ms. Nadel and Ms. Abendroth's intimacy, though Nussbaum's suggestion that he was a rejected suitor of one or both of them seems to err on the side of sensationalism.[5]

Effects on Abendroth and Her Work: A Mysterious End Game

At any rate, it was Ms. Abendroth who received Mehler's vitriol in public, and suffered from it tremendously. Her migraines grew more frequent and more pronounced; she restricted herself to her rooms when company called; she grew thin and listless, though she continued to produce work. Ms. Nadel was clearly anxious with concern, as evidenced by the number of doctor's bills in her household accounts for the years between 1857 and 1861; sadly, the numerous physicians she engaged proved to be of little help. In 1861, Ms. Abendroth's sensory uniqueness progressed into full-blown hallucinations, and she began to stab her pens into the wallpaper of her rooms, her bed, her paintings, and her own skin. One doctor's account suggested that she had taken to drinking her ink.[6] It was agreed that it would be best for all concerned if Ms. Abendroth should retire to the countryside and avail herself of the high standard of care for which Eberbach Abbey was renowned.

After a year of treatment—and, one suspects, protection from Mehler's constant attacks—Ms. Abendroth's condition improved to the point that the sisters of the abbey cautiously allowed her access to the tools of her trade, though always under their supervision. According to Kurtz, all the material she produced while incarcerated had one driving idea behind it, one unifying theme:

> *Leitfaden der Kritik* was to be Ms. Abendroth's opus, the last word in her seemingly relentless feud with Mr. Klaus Mehler. In it, she told Gertrude Nadel, she would create something so perfect, so pure, so unassailable that Mehler would be forced to put aside his scalpel of a pen and concede it unimprovable, a job well done. That she told Gertrude this from within the sanatorium at Eberbach Abbey did nothing to dampen her enthusiasm, though it did somewhat dim her loved one's confidence in her ability. Nevertheless, from 1862 until her death, most of her waking hours at Eberbach were spent in producing material for it.[7]

And yet, *Leitfaden der Kritik* never saw print; to this day, it exists only as a series of scattered papers that have yet to be assembled into one coherent whole. Kurtz reproduces some in support of his thesis: illustrations include savage caricatures of Mehler as a little teapot spewing tar, a Mehler-faced cushion being kneaded by a cat's extended claws, and a rather distressingly graphic image of Gren Ouille committing seppuku with a nib pen while Hop weeps over him. But the fact that Kurtz's selections are so limited speaks volumes about the morass of mixed metaphors and half-remembered French from which he chose them, and certainly Rothschild and Nussbaum don't consider the bulk of her creations during the Eberbach period to be anything more than the expiation of her tormented thoughts, finding the whole to be decidedly less than the sum of its remarkable parts.

Der singende Fisch, however, is not reproduced in Kurtz's book, and has never appeared in print until now.

According to Ms. Abendroth's will, only one copy was to be made of the image: the original was to be kept by Ms. Nadel, while the print was to be delivered, with compliments, to Mr. Klaus Mehler, beseeching his thoughts. Mehler received the letter and the print on Monday, May 10, 1869; by Monday, May 17, he had committed suicide. He was found slumped over a mess of illegible, blood-spattered notes, a pen embedded in his left eye, the copy of *Der singende Fisch* torn to shreds. An autopsy later found pieces of it lodged in his trachea. Gouged into the polished surface of his mahogany desk were the words *Die Palette hat keine Farbe,* which translates to "the palette has no colour."

Publicly, Ms. Nadel declared that his guilt over destroying Ms. Abendroth's mind and health had consumed him; privately, she insisted to friends and family members that *Der singende Fisch* was a curse eight years in the making, that Edith had confided in her the instrument of her revenge, and instructed her to produce copies for whichever critic should desire one. We must recall, however, that Ms. Nadel was a consummate actress, and her grief may have led to undue dramatization of the facts.

Still, it is surprising that there is no record of anyone publishing their thoughts on *Der singende Fisch;* Rothschild and Nussbaum remain far more interested in the facts of Abendroth's private life and analysis of her journals, and in the wake of Mehler's suicide, very few individuals applied to Ms. Nadel for copies, perhaps feeling that to succeed where he had so spectacularly failed would be unseemly. Nevertheless, it was rumoured that Stephen Kurtz had intended to produce a monograph focusing on *Leitfaden der Kritik* and *Der singende Fisch* alone, and had even applied to Ms. Nadel's estate for permission to see the original—but that project, like many others since the publication of *Frogs, Frocks, and Fol-de-Rol,* has fallen by the wayside while he recovers from his unfortunate boating accident.

Further Examination of *The Singing Fish*

Why, then, is the fish singing?

Certainly, divorced from its incredible history, *Der singende Fisch* is not particularly noteworthy: its lines are simple, its subject odd, if charming. All its cleverness lies in the recursivity of the meta-narrative—the fact that we, as critics, are observing a critic observing a fairly absurd creature, trying desperately to puzzle out its meaning. Just as the critic in the image is stymied by observing the fish, so must we be momentarily stymied by observing him observing the fish, and the dissonance produced by observing the fish in our turn, with all the calculated detail surrounding it.

Notice, for example, the thorns. Observe how one's gaze moves from left to right, to begin at the roses, tempting in the gentle wash of the watercolour, before thickening into thorns the closer one approaches the fish. Surely this symbolises the inaccessibility of the art object, the difficulty facing any critic who attempts to penetrate its mystery. Again, why is the fish singing? Why is it performing an act we cannot apprehend without the frame of the title? Is it triumphant? One could argue that its triumph is in its inscrutability, in the impossibility of seeing it as anything but what it is.

But the critic does not look cowed, only frowning in thought; he is sainted, even, he wears a halo! Could that indicate that the critic is dead? Is the Singing of the Fish synonymous with the Death of the Critic? Can the one exist without the other? *Finale,* spell the ribbons—or are they scarves? The looping of the letters is rather noose-like—hearkening back, perhaps, to Odin's gallows-heritage? The more answers one finds, the more thorns, or questions, one encounters!

This is terribly exciting work, you must understand. There is a terrible burden to be shouldered here, in being the first to offer a detailed analysis of the fish in print. Mehler's death-desk scribbles offer little in the way of illumination, except for his gouged-out exclamations about palettes and colour. These are useless. Of course the palette has colour on it—the whole piece is washed in a pale rose watercolour, and the palette is shaped for holding oils or acrylic. Ah, but is that irony at work? Oh, of course! It is a pen-and-ink drawing—and look, there, the inkwell and the feathers! She has *appropriated the critic's tools*! That is why the palette has no colour on it—the palette is her vulnerability, the colours her Achilles' heel! *The palette has no colour on it.* The fish has sprung fully formed from it—the fish *is* the palette's colour! The only colour is in the end—*Finale,* in colour, in the colour that the palette lacks—the colour the fish brings! The devilish detail of it! *Frogs begin as fish! They die and are resurrected as singing fish!* Oh, I see it all, Ms. Abendroth, I do, I see! I can hear it clear as a bell!

Such, at any rate, would likely have been Mehler's statements, had he been able to communicate them in something other than the blood and wood-dust beneath his fingernails. The piece seems very nice, and it is testament to Dr. Lambshead's discerning taste that he sought to preserve so excellent a thing in his Cabinet.[8]

ENDNOTES

1. Stephen Kurtz, ed. *The Early Journals of Edith Abendroth,* vol. III, p. 67 (Routledge, 1959)
2. Ibid., vol. VI, p. 98

3. *Die Spitzer Feder,* April 1856, p. 24

4. Ibid., October 1856, p. 32

5. Nussbaum, Ursula. *Loves That Did Not Know Their Names: Lesbian Desire in Edith Abendroth's Early Journals,* p. 134 (Ashgate, 1979)

6. Kurtz, Stephen. *Frogs, Frocks, and Fol-de-Rol: The Mirth and Madness of Edith Abendroth,* p. 91 (Routledge, 1961)

7. Ibid., p. 113

8. While the main body of this essay and all previous endnotes were the work of Amal El-Mohtar, the final paragraph was appended by a friend who has chosen to remain anonymous. This friend would like to make clear that Ms. El-Mohtar's unorthodox approach to the essay's conclusion is to be read as ironic, and certainly has nothing to do with the fact that she has since withdrawn into the seclusion afforded by a village in the southwest of Cornwall, where she spends her days in pursuit of garden fairies to dissect for her doctoral thesis, and her nights in tormented, guilt-wracked sobs for subjecting them to the cruelty of iron.

The Armor of Sir Locust

As Dictated to Stepan Chapman by Dr. Thackery Lambshead, 1998

Until recently, I looked forward to cataloging my collection of souvenirs and curios. Now, in retirement, I finally have the time, and it turns out that the job is an endless drudgery. It further turns out that I know nothing worth recording about my possessions. I only know that I acquired some of these things during my years of constant travel. Others could explicate them with better success than I. My memory is not what it was.

This thing, for example. I had to wire it together from various pieces. Bought it in a canvas box from an antique store in Cairo. Got it for peanuts. Had it appraised at the London Natural History. The docent said it was priceless. Hard to know what that means, coming from a docent.

It's unusual, these days, to own a suit of medieval armor, but this specimen is more than unusual, it's downright peculiar. The metal's been assayed. I'm assured that it's an alloy of tin and bronze characteristic of the Second Crusade. Copper grommets—probably a later addition. Scraps of leather, hung with buckles.

Ivica Stevanovic's "Armor Montage" incorporating Dr. Lambshead, as first published along with the doctor's account in the magazine *Armor & Codpiece Quarterly* (Winter 2000).

The first time you see this thing, a series of questions enter your mind. Such as: Is it armor for a man or for a horse? And if it's for a man, why has it got armor for four arms? And if it's for a horse, why has it got armor for six legs? That's three questions already, and they just keep coming. For as long as the legend of Sir Locust has been recited, there have been variants, and the variants raise questions of their own. Was he originally a soldier? Was he a priest? Was he a locust that grew and grew and somehow, by some bizarre spontaneous recombinant mutation, took on human attributes? Was he a man who was cursed, at puberty perhaps, with the attributes of a locust? Too many questions.

Sometimes I entertain the ghoulish notion that perhaps this armor is no artifact at all, but rather a mummified skeleton, scooped out subsequent to burial and grave robbery. But then I look closely at the hooks and loops and chain mail, and I remember that insects, of whatever size, are not made of metal. But a custom-forged spring-wound machine, an engine of war disguised as a person, *that* would be made of metal. Speculation is impossible. Let's examine the written records.

Sir Locust appears in several of the illuminated annals of the Second Crusade. His presence is noted at certain battles. One such text, which still exists in scattered fragments, is *The True Chronicle of Sir Locust the Unlikely.* It reports that Sir Locust had a nemesis, an opposite number on the Saracen side of the conflict, who was called the Mullah Barleyworm. This priest of Allah, so we're told, sent a series of three assassins against Sir Locust. None returned. At this juncture, the mullah confronted the French knight directly. They joined combat, and neither survived. I'm leaving out all the good parts. My time is limited, and my collection is extensive.

For instance, I'm leaving out the love interest. Evangelette of Lombardy was Sir Locust's lady. After his death, she cherished a bloodstained silk scarf, and so on. I'm sure that he wrote her countless sonnets from the front. If the Second Crusade *had* a front. The Christians lost that crusade, as you may recall.

So now we have a cast of characters all constellated around this dented suit of giant insect armor. Once, the Mullah Barleyworm traveled to France in disguise and kidnapped the Lady Evangelette. Word reached our hero. What a kick in the head for him. He followed his archenemy to Syria but could only effect his lady's release by giving himself into Barleyworm's power, as they say in gothic novels. Torture followed, and rooms filling with water, walls sprouting spikes, bottomless chasms, impregnable towers, the jaws of death, all the usual flummery. Also there was some question as to whether the lady actually *wanted* to be rescued, having fallen in love with her captor in the time-honored masochistic tradition. Legend has it she was drugged. That's just what Crusaders would expect from an infidel.

I remember one last thing about Sir Locust. I almost left this out. It's an alternative-origin story, which hinges on the third-century Syrian mystic, Saint Simeon Stylites.

Saint Simeon, as everyone knows, mortified his flesh by living for thirty-seven years at the top of a pillar. They say he subsisted on honey-dipped locusts, provided, I suppose, by respectful local peasants. I always wondered how the locusts got to the top of the pillar. Perhaps he had a bucket on a rope. I don't see why not. Simeon was so holy, they say, that even the fleas and horseflies refrained from biting him.

But one day, a great grey locust lighted on his sun-blistered nose, as bold as you please. This locust called out to Simeon. "Now I shall bite you, old hermit," it told him, "for excellent reasons. I can ignore your incessant consumption of my brethren bugs, soaked in the baby food of my cousin bugs, for such is the way of nature. But why should I excuse you from reciprocation? You may very well be considered a candidate for sainthood amongst the benighted Christians. But I, I'll have you know, am a good *Mussulman* locust." Whereupon the locust bit Simeon's nose, drank his blood, and flew away.

The saint might have been excused for cursing the locust. Being a saint, he did the opposite. He *prayed* for the proud heathen insect, and God was so impressed that He followed the saint's suggestions and blessed the locust with three boons. First, it grew as large as a horse—a miracle! Then it grew a human face on its head—an egregious miracle! The third boon, longevity, would only become apparent as the years went on. Saint Simeon had assumed that the locust would be grateful for its transformation. He hoped that it would convert to the true faith and save its tiny soul. (Saint Simeon didn't get out much.) The locust remained an unrepentant Muslim, and to compound its ingratitude, it outlived the saint by decades.

In fact, it lived in Syria for eight centuries, doing whatever it did without making any impression on the historical record. Then came 1144, the fall of Edessa, and the Second Crusade. The ancient creaking locust purchased a sword, commissioned a fine suit of armor, and joined the army of defense. It marched into legend as an illustrious soldier of Islam and died, in due course, a soldier's death.

The Christians, far from home, heard the story of the pious old locust from their wretched prisoners of war. And one Frenchman liked the story so well he stole it.

A Key to the Castleblakeney Key

Researched and Documented by Caitlín R. Kiernan

Excerpt from a postcard found among the correspondence of the late Dr. Thackery T. Lambshead, from Ms. Margaret H. Jacobs (7 Exegesis Street, Cincinnati, Ohio) to Lambshead; undated but postmarked January 16, 1979:

> . . . kind of you to give me access to the collection. Such marvels, assembled all in one place! It was like my first visit to the Mütter, so crammed with revelation. But the hand, the hand—well, I'll have to write you at length about the hand. I had a dream . . .

Excerpt from *Archaeological Marvels of the Irish Midlands* by Hortense Elaine Evangelistica (2009; Dublin, Mercier Press):

> . . . and is undoubtedly one of the more curious and, indeed, grisly side notes to the discovery of the "Gallagh Man" bog mummy. The hand clutching the key is severed just behind the wrist, bisecting the radius and ulna bones (short sections of which protrude from the desiccated flesh). The bronze skeleton key is held firmly between the thumb and forefinger in such a way as to give one the impression that the hand was lobbed off only moments before the key would have been inserted into the lock for which it must have been fashioned. The key measures just under seven centimeters, from the tip end of the shank all the way back across the diameter of the bow, and the bit has three prongs. As mentioned earlier, the hand clutching the key is exceptionally small, measuring not much more than nine centimeters, diminutive even for a small child.
>
> Littleway (2006) suggested the hand was not human at all, but, in fact, belonged to a species of Old World monkey (*Cercopithecidae*), probably a baboon or mangabey. This suggestion was subsequently rejected by Davenport (2007), who noted that no species of Old World monkey possesses claws, and even those few primitive New World species that do (*Callitrichidae*, the marmosets, and tama-

rins) lack opposable thumbs. Certainly, the sharply recurved claws at the end of each finger remind one more of the claws of a cat or bird of prey than anything even remotely human. After his thorough examination of the hand, Davenport (ibid) concluded it to be a hoax, a taxidermied chimera fashioned from the right hand of a primate and the talons of a barn owl, then treated with various acids, salts, and dyes so as to give it the appearance of having been excavated from the peat deposits at Castleblakeney. Prout (2007) agreed with Davenport that the hand wasn't that of a primate, but insisted it belonged to a three-toed sloth (despite the presence of five digits). Regardless, Davenport's hoax explanation appears to have run afoul of carbon-dating carried out at Brown University (Chambers and Burleson, 2009b), which indicated the hand likely dates from between 300–400 B.C.E., which would make it much older than "Gallagh Man." Also, a biochemical analysis of tissue samples taken from the hand reveal that it differs in no significant way from bog mummies known from Ireland and other locations across Northern Europe.

However, even if we accept that the strange hand from the late Dr. Lambshead's cabinet is almost twenty-five hundred years old, we're left with still another conundrum: the oldest known metal skeleton key (or passkey) dates back no farther than 900 C.E. Also, as Davenport was quick to point out, the only indication that the hand was recovered from the vicinity of Castleblakeney is a charred and faded label apparently written in Thackery Lambshead's hand.

As it stands, the matter may likely never be resolved to anyone's satisfaction.

Aeron Alfrey's eerie rendering of the Castleblakeney Key

Following a break-in on the evening of April 12, 2010, the hand and key were discovered to be missing from the collection of Brown University's Department of Anthropology, where the artifact was on long-term loan from the National Museum of Ireland (*Ard-Mhúsaem na hÉireann*). Reports indicate that the thieves took nothing else. . . .

Excerpt from "An Act of Rogue Taxidermy? Preliminary Report on the Morphology and Osteology of the 'Castleblakeney Hand,'" P. O. Davenport, *American Journal of Zooarchaeology*, vol. 112, no. 1 (2007):

. . . that evidence provided by these high-resolution X-ray CT images leads the author to the conclusion that the artifact is no more representative of the remains of a single animal than are other chimeric forgeries, including jackalopes, Barnum's "Feejee mermaids," the Minnesota iceman, the Bavarian Wolpertinger, Rudolf Granberg's skvader, or the fur-bearing trout of Canada and the American West. As will be demonstrated, these X-rays reveal fully intact terminal ungual phalanxes (bones and keratin sheaths) indistinguishable from those of members of the family Tytonidae (barn owls), articulated to the proximal metacarpophalangeal and ginglymoid surfaces of the phalanges of an adult Barbary macaque (*Macaca sylvanus*). It is not possible, at this time, to determine whether or not Lambshead himself was involved in fashioning the hand or whether he believed it to be authentic, having been duped by its creator, but that question is irrelevant to the current investigation.

The form and function of claws varies significantly among vertebrate species, though the composition of the claw sheath does not. Claw sheaths, nails, and hooves are comprised of an exceptionally tough class of fibrous structural protein monomers known as keratin (Raven and Johnson, 1992), which protects the bone of the terminal phalanx and assists in providing traction during such activities as climbing, defense, prey acquisition, and intraspecific combat associated with mating (brief review in Manning et al., [2006]). Mammalian claw sheaths are composed of a-keratin (helical), while those of avians, nonavian archosaurs, and non-archosaurian reptiles are composed of β-keratins (pleated-sheet) (Fraser and MacRae, 1980). The results of this study leave no doubt that the claw sheaths associated with the Castleblakeney artifact are composed of β-keratin and so cannot have originated from any primate or other mammal. Before addressing . . .

Excerpt from a letter found among the correspondence of the late Dr. Thackery T. Lambshead, from M. Camille Dussubieux (n°50, Rue Lepic, Paris) to Lambshead, dated November 17, 1957):

. . . do hope that your time abroad in the States was not in any way especially inconvenient, and that it proved helpful and productive in all your various researches. I hope to one day see Chicago and Manhattan for myself.

Setting aside casual pleasantries for another day and another letter, I am writing this evening to inform you that Monsieur Valadon and his circle of associates continue to press the matter of——, that *objet curieux* now residing in your care. Indeed, I begin to believe that you may have made a terrible error in taking the thing from *les carrières de Paris*. As you well know, I'm not a superstitious man, nor am I even particularly religious. But my concern is that Valadon's "warnings" that you may be visited by some mystic, infernal retribution are, in fact, thinly veiled threats of physical violence by members of his order now residing in Britain. If there's any truth to his unsavory reputation (and I have no reason to believe otherwise), these threats should be taken with the utmost seriousness. I would caution you to make such precautions as you may, if, indeed, I cannot persuade you to immediately divest yourself of that abominable relic.

It is beyond me what you hope to learn from ——, and seems far more likely, my dear friend, that you have merely convinced yourself it has added an additional measure of mystique to your cabinet. By now, I know you well enough to feel confident in drawing such a conclusion, and I hope you won't find it too presumptuous. You must not consider possession of —— to be a privilege or to carry any prestige. It is, at best, a burden.

I have taken the liberty of contacting our mutual acquaintance at the Musée Calvet à Avignon, who assures me that —— would be safe in that institution's care, even from the likes of Valadon, Provoyeur, and Rykner. She is also willing to travel to England to receive —— in person, rather than entrusting it to any courier or post. She only awaits word from me that you are agreeable to this arrangement.

Those passages you quoted from Balfour's *Cultes des Goules* are grim enough to rattle the nerves of even an old skeptic like myself. . . .

Excerpt from "Artifact, Artifice, and Innuendo" by Tyrus Jovanovich, *Art Lies: A Contemporary Art Quarterly* (no. 62, Summer 2009):

. . . and so have allowed questions of biological and historical "authenticity" to dominate the discussion. Insistent, unrelenting authority intervenes, and we are not allowed to view an *object* as a *work*. The potential for message is denied by the empirical demand for objective meaning. If we are to gain access to the intriguing conceptual dimensions and dialectics presented by this *hand* and this *key*, by the unity of hand *with* key, key *with* hand, it becomes necessary for us to invert, or entirely disregard, the inherent limitations of that scientific enterprise and its attendant paradigms. First off, we must cease to view the work—as it is now reconsidered, rescuing it from the mundane—as fragmentary or in any other sense lacking in fundamental wholeness, though questions of fundamental [un]whole[some]ness will be evaluated in light of complexities of the object-subject relationship.

As we refocus our attention from a normative default, it is neither the hand nor the key that consumes our need for understanding. Rather, we find, literally, new direction by *implication*. The hand holds the key, and the key moves our eyes from the visible towards the invisible. Here, a moment is brilliantly captured, and yet entirely escapes stasis. The hand is always and forever acting upon the key, and the key is ever pointing, moving, urging us towards the implicit *lock*, which is the truest *locus* in this configuration, even if the lock exists only by implication. So, too, the existence of a mind behind the hand and key and lock is unspoken, but no less essential. Finally, the efficacy and undeniable kinetics make themselves known, and we are drawn away. . . .

Excerpt from a letter found among the correspondence of the late Dr. Thackery T. Lambshead, from Ms. Margaret H. Jacobs (7 Exegesis Street, Cincinnati, Ohio) to Lambshead; undated but postmarked May 4, 1979:

. . . to put it out of my mind. But the dreams return night after night, each incarnation almost identical to every other, except that they grow worse, more horrifying. They're unrelenting. I've never suffered insomnia, but now I find myself afraid to sleep. I put off going to bed as long as possible. The thought of a catnap is enough to make me anxious.

As I've said, the dreams didn't begin until shortly after my visit with you last December. Don't get me wrong, Dr. Thackerey [sic]. I'm still grateful for having been allowed to view your collection and photograph the key. But I'm beginning to think I'm paying an awful price for that opportunity. Yes, I know how that must sound to a man of science such as yourself. By divulging my situation, I more than half-suspect I might find myself described in some future edition of your medical guide. But I don't know who else I would tell this to. Friends or family? No, they all think me odd enough already. They would dismiss it all, and ridicule me in the bargain. A psychiatrist? A priest? I can't abide the former, and, despite my Catholicism, have always been unable to open up to the latter.

That leaves just you, Doctor. I suppose it's like they say, and no good deed goes unpunished.

Please don't feel obligated to read what follows. Just because I had to write it down and send it to you doesn't mean you have to subject yourself to these grotesque, absurd ramblings. But I implore you again, please, *please* destroy the key (as I have destroyed the pictures I took). If I am certain of anything at all (and I doubt that more each day), I'm certain that the destruction of that thing will stop the nightmares, just as I believe my lifting it from its box, and daring to hold it, triggered them. And I suspect, too, there's something greater than my sanity at stake. How can I convince you that what you're harboring beneath your roof is more virulent than any disease? Burn it, Doctor. Melt the damned key to slag, and scatter the ashes of that mummified claw to the four winds.

The dream always begins with me looking out to . . .

Excerpt from "The Monkey's Paw Redux," Jones, Z . L . I. *Skeptical Inquirer,* vol. 30, no. 3 (May/June 2006):

. . . that has yet to be addressed by any of these investigators is the inconsistent nature of the second digit, even though it is obvious from the most cursory glance at photographs of the "Castleblakeney hand." On the thumb, and digits three, four, and five, the nails curve downward, exhibiting the normal condition for primates (and, for that matter, the ungues of all tetrapods). Yet, on the second digit, the nail displays a feat of anatomical gymnastics and curves *upwards.* Three possible explanations for this irregularity come to mind: (1) sloppiness on the part of the hoaxer; (2) a simple and intentional signal that the hand is indeed a hoax; (3) an attempt by the perpetrator of the hoax to make the hand/key contrivance seem even more bizarre.

For the moment, I'll focus on the second option, though it is probably the least likely of the three. I'll assume, for the sake of argument, that the hoaxer is an educated individual who would be well aware of the faux pas presented by the upturned nail. I will even go so far as to consider the possibility that it was his or her intent to embed in this intentional mistake some hidden meaning. Pause to consider the significance of the index finger in Western art and culture. For example, in Leonardo da Vinci's *St. John the Baptist* (c. 1513–1516), the right hand of the subject is raised, pointing heavenward, the index finger extended. In Michelangelo's *The Creation of Adam* (c. 1511), it is the index finger of the creator's right hand (*digitus paternae dexterae*) that is shown delivering the spark of life to the index finger of Adam's left hand. Comparable instances from Christian iconography are too numerous to list, though it is worth noting an altarpiece in the basilica of . . .

Excerpt from a letter found among the correspondence of the late Dr. Thackery T. Lambshead, from M. Camille Dussubieux (n°50, Rue Lepic, Paris) to Lambshead, dated January 23, 1954):

. . . only tell you what little I know of this odious thing, though surely there must be far less repellent subjects upon which you could fixate. It is a mummified hand, as small as a child's, gripping a bronze key. The fingers bear long talons, and the hand is so shriveled the bones show through. Both the hand and key are mottled with rot and verdigris, with a scab of long ages hidden away in darkness and damp. As for its provenance, I have heard a story told that it was discovered by Howard Carter in the spring of 1903, during his initial excavations at the entrance of the tomb of Thutmose I and his daughter Hatshepsut, though the key is clearly not of ancient Egyptian origin. I have also heard a claim that the hand is the remains of an homunculus created by John Dee, for Robert Dudley, 1st Earl of Leicester, and also that it came to France from China, and even that it was found in an Irish peat bog. I see no reason to give credence to any one of the tales; they seem equally outlandish.

I first saw it seven years ago, when it was very briefly on display in the Galeries de Paléontologie et d'Anatomie comparée on the rue Buffon. However, the Muséum national's former director, Achille Urbain, apparently ordered its deaccession from the museum's catalog, following a scandal of some sort (I confess, I do not follow such sordid affairs). In 1952, it resurfaced in a peculiar little antiquities shop on the rue de Richelieu, near the Bibliothèque nationale. Though some say this hand was no more than a clever counterfeit of the original. Either way, it was purchased by a Mlle. Dominique Provoyeur, an occultist who, in her younger days, is said to have had dealings with Crowley and others of his ilk. At this point, I caution you, we must descend into the sheerest sort of hearsay, but it may be that Provoyeur made a gift of the hand to another black magician, Erik Valadon.

There are rumors that the pair used it during profane rituals somewhere within the catacombs, perhaps l'Ossuaire Municipal.

By all accounts, Valadon is an especially execrable fellow, a drunkard and heroin addict, obsessed with various arcane texts and the notion that these texts contain rituals capable of summoning some manner of prehistoric deities, banished from the world before the evolution of mankind. Indeed, it is all quite completely ridiculous. Which is why I suggest you focus your energies elsewhere, Thackery. Your prodigious intellect should not be squandered on this sort of foolery. Let us speak no more of any . . .

Excerpt from a letter found among the correspondence of the late Dr. Thackery T. Lambshead, from Ms. Margaret H. Jacobs (7 Exegesis Street, Cincinnati, Ohio) to Lambshead; undated but postmarked March 12, 1981:

. . . by now, you must have stopped even opening my letters. I wouldn't blame you if that's the case. I wouldn't blame you if you write back and tell me please never send another. I think you've been too patient with me, too lenient, Doctor, these last two years, and it's difficult for me to imagine why. It must be wearing thin, and I picture you rolling your eyes at the arrival of every envelope bearing my name.

"Oh, good heavens. It's that dreadful woman from Ohio," you might say. Something like that. I truly have become "that dreadful woman," here in my own mind. That woman filled with little but dread.

Still and all, here I am, regular as clockwork, writing you again. Writing you again about my dream, my nightmare, which I cannot ever stop believing began with my visit to your home more than two years ago. But at least, this time, I'm writing to say that something has *changed*. Beginning last week, last Wednesday, a new wrinkle has been added to the dream narrative, which by now has become so threadbare and monotonous (but has lost none of its nerve-racking hold over me) any change is welcome.

It starts as it always does. Me waiting on the shore for the ferry, looking out across the sea, the waves thundering against the rocky jetty. The ferry arrives, and it delivers me to the island where the sickly yellow house stands alone amid that shaggy grove of hemlocks and the overgrown rose garden. Nothing's any different until after I've spoken with the ravens and the silver-eyed women and the Bailiff, until after the cannibalistic banquet and the disturbing images that old film projector spits out onto the parlor wall. But then, when I'm lead [sic] to the cellar door, the women both turn back and leave me to make the descent alone! Never before have they done this, but you know that. They shut the door behind me, and bolt it, and I go by myself down those creaking wooden steps.

I think, at least for a few moments, that I'm less afraid of what I'll see down there than I am surprised that they've allowed me to go without a chaperone. It'll sound strange, no doubt, but it makes me proud, as if I have been accepted as an equal, as one of the house's monstrous inhabitants. There is a sense of belonging. How can there be any comfort in such a thought? I can't say, only that this is what I feel.

As always, I reach the bottom of the stairs and find the cellar flooded by several inches of stagnant saltwater. The odor is overwhelming, and bloated fish and tangles of seaweed float all about me. Tiny crabs scuttle across the submerged cellar floor. This part is the same as always, of course. I try not to smell the rot, and splash between those moldering brickwork arches until I have come to the wall of grey granite blocks and grey mortar. Like always, it's encrusted with slimy moss and barnacles. Like always, the moss and barnacles have grown in patterns that make them look like leering skulls. All of this is the same.

But when I reach into my pocket for the skeleton key the Bailiff always gives me, it isn't there. There's nothing there, and for a moment I panic. They've trusted me to go down to this place *alone,* and I've managed to lose the damned key! I stop, trying hard to remember each step across the cellar, each step down, everything that occurred before the silver-eyed women lead [sic] me to the cellar door, how I might have possibly mislaid the key (which I always put in my dress pocket immediately, the moment the Bailiff places it in my palm). My mouth goes dry. My heart is hammering in my chest. They'll make me leave and never ask me back again, never again send the ferry for me (and, I know, I know, I should be glad, but in the dream I am mortified).

Then I look down, and there's something hideous crouched in the water not far from me. It's not much larger than a very large rat, and *it* has the key, clutched tightly in one hand. It isn't human, the thing with the key, and immediately I turn away, the sight of it enough to make me feel ill. Gone are those feelings that I've disappointed the Bailiff and his pale companions, that I *belong* here, below the yellow house. I only want to run back to the stairs and hammer on the door until they let me out again.

"Too late for that, Missy," the crouched thing with the key says. I don't look at it. I can't bear the thought of ever setting eyes on it again.

"Daresay, took you long enough to puzzle it out. Been waiting here so long

I've memorized the names of all the crayfish, and I think I might be water-logged."

"I don't want to see any more," I say, and it laughs at me. Or maybe it doesn't laugh *at* me, but it laughs. It's a small laugh, very small, and the sound makes me think of burning paper.

"Best be minding your P's and Q's, Missy. Come too far to go lily-livered on us now, don't you reckon?"

And I hear a clattering noise that I know is the crouched thing fitting the skeleton key into the keyhole in the granite wall. And I'm thinking how all this is wrong, that I should be at the keyhole, that the women should be with me, when the granite wall swings open wide, and the barnacles scream, and . . .

Excerpt from *Darkening Horizons: The American Supernatural Novel During the 1980s* by Gerald Hopkins (Austin: University of Texas Press, 1993):

. . . and, regrettably, the unjustly celebrated "Evil God, Out of Words" (*Twilight Zone* magazine #8, November 1981) isn't much better than Chalmers's earlier attempts to update the weird tale. Like Klein's *The Ceremonies*, this story adopts the basic framework and themes of Arthur Machen's "The White People"—a loss of innocence and the corruption of the untainted by way of induction into a secret witch cult—but does so far less effectively than Klein's revisiting of Machen's premise. And, to make matters worse, somehow, Chalmers has managed to write a story of only some eight thousand or so words that seems to go on forever, heedless of its size, not unlike the cursed real estate of Joseph Payne Brennan's "Canavan's Backyard."

The genesis of "Evil God, Out of Words" proves a good deal more intriguing than the story itself:

The entire plot coalesced indirectly around a single childhood memory, something I saw when I was ten years old. This would have been 1946 or '47. My mother and I accompanied my father on a business trip to Paris. We rarely took proper vacations, and I think he was trying to make up for that. Anyway, we saw the usual sights one sees in Paris, but we also visited a natural history museum, which delighted me far more than all the Eiffel Towers and Arcs de Triomphe combined. There was an enormous Victorian gallery filled with dinosaur skeletons! For a ten-year-old boy, how could the Louvre ever possibly hope to compete with *Diplodocus*,

Allosaurus, and *Iguanodon?* Of course, though, none of these served as the story's inspiration. But there was also a small glass case containing a sort of mummified hand, and the hand was gripping an old-fashioned key. I believe it was an Egyptian artifact of some sort, and it seemed entirely out of place there among the dinosaurs and mastodons. Perhaps this is *why* I recall it so clearly. The fingers had hooked nails or talons, and it reminded me immediately of W. W. Jacobs's "The Monkey's Paw," which I'd read by then, naturally. The odd thing is, decades later, I wrote the museum to inquire about the hand, wishing to compare my memories with the reality of what I'd seen. I received a somewhat terse response to the effect that there had never been any such artifact displayed at the museum. Now, I knew better. I'd seen it with my own eyes, hadn't I? I wrote a second time, and they didn't even bother to answer me. But what's important here is that it set me on the path leading to "Evil God, Out of Words."

Though the relic Chalmers may or may not have seen while in Paris as a child doesn't appear in the story, it is plainly echoed in the recurring motif of keys, both literal and figurative. Most notably, the terrible old man who first speaks to the story's *l'enfant innocent* of "the mysteries of the worm" describes nine magical keys. Each key bears the name of one of the muses of Greek mythology, as set forth in Cesare Ripa's *Iconologia* (1593). The old man tells the girl that the two most powerful keys, Polyhymnia and Calliope, are required for the ritual of resurrection ("shredding the veil, casting back, fetching up"). If Chalmers's choice of these two muses is meant to hold a particular symbolic meaning, it escapes repeated . . .

Excerpt from "The Thousand and Third Tale of Scheherazade: A Survey of the Arabian Ghûl in Popular Culture," Esther Kensky, *The Journal of Popular Culture,* vol. 42, no. 6 (December 2009):

. . . will, instead, quote at length from the summary provided by Niederhausen and Flaschka (1992): "This was the time before the war between the Ghûl (plural, Arabic غول) and the other races of the Djinn (جيني)—the Ifrit, the Sila, and the Marid. In those days, the men of the desert still looked upon all the Djinn as gods, though they'd already learned to fear the night shades, the *Ghûl,* and guarded their children and the graves of their dead against them. Among the fates that could befall the soul of a man or woman, to have one's corpse stolen and then devoured by the *Ghûl* was counted as one of the most gruesome and tragic conceivable. It was thought that to be so consumed would mean that the deceased would be taken from the cold sleep of *barzakh,* never to meet with the angels Nakir and Munkar, and so never be interrogated and prepared for Paradise (جنّة, Hebrew cognate *jannah*).

"It is said that these demons fear both steel and iron, like the other Djinn, and so people wear steel rings or place steel daggers where protection from Djinn and ghouls is needed. Salt is another means of protection, since ghouls hate it. The names of God, Qur'anic verses, magic squares (Muska), or that group of magical symbols known as 'the seven seals' are frequently worn by people or attached to their property to ward off the demons.

"One of the more obscure customs meant to provide a ward against the *Ghûl* is mentioned briefly in Jorge Luis Borges's *The Book of Imaginary Beings* (*Manual de zoología fantástica,* 1957). According to Borges, these creatures have an obsession with keys and locks, and can be thwarted by scattering a dozen or so keys near a locked door or gate, none of which actually fit the lock in question. The ghoul will try each key repeatedly (despite its purported fear of iron), so doggedly determined to find the correct match that it immediately forgets a given key has already been tested. It may continue this for hours, neglecting to watch for dawn, and be destroyed by the rising sun. It's believed that the severed hand of a ghoul dispatched in this manner, still holding tight to the last key it tried, is a powerful talisman against all manner of evils and misfortune. Interestingly, a similar predilection to arithmomania is ascribed to vampires in certain Chinese and European traditions, and to witches and other mischievous . . ."

Excerpt from a letter found among the correspondence of the late Dr. Thackery T. Lambshead, from Ms. Margaret H. Jacobs (7 Exegesis Street, Cincinnati, Ohio) to Lambshead; undated but postmarked May 25, 1981:

. . . the crouching thing, that goddamned horrid thing like a huge rat, and it scampers over the threshold that hadn't been there before it used the key. Its tiny claws scritch, scritch, scritch against the granite, a sound that makes me shudder whenever I remember it. I can be wide awake and driving to work, on a sunny day, and I recall that scratching noise and shudder. So, it crosses the threshold and calls for me to follow. I glance back at the flooded cellar, and see that the stairs have vanished, that it's not even a cellar anymore. It's a cave opening out onto the sea, a sea cave.

This is one of the new twists, Dr. Lambshead. Always before, always, when I'd pause and look back over my shoulder, the stairs would still be there. And they were a comfort to me, because the stairs implied a way out, that I could escape simply by retracing my steps. I could run back and hammer at the locked door until the silver-eyed women or the Bailiff came to let me out. It's awful, just awful, not having the reassurance of those stairs. I look at the entrance of the cave, and it's night outside, but I can see the water gets deep very fast out there. I've never been a very strong swimmer, Doctor.

"Stop dawdling," says the thing with the key. Its voice is as wretched as everything else about it. Have I ever mentioned that before? "Maybe you want to get yourself left behind, is that it? Maybe you want to be around for high tide and the sharks?" It has a dozen of these "maybe" questions. At least a dozen and sometimes a lot more than that. "Maybe you got gills I can't see?"

I tell it I'm coming, and I cross the threshold, too. This part's like before. But on the other side of the granite wall, everything's changed, the same way the cellar became a sea cave. Now, beyond the wall, where before there were only the winding tunnels, the Minoan maze where I used to wander for what seemed like hours before finding my way out into the cellar again, now there's an enormous chamber. We're still underground. That's obvious. The air is dank, musty, foul, but dry after the sea cave.

"This is the place it all begins," the wretched rat thing says. It sounds *proud*, like it's declaring some grand accomplishment, as if whatever begins here is *its* doing. Like that. "Now, was this anything that man, that Doc Sheepshead, ever told you about?" it asks me.

I know that it's getting your name wrong on purpose, but I correct it anyway. "Lambshead," I say, and it replies, in a singsong sort of way, "Shut up, Maggie. Sheep or lamb, ram or ewe, it hardly matters to me."

Yes, it knows my *name*. It knows my name, and it *speaks* my name. Surely, that should be enough to shock me awake, but I never wake until farther along.

"Beginnings are just as important as whatever comes along and happens after," it says. I want to cut its throat so I'll never have to hear that wretched voice again, but I look at the chamber, instead. It's an ossuary. I've never been inside an ossuary, but of course I've seen photographs of them. The floor below me is earthen, and there are two square pillars supporting the earthen roof. Between the pillars is a third column, made of blocks of granite held together with mortar and crowned with something like a huge bowl or basin or baptismal font or birdbath. I don't know the word for what it is, and it's not always the same. The wall beyond the three pillars is built entirely of the skulls and thighbones of human beings. The bones are very old. I know that just from looking at them.

"You pay close attention to all this," says the wretched not-rat thing. I tell it I want to go back. I ask it to take me back, but it doesn't reply. I think it is selectively deaf, if you get my drift.

And I realize there are two other people in the ossuary chamber with us. A man and a woman. Both are wearing heavy black robes with hoods. The robes and hoods are lined with purple silk. The man is holding an open book in his right hand and a silver cup in his left. The woman is holding a dagger of some sort. There's something dead on the floor between them, but I turn away before I can see what it might be. I don't want to know. I can't be blamed for not wanting to know that, can I?

The man and the woman are chanting. It might be Latin, but I'm not sure. I've never studied . . .

Excerpt from "The Castleblakeney Key: Unlocking an Example of the Importance of Uncertainty to Ontological Processes in Social Constructionism," Siegfried Glaserfeld, *Psyche: Journal of the Association for the Scientific Study of Consciousness,* vol. 12 (2006):

. . . the unfortunate case of Margaret Jacobs, that we quickly arrive at a position where it becomes obvious that the important questions here have nothing to do with the objective origins of the hand and whether or not it's genuine or a hoax. It makes no difference whether we say it came from an Irish peat bog or the Parisian catacombs, whether it belongs to a child, a monster, or a monkey. It doesn't matter if Lambshead knew it was a hoax or was duped by Dussubieux (or anyone else). Any answer regarding its "authenticity" is, by necessity, only provisional, open to correction or revision at any time, and, hence, far from being a direct representation of a preexisting singularity. All answers retain an inherently experimental character. Regardless of the hand/key's status as virtual construct/s, they remain, however, selections from our sensory fields that are causally linked to the real and, therefore, may surprise us at any time and without . . .

Excerpt from a letter found among the correspondence of the late Dr. Thackery T. Lambshead, from M. Camille Dussubieux (n°20, rue de la Chaussée-d'Antin, Paris) to Lambshead, dated August 2, 1961:

. . . that it pains me. The offer seemed more than equitable, considering you paid a mere 200 francs for ———. And to accuse me of secretly acting as an agent for Valadon and Provoyeur! Such an allegation strikes at the core of all our years of friendship and trust, and yet you make it so lightly. Am I supposed to put that out of my mind now?

Likewise, to accuse me of lying, when you can have no foreknowledge of my dreams, excepting to the degree I may divulge them. I tell you, Thackery, with no guile in my heart, that I *did* stand there in l'Ossuaire, at Crypte de la lampe sépulcrale, and I saw the foul beast come trundling through an opening in the wall, which it clearly used the key to fashion. I did not in the least exaggerate the repellent nature of the dwarfish creature, nor did I exaggerate the fear and confusion in the eyes of the poor woman who followed it through that doorway. She never once looked directly at me, but kept her eyes on the obscene ritual being performed (except once, when she glanced over her shoulder). But enough. I've told you this already, and in exacting detail. You may choose to believe me or not. The offer stands. And I will endeavor to set aside your last letter, in hopes of preserving our friendship. I pray you will do . . .

Excerpt from a letter found among the correspondence of the late Dr. Thackery T. Lambshead, from Ms. Margaret H. Jacobs (7 Exegesis Street, Cincinnati, Ohio) to Lambshead; undated but postmarked June 7, 1981:

. . . I can't imagine I'll ever write you again. Not because the psychiatrist has advised me to stop, and because of that very rude letter from your lawyer (if that's really who he is), but because I'm losing heart at your persistent refusal to respond. When we met, you seemed like such a good man, so forthright and generous. But now, I don't know.

So, probably this is the last time I'll bother you. I'm sure you're relieved at that news. Maybe I don't blame you for being relieved. If I were you, I might feel the same way. Only, I'm *not* you.

The dream has a new bit at the end. Toward the place I usually wake up, which I think of as the end. I've followed the wretched not-rat beast into the ossuary, and the two robed figures are waiting there. We've interrupted them again. I try not to dwell on what manner of witchcraft they might be up to. They don't look at me. They don't look at the wretched thing with the key. They turn and look at a man who has just entered (stage left).

He's a painfully thin man, and he looks like someone only half-awake, or like a sleepwalker, maybe. A somnambulist. He's barefoot. He's come down a flight of earthen stares [sic] at [sic] stands at the bottom, gazing directly at me and the wretched thing. He says something, but it's all French, and I'm not very good with

French. I only catch a few words. I'm almost pretty sure he says, *"Ne prenez pas cette route, Madame."* It's happened twice now, and I wrote that down as soon as I woke the second time. He also says, in English, "Please, turn around, go back!" He's very upset, and points at the hole the wretched thing made in the wall with the key. The robed figures are glaring at him now. The woman raises her dagger, taking a step towards him. The somnambulist turns and dashes back up the steps.

When he's gone, the wretched not-rat beast scrambles up to the man with the open book, and they whisper to one another. Then the man looks directly at me, and his eyes flash red-gold in the gloom, the way a cat's eyes will. He says, in English, "Heaven dost provide for all its children." I'm so scared, I finally do turn around, meaning to run back to the cellar or sea cave, whichever, because anything's better than this. But the hole in the granite wall is gone, and I'm *trapped* there. I slam my fists against the rock, over and over.

It shouldn't surprise you that I hardly sleep. . . .

Excerpt from a postcard found among the effects of Ms. Margaret H. Jacobs (7 Exegesis Street, Cincinnati, Ohio) following her suicide, from Lambshead, dated July 10, 1981 (postmarked July 13):

. . . can assure you, Ms. Jacobs, the letter in question did not come from my solicitors. I've inquired regarding this matter, and they've sent no such letter to you. Which is not surprising, as they aren't in the habit of taking such action unless I've requested that they do so. However, this said, I do think we might both be happier if these reports of yours ceased. I don't know what to make of them, and while I am obviously sorry if your visit set these unpleasant dreams in motion, I am not trained in psychoanalysis, and you'd be better served . . .

Excerpt from the obituary of Margaret Harriet Jacobs, *The Cincinnati Post*, July 8, 1981:

. . . a respected teacher and scholar, she was a tenured professor of Political Science at the McMicken College of Arts and Sciences, University of Cincinnati. She is survived by her sister, Dorothy Frost (née Jacobs), and her brother, Harold Jacobs. In lieu of flowers the family prefers memorial donations in the deceased's name to the Cincinnati chapter of the American Foundation for Suicide Prevention. Condolences may be expressed at . . .

Taking the Rats to Riga

A Critical Examination of Stigmata's Print

By Jay Lake

Perhaps the most quotidian detail of the print *Taking the Rats to Riga* (1969) is the eponymous rats themselves. This is somewhat uncharacteristic of the work of the artist Stigmata (b. Crispus Chang-Evans, Nanking, China, 1942; d. Khyber Pass, Pakistan, 1992). The artist was notorious for eschewing both representation and naturalism, noting in a 1967 interview with Andy Warhol, "The dial ain't set on sketch, and I'll never be a d**ned camera" (*artINterCHANGE*; vol. III, no. 4; 1968).

The unusual inclusion of such readily identifiable elements strongly hints that *Rats* is based on an actual event. The precise nature of this event is obscured by our distance in time from the origins of this print, as well as Stigmata's notoriously poor record-keeping. Lambshead's own acquisition notes on the print are strangely sparse as well. Art world rumor whispers that the print depicts a scene from *Karneval der Naviscaputer*, an occasional festival of deviant performance art held within East Berlin's underground club culture during the mid-to-late 1960s.

The astute observer would do well to attempt deconstruction of some of the other elements in *Rats*. Art unexamined is, after all, art unexperienced. In this case, even a close examination is unlikely to reveal the mundane truths behind the print. The emotive truths are, however, most certainly available.

Consider the chain that the rats are climbing. Why do they ascend? From where have they come? A hook dangles or swings not far below the lower rat. It appears ornamented in both shape and detail. Bejeweled, this cannot be an artefact of the working man. Nor does it conform to the Continental notion of *kunstbrukt*, that design should be both beautiful and functional. This hook is curious and attractive, but hardly something to lift a bale of opium from the decks of a shabby Ceylonese trawler. One must also consider the possibility hinted at in the print's title, that these are the plague rats Renfield carries into the world for his master Dracula, as depicted repeatedly in cinema.

Examine the chain itself. In Stigmata's rendering, this could just as easily be a motorcycle chain as a cargo chain or an anchor chain. Were that to be the case,

Taking the Rats to Riga, by Stigmata (1969); image from the collection of Eric Schaller.

we might assume the rats were being drawn upward, toward the top verge of the image. The dynamism of their forms suggests that they are more than mere passengers. Still, is that no different from a man walking up an escalator?

Once we have evaluated the context in which the rats appear, the image begins to lose its coherence. Most observers consider the smaller lines in the background to be more distant chains of the same sort the rats are climbing, but Priest has advanced the argument that those may be strings of lightbulbs (*Struggles in European Aesthetics,* Eden Moore Press, London, 1978). Her assertion is undercut by the strong front lighting on the primary figures in the composition, but given Stigmata's well-documented disregard for artistic convention, this is an inherently irresolvable issue.

The most visually dominant element in *Rats* is the tentacled skeleton in the left side of the image. Sarcastically dubbed "The Devil Dog" in a critical essay by Robyn (*Contemporary Images*, Malachite Books, Ann Arbor, 1975), this name has stuck, and is sometimes misattributed as Stigmata's title for the work. In stark contrast with the climbing rats, there is nothing natural or realistic about the Devil Dog. Rather, it combines elements of fictional nightmare ranging from Lovecraft's imaginary Cthulhu mythos to the classic Satanic imagery of Christian art.

Priest (op. cit.) nevertheless suggests that the Devil Dog may, in fact, be representational. Presuming even a grain of truth, this theory could represent the source of Lambshead's interest in acquiring *Rats* for his collection, given the doctor's well-known dedication to his own extensive *wunderkammer*. It is difficult for the observer to seriously credit Priest's notion, however, as she advances no reasonable theory as to what creature or artefact the Devil Dog could represent. She simply uses scare words such as "mutant" and "chimera" without substantiation. The burden of proof for such an outlandish assertion lies very strongly with the theorist, not with her critics.

Robyn and other observers have offered the far simpler hypothesis that the Devil Dog is an expression of Stigmata's own deeper fears. The open jaw seems almost to have been caught in the act of speech. While the eyes are vacant, the detail along the center line of the skull and above the orbitals can be interpreted as flames rather than horns or spurs. For a deep analysis of this interpretation, see Abraham (*Oops, I Ate the Rainbow: Challenges of Visual Metaphor*, University of New Mexico Press, Albuquerque, 1986). The tentacles dangle, horrifying yet not precisely threatening to either the artist or the observer. Rising above and behind is an empty rib cage—heartless, gutless, a body devoid of those things that make us real. This is a monster that shames but does not shamble, that bites but does not shit, that writhes but does not grasp.

The most important element in *Rats* is, without a doubt, the hand rising up to brush at the Devil Dog's prominent, stabbing beak. It is undeniably primate, and equally so undeniably inhuman. Still, a strong critical consensus prevails that this is Stigmata's own hand intruding to touch the engine of his fear. While the rats seek to escape up their chain, this long-fingered ape reaches deeper into the illuminated shadows, touching the locus of terror without quite grasping it.

The parallels to Michelangelo's *Creation of Adam* (ca. 1511) are inescapable and disturbing. Who is creating whom here? Is Stigmata being brought to life by his own fears? Or does he birth them into this print, as so many artists do, to release his creation on an unsuspecting world?

We can never answer those questions for Stigmata. Reticent in life, he, like all who have gone before, is thoroughly silent in death. Each of us can answer those questions for ourselves, however, seeing deeper into this print than the casual horror and blatant surrealism to what lies beneath. Much as Lambshead must have done when he bought the piece from the court-appointed master liquidating Stigmata's troubled estate, via telephone auction in 1993.

What wonder lies in yonder cabinet? *Taking the Rats to Riga* is a door to open the eyes of the mind. Like all worthwhile art, the piece invites us on a journey that has no path nor map, nor even an endpoint. Only a process, footsteps through the mind of an artist now forever lost to us.

The Book of Categories

Handled, Damaged, Partially Repaired, Damaged Again, and Then Documented by Charles Yu

0 What there is

1 Proper name

The full name for *The Book of Categories*[1] is as follows:

THE BOOK OF CATEGORIES
(A CATALOG OF CATALOGS
(BEING ITSELF A VOLUME ENCLOSING
A CONCEPTUAL STRUCTURE
(SUCH STRUCTURE BEING
COMMONLY REFERRED TO AS AN
(IDEA)-CAGE)))

2 Nature of

2.1 Basic properties of

The Book of Categories is composed of two books, one placed inside the other.

The outer book (formally known as *The Outer Book*) is a kind of frame wrapped around the inner book, which is known as, uh, *The Inner Book*.

2.1.1 Paper

The Inner Book's pages are made of a highly unusual type of paper, which is made of a substance known as (A)CTE, so-called because of its (apocrypha)-chemical-thermo-ephemeral properties, the underlying chemistry of which is not well understood, but the practical significance of which is a peculiar characteristic: with the proper instrument, (A)CTE can be sliced and re-sliced again, page-wise, an indefinite number of times.

2.1.1.1 Method for creation of new pages

Each cut must be swift and precise, and the angle must be metaphysically exact, but if the operation is per-

---

1 Which itself is listed in *The Book of Books of Categories*, vol. III, p. 21573, row K, column FF.

A photograph of pages from *The Book of Categories*, origin unknown.

formed correctly, there is no known lower bound to the possible thinness of a single sheet of (A)CTE paper.

2.1.1.1.1 Page count

To wit, as of the time of this writing, despite having total thickness (in a closed position) of just over two inches, *The Book of Categories* contains no less than 3,739,164 pages.[2]

3 Intended Purpose

3.1 Conjecture

This property of repeated divisibility is believed to be necessary for *The Book of Categories* to function in its intended purpose (the Intended Purpose).[3]

3.2 Theories regarding Intended Purpose

There are four major theories on what the Intended Purpose is. The first three are unknown. The fourth theory is known but is wrong.

The fifth theory of the Intended Purpose (the Fifth Theory) is not yet a theory, it's still more of a conjecture, but it has a lot of things going for it and everyone's really pulling for the Fifth Theory and thinks it's well on its way to theory-hood.

2 And counting.

3 The Intended Purpose is unknown, so this is basically just a wild-assed guess.

3.2.1   Unsubstantiated assertion (status: in dispute)

Whatever the Intended Purpose may be, this much is clear: the book is a system, method, and space for a comprehensive categorization of all objects, categories of objects, categories of categories of objects, etc.

4   What there is not

5   Mode of propagation

5.1   How the book changes hands

On the left-facing inside cover of The Framing Book, we find the word "DEDI-CATED," and underneath, two lines labeled

"From: _____ "

     and

"To: _____ ".

5.2   Each possessor of the book

attempts to impose his numbered ordering of the world by adding categories.

5.3   At some point whether out of frustration or a sense of completion, or a desire to impose such system on others,

a possessor will pass the book on to another user, by excising his or her name from the To line, placing the name in the From line, and then writing in the name of the next possessor of the book in the To line. The excision should be performed with the same instrument used to cut new pages.

6   As you may have realized

6.1   What this means is

The Book of Categories contains what is, in essence, its own chain of title. It is a system of world-ordering, which has, encoded into itself, a history of its own revision and is, in that sense, the opposite of a palimpsest. Nothing is ever overwritten in *The Book of Categories,* only interspersed, interlineated, or, to be more precise, inter-*paginated.*

7   Why

7.1   Why

would someone ever give this book away?

8 A man

8.1 Looking for what was there

8.1.1 Trying to name it

8.1.1.1 Naming being one way

to locate something not quite lost, and not quite found

8.1.1.1.1 A name also seeming

to be a necessary AND sufficient condition to possession of an idea, a name being a kind of idea-cage.

9 Something else you need to realize about the book

9.1 Is that

The sheer number of pages in the book is such that ordinary human fingers cannot turn the pages in a reliably repeatable fashion. Simply breathing in the same room as the book will cause the book's pages to flail about wildly. Even the Brownian motion of particles has been known to move several hundred pages at a time.

9.2 In fact, if you ever lose your place in the book,

it is unlikely that you will ever be able to return to the same page again in your lifetime

[INSERTED]

6.1.1 One reason

why someone would give this book away: at some point, whether out of frustration or a sense of completion, or a desire to impose such system on others, a possessor will pass the book on to another user, by excising his or her name from the To line on the

[INSERTED]

5.2.1 Each possessor of the book [4]

The various possessors of the book can be traced, from which[4]

---

[4] Lambshead himself has been the caretaker of the book on two separate occasions, each time receiving it from Bertrand Russell, and each time passing it to Alfred North Whitehead.

10 A man named Chang Hsueh-liang

has possessed the book seventy-three times. No other individual has owned it more than six times.

10.1   **Little is known about Chang, a general in the Chinese army,**

except that he is believed to have lost a child, a newborn daughter, in a freak accident while on a brief holiday with his family.

> 10.1.1   **The incident**
>
> Onlookers who witnessed the incident say there were no words in their language to describe what occurred, only that "the water took her" and that although "nothing impossible happened," it was, statistically speaking, a "once in a universe event."
>
> > 10.1.1.1 **His daughter**
> >
> > was five weeks old when she died. For reasons unknown, she had yet to be named.

10.2   **It is unclear whether Chang**

was repeatedly seeking out the book, or it kept finding its way back to him.

10.3   **A medal of some sort, and two insects**

are believed to have been placed inside the book by Chang.

> 10.3.1   **The general problem of categorization**
>
> Although it is worth noting that the location of these objects is unstable, due to a phenomenon particular to *The Book of Categories* known as "wobbling," which can result from stored conceptual potential energy escaping through the frame of *The Inner Book* and resonating with *The Outer Book*.

10.5   **It is clear from certain sites in the book**

that Chang remained obsessed with naming what had happened to his child.

> **10.5.1 Chang's last entry**
>
> is a clump of (A)CTE paper consisting of hundreds of thousands, maybe millions of blank pages, known as The Chang Region. On each page of The Chang Region of the book is written what appears to be an ancient form of a Chinese character. Scholars disagree as to the identity of the character.

11 Eventually, a possessor of the book comes to realize

how hard it is to find any given page, lost among the pages. Trying to find that slice, to cut through it on either side, before the page has been lost.

[INSERTED]

8.1.1.1.1.1 A name actually being

a memorial to the site where an idea once rested, momentarily, before moving on.

8.1.1.1.1.1.1 If you listen carefully,

you can hear it in there, but when you look inside, the idea-cage is always empty, and in its place, the concrete, the particular, something formerly alive,

now dead and smashed.

Objects Discovered in a
Novel Under Construction

Documented by Alan Moore

The following items have been retrieved from the construction site of an uncompleted novel, *Jerusalem*, where completion of the structure's uppermost level has been delayed by unanticipated setbacks that are unrelated to the project.

The site itself is gigantic in its dimensions, with more than half a million words already in place and the three-tier edifice as yet only a little more than two-thirds of the way into its lengthy building process. The intimidating silence that pervades the vast and temporarily abandoned landscape is exacerbated by the absence of the novel's characters and by the lack of any background noise resulting from the engineering and the excavation usually associated with such ventures.

Making a considerable contribution to the already unsettling ambience is the anomalous (and even dangerous) approach to architecture that is evident in the unfinished work: the lowest floor, responsible for bearing the immense load of the weightier passages and chambers overhead, seems to be built entirely of distressed red brick and grey slate roofing tiles with much of it already derelict or in a state of imminent collapse. Resting on this, the massive second tier would seem to be constructed mostly out of wood and has been brightly decorated with painted motifs that would appear to be more suited to a nursery or school environment, contrasted with the bleak and even brutal social realism that's suggested by the weathered brickwork and decrepit terraces immediately below.

The topmost storey, where work has been halted, seems again to be accomplished in a style that is entirely unrelated to the floors beneath. The building's lines and sweeping curves are unresolved, curtailed in jutting spars or girders that stand enigmatically against the skyline. Amidst these skeletal protrusions are two or three relatively finished works of decorative statuary, the most notable being a winged stone figure representing the archangel Michael, who is depicted

The Dead Dead Gang

A book discovered in Dr. Lambshead's cabinet, the bulk of it taken up by a false bottom, inside of which researchers found the text by Alan Moore and a tiny architectural structure consisting of several floors, somewhat akin to a doll's house, with a variety of odd objects inside each compartment or room.

standing with a shield held in his left hand and what seems to be a snooker cue clutched in his right.

The oddities listed below were all discovered in the confines of the structure's bottom two floors, and are labelled with an indication of which level and which individual chamber or compartment they were found in.

1. Deathmonger's aprons, two in number.
Found on ground floor; chamber 10.

These two aprons, which have been dated as originating from the first years of the twentieth century, have stitched-in tags identifying them as property of one Mrs. Belinda Gibbs. Supporting evidence suggests that Mrs. Gibbs's profession was that of an unofficial midwife/undertaker working in a badly disadvantaged neighbourhood located in the English midlands, persons of her calling being locally referred to as a "deathmonger."

One of the aprons is entirely black, being apparently the mode of dress appropriate for "laying out," or dealing with the bodies of the recently deceased. The other apron, meant for use on the occasion of a birth, is mostly white and yet around its edge is decorated with embroidered bees and butterflies in vivid, naturalistic colours.

In an inside pocket of the jet-black funeral apron, a discoloured handkerchief was found. Its sepia and burnt-umber stains suggest that Mrs. Gibbs was a habitual snuff-user, possibly as a precautionary measure to alleviate any olfactory distress occasioned by her work with cadavers.

2. Children's toys from dream, anagrammatically
derived. Found on first floor; chamber 13.

The second storey of the structure seems, from the inside, to border on the infinitely large, in terms of area, being much bigger than the floor below on which it somehow stands. Also, the actual substance of this second tier seems to be constantly in flux, with details of the landscape metamorphosing and shifting like the details of a dream. The overall appearance of this chamber is of an enormously wide wooden hallway or arcade, immeasurably long and with a grid of rectangular apertures set in its wooden flooring at regular intervals. These apertures look down upon the rooms and alleys of the floor immediately below, although for reasons that are as yet unexplained the holes are not apparent from beneath. Some of the spaces have entire (and massively expanded) trees growing up through them from the ground floor, with their upper branches reaching to the arcade's ceiling, a glass roof supported by Victorian ironwork beyond which vast geometric clouds, more like a diagram of weather than weather itself, appear to drift. The giant thoroughfare is thought to be known by its currently absented population as "The Attics of the Breath."

The hallway seems to be a magnified reflection of an ordinary shopping arcade found on the more naturalistic bottom level. Its endless walls are lined with shops, above which there are numerous wooden balconies. One of the businesses in the much smaller precinct on the lowest floor is a shop known as Chasterlaine's, dealing in toys and novelties. In the exploded reaches of the upper storey, though, this enterprise is subject to the creeping, dreamlike transformations that seem to afflict the second floor, its name moving through various anagrams to finally express itself as "The Snail Races" by the point at which work on the structure halted. In the window, displayed resting on their cardboard boxes in the manner of miniature 1950s Matchbox reproduction cars, was found a range of die-cast metal molluscs that were manufactured to incorporate the features of the scaled-down vehicles which they resembled: one snail has been painted white and has a red cross stencilled on its shell so that it calls to mind an English ambulance of the same vintage. Another has been liveried in navy blue with white calligraphy along its side, identifying it as a Pickford's removal van. A third has the snail's body dyed a brilliant post-box scarlet, while its spiral shell has been replaced by a tightly wound fireman's hose. All of the specimens discovered were roughly two inches long, two inches high, and an inch wide. Their value on the collector's market, if any, has proven impossible to calculate.

3. Solidified puddle of gold, three feet in diameter. Found on first floor; chamber 18.

Discovered in a typically oversized arena-like construction (which once more appears to be a massively expanded version of a site existing on the bottom floor), this smooth and flat ellipse of precious metal is reputedly a pool of scabbed, coagulated blood remaining from a brawl between two of the so-called Builders that are to be found amongst the structure's wildly variegated populace. According to reliable accounts, the Builders, upon this occasion, were perceived as being well over a hundred feet in height and were each armed with a proportionately massive snooker cue, their altercation having started in a nearby gaming parlour given over to the play of "trilliards," apparently a form of billiards undertaken by four players upon an impractically vast table with perhaps a thousand balls but just four pockets, situated at the corners. It would seem that local trilliards champion "Mighty Mike" emerged victorious from the colossal scrap, but since both combatants were wounded in the course of the engagement, it is not known from which Builder this specific pool of priceless blood was spilled.

4. Unusual fungal growths, found on ground floor in chamber 4; found widely distributed across first floor with specimens discovered in most of this second storey's chambers.

This peculiar variety of fungus seems to be a type that roots itself in higher mathematical dimensions, with the actual growth protruding down into the three-dimensional continuum below, where they are sometimes fleetingly apparent to a human viewer, despite being perceived very differently from a lower-dimensional perspective.

When viewed in their own environment, these growths have an attractive radiating symmetry, at first glance looking like some complex, delicately coloured form of starfish. Upon close inspection, though, it is apparent that the fungal bloom has taken the appearance of an interwoven ring of tiny naked women, all joined at the head with a communal tuft of "hair" (usually red, but sometimes black or blond) protruding from the centre of this strange, symmetrical arrangement. The bodies and the faces of these exquisite homunculi are overlapped in something of the manner of an optical illusion, so that three eyes will share two separate noses and two sets of rosebud lips, and that two distinct torsos will have only three legs with one limb shared by both.

Therefore, seen from above, these "fruit" have the communal tuft of usually crimson fibres at their centres, with a ring of glittering miniature eyes arranged around it, then a ring of noses, then lips, breasts, navels, and even dots of fibrous "pubic hair" set at the junctions of the radiating petal "legs." Turning the fungus over to inspect its underside, we have a scaled-down rear view of the conjoined female bodies with the decorative addition of small and translucent insect wings growing out from the beautifully sculpted miniature shoulder-blades. This would seem to explain why this form of the fungus is referred to as the "fairy" type, and would appear to represent the riper, more mature stage of the fungus's development. In its colouration, this mature form is astonishingly naturalistic in its mimicry of the nude human body, with a slightly carmine flush in the minuscule "cheeks" and bright green pinprick irises in the unusually animated-looking ring of eyes. The subtly graded pinks and creams have an appearance that is almost appetising, and the scent detectable upon the specimen is sweet and heavy, having notes of cardamom.

This is not true of the fungal growth's unripe or less mature form, known colloquially as the "spaceman" type. These growths are typified by a mildly unpleasant blue-grey colouring and an aroma that is sour and bitter, almost acrid. Rather than the visually pleasing ring of conjoined fairy figures found in more developed specimens, the miniaturised figures here are sinister and unappealing: spindly humanoids of no apparent gender, the smooth heads are disproportionately large and bulbous, and if these possess lips, ears, or noses, then these features are at best vestigial and practically unnoticeable. The eyes, however, are much bigger than those found in the mature and fully ripened "fairy" specimens, being a uniform and glassy black in colour, noticeably slanted and entirely lidless.

Where they are rooted on the building's second level, these growths are entirely visible and tangible. In the one instance where a specimen was found upon the ground floor, it was hidden to the ordinary senses and appeared to only manifest itself in brief consciousness-spasms that afflicted certain individuals, causing hallucinations where the compound figures of the higher-dimensional growth were perceived as independent tiny females in the manner of a fairy visitation. It may be imagined that the less-mature "spaceman" variety might bring about comparable dreams or mirages, but with black-eyed goblins substituted for wing-sporting naked women.

On the structure's upper floor, where the starfish-like blooms are easily detectable, they are known variously as Puck's Hats, Bedlam Jennies, Hag's Teats, or Mad Apples. It seems that the most important quality of these intriguing fungi is that they are the one foodstuff that such insubstantial and higher-dimensional beings as ghosts find edible. According to reports from these dimensionally displaced inhabitants of the unfinished structure's second storey, while the ripe "fairy" variety are the most flavoursome and sought-after, the "spaceman" form may be resorted to at times for want of any other sustenance. In either instance, the growth's "eyes" turn out to be small pips or seeds, hard and inedible, that must be spat out or excreted, thus ensuring that the growth . . . obviously not a fungus in the strict terrestrial sense . . . can propagate itself.

There are also reports that structures exist on some mezzanine level that's halfway between the ground and first floors, these being effectively the "ghosts" of long-demolished public houses. In these, revenant drinkers are alleged to congregate in mutual enjoyment of a form of alcohol that can be by some means fermented from the fungus to produce a rough home-made concoction known as Puck's Hat Punch. While enjoyably intoxicating in small quantities, it is believed that a prolonged exposure can wreak havoc with the mostly psychologically based "substance" of the phantom form, resulting in unstable physiologies that the sufferer will then have to endure perpetually. A local "character" known as Tommy Mangle-the-Cat is cited as evidence of this effect.

Down on the ground floor, where there may be many dozens of these growths existing undetected by the more prosaic population, it is said that the fungi prefer to root in places that have been associated either with intoxication or with mental illness. Public houses, drug dens, and, above all, psychiatric institutions are thus more than usually prone to infestation, and there have been anecdotal cases of the growths attaching themselves to a living human being's head, where they can bloom unseen by all but the afflicted party, while that party's consciousness is horribly afflicted by the visions that the fungus generates. Reportedly, Victorian patricide and fairy-painter Richard Dadd had an enormous "Puck's Hat" sprouting from his temple and affecting his behaviour tremendously, while it remained predictably invisible to Dadd's doctors and captors.

The display case containing these specimens appears to be empty, with its contents only viewable when situated on the structure's upper level.

5. Miscellaneous; found upon both completed floors, in various chambers.

One piece of burned cork, dated around 1910, supposedly used by Charles Chaplin as part of the makeup for his character "The Inebriate," performed with travelling comedy troupe Fred Karno's Army during that same year.

One gentleman's bicycle and two-wheeled trailer, also circa 1910, having no working brakes and being fitted with thick lengths of rope around the wheel-rims rather than the usual rubber tyres.

One printed pamphlet dating from 1738, titled "Submission to Divine Providence in the Death of Children recommended and enforced in a SERMON preached at NORTHAMPTON on the DEATH Of a very amiable and hopeful CHILD about Five Years old."

Imaginary children's book retrieved from dream of school, with green cloth boards and gold inlay illustration depicting a group of children including an older boy wearing a bowler hat. The book is titled *The Dead Dead Gang*, and its author is, apparently, one Marjorie Miranda Driscoll, a ten-year-old known more usually as "Drowned Marjorie."

Scrapbook of Princess Diana memorabilia, covering the period 1997–2005, belonging to Roberta Marla Stiles, an eighteen-year-old sex worker and crack cocaine addict who has decorated the book's cover with a collage of her own design, combining a sunset scene from a Sunday colour supplement with a picture of the late Diana Spencer's face pasted inexpertly onto the sun.

Artists' materials, circa 1865, thought to belong to Ernest Vernall, a worker employed in retouching the frescoes decorating the interior of the dome of London's St. Paul's Cathedral.

Artist's materials, circa 2015, belonging to Ernest Vernall's great-great-granddaughter, illustrator Alma Warren.

Sledgehammer, used in steel-drum reconditioning by Ernest Vernall's great-great-grandson and Alma Warren's younger brother, Michael.

THE ABOVE EXHIBITS, after cataloguing, have all been returned to the locations where they were discovered, ready and in place for when work once again resumes upon the structure, progressing towards its revised completion date of 2013.

VISITS and DEPARTURES

Visits

Over the years, several people visited Dr. Lambshead, and saw his cabinet. Few, however, can agree on its dimensions, exact location, or its contents. Sometimes, it isn't even clear that these visitors actually saw the core collection rather than just an overflow room on the first floor of the house. In three separate journal entries, Lambshead alludes to "a special room for the rubes," which he set up out of frustration at the number of requests to visit his cabinet. Many times he would relent and allow a visit, only to have his housekeeper lead the party in question to "the Rube Room" and then out the front door again.

A few notes on these entries, regardless of their accuracy. First, there is no truth to the claim that the chronicler of "The Singular Taffy Puller" simply "mistook Lambshead's kitchen for his cabinet," as put forward by Poe scholar S. J. Chambers. Nor is Mur Lafferty's failure to pass a polygraph test in 1965 relevant to her account. Those who doubt the testimony of Rachel Swirsky, meanwhile, should note that in 1994 she underwent a five-hour polygraph interrogation about her visit as part of misguided therapy for her "condition."

Finally, better investigators than the current editors have come up with inconclusive evidence as to the veracity of Lambshead's housekeeper, Paulette, whose account ends this section. Certainly, it's as good a story as any, even if it paints a rather narrow portrait of the good doctor.

As for more personal "visits and departures," Lambshead wrote on the subject in his journal while visiting newly independent Algiers in the late 1960s. He was no doubt thinking back to his involvement on the side of the National Liberation Front during the fight against the French a decade earlier.

"A visit presages its own departure, and almost no one makes it out," he wrote. "There's a hideous truth hidden in there—that sometimes *things* do the visiting for you and sometimes they're the message. Sometimes, too, whether it's a bullet or a collapsed roof or a fire or some other act of fate or chance, you don't always get to take out what you brought with you—even your own life."

Reports that a Greek woman, about a decade younger than Lambshead, was seen with him in Algiers that year, much as his wife, Helen, had in the 1950s, are entirely apocryphal. Certainly, no one matching the description appears in any of the official state footage of various public events. Indeed, Lambshead himself is rarely on display in these films—a matter of a few seconds here and there, his image soon gone and fading.

1929: The Singular Taffy Puller

As Told to N. K. Jemisin

I had traveled far—along the bustling coast by rail, then across the Atlantic by steamship, at great expense, I might add—on a matter of pride. Or, more specifically, dessert. You see, the cobbled and sweaty streets of my city would reek but for the exquisite aromas that offer relief from horse manure and overindulgence. Wrinkle your nose and you might miss the scent of the most delicate amaretto fondant, or creamy divinities solidifying to tooth-tenderness. And when the pecan harvest is brought—ah, me! You never tasted pralines like mine.

But those selfsame streets are crowded with eateries these days, and an old octoroon spinster looking to make a name for herself must employ more than the braggadocio that paler, maler chefs may indulge. Especially given that, of late, my business had suffered by its proximity to a flashy new restaurant next door. It was for this reason that I traveled to the house of the esteemed doctor, and was ushered into the renowned cabinet, so that I could at last behold the item that might—I hoped—save my business.

On entry to the doctor's home, I was momentarily stunned by the profusion of wonders within. These included the cabinet itself: a room of what had been handsome walnut wainscott and elaborately worked moulding (French rosettes and Egyptian cartouches, of all the mad combinations), though the lingering evidence of half-finished reorganization obscured the best of it. What remained of the chamber's treasures had been tossed, with no apparent regard for further cataloguing or even convenience, onto bookshelves, plinths, and racks, which quite crowded the space. Someone, however, had at least made an effort to group the items by purpose, so after some searching, I discovered the relevant rack. This was a baker's rack, naturally: three shelves of well-made ironwork fashioned into the most peculiar decorative geometries—what might have been lettering in some tongue of the far Orient, or the lost Toltec. But I will admit I spared less attention for the rack itself than for what it held.

All of the items were cooking implements of some sort: tongs for cooks lacking thumbs; an exceptionally large corkscrew; a strainer that, to all appearances, was solid but whose label indicated it could sift out bacterial particulates if given several days to work. There was also a fine Dutch oven, rather plainly enameled in white, whose lid had been securely tied with twine, then glued-and-papered over at each knot, then clamped with three vices, each of which appeared to have been welded so as not to turn. Like all the scions of Pandora who encompass my sex, I was most tempted to peel back at least one of the taped-over bits. My hand was stayed not by prudence, however, but by greed and impatience; the oven was not what I had come for.

At last I found it, behind a half-melted waffle iron: the Singular Taffy Puller.

Not much to look at, after all the effort I'd expended! The thing resembled nothing so much as an old-fashioned box iron of the sort my mother used when she took to laundering, after my father grew tired of keeping a *placée*. But where irons had a flat, tapered plate on the business end, this device had an irising cover that could be retracted by means of a clever mechanism on the handle. With the iris closed, the device was inert. When I opened it, however, and looked within the Puller, I beheld . . . nothing. No surface. Nothing that I could see, as I turned it to the light, save an unblemished, undifferenti-ated deepness of black. It was rather like a yawning, shadowless hole—but as I brought my free hand near it, I felt the powerful tug of the Puller's force. It was, for one moment, as though the Puller, not the ground beneath my feet, exerted the greater force of gravity. . . . Per my researches, I knew better than to move my hand much closer. And every journal I'd read on the object contained large-writ, dire warnings against ever breaching the horizon of its opening.

You may ask: of what use is such an item in taffy pulling? Well, as any con-fectioner can tell you, taffy must be pulled to achieve its proper consistency. When air bubbles are incorporated into the sugar matrix—yes, yes, science is of great relevance to cooking, but let us return to the matter of *taste*—the taffy be-comes lighter, softer, chewable rather than a jawbreaking knot. Unfortunately, when one pulls taffy with hands or even a standard machine, it is almost im-possible to keep contaminants from affecting the resulting substance. One of my best batches of Atlantic City Strawberry was utterly ruined when the stupid young potager of that damnable restaurant next door made a batch of gumbo with too much garlic. Just the scent of the stuff invaded my shop, but that was enough: invisible particulates of garlic worked their way into my candy, which I had flavored with real dried strawberries, and . . . Well, preventing such disas-ters was precisely why I had come all this way.

The Puller was capable of removing such particulates from the air. It would remove the air itself, if one pressed a different button on the handle, but as I fancied breathing, I resolved to test that one later. More important, my re-searches intimated that the Puller might improve my taffy in other ways. For the Puller did not just *draw in*. As I tilted the device, I noted a small glowing light near its tip. This was not part of the device, strictly speaking; rather, it was a sort of vent, covered over with leaded glass for safety's sake. However the Puller worked—and the books I'd found were as vague on its mechanics as they were regarding its origins—the by-products of its internal processes were said to include a peculiar form of emission, which appeared here as radiant light. If one could remove the glass and find a way to safely harness the emit-ted energy . . .

I make other sweets besides taffy, after all, and unique heat sources make for unique flavors. I would have to be careful regardless, as the Puller had had many, many owners over the years, some for ominously brief periods. One fact stood clear through all its shadowed history, though: those who mastered the Puller's secrets ranked among the greatest chefs and innovators of our art.

So I would test, and take great care in the testing. I would use every bit of knowledge and skill that I possessed, and some that I did not yet, to determine how best to employ this marvelous device. And if that thrice-damned potager next door ever again abused a bushel of garlic . . . Well, then I would have myself a fine new guinea pig.

So. When next you visit the city of the crescent, be certain that you come to the Vieux Carre, Toulouse Street, and ask for my shop. You will find the finest taffy in the city, to be sure—but if you find *new* desserts, then you will know my experiments have been successful. I shall owe it all, or at least its beginnings, to the good professor.

1943: A Brief Note Pertaining to the Absence of One Olivaceous Cormorant, Stuffed

By Dr. Rachel Swirsky

It was some sort of stuffed sea bird. A pelican or puffin or penguin . . . I'd never been good at birds. It stood with its feet awkwardly splayed and its wings raised in a threat display, neck curved and beak hissing. Black glass eyes shone murderously.

Dr. Lambshead (Thackery T.) thrust the dead thing forward. "This is it, you see! What did I tell you?"

"Doctor, I don't understand," I said. "What makes you think this seagull is the source of the phoenix mythology?"

"Gull? This is no gull!"

"I don't really do birds . . ."

"Note the slender body and long tail. This is a Brazilian olivaceous cormorant." He paused meaningfully. "Or looks superficially like one."

It was late 1943. I prickled in my cardigan suit and d'Orsay pumps; Dr. Lambshead looked breezy in his linen jacket and geometric tie. We stood in the basement of his Whimpering-on-the-Brook home, where he'd received me for the weekend, temporarily abandoning his post tending war wounded at the Combustipol General Hospital of Devon.

Readers who recognize me as a contemporary science fiction writer may be confused by my claims of visiting Dr. Lambshead in 1943. It's true, my body has only aged twenty-eight years at the time of this writing. This seeming contradiction is the result of a rare biological ailment, the nature of which Dr. Lambshead had been secretly helping me investigate, this comprising the bulk of our acquaintance.

You see, when I experience particularly extreme emotional states—sometimes joy, though usually pain or fear—my condition triggers a painful chemical process wherein I stiffen, contract, and shrink in on myself until I am reduced to infancy, and must re-embark upon the tiresome process of growing.

You must not take this for some airy supernaturalism. The matter is simple biology.

I maintain strict secrecy about my affliction; the world has always been hostile toward the unusual, and for centuries I've feared the historical equivalent of "alien autopsies." For this reason, I pressed Dr. Lambshead to keep his research confidential, which is why my affliction does not appear in any edition of his rare disease guide.

Dr. Lambshead was well aware that my condition had made me obsessed with legends of immortality, particularly those relating to the mythical phoenix, who—like me, and unlike the equally mythical vampire—must suffer periodic rebirth (with its loathsome necessity of periodic adolescence). Therefore, he had been sure to include the word "phoenix" in his invitation, knowing I would hasten to meet him immediately.

With this background, you may understand my disappointment as the distinguished scientific gentleman did nothing more dramatic than wave about the avian corpse while lecturing me on taxonomy.

"Of what possible interest," I asked with exasperation, "is this dead, grey thing?"

"That's just it!" he replied, excitement undimmed. "It's not grey at all!"

He pulled me nearer. Despite my natural disinclination toward being in such proximity to a corpse, I gasped—the feathers shone a strangely inorganic, metallic silver. Dr. Lambshead plucked one feather loose and held it to my eye. Even more remarkable! It shimmered with intense, beautiful colors that did not merely change in reaction to the light, but seemed to alter of their own accord. Gold, white, orange, rose, violet, and crimson danced together like the heart of a flame.

"Where did you find this?" I murmured.

The cabinet had a Victorian stiffness and eclecticism; I expected an answer in keeping with the air of pith helmets and mosquito nets. However, I must also report that I later felt that this was just a front or disguise of some sort for a more profound and eclectic collection.

"Some sprog found it in Gurney Slade. Sold it for thruppence."

"It's beautiful . . . but surely only superficially related to the phoenix mythos."

"You might think so! But my experiments have yielded other data . . ." Here, he digressed into such specialized, technical vocabulary that I cannot hope to repeat his lecture. At the completion of this torrent of obscurantism, he said, "I'll go fetch my notes."

Without further niceties, the doctor withdrew, taking the bird's corpse with him. Abruptly, I found myself alone in Dr. Lambshead's cabinet of curiosities.

A great deal of wordage has been spent describing the cabinet, but I will add my own. I've already mentioned that the rooms exuded a dark, musty air, crowded as they were with objects ranging from exquisite to disposable. A large number of preserved animal parts were affixed to brown velvet drapes that hung from the ceiling: malformed antlers, jagged horns, monstrous fish, paws and pelts and glowering heads. Bookcases crowded the walls, some filled with actual books, others piled high with specimen jars and music boxes and inscrutable devices.

My meandering took me to an archway blocked by a heavy, green-gold curtain. I admit I should not have swept it aside, but curiosity overcame my sense. As the fabric shifted, I saw a gleam in the shadows—something enormous and mechanical.

It will not surprise you that Dr. Lambshead attracted a great deal of gossip. In my social circle, it had long been suspected that Dr. L. was building some sort of war machine with which to aid the British effort. None of us doubted he could build such things; it was clear his genius extended beyond the medical.

It was such an armored monstrosity I expected to encounter when I stepped into the room. Imagine my surprise when I found myself nose to nose with a mechanical bull.

Don't mistake me. I don't mean the sort of crass rodeo relic on which inebriated young people struggle to maintain their equilibrium. This was a colossal bronze and silver construction, so large that its wickedly curved horns swept the ceiling. It was worked in excruciating detail, from muscular neck to powerful haunches. Only on close examination did I discern the evidence of clockwork mechanisms beneath its metal "skin."

I found myself drawn to the creature. I extended my hand, longing to stroke that vast, smooth muzzle.

At that moment, I heard Dr. Lambshead's returning footsteps. I snatched back my hand and turned toward the entryway. I expected him to be angry; instead, Dr. Lambshead seemed thoughtful as he looked between me and the bull.

He tucked the papers from upstairs under his arm. "My latest acquisition," he said. "More precisely, a loan from the Greek government. They want me to determine how it works."

"They don't know?"

"It was found at a recently discovered archaeological site containing a number of items typically used in the worship of Zeus. The bull appears to represent the god himself, who took a bull's form for seducing maidens. It's a sophisticated clockwork automaton and seems capable of independent motion, but I have not yet ascertained how to activate it."

"Archaeological site? This thing can't be more than a hundred years old!"

"The ancients appear to have possessed a great deal more technology than is commonly understood. For example, consider the Antikythera Mechanism, recovered at the beginning of the century from a shipwreck site. My more radical colleagues hypothesize it's a sophisticated clockwork-powered calendar, though they lack verification."

He paused to give me a significant look.

"Don't you remember?" he asked.

Dr. Lambshead was perpetually trying to discern when I'd contracted my ailment. "I may be old," I said, "but not that old."

The doctor gave me another strange look. "Sometimes you look quite young."

His gaze traveled briefly down my body. With a jolt, I realized the bull's allure had done more than draw me closer. Without noticing, I'd undone my jacket's top button. I ran my fingers through my hair; it tumbled untidily from my French twist.

"It's strangely beautiful," I said. "It seems so polished, so smooth." I reached toward its muzzle again. This time, my fingertips connected.

The bull blinked.

It let out an enormous snort. Metal rasped against wood as it pawed the floor. Its head swung back and forth, horns lowered and pointing straight toward us.

For a moment, we stood, stunned and still.

Then Dr. Lambshead screamed: "Run!"

Dr. Lambshead's papers tumbled to the ground as we bolted past the green-gold curtains, through the crowded rooms, up the basement stairs and out into the road. The bull crashed through walls as he barreled after us, the steam from his nostrils acrid in the air.

Our feet pounded the mud. "What happened?" I shouted, breathing hard as I ran.

"There must have been a chemical catalyst! Tell me, are you menstruating?"

"What a question!"

"I know the trigger can't be touch, because I've touched it. It can't be a woman's touch because I asked my cook downstairs for such an experiment. Are you a virgin?"

"An even worse question!"

"Zeus used his bull form to seduce maidens. Some womanly attribute must be key."

"If the bull seduced maidens, why is it trying to kill us?"

"Now *that* is a good question!"

We rounded past the hedge maze, pushing toward the chapel on the hill. The bull's footsteps thundered close behind. And yet Dr. Lambshead continued to ruminate aloud.

"The catalyst must be a complicated chemical interaction. Perhaps pheromonal. I've been experimenting with such things for treating Recursive Wife Blindness. I think—"

I was not to know his thoughts, for the bull had finally caught us. It reared, massive golden hooves raking the sky. I knew with sinking certainty that my long life would end there, trampled by those hooves and then gored for good measure by those horribly curved horns—

—as the terror overcame me, I felt the familiar shrinking sensation that meant only one thing.

I was about to be reborn.

Through my narrowing vision, I saw that, against all odds, Dr. Lambshead had rallied, having dredged up a square of red fabric from who knows where. He rounded on the bull with a wide, confident stance, flag rippling behind him.

I laughed. How could I have doubted a man like Doctor Thackery T. Lambshead? But the shrinking accelerated and I knew I would not see his victory, at least not in a way I could comprehend. Oh damn, I was going to have to be thirteen again. Oh damn, oh damn, oh damn.

I know not what happened next, only that Dr. Lambshead survived the encounter. That was the last I saw of the Grecian bull.

I have some suspicions, however. It is my belief that Dr. Lambshead bested the thing and then disassembled it, using the intricate technological secrets he derived to begin what's now known as the Information Age.

Don't scoff. As I've mentioned, Dr. Lambshead was clearly capable of such scientific feats. My explanation is at least as plausible as the traditional one that hypothesizes an exponentially accelerating pace of technological invention.

ALL THIS HAPPENED nearly seventy years ago. I've lived two lives since then. Nevertheless, there are two things I wish made known about the incident before I complete my notes.

First: Don't allow superstitions to cloud what I've written. Everything that occurred had a mundane, natural explanation. Honor Dr. Lambshead's memory. He would not want you engaging in tempting flights of fancy.

Second: There is no way to prove my assertions. I admit this suits my purposes as I remain dedicated to protecting my secrecy. It's only because of the recent conventions merging memoir and fiction that I can tell this story at all. I hide behind the edifice of literary convention, and its helpful construction of the unreliable narrator.

As for objects that might substantiate my claims, there are only two. One, the bull, was long ago disassembled. Two, the stuffed corpse of a mysterious sea bird, such as the one listed in your exhibit's inventory as One Tern, Stuffed, Moderate Condition—as to this latter item, I hope you will forgive me. I cannot risk you examining its feathers and concluding my claims are true. Therefore, I've relieved

269

your exhibit of one stuffed bird, though I hope you will equally enjoy the plastic flamingo I've left in its place.

Of course that's not my only reason for making off with your treasure. After being reborn in 1943, I was understandably too preoccupied to track down Dr. Lambshead for several years. I was unable to investigate as an adult, either, for reasons too complicated and personal to note here. I did attempt to pilfer both bird and notes after Dr. Lambshead's death, but the collapsed basement thwarted my attempts.

Thus it was with great pleasure that I received my invitation to preview the exhibit. It was with even greater pleasure that I discovered your security guards to be both affable and susceptible to drugs.

My consolations for your loss—and thank you for the bird.

1963: The Argument
Against Louis Pasteur

By Mur Lafferty

Is it odd that my clearest memory about Dr. Lambshead, world traveler, collector, and chronicler of the obscure, was his hatred of Louis Pasteur? I suppose when you connect a gastronomically violent reaction to a memory, that particular recollection sticks longer than others do.

It was 1963. I remember because I was to have been in Dallas to cover Kennedy's visit the following week, but I was unable to go because I was too weak due to my visit with Dr. Lambshead.

I had gotten a choice assignment to interview Dr. Lambshead, who agreed to meet me in his own home. I brought three notebooks and three pencils, but never thought to bring my own cream.

The doctor was polite yet distracted, as he poured my tea and added a dollop of cream without asking me if I preferred it (I didn't). I was focusing on my books and idle chitchat with Lambshead (I don't remember what about; that was erased by the next forty minutes), I took a large gulp of the Earl Grey. When the curdled cream hit my system, my skin broke out in a cold sweat and I found myself in the profoundly embarrassing position of needing, if not a toilet, a chamber pot where I could be politely ill.

The doctor took my request in stride, pointing me to the head and saying

Louis Pasteur, 1822–95

through the door that it was "only a bit of food poisoning, [I] should get over it posthaste and we can start the interview."

I'm sure I would have enjoyed looking at the fascinating drawings and pieces of art, including an odd anatomy chart that hung, water-wrinkled, in the curtainless shower, but I was too busy voiding the very fine salmon I'd just had for lunch. And the tea. And the wretched cream. And possibly some stomach lining.

When I returned to him, shaky and pale, but confident I could at least finish this rarest of rare interview opportunities (Lambshead was not often at home in the sixties), he started talking, not about his research but about Louis Pasteur. He derided the French scientist, saying that the world honored him for pasteurization, but Lambshead could easily name fourteen strains of bacteria that could figure out how to maneuver Pasteur's innovative S-shaped flask.

"You can't even call that a maze," he said, laughing.

I glanced at my teacup, with little lumps of curdled cream floating in it, and asked if that was why he refused to use pasteurized milk.

271

He waved me off, not answering, and motioned me to stand. "If you want to see a way to battle bacteria, come with me."

He led me back to the kitchen (the cream bottle sat on the counter, the cream clearly separated. I looked away) and out the back door. A cellar door sat flat in the lawn, surrounded by odd purple plants and prickly flowers. I was no botanist, but I was pretty sure they weren't native to England. I had no chance to ask about them, as he quickly hefted the door open and led me to the basement.

"There's no light right now, so just give me a second," Lambshead said. "Pasteur would have killed to see this. He would have eaten his *hat*."

There was indeed no light, but the basement was oddly dry and warm, something you didn't really see in an underground, English room made of stone. The dim daylight that dared to follow us into the basement tentatively touched a couple of shelves, and I gasped. The doctor had taken me to his cabinet, and I could see almost nothing! I could make out a large table in the corner with a single chair, both table and chair covered with various books, maps, and, I think, a taxidermed three-legged platypus.

One shelf had stuffed (although I could swear I saw one move, but it was dark) tropical birds. I tried to make out what was in some glass globes that looked as if they were full of mist and fireflies. Lambshead rummaged in a corner, murmuring to himself. I could make out, "If he'd just held out five years, we could have done so much together, but he died a moron."

(I later checked on this: Lambshead was born in 1900, and Pasteur died in 1895. I knew Lambshead was a child prodigy, but what he thought a seventy-eight-year-old man would have learned from a newborn, I did not ask.)

I reached out my finger to touch what looked like a finely crafted wooden horse, but then pulled back. Something had shifted, almost imperceptibly, inside.

An ancient spear sat propped in the corner opposite the door, and I peered at it. The spear was filthy, still bloody from the poor victim that had been pierced last. I shook my head. On the floor next to the spear lay at least twenty pots, most of them closed, but one on its side, shattered, with dust spilling out everywhere.

Something that looked like a bouquet of dried scorpions stuck up from another urn, and I decided I would not try to touch anything else.

Then Lambshead made an "aha!" sound, and I heard a crash as he tried to extricate something from a pile. He looked down at the floor and frowned. He said, "That was unfortunate, I should get Paulette to clean that up before it spreads," and then took my arm. I followed him reluctantly out to the sunny afternoon and watched as he closed the door.

But then I saw what he held, and the mysteries under the floor seemed unimportant. It was a most curious item; a flask, like Pasteur had created, but that was like saying a Chevy Sedan is a carriage much like Maximus Creed from Rome had cobbled together in 200 B.C. A large bulb at the bottom held a clear, broth-like liquid, but the neck of the flask swooped down in Pasteur's S shape, and then split in three, one swooping back up into a spiral that nearly reached two feet high, and then ended at a sealed glass nipple. Another branch of glass wound round itself, creating knots and curlicues; I counted at least three different sailor's knots and one Celtic knot, and seven more I couldn't identify, some seeming to actually have glass tubes entwined with it that started nowhere and ended nowhere. This whole complex mess wound round the bulb in a spiral, swooping back up to form the open mouth of the flask. The third branch was the strangest, stretching up and then coming back down to go back into the bottle, and, as far as I could tell, back out the bottom, only to fold back and actually form the bulb of the jar itself. This made it a Klein bottle (named for Felix Klein, d. 1882, and, unlike Pasteur, apparently a man *not* to be derided by Dr. Lambshead), sharing its inner and outer side.

I stared at it, flabbergasted by the sheer mastery of workmanship. It could have been my previous unfortunate upchucking situation, as I rarely find myself at a loss for words, but I simply looked from the flask to the doctor, and waited.

"You see, Pasteur managed a reasonable solution for everyday basic bacteria, proving that they can't pass a normal S bend. But you know he was killed by bacteria? Some say it was a stroke, but it was a bacterium with skilled navigational instincts, the kind of thing that laughs at the S bend, and is capable of trekking the fine capillaries, avoiding white blood cells, to attack at the most vulnerable areas in the brain. If he'd developed and learned about this flask in the years before I was born, he could have flummoxed the bacterium and lived longer." He pointed to one of the sailor's knots in the flask. "Here's where they usually get caught, in the Figure of Eight Stopper. Just get outright lost. They rarely make it to the Angler's Loop," he pointed to the final knot.

It was true, the open tubes had varying amounts of grime near the opening, with dead bugs caught in the knots, and some even having followed the dead-end tube and gathered in the nipple, but all of the glass near the bulb to the flask was perfectly clean. It was even clean on the outside.

I pointed to the bulb. "What do you have in there?"

He waved his hand again, and I wondered how many of my interview questions he would brush away. "Something pure, I can tell you that, untouched by neither smart nor ignorant bacteria. I'm saving it for a special occasion." He winked at me.

He took the flask with us inside and then offered me more tea, which I politely refused. We went on with the interview, not mentioning the cabinet again.

When I heard of his death in 2003, I wondered if he'd ever used what was in the flask, or if any of his journals would detail its contents. I also wondered if, perhaps, the flask died the same death as whatever crashed to the ground during my visit, and went from "something pure" to "something Paulette has to clean up before it spreads."

Regardless, in perusing the recent auction catalog for the few unearthed cabinet items that survived the fire, I was struck by the following description: "*Glass abstract sculpture.* Unknown origin. Composed of several curving and circular parts. Badly scorched and melted." Unfortunately, the item had already been bought, and I could not act on my sudden impulse to own it.

1972: The Lichenologist's Visit

As Told to Ekaterina Sedia by S. B. Potter, Lichenologist

As many readers of my novels know, I am also a professional lichenologist, and as such also part of a select and small community of fellow researchers. A few years back, when lichen taxonomy was revised based on new molecular data, it caused quite an upheaval—meaning that among fifteen people who've heard about it, ten cared. One of more vocal critics of the new taxonomic system was one S. B. Potter (not his/her real name), who has been active in the field for years, and who vigorously objected to redefining of some lichen genera. After one particularly heated Internet discussion, I received a snail-mail letter from S. B., containing the following story about a visit to Dr. Lambshead back in the 1970s. I'm afraid Potter has not communicated with me since, and I have no further information to offer. Although I do often wonder about the hand.—E. S.

I first visited Dr. Lambshead under a purely professional set of circumstances: I was recommended to him as the main lichenology expert of the area. At the time, Dr. Lambshead was just beginning to acquire a reputation for his acumen in the unusual diseases, and, like most men who are out to establish themselves, he was particularly impatient with anything that threatened to thwart his progress.

He called on me in secrecy, as if sharing his befuddlement would somehow diminish his stature: he had sent his letter with a messenger, the red wax of the seal reflecting the monogram of his signet ring, pressed with unnecessary vigor.

"Dear Dr. Potter," he wrote in his meticulous, small and square letters, "I loathe to impose on your time, but I suspect that I'm in need of your expertise. I have a patient, one Mrs. Longford, who has developed a persistent cough, and then, a week later, strange greenish-grey splotches on the backs of her hands. I took a sample of the tissue and subjected it to microscopic examination, and to my surprise, the tissue appeared to be of a plant origin. I sent samples to my friends in Oxford, and they confirmed that the sample is indeed a lichen. They also forwarded your name and address to me, and in that regard I am now seeking your advice.

"Would you be able to identify the specimen, and possibly suggest the ways to alleviate my patient's suffering? As time goes on, she is getting worse, with lichen now covering most of her extremities and spreading to her neck. Her cough has become rather fitful as well, and the sputum contains blood as well as lichen tissues. Yours sincerely, Dr. Thackery Lambshead."

At the time, I had just begun to stumble toward the discovery of the link between seemingly innocuous lichens and the disease, but I was still ignorant of the darker nature of this connection; despite my ignorance, however, I had developed a sense of foreboding, as if the part of me that was more perspicacious than the rest was trying to warn me of some unknown danger. However, being a man of

Lichen or Lambshead's new fingerprint?

science, I had dismissed such irrational thoughts and decided to travel to Dr. Lambshead's abode.

He resided in a large house, old and broad, fitting for a family doctor, I thought. The stones that composed its walls bore green and grey splotches, familiar to me—out of the habit, I gauged the age of the house by the lichen size. You see, lichens grow so slowly that many only increase their diameter by one millimeter a year; a lichen blemish the size of a penny is usually a hundred years old. The lichens on Lambshead's home, however, were enormous—if I was to believe them, his house was much older than Hadrian's Wall. Or at least the stones that composed it were—which was rather easier to believe, and I accepted this supposition as truth, reluctant (or unable) to continue thinking about the alternatives.

My next (unnoticed, unheeded!) warning came when the door swung open—it was a massive iron contraption, painted russet-red—and revealed a small man, his grey hair crusting over the dome of his variegated skull. His small eyes looked at me dully.

I asked to see the master of the house, and the man who answered the door turned, exposing the same powdery, unhealthily greenish aspect on the back of his neck as I had previously noted on his head.

Dr. Lambshead himself didn't seem to belong in the foreboding and dark atmosphere of the house—he, as you would well know, was a jovial, hearty man, and his appearance dispelled any doubts I might have had about coming there. He had not a trace of the sickly pallor about him, and at once I scolded myself for my overly active imagination.

I looked at the samples and was able to confirm that they were indeed soredia (asexual reproductive structures) of a lichen; I was even able to guess its genus as *Caloplaca*, but the species eluded me. I promised to conduct additional chemical tests to tease out the exact nature of the specimen, and, with the business concluded, agreed to join my host for tea.

Over tea, I started to feel mildly ill, and was unable to much concentrate on the words of Dr. Lambshead. Blood pounded in my ears, muffling his voice, and my right hand was throbbing. I glanced at my fingers holding the teacup, and noticed that they had grown swollen and powdery; moreover, small brown fruiting bodies were staring to open on my fingertips, like tiny ulcers.

I kept staring at my hand, paralyzed—the speed with which the lichen was growing was shocking, and I could not decide how I had managed to get myself exposed. I did not handle the specimen; it was presented to me on a glass slide. In fact, the only thing I had touched in that whole house was Dr. Lambshead's hand when I shook it—and the teacup.

A sudden realization shifted inside me, snapping like a string, forcing everything into focus. The butler, the blotches of lichen on the house itself . . . "Excuse me," I asked my host then in a trembling voice. "But that patient of yours . . . did you know her before she fell ill?"

Dr. Lambshead nodded. "Yes," he said, after a brief hesitation that told me that he was acquainted with the woman rather more than he wanted anyone to know. "I am friendly with the entire family." During this exchange, he looked straight at me, at my disfigured, bloated hand, and there was no possibility that he didn't see its state. And yet, he didn't make the slightest show of concern. "Is that important?"

"My hand is bothering me," I said, and splayed my blotchy fingers on the white tablecloth.

"It seems to be in order," he said. "Why do you think that my previous familiarity with the patient is relevant?"

His calm tone was the last shred of conviction I needed. I now knew—and I also knew the only reasonable thing to do. I grabbed the bread knife off the table and brought it hard over my wrist, for it is better to amputate one's appendage than to let the terrible contagion spread. The pain was surprisingly dull, even as I cringed at the impossible cracking of the bone and snapping of cartilage, as my blood stained the tablecloth and my host stumbled backward away from the table, his eyes and mouth opening wide.

I do not remember how I fled—the loss of blood weakened me, and I recovered my memory only a few days later, when I discovered myself in my own bed, light-headed but lucid. A neatly bandaged stump of my wrist proved that the events were not my imagination, and my renewed horror was soon soothed by relief once I discovered that *Caloplaca* or whatever accursed genus it was had not spread to the rest of my arm—I had acted just in time.

Despite the time that passed and the pestering questions of friends and relatives who wanted to know what happened to my hand, I have kept these events private until now. As much as I wanted to alert others to the danger, I also feared that my sanity would be questioned, and I did not relish the thought of involuntary commitment to the asylum. My story was as implausible as it was truthful, and really, who in their right mind would believe my discovery—that the man of such knowledge and medical expertise is not what he claims to be at all. You see, that day I realized that Dr. Thackery Lambshead was nothing more than a novel species of lichen, which somehow managed to impersonate a human being. I still believe that it belongs to *Caloplaca* genus.

1995: Kneel

By Brian Evenson

It should be no surprise that, in addition to his catalog of discredited diseases, Dr. Thackery T. Lambshead's collecting impulse extended to art, as exemplified by the galleries that form part of his cabinet of curiosities. His taste here ran to the mad and the mystical: at its best, *brut*ists like Adolph Wölfli and William Kurelek on the one hand, symbolists such as Carlos Schwabe and Mikalojus Konstantinas Ciurlionis on the other. In his galleries, I noted several pieces likely to cause a connoisseur's eye to glisten—for instance, a previously unknown minor Einar Jónsson sculpture or a particularly luminous landscape by Lars Hertervig. But for the most part, the work is mystical in a stately, dignified way, rarely shocking or surprising.

Or at least that is the case with the pieces most readily on display. If you navigate the twists and turns of Lambshead's galleries, if you begin to pay as much attention to your surroundings as to the work itself, you might stumble upon a certain plain white wall. If you take the time, as I did, to look carefully at this wall, you might glimpse a thin filament of light, nearly invisible, crossing it at about the level of your hips. And if you, intrigued, approach this wall and push at it and prod at it, you might well be rewarded, as I was, by the sound of a slight click and the opening of a panel.

An ordinary visitor to Lambshead's home might not be tempted to take the next steps: to fall to his hands and knees, peer into the opening revealed, and then crawl in. But I, as a trusted member of the organization hired by Lambshead to evaluate the artistic portion of his collection while he was away (an organization which, for the purposes of this report, must remain nameless), did take these next steps. On my knees, I peered into darkness. And then, taking a deep breath, I crawled in.

AT FIRST, I thought I had entered some sort of ventilation shaft. The passage was square, the floor and walls made of polished concrete, surprisingly warm to the touch. I was puzzled not to detect the fusty scent I often associate with such places; indeed, there was no smell to it at all. The passage itself sloped very slowly down, just enough that I could feel it. Glancing behind me, at first I could see the opening I had come through, but soon the passage had slanted enough that even that had vanished.

How long I crawled I cannot say. It seemed like some time: I had the impression that I had journeyed outside the confines of the house proper, down into the soil of the grounds surrounding it, but perhaps it was no more than a few dozen meters. Several times I nearly turned back—and indeed would have if the passage had not been too tight to negotiate turning around.

Then, abruptly, the passage reached its termination, concluding in a blank wall, a fact which, I have to admit, caused a certain amount of panic to well up within me. I pawed at the wall, looking for some hidden lever or some sign that what I was facing was not a wall but a door.

But I found nothing.

I AM GENERALLY not the sort to lose my composure. I am, in fact, known among my associates for my sangfroid, my ability to remain cool as a corpse no matter what difficulty I confront. I have no doubt that, despite my panic and the strangeness of the situation, I would have soon succeeded in mastering myself and proceeding in a calm and orderly fashion toward the nearest exit, backing my way slowly out. But in this task, I immediately encountered a complication. For as soon as I began to move backward, I discovered that not only was there a wall in front of me, but now a wall behind me as well.

THERE FOLLOWED A period that I cannot account for, in which I lost track of myself. Perhaps I lost consciousness. Perhaps in my panic I became, for a few seconds, for a few hours, another person entirely. I cannot account for this period. This fact troubles me more than any other.

Suffice it to say that, when I found myself again, my situation had changed. I was lying on the floor of a small, surprisingly modern room, architecturally dissimilar to the rest of the Lambshead residence. The contents of the room seemed to be an artistic installation. There was a painting hanging on the wall, with what I at first interpreted to be a sculptural object just before it, the word KNEEL inscribed in gothic script along the object's base.

Perhaps I was wrong in judging it to be an art installation, I thought, seeing this word. It had a dark, religious feel to it. Perhaps rather than a sculpture, this was an altar.

A rare view from inside Dr. Lambshead's cabinet, ca. 1995, showing Scott Eagle's art installation.

But, I wondered, *an altar to what?* I shook my head, told myself I was letting my time in the darkness get the better of me. Of course it was an art object, and I, as a member of the organization, was here to evaluate it.

The painting associated with the installation depicted a teapot, flame spurting from its spout, its body seemingly bloody. It rested on a mound of what might be tentacles or intestines, though they had a machinic aspect as well, and at least one of them terminated in a long-fingered, sharp-clawed hand. There was no signature that I could see, though the technique recalled for me the work of Scott Eagle, or Scott Aigle (as the French call him). The frame was irregular, strangely patched on one side. The longer I looked at it, the more I came to feel that the artwork did not end with the painting proper but extended into this frame. I heard, when I approached the painting, a strange humming, as if I might turn it over to find its reverse swarming with bees. But perhaps this was a quality of the room tone and not of the painting itself.

THERE WAS, BELOW the painting, what at first appeared to be a poem. A series of words, in any case. I read it, but once I had finished, found that I could not remember what it had said, nor, indeed, make any proper sense of it. I read it again, and a pressure began within my head, which, rightly or wrongly, I ascribed to the poem. I was tempted to read it a third time, this time aloud, but resisted, vaguely afraid of what might happen to me if I did.

And what was that at the bottom of the wall, that strange grouping of blood-red, unidentifiable objects? I crouched and examined them, picked one up and turned it round and about in my hand. It was like a small stone, but soft, and made of a substance I did not recognize.

I followed the line of objects back to the altar, for I had now begun in earnest to think of it as an altar. In the place of wooden spindles or legs, it rested on four simulacra of arms, lacquered. These supported a bottom platter, round, upon which rested sets of false (so I assumed) teeth, arranged in two rows. A top platter was cracquelured over with dried blood, and on this, other platters, other inexplicable disks, and finally, at the top, a glass bell, containing flecks of something like ice. Riding within the ice was an object of uncertain design.

What was the object? I could make out aspects of it, had something of a grasp of its shape and color, but still could not determine what it was. Truth be told, I remained unsure whether it should be considered art or something else, something ritualized and potentially threatening.

Kneel, the base of the altar commanded me. But I did not kneel. Instead I

Detail shot of Eagle's art installation

remained standing, hunched and leaning over the altar, my face nearly touching the glass bell. And then, on a whim, I reached up and lifted it away.

And here, I am afraid to admit, I suffered another lacuna, another moment of loss. There are things I remember. A roaring sound, but distant, as if miles away, as if there were still time to find shelter from whatever was coming. A horrible stench, like the air itself had been scorched. Brief flashes of motion and light, coming initially from the painting but quickly spreading all around me. And then nothing.

I returned to consciousness in the bushes next to one wall of the estate, unsure of how I had arrived there. One side of my body was sore, covered with scratch marks and scabs. My earlobe was stiff with dried blood, though I found no sign of any injury or wound. My tongue was scraped raw and sat heavy in my mouth.

When I stumbled back into the house, I discovered several days had passed and I had been replaced in my project of evaluating the collection.

When asked to justify my absence, first by my replacement and then by my betters in the organization, I recounted all that had happened. And yet, no matter how I searched, no matter where I looked in the galleries, I could find no hidden entry or door. I did my best to draw what I had seen, what I had perceived, but my interlocutors remained incredulous. There was, they told me, no secret room, no private altar of forearms and blood and teeth; I had dreamed it; I had imagined it.

When they told me this enough times, I stopped trying to convince them. Yes, I conceded, it was not real. I had merely fallen and hit my head. Nothing happened. I saw nothing.

BUT, OF COURSE, I had seen what I had seen, and as time went on, I found the memory of what I had seen working away at me. I saw it there before me: a painting of tubes and tentacles, an unknown object on a strange altar, balanced atop teeth and arms. And sometimes, in my thoughts, the teeth begin to chatter and the arms flex and stretch, the fingers moving, calling me, beckoning me. And though I had originally been repulsed, I now found myself more and more attracted, more and more drawn in.

Tonight I will break into the estate and then, with a sledgehammer, strike wall after wall until I find the vanished door. Once found, I will open it and again follow the passage slowly down until I find myself standing before the altar. This time, I will heed its advice and kneel. It will, I am certain, reward me. But how, and with what, and whether for better or worse, I do not know.

I am writing this record to stand in my place in case I do not return.

2000: Dr. Lambshead's Dark Room

By S. J. Chambers

About ten years ago, Dr. Lambshead published an article in the *Psychomesmeric Quarterly* about hypnotic techniques inherited from his grandfather, a great confidant of Monsieur Mesmer. Among Lambshead's mesmeric family legacy was the Valdemar Method, which enabled the doctor, so he claimed, "to extract from even the most cavernous subconscious those diseases that afflicted the soul, as demonstrated in the mesmeric stories of Edgar Allan Poe."

As I am a Poe scholar, the doctor's claims intrigued me and I wrote him requesting a demonstration. I knew the good doctor could not resist a challenge, so to further intrigue him, I mentioned that I felt riddled with a disease of influence that was affecting my work and love life, and offered myself up as the proverbial guinea pig. Within a fortnight, I received an invitation to his house, "the only place," he wrote, "where the Valdemar Method could be manifested."

Surprisingly, Dr. Lambshead appeared to have no maid or butler, and was already waiting at the door when I arrived. An ancient but spry man in a tailored silk bathrobe, he was headed down the hallway before I could put my bags down and greet him.

"To the matter at hand," he said. "Don't tell me a thing. That is for the Dark Room to show."

He waved me inside and led me to the back of the house, where he pulled aside a faded Turkish rug to reveal a trap door that fell open into a dark and dusty staircase. He descended into that darkness, and I followed him down several flights, feeling my way around the rocky walls, until he suddenly halted and clapped his hands repeatedly. When he stopped clapping, several floating orbs illuminated the basement.

"Will-o'-the-wisps," Lambshead said, "from the Iberian Coast. I caught them with one of Nabokov's butterfly nets." I looked at the floating lights, which graduated from green to purple, blue to red, like childhood's LED sparklers. I held out my hand and one alighted on my finger—its touch cool as the Mediterranean.

"How . . . how do they . . ."

"Float? Live? Glow?" He shrugged. "Curious, no?" This response disappointed me. It was unlike a man of science to pass up a chance to explain away the world. As if he knew my thoughts, he smiled. "Even in this century, there are still wonders beyond explanation. They are rare, but they do exist, and it has been my hobby, I suppose you could say, to collect all the world's true curios, as you will see. But no more words for now unless prompted; it disrupts the process!"

We continued through the hallway, and the will-o'-the-wisps grew brighter as we walked through the cabinet until we entered a dark chamber, empty but with the exception of two worn Louis XVI chairs.

"Ah, now we can really begin."

He sat in one chair and gestured for me to occupy the other. The will-o'-the-wisps floated out of our hands and hovered between our eyes. They undulated, glowing and dimming in tune with my heartbeat that swooshed through my ears.

"I want you to watch the wisps," he whispered, "and tell me: have you experienced these following symptoms: soaring soul, existential exigency, speaking in cryptically symbolic metaphor, vertigo caused by sublimity, vision heightened by chiaroscuro, dead-dwelling, or head-swelling?"

"Yes," I said.

"To all?"

"Yes."

"Hmmmm . . ." His disbelieving expression ebbed into a dare-to-hope.

The two will-o'-the-wisps glowed blindingly blue and I became dizzy and hot, and the doctor and the wisps became double-exposed, and somehow I was split twain by the sides until there were two of me. One sat in front of Lambshead and the undulating wisps, while the other, conscious and seeing, was free to traverse the room.

"Do you suffer from daydreaming reflex with reveries that include blackbirds, scents of an unseen censor, or aberrant alliterative applications?"

Beady eyes glowed from the wisps, and wings fluttered by my ears. I smelled dried flowers and cut grass, upturned earth and the fading waft of fabric softener. I looked at my sitting-self in the chair and heard her indolent "Yes."

"What else do you see?"

The wisps left Lambshead and my sitting-self to illuminate the corners of the empty room where ebon bookcases grew from the walls and within them appeared objects that my sitting-self described:

Jaundiced blueprints of a non-Euclidian pendulum; a stuffed cat with a hissing throat encircled in white fur; a fractured skull chilling a broken bottle of blood-thick sherry; a tailor's mannequin wearing a white, blood-soaked and dirt-streaked dressing gown, its neck a splintered pine plank engraved with claw marks.

Beside the cases stood a stuffed gorilla. I couldn't help but touch its fur, which turned to feathers and fluttered to the ground, revealing the tarred and malformed skeleton of a dwarf. Through its eye socket, a gold beetle climbed out and over to a shelf that held a jar of putrescence and nestled itself in an open locket containing a strand of blond hair speckled black.

At the very bottom of the bookshelves were several jorums filled with animated landscapes: tiny ships thrusting within a maelstrom pint; a littoral liter with a weeping willow tree overlooking a craggy shore; and a quart of electrified clouds in the shape of women hovering over an abandoned manse, crying dust and leaves.

"What are these?" I asked Lambshead. From his chair, he looked up to the ceiling, unsure of my voice's source.

"What do they look like?" he asked my sitting-self. I heard her describe the jorums, and he smiled.

"Mood," he spoke into the ether. "They are jars of mood."

I squatted at the bookshelf and selected one containing the cosmos. Several minute stars swam like strawberry seeds in a phosphorescent jam that churned and congealed into a sun that heated the glass. It burned my hand and I dropped it, and, with a loud bang, it exploded on the floor, incinerating all within the jar and melting the glass, which pooled and cooled into a Bristol blue fetus.

Before I could retrieve it, I heard Lambshead command me awake, and suddenly I was back in the chair—whole—and subject to his sherry-sweet breath. The bookshelves, the taxidermy, curios, and jars were all gone, but on the ground remained the glass fetus, which the doctor rushed to rescue.

He coddled it in his palm. "This—this is what ails you!"

"A child?"

"Of the imagination, yes. You thought you had a disease of influence, but it is much, much worse. You have a disease of the *imagination*, probably from too much Poe. But don't worry, this here is your cure."

"I thought you said it was what ails me?"

"You *are* cured," he said. "And I have another child for my cabinet!" He waved the wisps away and they dimmed in rejection. Before I could ask what the other children were, he all but rushed me from the basement and out of his house.

I did not see where he kept the Dark Room's offspring, and I suppose now I never will, but after I left Lambshead and his curious cabinet, I admit I felt a lot lighter. Before booting me off the steps, he gave me permission to write of my disease, which seemed to ameliorate my condition more.

Having been able to resume a normal, perhaps even an extra-normal life, I am forever indebted to that cabinet and to Dr. Lambshead. When I read of his death, just three years later, I mourned not only the loss of that great man but also of his Dark Room and its soul-ware nursery that has inevitably become overexposed and returned to the ether.

2003: The Pea

Related to Gio Clairval in 2008 at a Parisan Café,
by Dr. Lambshead's Housekeeper

Dr. Lambshead had told me not to dust the object resting on the third shelf from the floor, a collector's item hidden behind a maroon curtain. In my twenty years at the doctor's service, I had never contravened an order.

Nevertheless, my employer's days being numbered, it seemed to me that I should redouble my efforts in keeping the basement spotless.

Behind the curtain stood a bell jar of oxide-stained glass, iridescent with blues, pinks, and greens, as tall as my forearm, protecting a Smyrna-red velvet cushion the size of a full-blossomed rose. Golden tassels hanging from a crown of braided trimmings strangled the cushion into the shape of a muffin, the top of which appeared to be decorated with an embroidery of silver-coloured human hair stitched at regular intervals to form a lozenge pattern.

On the cushion sat a perfectly preserved pea.

I gasped, suddenly aware of my staring at a piece of Dr. Lambshead's secret collection, and lowered my gaze to examine the elegant pedestal. It was made of grey-veined marble carved into ovals framed by acanthus leaves. A slight suspicion of dust filled the carvings. After five seconds, I looked at the item again. How could a pea not shrink and shrivel, unless it was preserved in oil or in a vacuum? To judge by the colour, it was a young pea freshly spilled from its pod, full of water and life that made its skin turgid, ready to burst if squeezed between index finger and thumb.

My stomach clenched at the unprofessional thought. I concentrated on my task, passing my feather duster with the greatest attention on the delicate pedestal carvings, but my gaze wandered back to the pea. It had never happened before. In all those years, never had one single question about any of the objects crossed my mind. My deference to the doctor's wishes had always been absolute.

Dr. Lambshead had become all my family after my parents died. No sensible person can lend credence to the cook's rants; he attributes a selfish intent to each of the doctor's good actions. It is untrue that my legal guardian discouraged my interest in humanities to secure the services of an unpaid employee. When a paralysing timidity forced me to abandon my studies at Oxford, the doctor restored my self-esteem by assuring me I was the only person he could trust to keep his ever-growing collection mildew-free. He had always treated me with consideration. And dust was our enemy.

Dust, Paulette, dust hard and true, he used to say. Blessed be the stutter that forced you to forgo your wish to become a teacher. Dusting is a greater responsibility. Dusting must be your obsession. The professional Duster's mission is to make a stand against the particles that come out of the ether, the first step taken by Mother Nature in the process of smothering her children. Entropy, the doctor said, erases all differences, deconstructing complex matter into simple elements. Dust, full of vile microorganisms, is the harbinger of entropy and must be confronted with unrelenting determination. Forget the wonders gathered in this basement room. See only concave shapes and recesses and carvings as receptacles to choking death, headquarters where the enemy prepares for sorties. Don't let the soldiers of entropy regroup to launch the next offensive. Destroy them with your feather duster, moist rag, and badger-bristle brush. Wage war against the blanket of oblivion, Paulette. Make these shelves a testimony to Man's struggle for eternity.

With these words in mind, I would spend my days in the doctor's cabinet of curiosities, stroking precious items with my instruments. Never seeing the items themselves. Always considering these disparate objects in their mere quality of innocent victims to dust.

So why was I fascinated by the most humble among the doctor's treasures? Despite the glamorous presentation on the tasselled cushion, it was a simple pea—so round, so green, so impossibly glossy within the confined space of the bell.

It struck me that the pea, like other items protected by cloths, jars, bottles, cases, and sandalwood- or stone-inlaid boxes, didn't need me. Surely enough, the outer shell, the glass bell that protected it, would soon be marred by layers of particles, without my repeated interventions. But the pea itself flaunted its perfect round shape unblemished by the agents of annihilation. My chest ached as I realized how peripheral I was in the pea's destiny.

Dr. Lambshead's cook, a retired professor who philosophised while stirring sauces, once said my job epitomised the concept of empty instrumentality. He meant that once I had finished dusting, I would have to start it over again and there could be no lasting result of my toiling, ever. You're like the dust you fight, Paulette, a monument to impermanence. But I saw no problem in being a modest tool. Day after day, I won my battle against the dancing motes and went home happy, knowing that the enemy would infiltrate the basement during the night, laying a thin sheet of powdery specks on everything, but I would counter the attack the following day, and again, and I'd never be unemployed.

An immutable ritual. I wore a pristine white apron. Washed my hands at the sink concealed behind a drape in a corner of the one-room basement. Seized my instruments. Dusting, I crossed the strokes, swivelled before stepping toward the next spot, dedicated an entrechat to the smallest pieces and bowed to the tallest, seeing them as a continuum of surfaces to dust. I worked with enthusiasm, disputing my protégés to my opponent's domination. I was proud of my mission. I was content. Above everything, I was useful.

Until I saw the pea and its uncaring perfection.

The most fragile of pieces owed its safety to a transparent dome, an inanimate device, not to me. The doctor believed my work insufficient. He displayed the pea to prove the inanity of my task, and the cruel man had expected my curiosity to take over. He had wanted me to see the pea.

Brass clasps held the rim of the bell jar fixed to the marble pedestal. I fingered one, jerked my hand away. Overwhelmed by my audacity, I forced myself to step out of range, and glanced at other pieces that rested under their glass shields, forever impervious to the impalpable powders of time. One of the bells protecting a gilded mask had a spidery crack at the base that ended with a chink in the glass rim. The enemy had defeated all defences and penetrated the sanctuary. Trails of insectile feet crisscrossed the ebony floor around the mask. A fly had traced a series of doodling circles in the dust before extending its six legs in the rigour of death. What could my honest work do against such power of insinuation?

I spun other bells around and examined them under every angle. A few clasps were open or not fully cinched over the small indents in the pedestals. Worse still, I discovered a greater number of subtly broken glass surfaces. Bent on ignoring the pieces themselves, concentrating on the dust, I had never noticed any blemishes. Fear scratched tiny claws at my heart. At least one third of the stored bell jars had flaws that allowed decay to invade them. They were sly traitors collaborating with the armies of dissolution. I gripped the edge of the nearest table. Dr. Lambshead knew the shelves like his pockets. He had known the truth all the time. I was his alibi in an illusory resistance. I clenched my fists, fingernails digging into my palms.

And the pea, the only ordinary piece in that unbelievable collection. . . . The doctor couldn't trust a fragile glass case to protect it. To showcase a perfectly preserved specimen, he surely replaced it at the first sign of corruption, as a statement of short-lived flawlessness.

I went to fetch one of the tallow candles from the pantry. Back in the basement, I drew the drapes that concealed the sink and pushed the candle into the plastic siphon. I struck a long match used for the hearth and lit the wick. I counted on the flame to consume the plastic siphon and create a cloud of soot. It had happened to my cousin once removed when she had inadvertently dropped a candle in the sink after cleaning up the dinner table. The wick was still burning and the siphon had simmered all night, along with the plastic pipe, spitting out particles of soot. She and her husband had awoken to an apartment covered in a layer of greasy black stuff that stuck to every object.

The pea of record. On a cushion.

For the first time since I had begun working there, I opened jars, bottles, boxes, and set the objects free. The tour of the shelves took more than the usual three hours. By then, black particles fluttered about, spurting from the slow-burning plastic under the drain, blackening the unprotected pieces with myriad new soldiers of doom.

I rolled up my sleeves, plunged my rag into a bucket of soapy water, and smiled. Let the best one win.

My plan did not include sparks shooting out of the carbonized siphon. The drape took fire, which I noticed only when the fire reached an electric socket and the light went out. The auxiliary lighting bathed the basement in red. Petrified, I watched the flames lick a nearby shelf.

The side effect of my experiment shocked me at first and then thrilled me. I had intended to measure my skills against a formidable greasy black dust, but I had acted as an agent of purification by creating a cleansing fire.

I unclasped the bell, lifted it, and snatched the pea from under the protective dome. Now I held the doctor's most precious item between my index finger and thumb—the only symbol of life in a collection of dead objects. I pictured myself slipping the pea into an envelope, along with my resignation.

The pea was very heavy. The skin had lost its glossy polish, growing rough, lumpy. Unnaturally warm.

I threw the thing into the flames. It exploded like a firecracker, in a spray of blue sparks. I ran to the basement door and slammed it behind me.

Like every day before, I went home happy.

Happier.

A Brief Catalog
of Other Items

The discovery of the half-burned subterranean space devoted to Dr. Lambshead's cabinet of curiosities created an urgent need to sort through the wreckage and document "survivors." A number of experts helped catalog both the remains and the occasional miraculous find of an undamaged object. The most interesting of these items have been described below by the experts who discovered, cleaned, and researched them. Where appropriate, we have also included photographs, illustrations, and diagrams in support of these findings. Not every conclusion reached herein has been verified independently.

Bear Gun—Long-barreled flintlock rifle, four feet butt to muzzle, made from timber that traces back to a species of hickory previously abundant in the Appalachians and long thought to be extinct. When fired, it releases a live bear as a projectile. The bear expands in a matter of seconds from the size of a musket ball to full size, at which point it latches onto its target and devours it noisily. Documents found partly scorched in Dr. Lambshead's cabinet claim the use of the gun in the American Civil War for political assassinations. The scene of a vicious bear attack often permitted assassins an avenue for escape, while journalists and the government revised the facts of such events due to their absurd nature. A receipt wrapped around the barrel carries the signature of one John T. Ford, but the fire left the cost and date of the transaction unknown. (Adam Mills)

Bullet Menagerie—A clear surface two feet square and one inch in thickness, with the consistency of cold Vaseline. Metal shutters on each side, labeled A and B, may be opened or closed by button-press. When the A shutter is open, a projectile fired at the pane with a velocity greater than ten feet per second will remain trapped within the medium. Opening the B shutter will cause it to exit with its original length and velocity. Inscribed by the inventor: Chas. Shallowvat, 1788. An inventory sheet indicates that the menagerie preserves live bullets fired by French, Prussian, Ottoman, Hanoverian, Etrurian, Swedish, and unidentified forces, which Shallowvat managed to capture while traveling during the Napoleonic Wars. Upon acquiring the menagerie, Dr. Lambshead, perhaps thinking that opening the B shutter would also reopen an infelicitous period in the history of Europe, neglected to verify its contents. (Nick Tramdack)

Coffin Torpedo—Ostensibly of the Clover type, though considerably smaller

The very coffin torpedo from Lambshead's collection.

"This is one of only several existing images of a bear rumored to have been fired from a bear gun. That this bear was thus fired is assumed based on visible friction burns in its fur, most notably on one of its front legs and its back (the latter is evident in an accompanying photograph, not reprinted due to permission issues). The bear seems to have been shot with a taxidermy gun postmortem, as evidenced by stitches visible in hairless patches on its body. The bear's owner has so far ignored requests for fur samples, despite the need for carbon dating." (Adam Mills)

than other unexploded specimens originating in the latter half of the nineteenth century. Devices like these were used to discourage the very real threat of grave-violation by Resurrectionists, and their armament packages typically contained powder, shot, chain, etc. The triggering lever on this item is removed, thankfully, but it should be noted that the munition here is not of any recognizable type—warm to the touch, and emitting a surprising amount of detectable radiation for so small an object. (Jess Gulbranson)

Czerwatenko Whelk in Olive Oil—Preserved specimen of *Turpis pallidus*, a small whelk that once dominated the littoral fauna of the Czerwatenko Sea. The species disappeared when that body of water was drained in 1917 to create the International Saltworks Project. Within months, sixty-five salt-scrapers died, and company scientists traced the cause to the whelks. Upon desiccating, the delicate snails had crumbled—shell and all—into a highly toxic powder and mixed with the precipitated Czerwatenko sea salt, rendering it deadly. The saltworks was abandoned. In the 1920s, anthropologists discovered a group of indigenes who had once eaten the whelks as part of their staple diet. When asked how they had survived ingesting the toxic snails, they replied that any sort of oil or fat would neutralize the poison. The specimen in Lambshead's collection was purchased from a centenarian villager who claimed she had never developed a taste for the snails. (Therese Littleton)

Dander of Melville, The—Small crimson phial of biological ejecta sloughed from beard and waistcoat of one Herman M., inspector of customs. In cities prone to ship-rot and oracular drifters, admixture of same with barnacle flower was briefly regarded as a palliative for Vesuvian angers and scrimshaw-related injuries. In street parlance, more commonly referred to as "Red-burn's Rake" or godflake. (Brian Thill)

Decanter of Everlasting Sadness, The (*La decanter de tristesse qui dure pour toujours*)—Acquired in 1928 by Thackery T. Lambshead during an outbreak of blood poisoning at Le Moulin Rouge, this crystalline bottle includes a glass stopper in which an earlobe, purportedly that of Vincent van Gogh, has been chambered. An accompanying tag, attached to the neck of the bottle with braided cornsilk, indicates that imbibing any aperitif, properly aged within, will induce visions of a universe writ large. Earthy notes of potato, almond, and sunflower accompany a spectral show—in which the appetitive soul is riddled with starry starlight. On the base of the decanter, curving gracefully about the punt (and most easily read when the bottle is empty), a cursive admonishment is etched: *Use judiciously. The yeast of life's melancholy rises in proportion to the sedimentation of posthumous renown.* (William T. Vandemark)

Dinner Bell of the *Mary Celeste*, The—The bell, which was present when the *Mary Celeste* was towed into Genoa, was found to be absent when the ship was inspected in Gibraltar. The couple who presented the bell for auction in 1893 claimed to have snuck aboard the derelict ship as children, and to have taken the artifact as a memento. They asserted that ringing the bell caused a curious sensation in the back of the head, as well as a desire to go swimming, and as such was unsuitable as a dinner bell due to the dangers of swimming immediately after a meal. Experimentation at a boy's school next to a lake in the summer provided inconclusive data about the bell's efficacy in this regard, though it has been theorized by some that there must be a meal present to cause the bell's unusual effect. (Jennifer Harwood-Smith)

Dracula's Testicles—Unusual in size (they have a diameter of five inches apiece), these were a donation by Jonathan Van Helsing Jr. It is believed that the gigantic size of the testicles is due to their use while they were still attached to the body. According to Dr. Lambshead's hypothesis—enounced in a note glued to the jar filled with clear garlic juice in which the exhibits are stored—the testicles were used as reservoirs for the extra blood that the vampire had to suck before travelling, so as to be able to survive longer without drinking blood. According to the donor, the famous vampire-hunter's son, the testicles were a gift by Count Dracula's twenty-second wife to his father, in exchange for being allowed to collect and enjoy the vampire's life insurance (a fabulous sum, or so the rumors of the period said) after Dr. Van Helsing Sr. performed the staking of the four-hundred-year-old vampire. (Horia Ursu)

Ear Eye—This instrument functions in the same way as a periscope but is in the shape of a C, and therefore requires many more mirrors. It is apparently designed for looking into one's own ear. A transparent casing displays the mirrors inside. Inexplicably, one of them is tinted so dark as to be minimally reflective. According to Lambshead's journal, an employee of the caretakers of the doctor's house was testing the Ear Eye when he dropped it (fortunately, it doesn't appear to have been damaged) and ran away, yelling inarticulately and covering the ear he had just been looking into. He seemed to want no one to see into it. He has not reported back. No one has yet been found willing to further investigate the Ear Eye. (Graham Lowther)

Fort Chaffee Polyhedral Deck, The—This item consists of fifty-four uncoated paper playing cards in a cardboard sleeve printed with the slogan KNOW YOUR ENEMY. The cards resemble spotter decks used to train World War II pilots, but in place of aircraft silhouettes, each card is illustrated with a different stellated polyhedron and its Schläfli symbol. This is the only known copy of the Fort Chaffee deck and it is regrettably incomplete: the ace of spades was replaced with an ordinary playing card with a similar backing. It was discovered by Dr. Lambshead at a poker tourney hosted by an acquaintance, a professor of high-energy physics tenured at Los Alamos. According to his personal correspondence, Lambshead procured the Fort Chaffee deck with "haste and discretion," which may explain both his lack of inquiry into this apparent geometric incursion and the sudden end of his career as a cardsharp. (Nickolas Brienza)

A card carrier of the type used with the Fort Chaffee deck.

Harness & Leash for Fly—Harness fashioned from newspaper. Coiled, grey-colored leash of undetermined material. Possibly a relic from the Cult of the Fly, an obscure movement originating in the workingmen's clubs of nineteenth-century Lancashire. What little we know about the cult comes from a letter by a Miss Phyllis Grimshaw of Oswaldtwistle to a Mrs. Evelyn Hunt of Crewe (currently on display in the MOSI). She states: "Father has taken up with those ridiculous fly men and is growing a beard, to his knees, he says, so he can pluck a hair from it. Mrs. Cackett, at the shop, says some never-sweats have been plucking the tail hairs from passing horses." The precise nature of the ritual involving the flies is unknown, although it is unlikely the incumbent of this harness lived a full life: a fragment of wing remains attached to the newspaper. (Claire Massey)

Human Skeleton, Irregular—Adult male, 20th c. European, identity unknown. Acquired from the estate of noted dog breeder and occult hobbyist Mr. Comfort of Derbyshire, whose widow sold his collection and prized Schnauzers after his fatal hunting accident in 1952, the skeleton may be an example of an unclassified bone disorder or an elaborate anatomical hoax; Dr. Lambshead's records are inconclusive. Curious features include pronounced phalangeal keratin structures, twelve coccygeal vertebrae, rotated scapula and absent clavicle, convex frontal bone, and an elongated mandible with overlarge canines. A small hole in the occipital bone along with traces of silver and indentations in the cervical vertebrae suggest death by foul play rather than disease; scorching indicates posthumous exposure to fire. Mr. Comfort's journals contain no mention of the specimen and disclose no provenance. Mrs. Comfort's auction notes are brief: "Skeleton, male, possible medical interest. Nobody important. £3 starting bid." (Kali Wallace)

Ichor Whorl—Small, coarse, black object suspended in a yet-to-be-analyzed solution. Object is variable in size—averaging one cubic inch—and vortical in shape. Date of manufacture unknown. Lambshead journal fragment 729 notes the item's place of origin as "a polluted shoreline of a former Soviet republic." Dr. Lambshead sent the item to Tillinghast Laboratories, which provided the following report: "Keep organic matter one meter from contents. Empirical tests reveal living tissue placed within one meter is remotely hollowed (by undetermined means) to the limit of solidity without liquefying. Spectroscopic results inconclusive. Presence of organic matter within one-meter orbit is accompanied by slight phase change in object, from solid to non-Newtonian fluid, and extension of one spiral arm to three centimeters covered in half-centimeter protrusions. Authorization for further tests required." Donated to Dr. Lambshead by Maximilian Crabbe, 1989. (Ben Woodward)

Jug, Disgruntled, et al.—A series of cabinet artifacts, generally from antiquity, depicting human facial features that appear to differ in expression following the cabinet fire, based on records of their expressions prior to the fire. While the catalyst for the change may be apparent, the agency is not. (Art by Rikki Ducornet)

Kepler the Clock—Franz Kepler's rigorous attention to his many appointments made him susceptible to Chronometrophilia. Initially, the disease manifested in twitches of his right hand, as if

Rikki Ducornet's still-life mug shots, drawn from her encounters with disgruntled artifacts

he were reaching for a pocket watch. Had he sought treatment then, he may have been cured. But Kepler had no time for illness. Gradually, his features began to resemble a clock face. Within a month, his moustache would rotate to indicate the time. When his legs became mahogany, he adjusted by scheduling meetings in his office, ensuring none would fall on the hour, whereupon he would utter a loud "bong." One Monday, Kepler's colleagues arrived at work to find a grandfather clock behind his desk. Dr. Lambshead purchased the clock some years later from a private collector. Kepler is, we assume, still alive. He keeps excellent time and should continue to do so if he is regularly wound. (Grant Stone)

Kris ("The Assassin's Twist")—A kris whose every turn and twist on the blade is supposed to inflict a certain wound or an affliction upon the victim. However, unlike in all other krises, the twists in this one have been forged in a way that any attack by the tip or part of the blade will surely kill the target, yet when the large kris is pushed into one's body up to the hilt, it will leave the person alive (owing to a secret twist devised on the blade below the hilt). This geometric weapon increases the assassin's chance of killing the target (for even a single scratch would be enough) yet introduces a final plot twist to the weapon by leaving the target alive once it is pushed up to its hilt to the body. (Incognitum)

Leary's Pineal Body—This *epiphysis cerebri* was pickled in vivo by the late American psychologist most famous for his mantra "Turn on, tune in, drop out." Dr. Leary opened gates heretofore unknown beyond the speculations of H. P. Lovecraft, and this gland is noteworthy for its ability to have survived multiple encounters with beings from beyond—and otherwise. Research is pending on a way to safely experiment on it; the Stanford Asylum has a special wing for those who have attempted, to date. (Kaolin Imago Fire)

Mellified Alien—The enlarged head and oversized eyes of this diminutive, mummified humanoid creature would indicate that it is of the Grey type of extraterrestrial. That it has been preserved in honey is clear. What is less clear is if it feasted upon, willingly or unwillingly, "the golden stuff," before it died. For only if it had ingested honey in sufficient quantities over a number of days would its remains be truly mellified and impart their healing properties to whoever had been nibbling on it. The application of forensic dentistry may confirm the conjecture that this sweet confection once belonged to Sir Arthur Conan Doyle before coming into Dr. Lambshead's possession. (Julie Andrews)

Mooney & Finch Somnotrope—These sleep simulators (pictured on page 301) have become rare artifacts; even though they were mass-produced in the Mooney & Finch Sheffield facility, each one of them emerged as a unique object due to the pressures of the oneiric centrifuge. However,

The map for creating an Assassin's Twist (plot twist included).

PUTING KERIS/KERIS STEM

MATA KERIS/KERIS BLADE

Puting · Perut · Sepit Rotan · Ekor · Kepit · Aring · Janggut · Ganja · Kambing Kachang · Tulang Keris · Hujong Keris

Leher · Kepala Chichak · Dagu · Lambai Gajah · Belalai Gajah · Rigi · Gandik · Janggut · Mata Keris · Pamur · Tuntong Keris they were only sold for three months, prior to the first reports of somnambulance addiction and peripatetic insomnia. The idea of experiencing four or five hours of sleep within a mere few minutes held almost unlimited allure for the world's busiest captains of industry and harried matrons. But few were prepared for the intoxication of the Somnotrope's soothing buzz, the sheer pleasure of watching its central piston raise and lower, gently at first and then with increasing vigor, until your mind flooded with dream fragments and impression of having sailed to the nether kingdom and back, all in a few minutes. It only took a few unfortunate deaths for the whole line to be recalled. (Charlie Jane Anders)

Mother of Spirits—Drab olive in color, with copper flecking, this three-inch-long sessile organism resembles a desiccated asparagus spear mated with a tiny artichoke. Once rehydrated in a suitable measure of clean water, it manifests a most peculiar phenomenon. When placed into a vessel containing fermented alcoholic beverage—beer, wine, mead, etc.—the Mother of Spirits catalyzes a secondary fermentation up to 120 proof (provided sufficient sugars are available). The Mother extrudes rootlike growth during this process, which can last several months, and it is speculated these function in a symbiotic relationship with residual yeasts to effect the unusually high secondary fermentation. Daughters form at the root nodes once alcohol content surpasses 50 percent, as the Mother is spent during the process. The resulting liquor is of fine quality, but a distinct aroma and flavor of cilantro renders it unpalatable to some. (Jayme Lynne Blaschke)

Ron Pippin's optimistic vision of the Much Smaller Cabinet's contents.

Much Smaller Cabinet—This miniature cabinet is a duplicate of Dr. Lambshead's in nearly every respect, a 1/1000th-scale model incorporating scorch marks and splintered frame down to the smallest detail. A single variation: the door remains locked. The doctor dropped the diminutive key in his squid tank and failed to retrieve it before Longfellow's greedy tentacles snatched it from view. Peering through the keyhole—itself no wider than the head of a pin, with no room to spare for dancing angels or other divine revelers—one can glimpse a mere hint of the curios stored inside. Perhaps someday a scholar of all things underestimated will write a short story seeking to describe and comprehend the dwarf contents. (Paul Kirsch)

Night Quilt, American—A notable example of a hand-stitched night quilt featuring unusual subject matter: smallpox, penury, and death by hanging. The thread and dye indicate the quilt originated in the small farming communities of east-central Wisconsin around 1850.

The quilt was purchased during the 1902 decommissioning of Lake Covenant Church near Oostburg, Wisconsin. "Absolutely no return" is handwritten on the receipt. Two

The Steampunk Workshop/Jake von Slatt re-build of a Mooney & Finch Somnotrope

newspaper articles are attached to the receipt. The first, from the July 19, 1871, *Plymouth Herald,* reports on the acquittal of Samuel Ronde in his trial for the brutal murder of the Denne family in Oostburg and his unlikely escape from mob justice following his release. The second article is from the November 13, 1871, issue of the *Sheboygan Courier.* In reporting the great Peshtigo fire the previous month, the article reports that one S. Ronde, lately of Oostburg, is among those missing since the conflagration.

All three of the quilt's existing panels show exquisite and extensive detailing and remain in remarkable condition. Based on cut work, threading, and style, each of the panels was created by a different family member. The quilt's blue border is worked with alternating white stars and black circles, probably by the creator of the third panel.

In clockwise order, the appliqué panels show: first, a naked boy, covered in small sores, asleep atop a rough pine bed. The bed covering in the panel is worked with miniature red versions of the stars and circles that line the quilt's borders.

Second, a blond man at night, his felt pockets turned inside-out, standing in a fallow field. He appears to be holding a jug. A plow with empty traces is visible in the background. There is a waning quarter-moon visible in the night sky, but no stars.

Third, the same blond man from panel two, hanging from a leafless tree. On the right side of this panel, three women (wearing matching red bonnets) weep vibrant cloth tears. On the left side of the panel, a stout preacher wearing a black felt hat watches. What appears to be a sliver of moon is visible through the tree branches. Again, there are no stars.

The fourth panel is missing. (Tom Underberg)

Oneyroscope—A device designed by French inventor Louis Lumière after the invention of the cinematograph. His purpose was to record dream experiences, showing them on a screen, like motion pictures. Lumière's brother, Auguste, was the first subject of the experiment, and there is a silent movie directed by George Méliès registering the entire process. In the film, August Lumière is lying on his bed wearing a steel helmet on his head, connected by a bunch of wires to a strange machine operated by his own brother. Behind them, a silver screen is showing us what he's dreaming: a flock of clay pigeons flying underwater. On April 15, 1900, the first public demonstration of a prototype Oneyroscope was given at the Exposition Universelle held in Paris, France, becoming a huge success. At the time, Sigmund Freud, the father of the psychoanalysis, reportedly said that the Oneyroscope could be "the most revolutionary discovery in history." (Ignacio Sanz)

"Our Greatest President," Reel 3—A single reel of film with a yellowing, typewritten label that reads OUR GREATEST PRESIDENT—1939—REEL 3 OF 5. Notable for its size (38 millimeter instead of the standard 35 millimeter), the aging film is of interest for two other reasons. First, the movie features performances by Sarah Bernhardt, Marilyn Monroe, and someone who bears a striking resemblance to Steve Guttenberg. Second, and most intriguing, the plot of the movie seems to revolve around America's seventh president: a man called Ronald Smith Washington, purportedly the son of George Washington. The third reel tracks his last term in office and his struggle against the Japanese in the War of 1812. Despite the strange nature of the film's content, preliminary lab results have indicated the reel itself is consistent with other prints from the late 1930s. The other four reels have yet to surface. (Tucker Cummings)

Reversed Commas (box of)—The ordinary comma creates pauses in text; it logically follows that the reversed comma gives prose a push, accelerating it sometimes beyond the point of breathlessness into a blur or scream. A full box of these extremely rare punctuation marks turned up inside a volume on the laws of motion: the pages of that tome had been cut away to make a secret hollow space sufficiently large to securely hold the box. Dr. Lambshead does not remember how the book and thus the box came into his possession. He once sprinkled a handful of reversed commas into a copy of the *Highway Code*: the text immediately broke its own laws by exceeding the mandatory speed-limit in an urban zone. Reversed commas are more properly known as *ammoc*s, hence the phrase "to run ammoc." Serious attempts to create interstellar engines by composing entire books exclusively with reversed commas are destined to fail: nothing can exceed the speed of lightheartedness. (Rhys Hughes)

Sea Scroll, The—A live spiny eel (*Mastacembelus mastacembelus*) 40 centimeters long, the Sea Scroll has puzzled mystics and biologists alike. The scales' coloration and shape produce visible text in Akkadian cuneiform; more unusual yet, the fish continues to flop about in its small glass-and-teak aquarium, apparently unhindered by the absence of water and food for some years. Somehow imperishable, the eel shows no sign of age or illness, apart from its atypically molting scales. The message it bears changes regularly as new scales grow, attested to by accompanying diaries with nine centuries of transcriptions. The text has proven untranslatable thus far into Akkadian or any other language, and marginalia indicate that previous owners believed the writing was a divinely encrypted mystery time might uncover. Dr. Lambshead offers a different conjecture: "What if," the last entry in the notes reads, "the fish is merely illiterate?" (Hugh Alter)

Silence, One Ounce—Origins unknown. Found amongst the possessions of the recently deceased Frank Hayes, thirty-four, who tragically lost his life when he stepped in front of a public bus that failed to stop. Its provenance is thought to include M. Twain, W. Wilson, and the Marquis de Sade. Handle with care, not to be administered more than one drop at a time. Silence is golden, but too much will kill you. (Willow Holster)

Skull—Human, probably male. Physically unremarkable. Attached tag reads B. S. LONDON, 20/4/1912. The skull appears normal in all respects except during the new moon of every month, when it screams uncontrollably. (Amy Willats)

A Decadent-era example from Lambshead's prodigious and largely anonymous skull collection.

Skull, Parsimonious—The foul-smelling skull of a large owl, albeit with three eye-sockets, reputed to be of sentimental value to the doctor because of his dear departed mother's fondness for owls, particularly those possessing unusual congenital characteristics. Tufted with feathers and a patch of moldering owl flesh, the skull was lost on the moorlands of Tasmania after Lambshead's porter, a drunkard named Hendrick Carmichael, gambled it away on a wager with an unnamed fellow traveler. According to Carmichael's widow, the skull answered yes/no questions with astonishing accuracy and foresight, blinking with eerie illumination from within, once for yes and twice for no; this amounted to a useful basis for gambling and drinking games. Found unharmed in Lambshead's cabinet neatly wrapped in a pair of striped shorts thought to belong to legendary pugilist Gerald Jenkins, known to be on walkabout in Australia at the time of the doctor's travels to Tasmania. (Tracie Welser)

South American Insult Stone—This item came into the doctor's possession by way of his drawing-room window, through which the stone was hurled one evening. Six inches in diameter and almost perfectly spherical, one side of the stone had been carved into a stylized face reminiscent of Incan art. Upon picking up the stone, Dr. Lambshead was greeted by a voice emanating from within, which addressed him gruffly and at length in an obscure South American dialect, centuries dead. Transcribing and translating the words took over a week. It turned out that the stone had, in fact, been insulting the doctor, calling into question both his parentage and personal hygiene, among other things. Though the stone had obviously been thrown by a rival or malcontent, Dr. Lambshead was far too enamored of the device to dispose of it. (Nicholas Troy)

The St. Blais Toad at rest, as photographed by Dr. Galubrious.

St. Blaise's Toad—A 6-inch × 6-inch × 3-inch plastered and gilded wood, glass-and-taxidermied common toad. Referred to as "the miracle of the toad." In 1431, a vision of St. Blaise appeared to a farm boy catching toads near a spring in Bromley,

Kent. The saint called upon the boy to be kind to all amphibians. After the vision, an image of St. Blaise appeared on the back of a toad near the edge of the pool. The creature was skinned, stuffed, and enshrined by the church. This gilded toad reliquary was decommissioned by the church during the Calvinist reformation. The toad remained in the collection of Rawsthorne Family of Denbies Hall, Dorking, until won from Lord Rawsthorne by Dr. Lambshead in a game of skittles. Glass damaged in lower right corner resulting in mild molding and mouse damage to the epidermis. Papal seal on verso, canceled promissory note pasted on side. (Dr. Galubrious)

Tomb-Matches—Half a dozen square-stick lucifers, secured in a waxed-paper wrapping. The attached card indicates, in slightly shaky, faded handwriting, that these matches, when struck, produce not light, nor a means of igniting a cigarette, pipe, candle, or lamp, but instead a bloom of impenetrable, sound-muffling darkness. This darkness lasts for as long as the match burns. If, the card notes, members of the match-striker's party are missing when the light returns, it is only to be expected. (Nadine Wilson)

Tycho's Astronomical Support Garment—Designed by the sixteenth-century astronomer Tycho Brahe (1546–1601) as a device to combat chronic neck and back pain caused by years of stooping over observational instruments. The garment resembles an oversized corset stiffened by stays of horn, buckram, and whalebone. The center front is further reinforced by a busk made of ivory. The garment was fastened to the body via a complicated system of leather straps. How this was done remains a subject of controversy, as it is not obvious how certain straps were used. Tycho was not wearing the garment on October 13, 1601, when his bladder burst after he drank too much wine at a dinner party, which resulted in his eventual death. It is not clear that the abdominal support afforded by the garment could have prevented this tragedy. (Steven M. Schmidt)

Unhcegila's Scales—Vacillating between sickly virescent and rotted plum hues, these peculiar lamina are rumored to be found in the darkest corners of the North American Badlands' caverns. Thirty were found in Lambshead's cabinet, with each being roughly the size of a fig leaf. He said that he won them in a poker game with a hand of aces and eights in the Berlin Hellfire Club on April 28, 1945. The graybeard he won them from claimed to be the bastard son of Jesse James and said that he stole them from Bill Hickock as a boy. Hickock had told the boy that Sitting Bull gave them to him when they toured together in Buffalo Bill's Wild West shows. The scales are said to allow a man to make his enemies mysteriously disappear, when ground up and put into their food or drink. Curiously, his ledger shows he sold some to gangsters with connections to both Jimmy Hoffa and Elvis. (Christopher Begley)

Untitled Booklet—Consists of six bound pages obtained by Dr. Lambshead from a Prague antiquarian bookshop in January 1948, one month before the Czechoslovak coup d'état, donated to him for safekeeping. The booklet appeared to contain a short story in a Central Moravian Czech dialect. Dr. Lambshead, however, was assured the booklet was not what it appeared to be, but an insect able, through mimicry, to imitate any inorganic object placed within a short distance (including its smell). The creature was discovered in one of the "Stránska Skála" Upper Paleolithic caves in the northern outskirts of Brno not long after Professor Svoboda's archaeological excavations in the

Tartarus Press edition of Jean Lorrain's *Nightmares of an Ether-Drinker.* In this instance, the insect documented by Tony Mileman had insinuated itself under the dust jacket and wrapped itself around the pages, replacing the boards and simulating a cloth binding.

summer of 1946. Despite attempting escape many times, the insect was finally secured amongst a collection of obscure short stories by forgotten Czechoslovak writers of early twentieth-century Weird Fiction. The insect (booklet) is presumed dead. (Tony Mileman)

Von Slatt Harmonization Device—A system and method for cultural transmission scrambling, patent application number 15/603976. Assignee: Harmonization Incorporated. Summary of the Invention from the patent application: "Very soon, science will confirm that cultural information passes from one entity to another using devices accessed psionically via instructional facilities. It is the object of this device to locate, demodulate, and scramble cultural transmissions passing between hostile social formations. This novel device allows operators to inject false vernacular and traditions into cultural signals as they pass between entities. It can also hijack signals carrying historical intelligence by providing a stronger signal on the same frequency." (Annalee Newitz)

Wax Phonograph Cylinder, Unlabeled—Object appears to be over a century old, but is still functional. When played, the sound of a percussive instrument, possibly a large tubular drum, can be heard for approximately the first forty seconds of recording time. During this sound, the murmurings of a man's voice become interpolated with the beat. The syllables are indistinguishable, but as the drumbeat continues, the voice rises until it becomes a series of shouted plosives. At around the four-minute mark, both sounds stop completely and are replaced by a series of high-pitched cries, from which can be gleaned the only coherent word of the entire piece: "Alley-Caster," or perhaps "Snally-Gaster." The final sound heard on the recording is an extremely loud screeching whistle, which sounds reptilian in origin. An attached note indicates that Dr. Lambshead acquired the object from a motel-room drawer in Braddock Heights, Maryland. (Michael J. Larson)

An unprecedented panoramic view of the East End of Lambshead's cabinet, taken surreptitiously by photographer Bruce Ecker in 1999.

Artist and Author Notes

Story Contributors

Kelly Barnhill has had fiction published in *Fantasy, Weird Tales, Clockwork Phoenix,* and many other publications. Her first novel, *The Mostly True Story of Jack*—a lyrical fantasy for middle-grade readers—is set for a 2011 release by Little, Brown.

Holly Black is a best-selling author of contemporary fantasy novels for teens and children, including *The Spiderwick Chronicles* and the *Curse Workers* series.

S. J. Chambers has had fiction and nonfiction published by *Fantasy,* the *Baltimore Sun's Read Street Blog, Yankee Pot Roast,* and Tor.com. Her most recent projects include *The Steampunk Bible,* a coffee-table book coauthored with Jeff VanderMeer.

Stepan Chapman is the author of *The Troika,* which won the Philip K. Dick Award. His short fiction can be found in magazines and anthologies such as *Analog, Lady Churchill's Rosebud Wristlet, Leviathan, Polyphony,* and *Album Zutique.*

Ted Chiang is a multiple award–winning short story writer. His work has won the Nebula, the Hugo, the Locus Award, and others. His latest book is the novella *The Lifecycle of Software Objects,* published by Subterranean Press in 2010.

Michael Cisco's novels include *The Divinity Student, The Traitor,* and, most recently, *The Narrator.* His stories have appeared in *Leviathan 3, Leviathan 4, Lovecraft Unbound,* and many other anthologies.

Gio Clairval is an Italian-born speculative fiction writer who commutes between Paris and Lake Como. Several of her translations of iconic stories will appear in *The Weird: A Compendium of Strange and Dark Fictions* from Atlantic in 2011.

Amal El-Mohtar is currently pursuing a Ph.D. in Cornwall, England. Her poetry has won the Rhysling Award, and her fiction and nonfiction have appeared in *Weird Tales, Cabinet des Fées,* and *Shimmer.* She also coedits *Goblin Fruit,* an online quarterly of fantastical poetry.

Brian Evenson is the author of nine books, most recently the novel *Last Days* and the short story collection *Fugue State.* He directs Brown University's Creative Writing program.

Minister Faust is an Edmontonian writer, high school English teacher, union delegate, broadcaster, community activist, and novelist. His latest book is titled *From the Notebooks of Doctor Brain* and he is a past finalist for the Philip K. Dick Award.

Jeffrey Ford lives in South Jersey and is a multiple World Fantasy Award winner. His latest novel is *The Shadow Year,* and his latest collection of stories is *The Drowned Life* (both from HarperCollins).

Lev Grossman is a journalist for *Time* magazine and novelist living in New York City. His latest book is *The Magicians,* and the sequel is expected in 2011.

Will Hindmarch is a writer and graphic designer, with work published in various books, games, and magazines. Some of his work has appeared in *The Escapist, Atlanta* magazine, *Geek Monthly,* and *Everywhere.*

N. K. Jemisin is a Brooklyn-based author. Her short fiction has been published in *Clarkesworld, Baen's Universe, Strange Horizons, Postscripts, Weird Tales,* and many others. Her first two novels, *The Hundred Thousand Kingdoms* and its sequel, *The Broken Kingdoms,* have been published by Orbit Books.

Caitlín R. Kiernan was born in Ireland, raised in the southeastern United States, and now lives in Providence, Rhode Island. Her short fiction has been collected in several volumes, most recently *A Is for Alien,* and she's published eight novels, including *Daughter of Hounds* and *The Red Tree.*

Mur Lafferty is a writer, podcaster, and blogger. She has written for various RPGs, Tor.com, *Scrybe Press, Murky Depths,* and *Hub Magazine.*

Jay Lake lives in Portand, Oregon, where he writes, edits, and generally misbehaves. His latest novels are *Green* and *Madness of Flowers.*

China Miéville lives and works in London. He is three-time winner of the prestigious Arthur C. Clarke Award. His novel *The City & The City* recently won the British Science Fiction Award, the Arthur C. Clarke Award, the World Fantasy Award, and the Hugo Award. In addition to fiction, he has also contributed his art to this book.

Michael Moorcock is an iconic figure in literature, having written in perhaps every genre as well as published such classics as *Mother London.* A multiple-award winner, he lives in Texas with his wife, Linda, and several cats.

Alan Moore is an English writer primarily known for his work in graphic novels. Some of his more well-known series include *Watchmen, From Hell, V Is for Vendetta,* and *The League of Extraordinary Gentlemen.*

Reza Negarestani is an Iranian writer working in diverse fields of contemporary theory, ancient Greek and contemporary philosophy, and politics. His latest novel is *Cyclonopedia: Complicities with Anonymous Materials.*

Garth Nix is a best-selling, multiple award–winning Australian writer best known for his young adult fantasy novels. He has also written for RPGs and magazines and journals. His latest book is *Lord Sunday.*

Naomi Novik is a *New York Times* best-selling writer. She was awarded the John W. Campbell Award for Best New Writer in 2007. Her latest book is *Tongues of Serpents.*

Helen Oyeyemi is a Nigerian writer living in the United Kingdom. Her latest novel, *White Is for Witching,* was nominated for the Shirley Jackson award.

Cherie Priest is the author of seven novels published by Tor and Subterranean Press, including the Nebula Award nominee *Boneshaker, Dreadful Skin,* and the Eden Moore trilogy. Her short stories and nonfiction articles have appeared in such fine publications as *Weird Tales, Subterranean Magazine, Publishers Weekly,* and the Stoker-nominated anthology *Aegri Somnia* published by Apex.

Ekaterina Sedia has published three novels—*The Secret History of Moscow, The Alchemy of Stone,* and *The House of Discarded Dreams.* Her short stories have been published in *Analog, Baen's Universe,* and *Clarkesworld.*

Rachel Swirsky has had short fiction appear in venues including Tor.com, *Subterranean Magazine, Fantasy Magazine, Weird Tales,* and the *Konundrum Engine Literary Review.* Her latest book, *Through the Drowsy Dark,* is a mini-collection of feminist poems and short stories, available from Aqueduct Press.

Carrie Vaughn is the author of the popular urban fantasy Kitty Norville series. She has published over forty short stories in magazines such as *Weird Tales, Strange Horizons, Realms of Fantasy,* and *Asimov's Science Fiction.*

Tad Williams is a best-selling writer who lives in California. His latest book is *Shadowheart,* the fourth book in his Shadowmarch series.

Charles Yu is an American writer whose first novel, *How to Live Safely in a Science Fictional Universe,* has been added to many year's best lists for 2010. His short fiction has been published in a number of magazines and literary journals, including *Oxford American, The Gettysburg Review, Harvard Review, Mid-American Review, Mississippi Review,* and *Alaska Quarterly Review.*

Artists

Aeron Alfrey creates unique imagery inspired by strange fantasy worlds filled with monsters, magic, and death. His art has been published in numerous books and shown in galleries around the world.

Kristen Alvanson is an American artist based in Malaysia and Iran. She has participated in group/solo shows in New York, Tehran, London, Istanbul, Berlin, Belgium, and Vilnius, including a solo exhibition of her work at Azad Gallery (Tehran) and at the International Roaming Biennial of Tehran.

Greg Broadmore is a New Zealand illustrator, writer, and conceptual designer for Weta Workshop and has designed for the motion pictures *District 9, King Kong, The Lion, the Witch and the Wardrobe,* and *Black Sheep,* among many, many others.

John Coulthart is a world-recognized illustrator, graphic designer, and comic artist, who lives in Manchester, England. He has designed and provided art for several classic books, including *The Thackery T. Lambshead Pocket Guide to Eccentric & Discredited Diseases*. Find more of his work at johncoulthart.com.

Scott Eagle is a professor of painting and drawing at East Carolina University in Greenville, North Carolina. His paintings have graced the covers of many books, including *City of Saints and Madmen* and *Secret Life* by Jeff VanderMeer. His illustrations have appeared in a number of national magazines.

Vladimir Gvozdariki, a Russian artist who also works under the moniker Gvozd (which means "Iron"), is known for his whimsical and mechanical illustrations and sculptures. His Web museum can be found at gvozdariki.ru.

Yishan Li is a professional manga artist living in Edinburgh, Scotland. She has been published internationally, including in China, the United States, France, and the United Kingdom. Her latest book is *The Complete Shojo Art Kit*.

Mike Mignola is an artist known for graphic novels such as *Hellboy* and *The Amazing Screw-on Head*. He was also the production designer for the Disney feature film *Atlantis: The Lost Empire*.

Jonathan Nix is an award-winning director, animator, artist, and musician. He lives in Sydney, Australia.

Eric Orchard is an award-winning illustrator and cartoonist living in Canada. He most recently illustrated the children's book *The Terrible, Horrible, Smelly Pirate*. His work has been recognized in the Spectrum Annual of Fantastic Art and the Society of Illustrators annual exhibit.

James A. Owen is an American comic book artist, publisher, and writer. He is the author of the popular Chronicles of the Imaginarium Geographica series and the creator of the critically acclaimed *Starchild* graphic novel series. His most recent book is *The Dragon's Apprentice*.

Ron Pippin's artwork has been shown around the world in solo shows as well as group exhibitions. His art has also been seen in various movies and TV shows such as *Spider-Man*.

J. K. Potter is an iconic photographer known mostly for his work in the horror, science fiction, and fantasy world, as well as his album/CD covers. He has produced art for many book covers, including the recent Subterranean Press limited editions of *Ebb Tide* by James Blaylock and *Last Call* by Tim Powers.

Eric Schaller is an artist, writer, and scientist. His stories have appeared in *Postscripts*, *New Genre*, and *Nemonymous*, and his artwork in *The White Buffalo Gazette*, *Lady Churchill's Rosebud Wristlet*, and Jeff VanderMeer's mosaic novel *City of Saints and Madmen*.

Ivica Stevanovic is a Serbian artist. He has won several prizes in the fields of design, illustrations, cartoons, and comics. His specialty is graphic novels and art book projects. His latest book is *Katil* (Bloodthirsty Man) and he also recently contributed to the anthology *Steampunk Reloaded*.

Jan Svankmajer is a famous Czech surrealist artist and filmmaker. His first feature film in 1987 was *Alice,* based on Lewis Carroll's *Alice in Wonderland.* His most recent film is the Czech comedy *Surviving Life* (2010), which he claims will be his last.

Sam Van Olffen is a French artist best known for his surreal depictions of steampunk and/or dieselpunk images. His work has been featured in many books as well as gallery exhibits around the world.

Myrtle von Damitz III is a painter living in New Orleans who sees her work as a form of storytelling. She has had numerous solo exhibits as well as group gallery showings around the country. She is the founder and curator of Babylon Lexicon, an annual exhibition of artists' books and local independent presses.

Jake von Slatt is a steampunk contraptor and proprietor of the popular Web site The Steampunk Workshop (steampunkworkshop.com); he lives in Boston. He and his projects have been featured in Boing Boing, *WIRED, Nature, Newsweek,* and the *New York Times.*

Catalog Contributors

Hugh Alter is currently working on novels that you will recognize as award-winning best-sellers from the future. He is also working on retrieving coins from inside his couch. **Charlie Jane Anders** blogs at io9.com and organizes the Writers with Drinks reading series. Her work has also appeared at Tor.com and the *McSweeney's Joke Book of Book Jokes.* **Julie Andrews** is a 2007 graduate of the Clarion Writers' Workshop and is a member of both Broad Universe and The Outer Alliance. **Christopher Begley** is thirty and lives in Worcester, Massachusetts. This is his first published work. He wouldn't call his writing Moore-ish or Gaiman-esque but will not stop others from doing so. **Jayme Lynn Blaschke** writes science fiction, fantasy, and related nonfiction. He has authored a book of genre-themed interviews, titled *Voices of Vision: Creators of Science Fiction & Fantasy Speak.* **Nickolas Brienza** is a Seattle resident; all further CV may be confidently extrapolated via the usual statistical methods. **Tucker Cummings** has been writing strange stories since the day she developed sufficient hand-eye coordination to hold a crayon. Previous microfiction efforts garnered accolades during competitions held by HiLoBrow.com and MassTwitFic. **Rikki Ducornet** is one of her generation's best surrealists, with books including *The Word Desire* and *The Fountains of Neptune.* She is also the Rikki in the Steely Dan song "Rikki Don't Lose That Number." **Kaolin Imago Fire** is a conglomeration of ideas, side projects, and experiments. He has had short fiction published in *Strange Horizons, Crossed Genres, Escape Velocity,* and *M-Brane SF,* among others. **Jess Gulbranson**, a hyperminimal neoplastic bricoleur from Portland, Oregon, is an author, musician, critic, artist, and family man. He has swell hair. **Jennifer Harwood-Smith** is a Ph.D. student at Trinity College Dublin. She won the 2006 James White Award and has been published in *Interzone* magazine. **Willow Holser** is a twenty-six-year-old daydreamer with delusions of adulthood, gainful employment, and grammatical correctness. However, she does have what has been called a "Quite Suitable Hat." **Rhys Hughes** is a writer of absurdist fantasy; he lives in Wales. His most recent book is the novel *Twisthorn Bellow*, and he contributed to the first Lambshead anthology. **Incognitum** has long been part of a secret society dedicated to the subversion of reality through the recontextualization of museum exhibits and various other contaminations of meat-minds through subtextual viruses. **Paul Kirsch** grew up on an unhealthy diet of grilled cheese and ghost stories. He's been tinkering with a steampunk/fantasy series, and writes book reviews at paul-kirsch.com. He lives in Los Angeles. **Michael J. Larson** lives in Minneapolis when he's not on his private dirigible, holding wild midair parties and getting involved in international intrigue. **Therese Littleton** is a curator and writer who lives in Seattle, Washington. **Graham Lowther**, born in Vermont, now lives in Maine, where he is building his own house. He has long been a fan of horror and surreal fiction, and sometimes writes it. This is his first appearance in print. **Claire Massey** lives in Lancashire with her husband and two young sons. Her short stories have been published in a variety of places and she is the founding editor of online magazine *New Fairy Tales*. **Tony Mileman** lives and works in the Czech city of Brno. His pleasures include translating Czech supernatural fiction. His previous short fiction has appeared in *Nemonymous*. **Adam Mills** lives in a town in the Missouri Ozarks, one you can only see if you pay attention and pass by at the right time of night. He writes coded messages, teaches college English, and lives in a bowling alley. **Annalee Newitz** is the editor in chief of io9.com. She's published her work in *Wired*, the *Washington Post*, *Flurb*, and *2600*. She used to be a professor who studied monsters. **Ignacio Sanz** was born in Madrid, Spain, in 1977, and is a sci-fi and fantasy aficionado. Until now, he has written some short pieces, but this is the first time he has competed in an international writing contest. **Steven M. Schmidt** is a person of no importance whatsoever. He is working to correct this appalling state of affairs but it may take some time. **Grant Stone**'s stories have appeared in *Shimmer, Andromeda Spaceways Inflight Magazine,* and *Semaphore*. He lives in Auckland, New Zealand. Which is handy, since that's where all his stuff is. **Norman Taber** (aka Dr. Galubrious) teaches graduate studies in ethereal anthropology and at Exeter University in Putney, Vermont. He is the world's foremost expert on toad-scrapings. Galubrious is represented in the United States by Norman Taber, a professor of design at SUNY Plattsburgh. **Brian Thill** is the director of the Humanities Core Writing Program at UC Irvine, where he completed his Ph.D. in English. His research focuses include American literature, art, and politics. **Nick Tramdack** was born in 1985 and grew up in New Jersey. He works in the stacks of a Chicago library, where he has developed a Grendel-like hatred for noise. **Nicholas Troy** was born in Washington, D.C., grew up a bit in Germany, then grew up some more in Boston. He has always loved stories, and is currently a part of the Illiterati writing group. **Tom Underberg** lives with his wife and children in an old house. Standing on his roof, you can see Lake Michigan. He has been an economic consultant (excellent), bartender (disastrous), and dishwasher (promising). **Horia Ursu** is a Romanian publisher, translator, and (sometimes) writer of science fiction and fantasy. He is also senior editor of *Galileo*, a digest-size F&SF magazine. He lives in Satu Mare with his wife and daughter. **William T. Vandemark** can be found wandering the backroads of America in a pickup truck. His fiction has appeared in *Apex Magazine, InterGalactic Medicine Show,* and in several anthologies. **Kali Wallace** is inconveniently overeducated and underemployed. She lives in Colorado with her family, four cats, and a turtle. **Tracie Welser** is a speculative fiction writer and instructor of women's studies. She's quite fond of owls. In 2010, she was fortunate enough to survive the Clarion West Writers' Workshop. **Amy Willats** is originally from California, although she has also been seen in Texas and Maryland. Currently residing in the San Francisco Bay Area, she tries not to scream uncontrollably, although sometimes she just can't help herself. **Nadine Wilson** is a reader of books, scribbler of stories, taker of photographs, mother of one, big sister to many, pet of cats, lover of oddities, seminomadic and vaguely ambitious. She loves the world, even you. Especially you. **Ben Woodard** recently completed a master's in philosophy at the European Graduate School. He blogs at naughtthought.wordpress.com, and his first monograph, *Slime Dynamics: Generation, Mutation, and the Creep of Life,* is forthcoming from Zer0 Books.

About the Editors

Hugo Award–winner Ann VanderMeer and World Fantasy Award–winner Jeff Vander-Meer have recently coedited such anthologies as *Best American Fantasy #1 & 2, Steampunk, Steampunk Reloaded, The New Weird, Last Drink Bird Head,* and *Fast Ships, Black Sails.* They are the coauthors of *The Kosher Guide to Imaginary Animals.* Future projects include *The Weird: A Compendium of Strange and Dark Fictions,* for Atlantic. Jeff's latest books are the novel *Finch,* a World Fantasy Award and Nebula Award finalist; the story collection *The Third Bear;* the nonfiction collection *Monstrous Creatures;* the coffee-table book *The Steampunk Bible* (with S. J. Chambers); and the writing strategy guide *Booklife.* Ann is the editor in chief of *Weird Tales* magazine and has a regular art column on the popular SF/fantasy Web site io9. Together, they have been profiled by National Public Radio and the *New York Times'* Papercuts blog. They are active teachers, and have taught at Clarion San Diego, Odyssey, and the teen writing camp Shared Worlds, for which Jeff serves as the assistant director. They live in Tallahassee, Florida, with too many books and four cats. For more information, visit jeffvandermeer.com.

Acknowledgments

First and foremost, a huge thank-you to Diana Gill, our editor, for being wonderfully supportive of this project and letting this three-ring circus reach its full potential. Thanks also to Will Hinton at Harper Voyager, who put up with a constant stream of e-mails and image downloads, among other impositions—as well as everyone else involved in this project, including the book designer. Huge thanks as well to John Coulthart for acting as an image consultant to this anthology, while also providing his own art/design and found art—you're the best and we couldn't have done it without you. Thanks to the gang at Brueggers, Hopkins, and Monks for good company, and for keeping us fed and caffeinated during the process. Thanks to our friends at the Leon Station post office for laughs and over twenty years of great service. We would also like to thank Myra Miller and Arthur Burns at Alpha Data Systems for continuing support (and a special shoutout to Arthur for keeping all our technology running smoothly).

Acknowledgments

We're also indebted to Stepan Chapman and Michael Cisco's contributions to *The Thackery T. Lambshead Pocket Guide to Eccentric & Discredited Diseases,* as this volume makes use of some of their ideas and writings from that prior volume. We're also forever indebted to our *New Weird* editor in the Czech Republic, Martin Šust, for his help in acquiring art from Jan Svankmajer. Finally, thanks to all of the contributors for making this anthology so special for us.

Credits

ARTISTS

All images copyright 2011 to the individual creators and original to this anthology, unless otherwise noted. All public-domain art and photography provided by and/or Photoshopped by John Coulthart. All title pages copyright 2011 John Coulthart.

"Mecha-frog" and "Mecha-fish" on pages 18 and 19, Vladimir Gvozdev, copyright © 2008

Introduction

"just one shelf in Lambshead's study"—Jennifer and J. K. Potter, photograph from their "knickknack collection," as arranged by Jennifer

"stage set for musical of Dr. Lambshead . . ."—Sam Van Olffen, "Travailleurs de lacier," copyright © 2008

"secret medical laboratory stage set . . ."—Sam Van Olffen, "Dissecator," copyright © 2007

"One of Lambshead's few attempts at art . . ."—Myrtle von Damitz III, detail shot from "Family Portrait" with Michael, Michelle, and Sydney Holdman pictured, copyright © 2010

"One of the few museum exhibit loans . . ."—Vladimir Gvozdev, "Mecha-Rhino," copyright © 2008

"Spell or secret communication?"—Kristen Alvanson, "Constructing an Elysian Pod for the Last Journey," copyright © 2007

"so-called 'Skull Cucumber' hoax . . ."—Jan Svankmajer, cryptozoology print, copyright © 1975

"demonstrating the doctor's commitment to the future . . ."—Jake von Slatt, "Bassington & Smith Electro-Mechanical Analog Brain," copyright © 2010, first publication herein

"More evidence of the disarray . . ."—J. K. Potter, originally end papers for James Blaylock's *The Adventures of Langdon St. Ives* from Subterranean Press, copyright © 2008

The Broadmore Exhibits

"Electrical Neurheographiton," "St. Brendan's Shank," "The Auble Gun," and *"Dacey's Patent Automatic Nanny"*—Greg Broadmore

"Nikola Tesla ca. 1890"—Wikipedia Commons

"The Tasker Battle Carriage"—Sam Van Olffen, "Cours Lapin, cours!" copyright © 2008

Honoring Lambshead

"medieval tapestry . . ."—James A. Owen

"Tree Spirits Rising"—Jonathan Nix, copyright © 2006

"Relic with Fish"—Ivica Stevanovic

"Lord Dunsany's Teapot"—Yishan Li

"Portrait of a Bear Unbound (with speaker)"—Eric Orchard

"The Meistergarten"—John Coulthart

The Mignola Exhibits

"Addison Howell on his Clockroach," "Sir Ranulph Wykeham-Rackham," "Shamalung," and *"Pulvadmonitor"*—Mike Mignola

The Miéville Anomalies

"The Very Shoe" and *"Gallows-horse"*—China Miéville

The Further Oddities

"Thing in Jar"—Aeron Alfrey

"Frog Resurrection"—Ron Pippin, copyright © 2008

"Armor Montage"—Ivica Stevanovic

"Castleblakeney Key"—Aeron Alfrey, copyright © 2009

"Taking the Rats to Riga"—Eric Schaller

"The Book of Categories"—Ron Pippin, copyright © 2008

"The Dead Dead Gang book cover"—John Coulthart

Visits and Departures

"Kneel" (full and detail views)—Scott Eagle, "Meditation on Power" installation, copyright © 2009

Catalog of Additional Items

"Bear Gun/Taxidermy Gun"—Eric Orchard

"Coffin Torpedo"—Jess Gulbranson

"Disgruntled Artifacts"—Rikki Ducornet

"Mooney & Finch Somnotrope"—Jake von Slatt, "Chronoclasmic Inhibitor," copyright © 2010, first publication herein

"Much Smaller Cabinet"—Ron Pippin, Archive Box #2, copyright © 1999

"Skull"—John Coulthart, copyright © 1995

"The St. Blais Toad"—Norman Tabor

"Jean Lorrain's Nightmares of an Ether-Drinker"—R. B. Russell, Tartarus Press designer/artist for dust jacket and boards, copyright © 2003

"Panoramic view of the Lambshead's cabinet"—Bruce Ecker, The Obsolete Gallery, copyright © 2007

TEXT

"Introduction: The Contradictions of a Collection, Dr. Lambshead's Cabinet" and all image captions, unless otherwise noted, copyright © 2011 Jeff & Ann VanderMeer. The character of Thackery T. Lambshead is a creation of Ann & Jeff VanderMeer, copyright © 2003.

The following subsection introductory text copyright © 2011 Jeff VanderMeer: "Holy Devices and Infernal Duds: The Broadmore Exhibits," "Honoring Lambshead: Stories Inspired by the Cabinet," "Microbial Alchemy and Demented Machinery: The Mignola Exhibits," "The Miéville Anomalies," "Further Oddities," "Visits and Departures," and "A Brief Catalog of Additional Items."

Additional text: caption for Jake von Slatt image in the introduction, *"demonstrating the doctor's commitment to the future,"* copyright © 2011 Annalee Newitz; caption for *"Bear Gun/Taxidermy Gun"* at beginning of "A Brief Catalog" copyright © by Adam Mills. *"Disgruntled Artifacts"* text attributed to Rikki Ducornet (with her permission) in "A Brief Catalog" copyright © 2011 Jeff VanderMeer.

In order of appearance in the anthology:

"The Electrical Neurheographiton" copyright © 2011 by Minister Faust

"St. Brendan's Shank" copyright © 2011 by Kelly Barnhill

"The Auble Gun" copyright © 2011 by Will Hindmarch

"Dacey's Patent Automatic Nanny" copyright © 2011 by Ted Chiang

"Threads" copyright © 2011 by Carrie Vaughn

"Ambrose and the Ancient Spirits of East and West" by Garth Nix

"Relic" copyright © 2011 by Jeffrey Ford

"Lord Dunsany's Teapot" copyright © 2011 by Naomi Novik

"Lot 558: *Shadow of My Nephew* by Wells, Charlotte" copyright © 2011 by Holly Black

"A Short History of Dunkelblau's Meistergarten" copyright © 2011 by Tad Williams

"Addison Howell and the Clockroach" copyright © 2011 by Cherie Priest

"Sir Ranulph Wykeham-Rackham, GBE, a.k.a. Roboticus the All-Knowing" copyright © 2011 by Lev Grossman

"Shamalung (The Diminutions)" copyright © 2011 by Michael Moorcock

"Pulvadmonitor: The Dust's Warning" copyright © 2011 by China Miéville

"The Very Shoe" copyright © 2011 by Helen Oyeyemi

"The Gallows-horse" copyright © 2011 by Reza Negarestani

"The Thing in the Jar" copyright © 2011 by Michael Cisco

"The Singing Fish" copyright © 2011 by Amal El-Mohtar

"The Armor of Sir Locust" copyright © 2011 by Stepan Chapman

"A Key to the Castleblakeney Key" copyright © 2011 by Caitlín R. Kiernan

"Taking the Rats to Riga" copyright © 2011 by Jay Lake

"The Book of Categories" copyright © 2011 by Charles Yu

"Objects Discovered in a Novel Under Construction" copyright © 2011 by Alan Moore

"1929: The Singular Taffy Puller" copyright © 2011 by N. K. Jemisin

"1943: A Brief Note Pertaining to the Absence of One Olivaceous Cormorant, Stuffed" copyright © 2011 by Rachel Swirsky

"1963: The Argument Against Louis Pasteur" copyright © 2011 by Mur Lafferty

"1972: The Lichenologist's Visit" copyright © 2011 by Ekaterina Sedia

"1995: Kneel" copyright © 2011 by Brian Evenson

"2000: Dr. Lambshead's Dark Room" copyright © 2011 by S. J. Chambers

"2003: The Pea" copyright © 2011 by Gio Clairval

The flash fictions in "A Brief Catalog of Additional Items" are copyright © 2011 to the writer noted in parentheses at the end of each entry: Hugh Alter, Charlie Jane Anders, Julie Andrews, Christopher Begley, Jayme Lynn Blaschke, Nickolas Brienza, Tucker Cummings, Kaolin Imago Fire, Jess Gulbranson, Jennifer Harwood-Smith, Willow Holser, Rhys Hughes, Incognitum (aka Reza Negarestani), Paul Kirsch, Michael J. Larson, Graham Lowther, Claire Massey, Tony Mileman, Adam Mills, Annalee Newitz, Ignacio Sanz, Steven M. Schmidt, Grant Stone, Norman Taber (aka Dr. Galubrious), Brian Thill, Nick Tramdack, Nicholas Troy, Tom Underberg, Horia Ursu, William T. Vandemark, Kali Wallace, Tracie Welser, Amy Willats, Nadine Wilson, Ben Woodard.